THE appearance in ... ... *Arabian Nights' Entertainm* ... ...ntury accompanied a fashi... ...astern' or 'Persian' elements in architec..., furniture, fashion, and the decorative arts, and introduced into the English literary tradition what was soon to prove one of its most versatile forms of prose fiction, the oriental tale. Some of the most imposing and influential of the so-called Augustan authors tried their hand at the form at one time or another, and throughout the period essayists and novelists—many of them women—supplied a long line of treacherous genii, enigmatic princesses, and adventurous sultans to an eager reading public. This volume brings together in a single edition four of the most influential and intriguing of these oriental tales: John Hawkesworth's *Almoran and Hamet* (1761), Frances Sheridan's *History of Nourjahad* (1767), Clara Reeve's *History of Charoba, Queen of Ægypt* (1785), and Maria Edgeworth's *Murad the Unlucky* (1804). While together exemplifying the oriental taste of eighteenth- and early nineteenth-century England, each of these stories makes different use of the frame provided by the oriental tale, and sheds unique light on the genre's contributions to the larger development of the English novel. These works similarly demonstrate the protean capacity of the oriental tale as a literary form in its own right, in a way not necessarily in evidence to those familiar only with the philosophical satire of other eastern tales such as Samuel Johnson's popular *Rasselas* (1759), or the highly idiosyncratic, imaginative vision of William Beckford's *Vathek* (1786).

ROBERT L. MACK is an Assistant Professor of English at Vanderbilt University. His publications include an edition (in collaboration with Margaret Anne Doody and Peter Sabor) of Frances Burney's *The Wanderer*. He is currently writing a book on Restoration and eighteenth-century parody, and editing *The Arabian Nights' Entertainments* for World's Classics.

THE WORLD'S CLASSICS

Oriental Tales

Edited with an Introduction by
ROBERT L. MACK

Oxford · New York
OXFORD UNIVERSITY PRESS
1992

Oxford University Press, Walton Street, Oxford OX2 6DP

Oxford New York Toronto
Delhi Bombay Calcutta Madras Karachi
Petaling Jaya Singapore Hong Kong Tokyo
Nairobi Dar es Salaam Cape Town
Melbourne Auckland

and associated companies in
Berlin Ibadan

Oxford is a trade mark of Oxford University Press

Editorial material © Robert L. Mack 1992

First published as a World's Classics paperback 1992

British Library Cataloguing in Publication Data

Data available

Library of Congress Cataloging-in-Publication Data

Oriental tales / edited with an introduction by Robert L. Mack.
p.   cm.—(World's classics)
Includes bibliographical references (p.   ).
Contents: Almoran and Hamet / by John Hawkesworth—The history of Nourjahad / by
Frances Sheridan—The history of Charoba, Queen of Ægypt / by Clara Reeve—Murad
the Unlucky / by Maria Edgeworth.
1. English fiction—18th century. 2. Orient—Fiction. I. Mack, Robert L. II.
Series.
PR1297.075 1992 823'.6083256–dc20 91–45856

ISBN 0-19-282764-2

Typeset by Cambridge Composing (UK) Ltd.
Printed in Great Britain by
BPCC Hazells Ltd.
Aylesbury, Bucks

CONTENTS

INTRODUCTION

ON 1 August 1716, Lady Mary Wortley Montagu left
London to accompany her husband, the recently appointed
Ambassador Extraordinary to the Court of Turkey, on the
long and arduous overland journey to the Ottoman Court,
then at Adrianople. Lady Mary, a member of fashionable
London society who once commented that she prided
herself on the thought of 'going farther than most other
people go', professed later in life from the start to have
been 'charmed with the thoughts of going into the East'.[1]
She was not to be disappointed by what she found there.
Styling herself as an intrepid and pioneering explorer—and
(rather hyperbolically) as the first woman to undertake a
journey 'that has not been undertaken by any Christian
since the Time of the Greek Emperours'—she soon initiated
a correspondence which offered with a degree of detail yet
unknown to most of her English acquaintances a description
of the 'marvels' of the East.[2]

The main purpose of her husband's appointment as
Ambassador was to negotiate a settlement between the
Turkish Sultan Achmet III and the representatives of the
Holy Roman Empire.[3] Wortley Montagu's diplomatic
efforts in fact turned out to be a dismal failure. He would,
to the great disappointment both of himself and of his wife,

[1] Lady Mary's remarks are recorded in a letter by the anecdotist Joseph
Spence to his mother, dated 25 Feb. 1741. The passage is reprinted in
Robert Halsband's biography *The Life of Lady Mary Wortley Montagu*
(Oxford, 1956), 56.

[2] *The Complete Letters of Lady Mary Wortley Montagu*, ed. Robert
Halsband, 3 vols. (Oxford, 1965), i. 310.

[3] The circumstances of Wortley Montagu's appointment as Turkish
Ambassador are briefly recounted in Halsband, *Life of Lady Mary Wortley
Montagu*, 57.

be recalled from his post after less than two years—long before a new appointment was due. The truly long-lasting legacy of Wortley Montagu's embassy to Constantinople would prove to be not his own futile diplomatic manœuvring, but rather the carefully documented and passionately detailed journals and correspondence of his wife. Lady Mary seems to have been determined to enjoy every moment of her stay in the East and set about making the most of her time there. Although the heavy formalities and lengthy ceremony of the Turkish court at times struck her as a trifle tedious, she lost no time in acquiring some familiarity with what she called 'Oriental Learning'. Dressed in a colourful and richly embroidered native habit, she was soon exploring scenes of Turkish life hitherto off limits to the most inquisitive of her male counterparts. 'I ramble every day', she wrote, 'wrapp'd up in my ferigé and asmak, about Constantinople and amuse my selfe with seeing all that is curious in it.'[4] In the months following her breathless arrival in the East, Lady Mary offered her correspondents first-hand accounts of the luxury and beauty of the women in the Bagnio—the hot baths—in Sophia, detailed the fabulous dinners and evening entertainments in the richly decorated harem of the lady of the Grand Vizier and the lady of the Kahya (the second minister), described 'the luscious passion of the seraglio', and marvelled at the fantastic, uneven landscape of palaces, mosques, and minarets which stretched, towards the Asian hills, beyond the window of her own palatial home in Constantinople. She even managed to gain entrance to the great Byzantine mosque of St Sophia, a privilege then generally forbidden to Christians (she later claimed to have been dressed 'in men's clothes' at the time). 'Now do I fancy', she once paused in a letter to her sister Lady Mar,

---

[4] *Complete Letters*, i. 405.

that you imagine I have entertain'd you all this while with a relation that has (at least) receiv'd many Embellishments from my hand. This is but too like (says you) the Arabian tales; these embroider'd Napkins, and a jewel as large as a Turkey's egg!— You forget, dear Sister, those very tales were writ by an Author of this Country and (excepting the Enchantments) are a real representation of the manners here.[5]

Lady Mary's adventures in the fifty-two Turkish Embassy Letters often, in fact, read like an episode straight out of the *Arabian Nights*—like an Eastern romance, an oriental tale.[6] Although she took a great deal of pleasure in correcting the many fallacious accounts of the East then in print, it is striking that Lady Mary turned to the most popular *literary* representation of the Orient available to her French and English correspondents when attempting to validate and to legitimize her own account of life in Turkey. Antoine Galland's translation of the Near Eastern tales collected together in the *Alf Layla wa-Layla* had begun appearing in French as *Mille et Une Nuit* in 1704. An anonymous English translation of Galland's text—the so-called 'Grub Street' version—was available soon thereafter. The *Arabian Nights' Entertainments*, as the popular collection was soon known in England, was to accelerate a taste for what would alternately be described as 'oriental', 'Arabian', 'Persian', or 'Moorish' fashions and designs which would enliven literature and the arts in England throughout the eighteenth century.

Lady Mary's unusually well-documented fascination with the Ottoman court of the early eighteenth century (and by extension with the vaguely designated 'Orient' which seemed at times, in the popular imagination, to stretch

[5] Ibid. i. 385.

[6] On the connection between the Embassy Letters and the *Nights* see Cynthia Lowenthal, 'The Veil of Romance: Lady Mary Wortley Montagu's Embassy Letters', in *Eighteenth-Century Life*, 14 (1990), 66–82.

from North Africa to as far as China and Japan) is in fact representative of the attempts of an entire generation to understand the Muslim East. Europeans in the eighteenth century were faced with the difficult task of assimilating a rapidly increasing amount of information about the peoples, customs, and beliefs of a diverse culture which had, until the very recent past, been only slenderly known in the West. To be sure, there are many traces of Islam in the Western literary tradition, and classical works as well as texts from the Middle Ages and the Renaissance can at times betray a profound debt to the East. Wallace Gray has correctly pointed out that even Homer's *Iliad* (c.700 BC), a work which is perceived by many to be the founding text of the *Western* literary tradition, is itself 'an oriental work, facing the East', and further reminds us that the very action of the epic takes place not in Europe, but on the coast of Asia Minor, in what is now Turkey.[7] On much the same note it is worth pointing out that the action of Heliodorus' *Aethiopica* (c.AD 250) likewise opens with a spectacular scene set at the Canopic mouth of the river Nile, near the Libyan desert. An earlier Greek writer, Herodotus, had similarly 'faced' the East for much of his *Histories* (c.446 BC), discovering in Persia and in Egypt centuries-old civilizations which rivalled and even surpassed his own.

There are times when the debt of the Western literary tradition to Eastern narratives is a prominent one. It has long been recognized, for example, that Chaucer's 'Squire's Tale' in his *Canterbury Tales* (c.1388–1400) draws on narrative material similar to that contained in the *Nights*, as does the Christopher Sly dramatic frame which inducts the audience into Shakespeare's *The Taming of the Shrew* (1594). *The Song of Roland* (c.1100), *The Cid* (c.1250), and Boccaccio's *Decameron* (1348–58) are all texts which owe something to the Muslim Orient. More frequently, how-

[7] Wallace Gray, *Homer to Joyce* (London, 1985), 25.

ever, the East after the advent of Islam has a way of turning up in the odd corners of texts, of hanging in the background. In the Middle English *Sir Gawain and the Green Knight* (c.1250), for example, it quite literally hangs over the heads of the poem's Christian protagonists, in the form of richly embroidered 'Turkish' tapestries which form the canopy over the dais at the court of King Arthur. Here as elsewhere within the context of the overtly religious struggle which forms the background for so much of the drama of the Middle Ages, the East seems to be invoked as the locus of excessive, crippling luxury and pagan infidelity. It is the centre of all that is opposed to the values and achievements of 'Christendom'. It is no accident that the towers of the city of Dis in Dante's *Inferno* (c.1314–21) are said to glow red like 'meschite' or mosques, or that Milton's Satan, seated on a 'throne of royal state' reminiscent of those in the 'gorgeous East', is described as a kind of oriental despot. At other times more positive images of Islam managed to write themselves into the traditions of Western literature. Cervantes, in Part I of his *Don Quixote* (1605), describes the busy silk market of Toledo in Moorish Spain as a lively place of bustling and colourful activity, and even tells us that the story of the knight errant of la Mancha was originally written by an 'Arabic historian'—Cide Hamete Benengeli. The enormously popular French romances of the mid-seventeenth century, such as Madeleine de Scudéry's *Ibrahim* (1641) or *Artamène; ou, Le Grand Cyrus* (1649–53), or the pseudo-Islamic dynasties of Restoration heroic dramas such as John Dryden's *The Conquest of Granada* (1670–1) and *Aurung-Zebe* (1676), also offer their readers or spectators an attractive (if highly romanticized) vision of Eastern luxury.

The appearance of Galland's *Nights* beginning in 1704, however, presented to the larger European public what amounted to a genuinely new vision of the Muslim world, and its impact cannot be overstated. The European West was soon producing its own indigenous versions of this perceived Eastern splendour, and the fashion for oriental fables, costumes, accessories, and pastimes reached into nearly every facet of English life. The romantic, fancy-dress portraiture of the late seventeenth and eighteenth centuries testifies to a desire among the fashionable classes to include in their own wardrobes items of oriental design or origin, including richly embroidered robes of brilliants and tight-fitting silk caftans. Eastern dress became a favourite among frequenters of masquerades, and certain items of oriental fashion (most notably lavishly trimmed turban caps, crowned later in the century with ostrich feathers, coloured roses, or an aigrette) remained permanent articles of dress.[8] Men's fashions likewise reflected the oriental vogue. Designs on men's waistcoats were inspired by the elaborate patterns of silk imported from the East, and later in the century long silk or cotton nightgowns of oriental fashion were popular as 'undress' wear.

Nor was the English oriental taste of the eighteenth century to be without its influence in such areas as landscape gardening and architecture. Sir William Chambers, whose 1772 *Dissertation on Oriental Gardening* would champion the 'surprise' and 'variety' of the Chinese garden as opposed to the more indigenously natural designs of the likes of 'Capability' Brown, in 1762 constructed a fifty-metre-tall pagoda, complete with gilded dragons, to tower over the placidity of an increasingly suburban Kew Gardens. The early years of the nineteenth century would witness the equally bizarre Taj Mahal-like domes and spires of John Nash's Royal Pavilion rising over the staid English strand at Brighton. The oriental vogue would influence interior design as well. Chairs, cabinets, screens, delicate lacquer-work tea and coffee tables (the 'shining Alters of

---

[8] See Georgine de Courtais, *Women's Headdresses and Hairstyles in England from AD 600 to the Present Day* (London, 1973), 98.

Japan', as Pope calls them in *The Rape of the Lock* (1714))—indeed, entire rooms—would be designed 'à la chinoise'. The London pleasure gardens of Vauxhall and Ranelagh cultivated an exotic look with 'oriental' and 'Chinese' buildings, and no doubt recalled for many visitors, as for the fictional Lydia Melford, of Tobias Smollett's *Humphrey Clinker* (1771), 'the inchanted palace of a genie'.[9] The young Miss Melford is in fact moved upon her first visit to the capital to describe London itself as the realization of 'all that you read of wealth and grandeur, in the Arabian Night's Entertainment, and the Persian Tales, concerning Bagdad, Diarbekir, Damascus, Ispahan, and Samarkand'. The fact that Smollett's giddy young romantic heroine, a country girl new to London, should be able to reel off without difficulty (and spell correctly!) the names of Near Eastern cities is one indication of just how thoroughly the vogue for oriental tales had entered the popular imagination.

By the time Maria Edgeworth publishes *The Absentee* in 1812, such an oriental taste is seen by some to have become a trifle outdated. The conceited interior designer Mr Soho, who recommends the purchase of 'Turkish tent drapery', 'Seraglio ottomans', 'Alhambra hangings', and 'Chinese pagoda paper', is dismissed by one fashionable lady in the novel as an 'abominable' man who imposes yesterday's fashions upon his credulous clients.[10] The so-called 'Arabian tales' themselves, however, are respectfully presented to the young heroine by the hero in the same novel in 'a beautiful edition'—surely a sign that the fashion for and propriety of oriental fables was still as strong as ever. The strictly literary appeal and influence of the *Arabian Nights'*

[9] Tobias Smollett, *The Expedition of Humphrey Clinker*, ed. Thomas R. Preston (London, 1990), 91.

[10] Maria Edgeworth, *The Absentee* (World's Classics edn., Oxford, 1988), 35.

Entertainments would in fact prove no less staggering—and in many ways more enduring—than the vogue for orientalism in general. The later translations and editions of E. W. Lane, John Payne, and Sir Richard Burton would carry the oriental inheritance of the *Nights* well into the twentieth century. Galland's collection hastened the appearance of other pseudo-Arabian story cycles, some based on actual Eastern material, others completely the products of their French and English 'translators' and authors. The libraries of Europe (and it is important to remember that both men and women read these books) were filled with volumes with titles such as *Turkish Tales* (1708), *Persian Tales* (1714), *Chinese Tales* (1725), and *Mogul Tales* (1736); collections of pseudo-oriental correspondence such as Montesquieu's *Lettres persanes* (1721) and Lyttelton's *Persian Letters* (1735) would also prove enormously popular.

The exotic machinery of the *Nights*—the moonlit seraglios, the baths, the genii, the magic rings and caskets, the mysterious, blushing princesses and imperious sultans—would also be reincarnated in the many shorter, self-contained oriental tales which began appearing in the first decade of the eighteenth century. Linda Degh has commented that fairy tales make use of magic and enchantment because such magic speaks 'the language of . . . fantasy'.[11] A near relation to the fairy tale, oriental fables speak this 'language of fantasy' as well, and Eastern fictions are a sub-genre of English fiction to a large degree defined *by* their magical machinery. 'Oriental tales' are set in exotic Eastern locations, often—like many of the narratives in the *Nights* themselves—in Baghdad or in Persia. The stories are characterized by supernatural events and enchantments—

[11] Linda Degh, 'Grimm's *Household Tales* and Its Place in the Household: The Special Relevance of a Controversial Classic', *Western Folklore*, 38 (1979), 83–103; repr. in Michael M. Metzger and Katharin Mommson (eds.), *Fairy Tales as Ways of Knowing* (Berne, 1981), 21–53.

the appearance of genii and 'shaytans' or demons—and by magical objects: rings, talismans, and charmed lanterns. Like the stories in the *Nights*, these shorter oriental tales usually tell the story of a single individual (e.g. Aladdin, Ali Baba, Sindbad, Rasselas, Vathek) although the narratives can range from tales of romantic passion to simple 'action and adventure' stories. Some sort of reference is usually made to the 'stuff' of Eastern life (caravans, khans, dates, sherbet, coffee, dinars), to the Islamic religion (the 'prophet', Khadija, pilgrimages), and to the centres of the Islamic world (Mecca, Medina, Balsora, 'Grand' Cairo). Joseph Addison, in his *Spectator* (1711–14), is among the first in England to begin writing such Eastern fictions, with their conscious and acknowledged debt to the *Nights*. By the end of the century such noted authors as Ambrose Philips, Eliza Haywood, Samuel Johnson, Oliver Goldsmith, Horace Walpole, and Mary Pilkington all write oriental tales of some sort or another.

A handful of these stories, most notably Johnson's *Rasselas* (1759) and William Beckford's *Vathek* (1786), have tended to monopolize the attention of scholars and critics since the late nineteenth century, and in so doing have presented a somewhat skewed picture of what was in fact a highly diverse and influential sub-genre of English prose fiction in the eighteenth century. The most substantial study of the subject, Martha Pike Conant's 1908 *The Oriental Tale in England in the Eighteenth Century*, viewed the oriental tale primarily as a 'natural reaction' against 'the dominant classicism of Boileau'.[12] Although undertaking to survey the wide range of eighteenth-century oriental fiction, Conant's study primarily regarded the oriental tale as 'a tendency itself a part of the larger movement of English Romanticism', and so focused on familiar favourites such

---

[12] Martha Pike Conant, *The Oriental Tale in England in the Eighteenth Century* (New York, 1908), pp. xv–xxvi.

as Beckford's *Vathek*. It has only recently been asserted that, following the publication of *Rasselas*, 'nothing of any great literary profundity was achieved in the pseudo-oriental genre until the publication of *Vathek*'—and this from a critic who is in fact seeking to restore the *Nights* to its proper eminence in the history of literary influence and allusion in English![13]

Our notions of eighteenth-century literary history have undergone some substantial changes in recent years. We need no longer classify oriental tales simply as the voluptuous harbingers who sought riotously to deface the calm and unruffled surface of a bankrupt English neo-classicism. Nor, however, need we view them as consistently 'moral' tales and apologues wrapped in the garb of Eastern exoticism only to render them unfamiliar (and hence more appealing) to a European audience. One senses rather that the oriental tale has been swept under the carpet of literary history by those who saw something genuinely dangerous in it—by those who recognized in the genre a threat of some sort beneath the exoticism and free play of alternative cultural archetypes. It is certainly odd that a genre of prose fiction which—from Scheherazade on down—so prominently included figures of *female* story-tellers, and which was in fact dominated by a number of prominent female writers, should be remembered by later generations as a form of fiction in which the greatest achievement is a text such as Johnson's *Rasselas*—so often praised for its 'masculinity'. Oriental tales, as *Rasselas* and the earlier work of Addison, or the Revd James Ridley's later *Tales of the Genii* (1764), demonstrate, could indeed be morally, politically, and sexually conservative. Ridley's stories are recommended by one early editor as being 'among the purest and

---

[13] Peter L. Caracciolo, 'Introduction: Such a Store House of Ingenious Fiction and of Splendid Imagery', in Peter Caracciolo (ed.), *The Arabian Nights in English Literature* (New York, 1988), 4.

most beautiful of our Oriental fictions' precisely because 'they uniformly inculcate religion and virtue'.[14] Yet the oriental tale, as Beckford's *Vathek* itself and the oriental *jeux d'esprit* of authors such as Horace Walpole, Thomas Gray, and Matthew Lewis reveal, was also an ideal, boundary-less form for those authors whose own sexuality in some way prevented them from feeling comfortable with other, more 'probable' forms of fiction. Homosexual writers are at home in the oriental tale, as are female authors; it is a place to be free of the restrictions of the mundane realism tied to the demands of the market-place and the goings on of 'real' society. The spectacular effects of its 'enchanting' conventions—of its genies and its demons and its magic spells— are themselves the symptom of a larger freedom and magic at work in these texts: the freedom of fictional explorations of alternative possibilities, of fearless sexuality, and of a possibility of expression beyond the limitations of ordinary, day-to-day life.

Critics early on in the tradition attempt to contain the effects of the oriental tale. It is dismissed as effeminate, insipid, and simply not worth reading. Jane Austen's brother James, writing under the guise of the silly female correspondent 'Sophia Sentiment' in his Oxford literary periodical the *Loiterer* in 1789, effectively satirizes the taste for these tales, suggesting they are suitable only for the least demanding readers. 'Only conceive,' Sophia Sentiment writes of James's periodical, 'in eight papers, not one sentimental story about love and honour, and all that.— Not one Eastern tale full of Bashas and Hermits, Pyramids and Mosques . . .'[15] For the privileged male Austen—a college Fellow—the oriental tale could be dismissed as so much fictional paraphernalia: 'Pyramids and Mosques'. The young Jane Austen herself, however, clearly enjoyed the

[14] James Ridley, *Tales of the Genii* (London, 1873), p. v.
[15] *Loiterer*, 9 (28 Mar. 1789).

Arabian Nights and its successors, playfully referring at one point in her own *juvenilia* to 'the Princess Badroulbadour in the 4th volume of the Arabian Nights', and listing with an obvious appetitive glee all the 'Rubies, Emeralds, Toppazes, Sapphires, Amethysts, Turkeystones, Agate, Beads, Bugles & Garnets' which seem inevitably to surround the heroines of these oriental tales.[16] Austen was not beyond burlesquing the taste for Eastern fiction herself; there is even a slight possibility that she is herself the *Loiterer*'s 'Sophia Sentiment'. Yet, as her complex parodies of the conventions of the Gothic novel in *Northanger Abbey* (1818) demonstrate, Austen was eminently capable of discriminating between a genial and well-intentioned parody of the excesses of the individual forms of prose fiction (and their readers) on the one hand, and an uncomprehending dismissal of the implications of the subtexts of these works on the other. Writing of Austen's parodies of the conventions of the Gothic in *Northanger Abbey*, Claudia Johnson has noted that while she 'may dismiss alarms concerning stock gothic *machinery*—storms, cabinets, curtains, manuscripts,—with blithe amusement, alarms concerning the central gothic *figure*, the tyrannical father . . . are commensurate to the threat they actually pose'.[17] One senses that Austen herself would draw much the same distinction between the 'machinery' of the oriental tale—'Bashas and Hermits, Pyramids and Mosques'—and the political resonance of a form which presents a potentially powerful critique of the conservative ideology implicit in the then-dominant forms of realistic prose fiction. Horace Walpole, writing in the same year as James Austen, suggested to a female correspondent that she should 'read Sindbad the

---

[16] *The Oxford Illustrated Jane Austen, Minor Works*, ed. R. W. Chapman, with revisions by B. C. Southam (London, 1969), 52.

[17] Claudia Johnson, *Jane Austen: Women, Politics and the Novel* (London, 1988), 35.

Sailor's voyages, and you will be sick of Aeneas's'.[18] The *Arabian Nights* and its progeny can be seen throughout the eighteenth century as forming a counterpart of sorts to the great male tradition. Readers of the *Arabian Nights* and of other oriental tales are, in some respects, already 'sick of Aeneas'—they have at least grown tired of his divinely and patriarchally sanctioned singularity of purpose, and ask for a narrative which offers multiplicity rather than singularity, for a narrative which replaces the national purpose characterizing Aeneas' *one* great voyage with the rambling, multi-cultural experiences captured in Sindbad's seven. Walpole further comments in the same letter that while he does not think the narratives of the *Nights* to be either very 'natural' or 'probable' (he does not think, in other words, that they fulfil the expectations of the realistic novel), he nevertheless feels that 'there is a wildness in them that captivates'. The best oriental tales continue to walk on this 'wild' side. Offering on one level the moral tales and apologues demanded by a certain portion of the eighteenth-century reading public and familiar to other forms of prose fiction, on another level the oriental tale retains the right to break down the restrictions of probability, and to open wide the seraglio doors to the unpatterned and unpredictable world of play.

Almoran and Hamet

The first of the stories presented here—John Hawkesworth's *Almoran and Hamet*—has most often been discussed in conjunction with Samuel Johnson's *Rasselas*, a work which appeared just two years before Hawkesworth's tale, and together with which it was subsequently republished several times in the late eighteenth and early nineteenth

---

[18] Horace Walpole, *Letters*, ed. Mrs Paget Toynbee (Oxford, 1903–18), xiv. 140.

centuries. The tendency to bring the two works together is quite natural; Hawkesworth was a close personal friend of the 'great Cham' in the 1750s, and enjoyed a literary career which was in many ways remarkably similar to Johnson's own.

Born in London in 1720, Hawkesworth was apprenticed at the age of 16 to an attorney in Grocer's Alley in the Poultry.[19] He married in 1744, and soon afterwards moved to Bromley, in Kent. At about the same time, he succeeded Johnson as the compiler of the parliamentary debates in the *Gentleman's Magazine*. Hawkesworth had already, in 1741, published his first poem in the same periodical, and throughout his career the connection with the *Gentleman's Magazine* was to prove an important one; beginning in 1756, he would serve as its literary and dramatic editor. The first number of his *Adventurer*, a periodical written in emulation of Johnson's *Rambler*, appeared in 1752. Although Hawkesworth would write the majority of the numbers, the *Adventurer* was to include contributions by Johnson himself, and by Richard Bathurst and Joseph Warton. Hawkesworth followed the success of the *Adventurer* with an impressive and well-received edition of the works of Jonathan Swift, to which he contributed a 'Life'. His later writings include a collaboration with David Garrick for the theatre, an original stage comedy, and a translation of Fénelon's *Les Aventures de Télémaque* (1768). Hawkesworth's oriental tale, *Almoran and Hamet*, was published in 1761. In 1771 he was appointed by Lord Sandwich to write an account of Captain Cook's recent voyages to the South Seas. The *Voyages*, for which Hawkesworth was paid the astronomical sum of £6,000, were published in 1773. Much to his dismay, the volumes were

[19] Biographical information on Hawkesworth is based on John Lawrence Abbott's *John Hawkesworth: Eighteenth-Century Man of Letters* (Madison, Wis., 1982).

sharply criticized for their supposed indecency and unreli-
ability. When Hawkesworth died just a few months later,
there was little doubt among most of his friends and
acquaintances that the mean-spirited criticism of this last
effort only helped to hasten his death.

Although the two were to have a falling-out in the 1760s
Johnson remained a profound influence on Hawkesworth's
literary style and choice of subject. One need only read the
opening sentence of Hawkesworth's story to see that
Almoran and Hamet in many ways seems deliberately to
model itself on Johnson's *Rasselas*. Hawkesworth appears
to adopt much the same moral tone as his predecessor (both
works, Hawkesworth's biographer John Lawrence Abbott
has observed, 'are philosophical investigations of the
choices life offers and the means by which happiness can be
achieved'), and there are moments when Hawkesworth—
no stranger to Johnson's periodic style—himself very suc-
cessfully mimics the weighty, instructive rhythms of John-
sonian prose.[20] Such imitation was no doubt intentional,
and in time Hawkesworth perhaps did see himself as
rivalling Johnson. One of his early critics, writing in the
Universal Magazine, even suggested that Hawkesworth had
been so 'intoxicated' by the popularity of his *Adventurer*
that he 'no longer esteemed Johnson to be, in natural
talents, at all superior to himself'.[21] The same critic goes on
to assert that *Almoran and Hamet* was merely an attempt to
go one better than Johnson—to 'out-Rasselas' *Rasselas*, as
it were. Thomas Percy, writing soon after the novel's
publication, similarly contended that *Almoran and Hamet*
was 'intended as a rival to *Rasselas*', but goes on to suggest
that while Johnson's style remained superior to Hawkes-

[20] Abbott, *John Hawkesworth*, 114.
[21] 'Memoirs of the Life of Dr. John Hawkesworth', *Universal Magazine*,
111 (1802), 237; cited in Abbott, *John Hawkesworth*, 113.

worth's, the 'very pleasing love-story' of *Almoran and Hamet* made it ultimately the more appealing of the two stories.[22]

While *Almoran and Hamet* may well look towards Johnson's work as a forerunner and possible model, it is worth remembering that by the time he came to pen the story, Hawkesworth was himself an experienced writer of Eastern or oriental tales. The *Adventurer* contains no less than eight oriental tales (most of them written by Hawkesworth himself) in the manner of earlier essayists in the *Spectator* and the *Guardian*. Johnson's early biographer Sir John Hawkins even observed that Johnson was himself so impressed by the popularity of the 'Eastern Tales' which had appeared in his own *Rambler*, 'and by Hawkesworth in his *Adventurer*', that it led him to consider writing 'a fictitious history, of a greater extent of any than had appeared in either of those papers'.[23] Such a comment would appear to stand the generally perceived pattern of literary influence on its head, rendering Johnson to some extent the beneficiary of Hawkesworth's experience as a writer of oriental apologues, rather than the other way around. Hawkesworth had in fact gone on record some considerable time before the publication of *Rasselas* with the observation that oriental tales were 'perhaps the most generally pleasing of all literary performances'.[24]

The stated aim of *Almoran and Hamet* too was very different from that of *Rasselas*. The very genesis of the tale tends to argue against the specific influence of Johnson's volume. Hawkesworth had originally intended *Almoran and Hamet* to be a drama, but his friend and sometime collaborator David Garrick was, as Hawkesworth's wife Mary

---

[22] *The Correspondence of Thomas Percy and William Shenstone*, ed. Cleanth Brooks, vol. vii of *The Percy Letters*, ed. Cleanth Brooks and A. F. Falconer (New Haven, Conn., 1977), 101–2; cited in Gwin Kolb, *Rasselas and Other Tales* (New Haven, Conn., 1990), p. lvii.

[23] John Hawkins, *Life of Samuel Johnson, LL.D* (London, 1787), 366.

[24] *Adventurer*, 4 (14 Nov. 1752).

would later put it, 'staggered' by the cost which would be necessary to bring the fabulous effects of the oriental tale to life on the stage. (Samuel Pratt, who was to use *Almoran and Hamet* as the basis for his drama *The Fair Circassian* in 1781, would similarly reject the 'machinery' of Hawkesworth's tale, ostensibly on the grounds that 'it would have been too daring an attempt to intertwine it with the fable of a modern composition', though one suspects a financial motive here as well.[25]) Hawkesworth lost no time in turning the drama of *Almoran and Hamet* into prose fiction, and readers can still see traces of the original dramatic structure of the narrative in the published version of the story. The transformation of *Almoran and Hamet* into its final form allowed Hawkesworth to state his moral and political agenda more clearly and at greater length, and presented him as well with the opportunity to dedicate the work to the new King George III, who had ascended the throne less than one year before the volume was published.

The machinery and situations of oriental fiction (e.g. a 'genius', a magic signet or ring, ominous pronouncements, the intrigue of the seraglio, the advice of a venerable elder counsellor) are present much more clearly and effectively in Hawkesworth's tale than in tales such as *Rasselas* and, as John L. Abbott has pointed out, Hawkesworth's story 'is defined by them'.[26] Hawkesworth does not shy away from the supernatural forms and devices of Eastern fiction and (unlike Johnson and Goldsmith) he is clearly participating in the more elaborately exotic and fantastic tradition of the oriental tale. His story deliberately includes 'enchantments', particularly in the shape of a 'genius . . . convoked from the middle region', as well as in the form of magical transformation and shape-shifting. *Almoran and Hamet* also recalls several of the narratives of the *Arabian Nights* in

[25] Samuel J. Pratt, *The Fair Circassian* (London, 1781), p. iii.
[26] Abbott, *John Hawkesworth*, 114.

which brother is pitted against brother, and in which an attractive young Circassian slave is the 'prize' to be awarded to one of two rivals. Like Johnson, Hawkesworth appears to be using the trappings of orientalism in order to mask a moral lesson which could just as well be at home in any other form of prose fiction—'to show', as his early editor Anna Laetitia Barbauld put it, 'that no outward circumstances, even such as may be produced by changing the course of nature, are sufficient to procure happiness'.[27] Rather than attempting to decode Hawkesworth's narrative *out* of its orientalism, however, we might more profitably ask ourselves what the aura of Eastern exoticism allows Hawkesworth to accomplish in his story—what it permits him to write that he might not otherwise have been capable of writing in a more realistic form of fiction.

The story of *Almoran and Hamet* is an exciting one, characterized by the ominous pronouncements of a powerful and threatening genius (recalling the angry genius in 'The Story of the Fisherman and the Genie' in the *Nights*), and the unspoken desire of fraternal twins. Tales about twins and twinning are never simple or straightforward; they touch too closely on the potential for duality and division—on the 'dark side'—within all of us. *Almoran and Hamet* is no exception. The pretence of setting his tale in 'Persia' rather than in any European country allows Hawkesworth to place not one but *two* princes on the throne. The possibility of such a rival or 'pretender' to *any* throne was not, even by 1761, a pleasant prospect for any Englishman to contemplate. In a work the stated purpose of which is to 'recommend the practice of virtue, as the means of happiness' to 'a Prince, who illustrates . . . the precepts of the moralist by his life', it is striking that from the outset the reader is alerted to the fact that *neither* of the

[27] Anna Laetitia Barbauld, introduction to *Almoran and Hamet*, *The British Novelists*, xxvi (London, 1820), ii.

two crown princes is entirely suited for the task which lies before them. Hawkesworth initially makes it clear that the 'gentle, courteous, and temperate' Hamet is the more virtuous and consistent of the two. Solyman before his death suggests the joint tenure of his sons only because, having considered the dispositions of each of them, he has decided that 'if they had been blended in one person, they would have produced a character more fit to govern in his stead, than either of them alone'. Hamet, in other words, has faults no less detrimental to a successful reign than Almoran's. Solyman worries, for example, that Hamet will 'sink into inactivity for want of spirit'. He fears Hamet's 'fondness for retirement' and his 'placid easiness of temper, which might suffer the reins of government to lie too loose', no less than he fears Almoran's 'quickness of resentment' and 'jealousy of command'. Solyman's attempts to forge unity out of the unreconciled differences in temperament— quite literally to forge a *mon*arch—in the end result only in disaster. The talisman of the genius (who is ultimately revealed to be one 'of the spirits that rejoice to fulfill the purpose of the Almighty'), permits Almoran to pursue a casual, corporeal schizophrenia which, far from uniting the virtues of each brother in a balanced and coherent ruler, leads to a further disintegration and splintering of the royal personalities. Rather than bringing the persons of Almoran and Hamet together, as Solyman had desired, the talisman allows a motley integration of outward form and inner substance which threatens to destroy *both* princes.

The sage and virtuous Omar is meant to provide some sort of balance to the extremes of Solyman's sons. He initially objects to the joint tenure of Almoran and Hamet, but, Hawkesworth writes, 'he at length acquiesced'. There is perhaps a shade too much of the politician in Omar's deference to Solyman; he in fact ends up siding with Hamet in the inevitable struggle for power played out between the two brothers, a partiality which tends to cast doubt on his original commitment to honour and uphold the will of Solyman. Almeida similarly oscillates between the two princes, declaring at one moment her loyalties for Hamet, the next for Almoran, and then again for Hamet (Almeida is at least consistent in her chaste desire for the mind and personality of Hamet even when it is trapped in the form of Almoran). The movement of loyalties and affiliations in the story leaves the reader with a slightly queasy, sickening movement of uncertainty. Love, loyalty, and obedience in the political world are all as easily transcended and transformed as the bodies of Almoran and Hamet, if only because one never quite knows the real nature of the person with whom one is dealing. The abrupt metamorphosis which concludes Hawkesworth's tale, and the lack of any real reason for the genius's entrapment of Almoran, leave the reader with a perfunctory 'sense of an ending'. The ossification of Almoran allows Hawkesworth to end the story on a positive note, but that note rings false. Hawkesworth's story pretends to offer a straightforward moral lesson which preaches the advantages of temperance, honesty, patience, and quiet affection; the real political lesson of the story, however, emerges from between the gaps and cracks of communication between Almoran, Hamet, Omar, and Almeida, inculcating with equal force the values of privacy, reticence, circumspection—and even distrust—in the royal person. *Almoran and Hamet* asks on one level to be read as an Eastern apologue—an oriental tale with a simple moral. But Hawkesworth's stated didactic purpose conceals a deeper anxiety regarding the transference of political power and the environments and circumstances of political action. For every Hamet, there is an Almoran, for every Osmyn, a Caled. Hawkesworth's pessimism even seems to be cryptically encoded in the very names of the characters; that of the unscrupulous prince sounds in our ears like 'all men', while Hamet's name suggests the philosophical withdrawal of the 'hermit'. The possibilities of virtuous action are restricted to those living the *vita contemplativa*. The task which lay before the young King George III was to be perhaps greater than Hawkesworth cared consciously to admit.

The History of Nourjahad

Nourjahad is one of those rare, evocative volumes which tend to recall no one single source or literary model, but rather conjure an entire galaxy of texts. *Nourjahad* is undoubtedly to be classified as an 'Eastern tale'; the familiar cast of characters—sultans, faithful viziers, eunuchs, ladies of the seraglio, loyal slaves—are all here, as are the topoi of oriental fiction. There are, for example, magic potions to be consumed, a guardian 'genius' who (again) seems to appear inexplicably and 'magically' at moments of great crisis, and improbably large urns filled with gold and jewels of an equally improbably large size. Yet Sheridan's tightly constructed volume takes these fundamental building blocks of oriental fiction far beyond the range of most of her fellow orientalists, and in so doing achieves for her story the privileged status of those grand, resonant literary fables which seem to find their complement and echo in any tale which details the furthest reaches of human hopes and aspirations, and the inevitable consequences of human folly.

Frances Sheridan was born Frances Chamberlaine in Ireland in 1724.[28] Her mother died shortly after her birth, and her upbringing was subsequently entrusted to her father, the Revd Dr Philip Chamberlaine, a clergyman whose particular views on the unnecessary education of women were likely to leave his daughter virtually illiterate. While it was perhaps necessary to teach young ladies how to read, any instruction in the way of writing, Dr Chamber-

---

[28] For a full account of Sheridan's life and writings see Alicia Le Fanu, *Memoirs of the Life and Writings of Mrs. Frances Sheridan* (London, 1824).

laine was said to believe, 'tended to nothing but the multiplication of love letters, and the scarcely less dangerous interchange of sentiment in the confidential effusions of female correspondence'.[29] The young Frances had the good fortune to have three brothers who were said to have 'vied with each other in averting the effects of her father's injudicious prohibitions'. Her eldest brother, Walter, soon found his precocious sister to have a mind which led her to 'look beyond the usual routine of female education', and promptly began instructing her in Latin. She started writing fiction at an early age, and completed a two-volume romance, *Eugenia and Adelaide*, when she was only 15. Like Frances Burney after her, who would on *her* fifteenth birthday destroy the manuscript of her early novel *The History of Charlotte Evelyn* because she had so impressed herself with 'ideas that fastened degradation' to the writing of novels, Frances Chamberlaine likewise felt compelled to keep *Eugenia and Adelaide*—her 'first literary sin'—a secret from her father (the work would not be published till many years after her death). In 1747 Chamberlaine, aged 21, married the actor and theatrical manager Thomas Sheridan. The couple divided their time between Dublin and their country property of Quilca in County Carn before settling permanently in London in 1758. It was in London, where she received the warm encouragement of the novelist Samuel Richardson, and found herself surrounded by the literary and theatrical society which included Samuel Johnson, James Boswell, and David Garrick, that Sheridan finally cast off the fear and guilt which she had been led early in life to associate with the writing of fiction. She completed two comedies for the stage and, in 1761, published her novel *The Memoirs of Miss Sidney Bidulph* (though she still felt compelled to keep the latter a secret from her husband until the novel was actually in print). *Sidney*

---

[29] Le Fanu, *Memoirs*, 4.

Bidulph was a spectacular success, and a three-volume sequel or continuation was published in 1767. Sheridan's life in London was far from easy, however, and it was not without reason that her granddaughter noted with equal weight that 'the authoress of some of the most admired products of her time, was also acknowledged to excel in every branch of domestic economy'.[30] She bore six children, four of whom survived. Her husband's financial misfortunes and her own ill health eventually forced the family to move to Blois, in France. In the last year of her life she completed yet one more stage comedy—*A Journey to Bath*—and *The History of Nourjahad*, which was published posthumously in 1767.

In her *Memoirs of the Life and Writings of Mrs. Frances Sheridan*, Le Fanu recalls that Sheridan had originally intended *Nourjahad* to be 'the first of a series of instructive moral fictions, which the author was to have obtained permission to dedicate to His present Most Gracious Majesty, then the young Prince of Wales'.[31] Like Hawkesworth, therefore, Sheridan similarly saw her tale as operating within the traditions of the *speculum principis*—the education of Nourjahad is meant to be of practical value to a young prince. Again like Hawkesworth, however, what Sheridan creates turns out to be something far more lasting and resonant than an occasional moral fable. There are many times in the story when we seem to hear other texts speaking *through* Sheridan's tale—not merely eighteenth-century texts, but texts from every period of English literary history. Nourjahad's early, defiant speeches in which he speculates on the 'constant succession of new delights' to be procured through his sudden acquisition of unlimited wealth, for example, recall the similarly appetitive desires of the memorable overreachers in the plays of Christopher

---

[30] Le Fanu, *Memoirs*, 88.
[31] Ibid. 296.

Marlowe. Nourjahad himself is a kind of Faustus figure. His boast that he will visit every 'spot of the habitable world, which contains anything worthy of . . . [his] curiosity', is very like Faustus's determination to 'search all corners of the new found world' in search of sensory pleasures. Like Faustus, Nourjahad will watch these anticipated pleasures dwindle into shabby spectacle and violence. The global and titanic ambitions of Marlowe's earlier Tamburlaine also lurk in the background of Nourjahad's desires (the gleeful pleasure he takes in spurning the generous Schemzeddin even reminds us of the Marlovian hero's attempts to humble another Eastern prince, Bajazet). Shakespeare's plays are also evoked by *Nourjahad*. The surprise denouement of Sheridan's fable recalls nothing so much as the similarly 'miraculous' endings of the late Romances—particularly *The Winter's Tale* (1611)—while Schemzeddin's desire surreptitiously to educate his friend and subject similarly recalls the tactics of the Duke of Vienna in *Measure for Measure* (c.1604). Nourjahad's misplaced desire for immortality, too, recalls Gulliver's account of the Struldbrugs in Swift's *Gulliver's Travels* (1726). Reading into the future, the tripartite structure of Sheridan's tale (with its three periods of sleep and the progressively introspective journey of its protagonist) anticipates the moral lessons of Charles Dickens's *A Christmas Carol* (1843), and the long periods of Nourjahad's 'trances'—the passing of vast periods of time in a state of sleep or suspended animation and the experience of what Dorothy Van Ghent has called 'atemporal time'—recall the eerie oblivions suffered by the heroes and heroines of tales ranging from traditional fairy stories such as Snow White and Sleeping Beauty, to Rip Van Winkle and *Brigadoon*.[32]

---

[32] Dorothy Van Ghent, *The English Novel: Form and Function* (New York, 1953), 286.

Sheridan seems, in other words, to have found in *Nourjahad* a story of mythic dimensions.

Sheridan's account of the composition of *Nourjahad* would seem to encourage this notion that she was in some way tapping into archetypal narrative concerns which lurk just beneath the conscious mind. The plan of the novel, Le Fanu recalls her grandmother telling her,

was suggested to her mind one sleepless night, when from reflecting upon the inequality in the conditions of men, she was led to consider that it is in the due regulation of the passions, rather than on the outward dispensations of providence, that true happines [*sic*] or misery depends; and she conceived the idea of the probable condition of a human being of a violent and perverse disposition, supposing his wealth to be inexhaustible, and his days extended to infinity. In fancy she beheld this being, possessed of the two greatest apparent goods, riches and immortality, yet devoid of any inward principle to restrain the unbounded indulgence of his passions. Nourjahad finds in those gratified, yet still importunate passions, his tormentors, and the two blessings he had impatiently coveted transformed into insupportable evils. As this idea acquired form and consistency, Mrs. Sheridan represented it as entering her mind like a kind of vision or dream, between sleep and waking. . . . She communicated the skeleton of the story the next morning to her eldest daughter, whose promising talents and opening mind Mrs. Sheridan began to take great delight in cultivating.[33]

Sheridan's language in this recounting—'a kind of vision or dream, between sleep and waking'—anticipates phrases used by the Romantic poets (particularly, of course, Coleridge's description of the circumstances of composition of 'Kubla Khan' (1816), and the final lines of Keats's 'Ode to a Nightingale' (1820)), when attempting to describe the nature of poetic inspiration. The similarity is, in some ways, strikingly appropriate; *Nourjahad* possesses a lush

[33] Le Fanu, *Memoirs*, 295–6.

physicality—a delight in the voluptuous descriptions of sensuous excess—akin to that of Keats's poem, and shares with 'Kubla Khan' an equally sensuous delight in the landscapes of orientalism. Like these works, however, the architectonic skill with which *Nourjahad* is constructed belies the account of its casual and 'inspired' composition. The narrative secrets of *Nourjahad* require an immense amount of control and precision, and Sheridan never allows her grasp on the story to slip. Only once—immediately prior to the first of Nourjahad's 'sleeps'—does the narrator intrude into the story. Nourjahad has gathered the women of his seraglio and his musicians together for a sumptuous feast, she writes,

Himself attired in robes, such as the kings of Persia were used to wear, was seated under a canopy of silver tissue, which he had put up for the purpose; and assuming the pomp of an Eastern monarch, suffered the illusion to take such possession of his mind, that if he were not before mad, he now seemed to be very near distraction.

Intoxicated with pleasure, the historian who writes his life, affirms that this night Nourjahad for the first time got drunk.

Be that as it may, it is certain that having retired to rest, he slept sounder and longer than usual; for on his awaking, and missing Mandana from his side, whom he had made the partner of his bed, he called out to the slave who always attended in his antichamber, in order to enquire for her, resolving to chide her tenderly for leaving him.

Sheridan's wonderfully equivocal 'be that as it may' (and her scrupulously precise 'it is *certain*') is deft and unobtrusive. Only on re-reading the story do we see how skilfully the 'historian' who writes Nourjahad's tale maintains the fictions of Nourjahad's enchantments so that the reader as well as the fictional character himself is swept up and overwhelmed by the unexpected anagnorisis of the story. There are few passages in eighteenth-century literature which possess the sheer exhilaration of the final pages of

Nourjahad. If one of the strengths of the oriental tale as a sub-genre of English prose fiction is its ability to present readers with a range of alternative cultural possibilities, *Nourjahad* works as well to present alternative possibilities for *each* of our own lives. Nourjahad participates in a remarkable 'drama' of life, which allows him to treat his real life with greater value and attain, as Sheridan would have it, 'true happiness'.

Of what does this happiness consist? Sheridan pretends to end her tale on a conventionally romantic note. Schemzeddin offers the 'amiable Mandana' to Nourjahad as his wife, and the 'fixed confidence and love' of Schemzeddin as a reward for his reformation. The real 'love story' of *Nourjahad*, however—the erotic and romantic power which drives the tale—is that between Schemzeddin and Nourjahad themselves. Nourjahad's original confession to Schemzeddin that he desires to possess 'inexhaustible riches' is made in the deeply romantic setting of the seraglio gardens. The lush language of the passage ('the mild lustre of the moon now at full', 'the exhalations which arose from a thousand odoriferous shrubs', 'throwing himself down on a bank of violets') deliberately recalls the opening lines of Shakespeare's *Twelfth Night*, in which the love-sick Duke Orsino—prostrate with infatuation—lies incapable of action before a romantic object of affection who to him remains unattainable. Perhaps Sheridan wishes us to recall the issues of gender and sexuality—the seemingly random and haphazard directions of love and desire—which are raised in Shakespeare's comedy as well. At the very least, her tale presents a fable the centre of which *is* articulated by the otherwise silly Orsino; Schemzeddin creates the contexts within which the appetite of Nourjahad may indeed be satisfied by excess 'and so die'. Schemzeddin states that his real purpose in practising the elaborate imposture on Nourjahad was to demonstrate to him 'what the heart of man is capable [of], when he shuts his eyes

against the precepts of our holy prophet'. Yet Schemzeddin's true aim is to keep Nourjahad close to himself—'an
ornament and support to the throne of Persia'—in the face
of strong and (it must be admitted, in retrospect) legitimate
political opposition. At the end of the story Schemzeddin
has been able to keep his beloved Nourjahad at his side.
Nourjahad's appetite has merely realized the proper object
of its affections; the only real transformative magic in the
story is the 'genius' of the human heart.

The History of Charoba, Queen of Ægypt

In sharp contrast to Frances Sheridan who, as we have
seen, struggled at an early age against patriarchal injunctions which begrudged her the most elementary education,
Clara Reeve—born in Ipswich, Suffolk, in January 1729—
spent her earliest years surrounded by books, and by a
close and supportive family which, rather than hindering
her, encouraged her learning as much as possible.[34] Reeve
in fact once observed to a friend that, 'at an age when few
people of either sex can read their names', she was already
familiar with the Greek and Latin classics, as well as with
the recent histories of England, and the parliamentary
debates recorded in the newspapers (written by Johnson
and Hawkesworth) and popular magazines. Upon the death
of her father in 1755, Reeve moved from Ipswich with her
mother and sister and resettled in Colchester, where she in
time devoted herself to her writings. Her first effort, a
collection of poetry, was published in 1769; an ambitious
translation of John Barclay's 1621 Latin romance *Argenis*
followed in 1772. Her popular first novel *The Champion of
Virtue* (soon retitled *The Old English Baron*) appeared in

---

[34] Biographical information here is drawn partly from Elizabeth
Napier's entry in the *Dictionary of Literary Biography* (New York, 1985),
372–7.

1777. Later in life she wrote a series of novels, including *The School for Widows* (1791) and its sequel *Plans for Education* (1792), which concerned themselves with questions of practical pedagogy. She died in Ipswich in December 1807.

Reeve's *History of Charoba, Queen of Ægypt* first appeared in 1785, when it was published as an appendix to her critical dialogue *The Progress of Romance*. *Charoba* was Reeve's own redaction of a tale which had originally been included in Murtada ibn al-Khafif's history of Egypt. The story had in time been translated from the Arabic by Pierre Vattier and—finally, in 1672—into English by John Davies, the busy seventeenth-century translator who would eventually render both Mlle de Scudéry's *Clélie* and Honoré d'Urfé's *Astrée* (1607–27) into English. Reeve freely admits her indebtedness to Davies's *Egyptian History* in her Preface, claiming only to have 'compiled and methodised' the existing account. Reeve in fact made several significant changes in the story before including it in her own volume, elaborating on the received biblical narrative as well as altering her immediate source.

Charoba might initially appear to have been included in Reeve's volume as little more than an afterthought to the larger dialogue. Reeve herself notes that she includes the story merely in order to demonstrate that 'Romances are of universal growth, and are not confined to any particular period or countries.'[35] On closer examination, however, *Charoba* has an important part to play in Reeve's analysis of the novel. *The Progress of Romance* on the whole argues for the significance of the romance tradition; it is among the first critical works to recognize that the traditions of romance are an integral part of what we have since characterized as 'the rise of the novel' in English—it is among the

---

[35] Clara Reeve, *The Progress of Romance . . . through Times, Countries, and Manners* (Colchester, 1785), xv–xvi.

first to recognize that the 'novel' itself, as Reeve puts it, has 'sprung out of [the] ruins' of the Romance.[36] Theorists of the novel since Reeve have tended to minimize the role of the romance in the formulation of modern forms of prose fiction. We have repeatedly been told that the development of what the critic Ian Watt some time ago labelled the structures of 'formal realism' in the eighteenth-century novel involved a repudiation of the techniques and conventions of the sprawling prose romance. Reeve's early analysis of this 'rise of the novel', however, demands that the romance be examined as the foundation upon which the modern novel has been built. Reeve's is a vision which sees the novel arising not out of the narrow economic, social, or religious circumstances of a particular moment in the early eighteenth century in England, but which desires, rather, generously to view the history of prose fiction in all its grand, polyglot inclusivity. Romance, Reeve tells us, has been with us since the beginning of story-telling itself. While it may well be necessary to distinguish between forms of prose fiction (romances, she decides, are heroic fables which treat of fabulous persons and things—they describe 'what never happened nor is likely to happen'; the novel, on the other hand, is a picture of real life and manners; it gives us 'a familiar relation of such things, as pass every day before our eyes'), the thrust of her argument works constantly to break down the generic and sub-generic distinctions which have worked to privilege one particular form of prose fiction over another.[37] The dialogue emphasizes that romance has always been with us and—in one form or another—always *will* be with us. At their best romances are no less capable than other kinds of prose fiction of 'improving the morals and manners of mankind'. Reeve rather scandalously insists that works operating in

[36] Ibid. i. 8.
[37] Ibid. i. 111.

the tradition of romance such as the *Arabian Nights* itself
are worthy of comparison with Homer's *Odyssey* ('You
cannot be in earnest in this comparison', gasps one stunned
male participant in the dialogue). She even allows the
participants in her 'dialogue' to praise Eastern tales as being
among the most readable and consistently entertaining
forms of prose fiction. *Rasselas*, *Almoran and Hamet* and
Nourjahad ('a very pretty Eastern Tale') are all mentioned
by name. 'There is a kind of fascination in them,' one of
the interlocuters says of oriental tales in general, '—when
once we begin a volume, we cannot lay it aside, but drive
through to the end of it'.[38] While there is thus 'something
very pleasing in *Eastern Stories* well told', the character of
Hortensius in Reeve's dialogue contends that they are
nevertheless 'dangerous books for youths,—they create and
encourage the wildest excursions of imagination which it is,
or ought to be, the care of parents and preceptors to
restrain, and to give them a just and true representation of
human nature, and of the duties and practice of common
life'.[39] The character of Euphrasia, however, who more
frequently appears in the dialogue to give voice to opinions
closer to those held by Reeve herself (her name tells us,
after all, that she 'speaks well'), ridicules the value of a
pedagogical method which renders youth '*old* before their
days are half spent', and concludes that such Eastern tales
represent a healthy narrative passion as ancient as civilization itself. *Charoba* becomes the keystone not only of
Reeve's defence of Eastern tales, but of her larger argument
for the romance as being 'of human growth'—of being
indigenous to *all* mankind. It is the 'curious story' which
draws together the seemingly varied strands of biblical,
Eastern, and classical narratives in order to demonstrate
that it is only custom and prejudice which blind us to the

---

[38] Ibid. ii. 58–61.

[39] Ibid. ii. 59

underlying similarities in the passion of all peoples for 'tales and stories'. Reeve is—in this respect at least—an archetypal critic (one who recognizes the interconnectedness and interdependency of *all* narratives) far ahead of her time.

Charoba is less obviously 'oriental' than Hawkesworth's *Almoran and Hamet* or Sheridan's *Nourjahad*. There is some recollection of the stories in the *Arabian Nights* (particularly 'Aladdin; or, The Wonderful Lamp') in the description of the subterranean cavern through which Gebirus must pass in order to obtain the riches necessary to complete his city, yet the narrative world of the story is a more ancient one. In the place of turbaned genii and magic talismans, the reader is presented with a setting in which the wonders and enchantments more readily recall the miracles of the Old Testament. *Charoba* in fact presents itself as biblical apocrypha—at least it begins by offering its readers a narrative concerning Abraham and Sarah which does not belong to the mainstream of the Judaeo-Christian tradition. Yet it is also *classical* apocrypha. We everywhere hear echoes, for example, of Homer's *Odyssey*. The strategy of Charoba and the nurse literally to deconstruct the diurnal progress of Gebirus' city calls to mind the contrivances of Homer's Penelope (whose household is also assisted by a faithful 'nurse' in the form of Eurykleia), who picks apart the progress of her weaving so as likewise to avoid unwelcome suitors. The elusive and mysterious 'lady of the sea' who wrestles the young shepherd out of his flock and then helps Gebirus to complete the city similarly recalls the action of Book IV of the *Odyssey*, in which Menelaus recounts to Telemachus a similar experience (which also took place in Egypt) of having to outwit the old man of the sea Proteus with the help of his daughter Eidothea, before being allowed to return home.

It is precisely Reeve's purpose to draw together and to connect the seemingly disparate strands of narrative invention—to demonstrate the progress of romance not only through but *across* 'times, countries, and manners', as the extended title of her volume puts it. Having lost sight of the extensive genealogy of the novel in Europe and—indeed—in the East as well, Reeve seems to be saying, we have narrowed and falsified our understanding of prose fiction, and effectively created 'chasms' in our literary history. Charoba is proof that 'romances are of human growth', and it is proof as well that the romance tradition is not so easily to be pushed aside and appropriated. Margaret Anne Doody has argued persuasively that the reading of romances was an important part of the literary education of both male and female readers in the early eighteenth century; it is only from the early 1750s that the constraints of so-called 'formal realism' begin to exclude the romance from the taxonomies of respected and respectable fiction.[40] A 'revised notion of probability' works to exclude the romance from the accepted genealogy of the novel. In light of this puzzling 'repudiation of romance' in the mid-eighteenth century, the narrative of *Charoba* itself becomes a metaphorical demonstration of the struggle of the female story—the struggle of the romance—to be heard in a world which all too frequently acknowledges and inscribes only the voice of the male. Charoba insists that her struggle too be 'engraven' on a pillar. The 'high tower' which rises above the city of Gebirus bears not only the name of the man who erected it, but also that of the rival who insisted on remaining 'a virgin to the end of her life'. Upon her death the crown is passed to a female successor (who likewise insists on remaining unmarried), but this line of descent is later obscured, and the laurels are passed to successors who wear the crown of Egypt 'for many generations'. Reeve fights in her own day against the stern and pedantic 'Hortensius' who insists on a form of fiction which

---

[40] Margaret Anne Doody, 'Introduction' to Charlotte Lennox's *The Female Quixote* (World's Classics edn., Oxford, 1989), pp. xvii–xix.

inculcates in its reader the 'duties' of 'common life'. Like Charoba herself, Reeve deconstructs the work of the despotic male, taking it apart and working to turn it to her own ends. Including *Charoba* in her *Progress of Romance*, she reinscribes the magic and peculiarly female traditions of romance within the 'older and better' language of the ultimate document of the patriarchal tradition—the Bible itself.

Murad the Unlucky

The last of the authors whose work is included in the present volume, Maria Edgeworth, has received by far the greatest amount of attention. Edgeworth has been the subject of an excellent literary biography and of numerous critical studies. While the author of such important 'regional' novels chronicling life in Ireland as *Castle Rackrent* (1800) and *The Absentee* was never quite allowed to disappear from the established literary canon, recent years have seen the republication as well of some of her other important and influential works, including *Belinda* (1811) and *Patronage* (1814). Two of Edgeworth's most recent editors note that there has likewise been a belated and well-deserved revival of recognition for the third of the novelist's 'reputations'—and the one for which she was best known in her own lifetime—as a 'pioneer in the field of education and of writing for children'.[41]

It is this last category to which *Murad the Unlucky* belongs. *Murad* was first published in 1804 as part of a three-volume collection of sketches and short stories entitled simply *Popular Tales*. The collection was the third of Edgeworth's attempts—following *The Parent's Assistant* (1796; 1800) and *Moral Tales* (1801)—to bring together a

---

[41] W. J. McCormack and Kim Walker (eds.), Maria Edgeworth's *The Absentee* (World's Classics edn., Oxford, 1988), p. ix.

series of novellas and short fictions which inculcate the specific moral values she was to set out at greater length in the treatise on pedagogy she would write with her father Richard Lovell Edgeworth, *Practical Education* (1798). Incorporating the ideas of educational thinkers earlier in the century such as Locke and Rousseau, *Practical Education* is a work of considerable reformist practicality. The individual chapters of the book (e.g. 'Toys', 'On Attention', 'On Obedience', 'On Truth', 'On Rewards and Punishments', 'Memory and Imagination', 'Wit and Judgement') deal with an impressive range of pedagogical issues, and together stress the idea that, while discipline may be important to the upbringing of a child, the ultimate goal of the successful education of children is to 'let them be left as free as the air' or, in more practical terms, to render them capable of making their own reasoned and responsible moral decisions.[42]

The short stories brought together in the *Moral Tales* and the *Popular Tales* reflect a central observation of *Practical Education*: that 'without particular examples, the most obvious tasks are not brought home to our business'.[43] The *Tales* reflect as well the Edgeworths' belief, again following Rousseau, that different narratives are suited to different ages and audiences. The stories collected in the earlier *Parent's Assistant* had been designed and written specifically with the youngest readers in mind. The most memorable of the stories—'Waste Not, Want Not', for example, or 'Simple Susan'—are told in a manner which clearly articulates the moral and didactic purpose of the tale, yet at the same time entertains with its simple but effective attention to small narrative detail, and its genuine comprehension of 'what really matters' in the eyes of a child. The *Popular Tales*, by contrast, are designed for a slightly older audi-

[42] *Practical Education* (London, 1798), ii. 287.
[43] Ibid. i. 291.

ence—they are 'stories for young men and women'.[44]
Richard Lovell Edgeworth again notes, however, that they
are meant clearly to be didactic tales, to present 'instruction, in the dress of innocent amusement'.

Murad is the seventh of the eleven tales in the collection.
It is not surprising that Edgeworth chose to 'dress' one of
her stories as an oriental tale. One of the earliest tasks of
composition she had been set by her father—who had
apparently been disappointed by her uncommunicative
letters sent from school when she was only 10 years old—
was to complete, in her own language, a popular 'Arabian
tale' begun by himself. Like her contemporaries, Edgeworth had grown up surrounded by the narratives of the
Arabian Nights, the *Persian Tales*, and other Eastern fictions. Yet while *Practical Education* itself lists with approval
Hawkesworth's *Adventurer* essays ('found interesting' it is
noted, 'to children from seven to nine or ten years old'),
the same volume notes that a greater care needs to be
exercised when placing the *Nights* themselves in the hands
of younger readers; the *Nights*, it is warned, belongs to 'a
class of books which amuse the imagination of children,
without acting upon their feelings'.[45] 'A boy, who at seven
years old longs to be . . . Sindbad the sailor,' Edgeworth
writes,

may at seventeen, retain the same taste for adventure and enter-
prise, though mixed so as to be less discernible, with the incipient
passions of avarice and ambition; he has the same dispositions
modified by a slight knowledge of real life, and guided by the
manners and conversation of friends and acquaintance. Robinson
Crusoe and Sindbad will no longer be his favourite heroes; but he
will now admire the soldier of fortune, the commercial adventurer,
or the nabob, who has discovered in the east the secret of Aladdin's

---

[44] Richard Lovell Edgeworth, Preface to *Tales of Fashionable Life*, 1st
series (London, 1809); cited in Marilyn Butler, *Maria Edgeworth: A
Literary Biography* (Oxford, 1972), 286.
[45] *Practical Education*, i. 299, 304.

wonderful lamp; and who has realized the treasures of Aboulcasem.[46]

Such criticism recalls the warnings of Clara Reeve that the *Arabian Nights* is a 'dangerous' book for youths. Yet Edgeworth's language in this passage is more startlingly revealing. 'Commercial adventurers' and 'soldiers of fortune' were plunderers and fortune-hunting thieves; 'nabobs' or 'nabob plunderers', in the more recent sense in which Edgeworth is using the term, were Englishmen who returned from the East with great (and more frequently than not ill-gotten) wealth. Edgeworth's clear implication is that the spoils of colonialism—the stolen 'secrets of Aladdin's lamp'—are the results of a misguided avarice and ambition. Edgeworth is presenting in the passage nothing less than a not-so-subtle critique of British imperial policy, with a critique as well of the pedagogical misadventures which encouraged the English to think of the world as a rich 'object' ripe for spoil.

Murad is itself a story from the *Arabian Nights* rewritten to correct such an impression; it is a corrective oriental tale. Neglected by the earliest reviewers of the *Popular Tales* and by almost all of Edgeworth's subsequent critics, *Murad* has been dismissed by those who care to mention it as a simplistic moral fable with an all-too-obvious message: prudence and good judgement, rather than luck or chance, are the governing factors of human life. The story has been condemned as the least interesting and least efficacious of the *Popular Tales* by at least one critic, who has maintained that 'it is impossible to beguile the reader into accepting a practical lesson on the basis of such bizarre facts and striking occurrences'.[47] From its opening paragraphs, however, Edgeworth has set up a careful contrast between

---

[46] Ibid. i. 302.

[47] Elizabeth Harden, *Maria Edgeworth's Art of Prose Fiction* (The Hague, 1971), 131.

Murad and the stories in the _Nights_. It can even be argued that the real concern of _Murad_ is not so much the obvious argument for prudence as opposed to luck, but rather the same condemnation of political ambition which Edgeworth has so forcibly stated in _Practical Education_—a condemnation which is implicitly echoed in Saladin's protestations in the final paragraph of the story that he is 'perfectly happy in his present situation', and his rejection of the 'ambition' which could make him a governor. The full irony of Saladin's name, recalling as it does the twelfth-century Islamic warrior (see p. 216 and note) becomes evident only in this final passage, as he spectacularly rejects worldly and political ambitions for his quiet life as a merchant. In a section of _Practical Education_ entitled 'On Vanity, Prudence, and Ambition', Edgeworth had written,

The ambition to rise in the world, usually implies a mean, sordid desire of riches, or what are called honors, to be obtained by the common arts of political intrigue, by cabal to win popular favor, or by address to conciliate the patronage of the great. The experience of those who have been governed during their lives by this passion, if passion it may be called, does not shew that it can confer much happiness either in the pursuit or attainment of its objects.[48]

Edgeworth's condemnation of the _Arabian Nights_ as a text which at its worst reinforces in its young readers the meanest habits of vulgar ambition—'the sordid desire of riches'—is implicit in her _own_ oriental tale, which pushes the dubious (as she sees them) moral values of its narrative progenitor to one side.

If the fate of Saladin suggests that one who has pursued the 'noiseless tenor' of his way is to be preferred to the careers of those entranced and entrapped by the delusive fantasies of political and material success prompted by the _Nights_, the fate of Murad—left to die a horribly painful

48 _Practical Education_, i. 281.

death in the opium markets of Constantinople—would likewise seem to suggest that Galland's *Nights* is, in any event, no longer a viable source for images of exotic Eastern riches, nor, for that matter, of legitimate images of Eastern culture in general. The *Arabian Nights does* remain an important text throughout the nineteenth century, but it is a *Nights* tempered by increasing travel to and contact with the East; it is in the *Nights* of Sir Richard Francis Burton, not of Galland. *Murad* reflects the growing tendency of oriental tales very early in the nineteenth century to respond to the (by then) truly overwhelming amount of information about the East—travellers' accounts, letters, maps, even guide books—in circulation. If the early eighteenth century had witnessed a fascination with Islamic culture prompted by the work of scholars and orientalists such as Galland, the corresponding years of the nineteenth century see the last successful attempts by writers in the West consciously to romanticize and to transform the East into an exotic land of oases, harems, and seraglios. The world of Edgeworth's tale is emphatically *not* the hazy, opulent landscape of the earliest Eastern tales; it is a world ravaged by the plague, threatened constantly by natural disasters and social unrest, and inhabited by the forces of a foreign occupation; it is a world which is well on its way to the East of Lord Byron's *Don Juan* (1819–24). Gone are the romantic and colourful market-places of the *Nights*, and the moonlit gardens of Hawkesworth's *Almoran and Hamet* and Sheridan's *Nourjahad*; in their stead is the crowded, urban setting of a Constantinople poised on the edge of the modern world, with its mobs, its riots, and its insurrections. The movements of the European forces then deciding the fate of the Ottoman empire circle ominously on the borders of Edgeworth's narrative. While certain aspects of her tale deliberately evoke the world of the *Nights*, they do so only to deconstruct it, exposing beneath the lush romanticism of eighteenth-century orientalism the harsh realities of life in the 'gorgeous East'.

The surprisingly lengthy explanatory glosses which support Edgeworth's text are part of this conscious attempt to deconstruct earlier Eastern narratives. Edgeworth quotes at length from François, Baron de Tott's *Memoirs concerning the State of the Turkish Empire and the Crimea* (1785) and John Antes's *Observations on the Manners and Customs of the Egyptians* (1800). Antes was a missionary who published his *Observations* as a complement and corrective to the more wide-ranging and inclusive travel narratives of Savary and Volney. He lived in Egypt for several years, and the *Observations* provide Edgeworth with an extensive amount of material for *Murad* detailing the spread and transmission of the plague. Baron de Tott, whom Edgeworth quotes at even greater length in her glosses, was a French diplomat who spent a significant portion of his life in Constantinople. His *Memoirs* provided Edgeworth with descriptions of an 'Orient' plagued by violence and political turmoil. Her descriptions were effectively underscored by quotations from de Tott and Antes which work to undercut the dramatic unity of the familiar form of the oriental tale. Beneath the surface of Edgeworth's seemingly conventional oriental apologue—beneath the trappings of its exoticism— lies a brutally real picture of despotism, intolerance, and human misery. There may very well be legitimate ways in which the East differs from the West, Edgeworth seems to say, but the inconsequential enchantments of the *Arabian Nights* are not among them. It is no longer possible to use the East as a convenient and mysterious repository of a world governed by genii and magic; in *Murad* we see at least one writer beginning to come to grips with the realization that the orientalism of the nineteenth century will have to be less fanciful and more culturally responsible.

* * *

It has been argued very convincingly in recent years that the ideology of orientalism works 'in the service of imperialism'—that orientalism itself, an effort to 'comprehend the civilizations, cultures, and religions of the East', creates a world which is 'a singularly subjective creation seen and measured through ethnographic perceptions and criteria'.[49] The most severe and articulate critic of Western complacency regarding the image of the Orient has of course been Edward Said. For Said, orientalism is 'a kind of western projection onto and will to govern the Orient', 'a collective notion identifying "us" Europeans as against all "those" non-Europeans'.[50] For Said and other critics of orientalism, as Kathryn Tidrick has put it, 'writers on the Middle East'—and we may here most certainly include the English orientalists of the eighteenth century—'are primarily to be understood as prisoners of an institutionalized system of discourse which makes it impossible for them to regard Orientals as human beings like themselves'.[51]

While there is no doubt some degree of truth to what Said and others have thus written about the structures of orientalism, the tales brought together in this volume would seem to argue for an analysis which necessarily involves fewer such sweeping generalizations. In her study of the masquerade in eighteenth-century English culture and fiction, Terry Castle notes that the vogue for oriental costumes in the period could be seen as 'a mere displacement of imperialist fantasy'.[52] 'The popularity of the masquerade', she observes, 'coincided after all with the expansion of British imperialism, and the symbolic joining of the races could conceivably be construed as a kind of perverse

---

[49] 'Introduction', in Asaf Hussain, Robert Olson, and Jamil Qureshi (eds.), *Orientalism, Islam, and Islamists* (Brattleboro, V., 1984), 1–4.

[50] See Edward Said, *Orientalism* (New York, 1979), 31–110.

[51] Kathryn Tidrick, *Heart-Beguiling Araby* (Cambridge, 1981), 2.

[52] Terry Castle, *Masquerade and Civilization: The Carnivalesque in Eighteenth-Century English Culture and Fiction* (Stanford, Calif., 1988), 61.

allusion to empire'. Undoubtedly this is the manner in which the critics of orientalism *would* construe it. Yet, as Castle goes on to point out,

> at a deeper level, such travesties were also an act of homage—to otherness itself. Stereotypical and inaccurate as they often were, exotic costumes marked out a kind of symbolic interpenetration with difference—an almost erotic commingling with the alien. Mimicry becomes a form of psychological recognition, a way of embracing, quite literally, the unfamiliar. The collective result was a utopian project; the masquerade's visionary 'Congress of Nations'—the image of global conviviality—was indisputably a thing of fleeting, hallucinatory beauty.[53]

At their best, oriental tales are also an act of homage to the Orient. They too have been dismissed as stereotypical and mistaken in their picture of Eastern life. But Hawkesworth, Sheridan, Reeve, and Edgeworth all use the oriental tale in remarkable different ways. It is certainly less their concern to offer a reductive vision of life in the 'elusive East' than to exploit the *form* of the oriental tale to their particular advantage. Hawkesworth's tale presents a moral lesson to a young monarch which conceals within it a vision of the political world which is far from optimistic; Sheridan advances a homoerotic love story which spectacularly plays with the conventions of narrative and reader awareness; Reeve draws the oriental tale within the wide and encompassing fold of the 'romance'; Edgeworth tells us that we shall have to rethink the *Arabian Nights* if we are ever to understand the East. To each the oriental tale is an enabling form of prose fiction, and to all the Orient not a 'family of ideas' but a forum for the widest possible stretches of the human imagination. The plasticity of the oriental tale opens the form up to a startling variety of agenda—political, sexual, revisionary—and the writers in this collection picked up the genre because it allowed them to do some-

[53] Ibid. 60–1.

thing different. What draws these tales together is not only contemporary popularity—the fact that there was an audience for them—but the licence provided by the oriental tale as a genre.

NOTE ON THE TEXTS

ALTHOUGH at least two of the stories included here enjoyed a considerable degree of popularity among eighteenth-century readers (*Almoran and Hamet* had passed through six editions by the end of the century, for example, while Sheridan's *Nourjahad* appeared no less than five times), a collation of the several editions published during the authors' lifetimes revealed no evidence of substantive changes or authorial revisions. The text of John Hawkesworth's *Almoran and Hamet* is that of the first edition, published in two volumes by Payne and Cropley in 1761. The text of Frances Sheridan's *History of Nourjahad* has been set from a copy of the first edition, published by Dodsley in 1767. Clara Reeve's *History of Charoba, Queen of Ægypt* first appeared in 1785 with her dialogue *The Progress of Romance*, and the text of the first Colchester edition has been used. The present text of Maria Edgeworth's *Murad the Unlucky* is taken from the first (1804) edition of her collection of *Popular Tales*. All of these texts have been set from copies now in the Bodleian Library, Oxford.

For the convenience of the modern reader a number of changes have been made to the texts according to the following general principles:

1. The long eighteenth-century 's' (ʃ) has been modernized throughout.

2. Eccentricities of grammar, spelling, and punctuation have been retained, except that quotation marks have been systematized to conform with modern custom.

3. Capitalization and italicization have been retained as in the original, except that the continued capitalization of proper names in *Nourjahad* and the similar italicization

of proper names in Reeve's *Charoba* have been normalized.

4. Obvious typographical errors, misprints, and anacoluthon have been silently corrected. The modest errata printed at the end of the first volume of the first edition of Hawkesworth's *Almoran and Hamet* have been included in the present text.

SELECT BIBLIOGRAPHY

Editions: There have been no modern editions of John Hawkesworth's *Almoran and Hamet*, although the 1761 edition has been reprinted in a facsimile text in the Garland series 'The Flowering of the Novel: Representative Mid-Eighteenth-Century Fiction' (New York, 1974). Frances Sheridan's *History of Nourjahad* was reprinted in the same series (New York, 1974). *Nourjahad* had appeared in another edition earlier this century with a modest introduction by H. V. Marrot and illustrations by Mabel R. Peacock (London, 1927), and more recently with an introduction by Maurice Johnson (Norwood, Pa., 1977). The Facsimile Text Society reissued Clara Reeve's *The Progress of Romance and the History of Charoba, Queen of Ægypt* in a facsimile reproduced from the Colchester edition of 1785. Maria Edgeworth's *Murad the Unlucky* has appeared with the rest of the *Popular Tales* in the second volume of the ten-volume Longford edition (London, 1893), which has twice been reprinted (New York, 1967; Hildesheim, 1969).

Biography: John Hawkesworth has found an able biographer in John Lawrence Abbott, whose *John Hawkesworth: Eighteenth-Century Man of Letters* (Madison, Wis., 1982) offers a clear account of Hawkesworth's literary activity ranging from his early contributions to the *Gentleman's Magazine* to the final, dispiriting reception of his *Voyages* of Captain Cook in 1773. The only full-length biographical study of Frances Sheridan is the *Memoirs of the Life and Writings of Mrs. Frances Sheridan* (London, 1824) by her granddaughter Alicia Le Fanu. Also noteworthy is Margaret Anne Doody's concise entry in the *Dictionary of Literary Biography*, vol. xxxix, pt. II (New York, 1985), 428–33. Elizabeth Napier's discussion of Clara Reeve, again in the *Dictionary of Literary Biography*, vol. xxxix, pt. II (New York, 1985), 372–7, is one of the very few extended accounts of Reeve's life and work. Maria Edgeworth has benefited from the attention of Marilyn Butler, whose authoritative *Maria Edgeworth: A Literary Biography*

(Oxford, 1972) provides a thorough background to Edgeworth's career as a novelist.

Oriental Tales: Readers wishing to acquaint themselves more thoroughly with the genre of the oriental tale will probably want to begin with *The Arabian Nights' Entertainments*. Antoine Galland's original French translation (*Mille et Une Nuit*) of the tales collected in his Arabic original is currently available in three volumes (Paris, 1965), with an introduction by Jean Gaulmier; the earliest English translation of Galland's text is currently being edited for the World's Classics series. The appearance of Galland's work in English is discussed by James Hanford in 'Open Sesame: Notes on the *Arabian Nights* in England', *Princeton Library Chronicle*, 26 (1964–5), 48–56. Henry Weber's invaluable three-volume *Tales of the East* (London, 1812) reproduces not only the English translation of Galland's *Nights*, but also the *New Arabian Nights*, *Persian Tales*, *Tales of Inatulla of Delhi*, *Oriental Tales*, *Mogul Tales*, *Turkish Tales*, *Tartarian Tales*, *Chinese Tales*, *Tales of the Genii*, and *Tales of Abdallah, the Son of Hanif*. Other oriental tales and Eastern fictions remain widely available. Montesquieu's *Lettres persanes* has been published with a preface by Jacques Roger (Paris, 1964), and Lord Lyttelton's *Persian Letters* has been edited by Roderick Boyd Porter, with an introduction by Pat Rogers (Cleveland, 1988). Samuel Johnson's *History of Rasselas, Prince of Abissinia* has appeared in an authoritative edition edited by Gwin Kolb, *Rasselas and Other Tales* (New Haven, Conn., 1990), which contains an introduction placing Johnson's philosophical satire within the larger context of the oriental tale. William Beckford's *Vathek* has been edited by Roger Lonsdale (Oxford, 1983). Also available is Beckford's *Episodes of Vathek*, edited by Robert J. Gemmet (London, 1975); the volume contains Beckford's remaining oriental fictions, originally published posthumously in 1912.

There have been very few discussions of the oriental tale as a sub-genre of eighteenth-century prose fiction. The most substantial include: Martha Pike Conant, *The Oriental Tale in England in the Eighteenth Century* (New York, 1908); volume v of Ernest A. Baker's *History of the English Novel* (London, 1929), which includes a chapter on 'The Oriental Tale from Rasselas to Vathek';

Kokab Saffari, *Les Légendes et contes persans dans la littérature anglaise des XVIIIe et XIXe siècles jusqu'en 1859* (Paris, 1972); Rochelle Suzette Ekhtiar, 'Fictions of Enlightenment: The Oriental Tale in Eighteenth-Century England', Ph.D. diss. (Brandeis University, 1985). Benjamin Boyce's 'English Short Fiction in the Eighteenth Century: A Preliminary View', *Studies in Short Fiction*, 5 (1967–8), 95–112, acknowledges the oriental tale to have been one of the major 'kinds' of short fiction in the eighteenth century. Peter L. Caracciolo has edited *The Arabian Nights in English Literature* (New York, 1988), a collection of essays which together examine the formative influence of the *Nights* on the imaginations and literary productions of English authors.

There are very few studies of the particular oriental tales included in the present volume. *Almoran and Hamet* is discussed with reference both to Johnson's *Rasselas, Prince of Abissinia* and to Hawkesworth's other work in Abbott's biography of the author, noted above. Robert D. Mayo's *The English Novel in the Magazines, 1740–1815* (London, 1962) contains a short analysis of the relation between Hawkesworth's full-length oriental fiction and the earlier Eastern stories contained in his *Adventurer*. Gwin Kolb's *Rasselas and Other Tales*, also noted above, offers some brief points of comparison between Hawkesworth and Johnson. Margaret Anne Doody's 'Frances Sheridan: Morality and Annihilated Time' in Mary Anne Schofield and Cecilia Macheski (eds.), *Fetter'd or Free: British Women Novelists, 1670–1815* (London, 1986), relates Sheridan's treatment of time in *The History of Nourjahad* to a similar treatment in her realistic fiction. Brief discussions of *Murad the Unlucky* are included in Elizabeth Harden's *Maria Edgeworth's Art of Prose Fiction* (The Hague, 1971), as well as in her *Maria Edgeworth* (Boston, 1982). Edgar Rosenberg's *From Shylock to Svengali: Jewish Stereotypes in English Fiction* (Stanford, Calif., 1960) contains an analysis of Edgeworth's unflattering portrait of the treacherous Jew Rachub in the tale.

Orientalism, Islam, and the West: Edward Said's *Orientalism* (New York, 1978) has prompted a sometimes heated debate regarding images of Islam in the European West, a debate which is ultimately of interest to any reader attempting to understand the role of the *Arabian Nights* and the eighteenth-century oriental tale in the construction of those images. The controversy initiated by Said is continued in volumes such as Asaf Hussain, Robert Olson, and Jamil Qureshi (eds.), *Orientalism, Islam, and Islamists* (Brattleboro, Vt., 1984). Two contributions to the discussion particularly worth noting are Bernard Lewis's 'The Question of Orientalism', *New York Review of Books*, 29 (1982), 49–56, and Said's own revaluation, 'Orientalism Reconsidered', *Cultural Critique*, 1 (1985), 89–107. Earlier studies of the subject addressed by Said include Norman Daniel's volumes *Islam and the West: The Making of an Image* (Edinburgh, 1960), which explores the foundation of Christian attitudes towards Islam in the European West, and his *Islam, Europe, and Empire* (Edinburgh, 1966), which continues the study through Europe's relation to Islam in the late eighteenth and nineteenth centuries. Accounts of travellers and explorers in the Near East whose writings were to prove influential on English orientalists in the eighteenth and nineteenth centuries include: Sari J. Nasir, *The Arabs and the English* (London, 1976); Zahra Freeth and Victor Winstone, *Explorers of Arabia: From the Renaissance to the End of the Victorian Era* (New York, 1978); Raymond Schwab, *The Oriental Renaissance: Europe's Rediscovery of India and the East, 1680–1880*, trans. Gene Patterson-Black and Victor Reinking (New York, 1984); Rana Kabbani, *Europe's Myths of Orient* (Bloomington, Ind., 1986). Kathryn Tidrick's *Heart-Beguiling Araby* (Cambridge, 1981) concentrates on the work of nineteenth-century orientalists, such as Richard Burton and Gifford Palgrave. Alternatively, literary contact with the East prior to the flourish of English orientalism in the eighteenth century— and the extent of the West's literary indebtedness to Arabic culture—is documented in Dorothee Metlitzki's *The Matter of Araby in Medieval England* (London, 1977), and Maria Rosa Menocal's *The Arabic Role in Medieval Literary History: A Forgotten Heritage* (Philadelphia, 1980). On the general eighteenth-century vogue for the oriental see B. S. Allen, *Tides in English Taste, 1619–1800* (Cambridge, Mass., 1937); Hugh Honour, *Chinoiserie: The Vision of Cathay* (London, 1961). Lynne Thornton's *Woman as Portrayed in Oriental Painting* (Paris, 1985) likewise contains some discussion of the vogue for *turqueries* in the eighteenth century.

A SELECT CHRONOLOGY OF THE ORIENTAL TALE AND RELATED WRITINGS IN ENGLISH

WHAT follows is an attempt to give some idea of the range of Eastern or oriental fiction in the eighteenth and early nineteenth centuries. While this chronology is necessarily highly selective, particular care has been taken to include those works which were to prove formative influences on poets and novelists in England well into the twentieth century. Bibliographical sources have included the yet valuable Appendix (B. I) to Martha Pike Conant's study *The Oriental Tale in England in the Eighteenth Century*, and Robert D. Mayo's exhaustive survey *The English Novel in the Magazines, 1740–1815* (see Bibliography). I have also consulted the *Dictionary of Literary Biography*, vol. xxxix, ed. Martin C. Battestin (New York, 1985).

1687–93 English translation of Giovanni Paolo Marana's *L'Espion turc* (*Letters Written by a Turkish Spy*), first published in France in 1684–6. Marana's work supposedly records the observations of a foreigner—Mahmut, a Turk—concerning affairs in European courts from 1637 to 1682. The appearance of Marana's volume initiates a fashion for a new genre of satirical fiction, the pseudo-oriental letter, later examples of which will include Montesquieu's *Lettres persanes* (1721), Lyttelton's *Persian Letters* (1735), and Goldsmith's *Citizen of the World* (1762).

1697 Publication of Barthelemy d'Herbelot's *Bibliothèque orientale; ou, Dictionnaire universel, contenant généralement tout ce qui regarde la connaissance des peuples de l'Orient*. Eventually translated into English, d'Herbelot's constantly expanding encyclopedia of the 'Orient' (initially completed by Antoine Galland) will prove an authoritative source for many eighteenth-century writers both in France and in England seeking to attain a practical and reliable knowledge of Persian and Arabian customs and history.

1704 Antoine Galland, French orientalist, begins his translation of the Arabic *Alf Layla wa-Layla*. A total of twelve volumes of his *Mille et Une Nuit* will appear by 1717. An English version of Galland's text—the work of an anonymous 'Grub Street' translator—appears as *The Arabian Nights' Entertainments* very soon after its initial appearance in French. Galland's incalculably influential collection includes 'The Story of Sindbad the Sailor', 'The Story of Aladdin; or, The Wonderful Lamp', and 'The Story of Ali Baba and the Forty Thieves, Destroyed by a Slave'.

1708 The *Turkish Tales*, translated into English from the French of François Petis de la Croix. A collection resembling the *Arabian Nights*, the *Turkish Tales* contains the 'History of the Santon Barsisa' which eventually serves, via Steele's *Guardian* 148, as the inspiration for Matthew Lewis's Gothic novel *The Monk* (1796).

1711 The Fables of Bidpai collected in *Æsop Naturaliz'd; in a Collection of Diverting Fables and Stories from Æsop, Lockman, Pilpay, and Others*. Bidpai (variously 'Bidpay' or 'Pilpay') is the name given to the narrator of the *Panchatantra*, a collection of Indian beast fables which had been known to European authors as early as the 11th century AD. The stories, which possibly date from as early as the first century BC, remained, with those of Aesop, one of the more commonly circulated bodies of fables, tales, and folklore; the so-called 'Fables of Bidpai' will be reprinted several times in the eighteenth century.

The *Spectator*, a periodical written and edited by Joseph Addison and Richard Steele, begins a publishing history which will continue until December 1714. Eventually containing over 600 essays, the *Spectator* will include some of the most influential retellings and redactions of the oriental tales contained in the *Arabian Nights*, as well as a number of important, original Eastern stories. These include 'The Vision of Mirza' (159), and 'The Story of Shalum and Hilpa' (584–5).

1714   *The Persian Tales*, also known as *The Thousand and One Days*, translated by Ambrose Philips and others from the French of François Petis de la Croix. Along with Galland's *Arabian Nights*, the 'feigned' oriental narratives of the *Persian Tales* will prove some of the most widely read and influential oriental fictions in the eighteenth century.

1725   Appearance in English of Thomas Simon Gueullette's *Chinese Tales; or, The Marvellous Adventure of the Mandarin Fum-Hoam*. The *Chinese Tales*, which first appeared in French in 1723, is the first of the prolific Gueullette's several collections inspired by the *Arabian Nights*.

1729   Appearance in English of John Paul Bignon's *Tales of Abdallah, the Son of Hanif*, detailing the title character's quest for 'the happy fountain of life' on the isle of Borico; originally published in French in 1713.

1730   First English edition of Baron de Montesquieu's *Lettres persanes*, which originally appeared in French in 1721. The *Persian Letters* pretend to record, in over 100 letters, the observations of two Persians at the court of Louis XIV.

1734   George Sale publishes his exhaustive and influential *Preliminary Discourse* to his translation of the Koran. Sale's introduction to the sacred Islamic text offers a description of the religion, language, and customs of the Arabs.

1735   Lord Lyttelton's *Persian Letters*. Modelled after Montesquieu's *Lettres persanes* (see above), Lyttelton's collection of missives likewise pretends to present the correspondence of a foreigner in Europe.

1736   Thomas Gueullette's *Mogul Tales* appears in English. Includes 'The History of Aboul Assam, the Blind Man of Chitor', which contains narrative material eventually used by William Beckford in his *Vathek*. The *Mogul Tales* first appeared in French in 1723.

Eliza Haywood's *The Adventures of Eovaai, Princess of Ijaveo*, reprinted in 1740 as *The Unfortunate Princess*. Haywood's story details the trials of the virtuous Princess Eovaai at the hands of the pseudo-oriental magician Ochihatou.

1749   Voltaire's philosophical satire *Zadig; or, Destiny: A Tale of the Orient* published in English. The tale, although essentially a satire and *conte philosophique* along the lines of *Candide*, contains a liberal sprinkling of oriental references ('Babylon', 'Balzora') and characters ('Astarte', 'Cador').

1750   Samuel Johnson begins publication of the *Rambler*, a periodical which will have a run of two years. Eastern tales recounted in Johnson's popular and frequently reprinted series will include 'The History of Abousaid' (190), and 'The History of Seged' (204–5).

1752   John Hawkesworth begins publication of the *Adventurer*, which will continue until early 1754. Hawkesworth's oriental tales will include 'The Ring of Amurath' (20–2), 'Omar, the Hermit of Mecca' (32), and 'The Story of Bozaldab' (76).

1757   Horace Walpole's *Letter from Xo Ho, a Chinese Philosopher at London, to his friend Lien Chi at Peking*. Like earlier pseudo-oriental letters Walpole's *Letter* conceals a satire on contemporary English customs and politics.

1759   Samuel Johnson's *Rasselas, Prince of Abissinia*; Thomas Gueullette's *Tartarian Tales; or A Thousand and One Quarters of Hours*, translated into English. Gueullette's work had originally appeared in French in 1723.

1760   Oliver Goldsmith's 'Chinese Letters', which will be collected and published as *The Citizen of the World* in 1762, begin appearing in John Newberry's *Public Ledger*. One year earlier, Goldsmith's *Asem* (or 'The

Proceedings of Providence Vindicated: An Eastern Tale') had appeared in the *Royal Magazine*.

1761   John Hawkesworth, *Almoran and Hamet*.

1764   Thomas Gueullette's *Peruvian Tales* appears in English. Also James Ridley's *Tales of the Genii*, a moralized collection of pseudo-oriental fictions purportedly the teachings of one 'Horam', inculcating 'the virtues of truth, wisdom, justice, and moderation'.

1767   Frances Sheridan, *The History of Nourjahad*.

1768   Alexander Dow's *Tales ... of Inatulla of Delhi*, a translation of a collection of ribald oriental tales.

1774   Charles Johnstone, author of the popular *Chrysal; or, The Adventures of a Guinea* (1760–5), publishes his *History of Arsaces, Prince of Betlis*, an extended chronicle (not unlike *Chrysal*) which follows the adventures of an Arab named Selim across an ill-defined oriental landscape. Johnstone will again attempt to add an Eastern colour to his fiction the following year, when he publishes his *The Pilgrim; or, A Picture of Life in a Series of Letters*, a selection of pseudo-oriental correspondence.

1785   Clara Reeve, *History of Charoba, Queen of Ægypt*, included in *The Progress of Romance*; Horace Walpole's *Hieroglyphic Tales*, containing 'A New Arabian Nights' Entertainment' and 'Mi Li: A Chinese Fairy Tale'.

1786   William Beckford, *Vathek*.

1787   Robert Bage's second novel, *The Fair Syrian*, including the chronicle of Honoria Warren, who has been kept in a harem in the East, and the adventures of the Marquis de St Claur, a French aristocrat, in Turkey.

1790   Ellis Cornelia Knight's *Dinarbas; A Tale: Being a Continuation of Rasselas, Prince of Abissinia*, an optimistic continuation of Johnson's oriental fable.

1792   *The New Arabian Nights*, translated from the French of Dom Chavis and M. Cazotte. The collection, often referred to simply as *The Arabian Tales*, contains the influential tale of 'The Robber Caliph'.

1800 Mary Pilkington's *The Asiatic Princess: A Tale* published in three volumes.

1804 Maria Edgeworth's *Murad the Unlucky* published in her three-volume *Popular Tales*.

1808 Matthew 'Monk' Lewis's *Romantic Tales*, including 'The Anaconda: An East Indian Tale', and 'The Four Facardins', a translation and continuation of Antoine Hamilton's complex *Les Quatre Facardins* (1760).

1812 Henry Weber's three-volume *Tales of the East* offers a comprehensive anthology of English oriental fiction, ranging from Galland's original *Arabian Nights' Entertainments*, to Sheridan's *Nourjahad* and the *New Arabian Nights* of 1792.

ACKNOWLEDGEMENTS

I OWE thanks to the Bodleian Library for allowing me to reproduce the texts upon which this edition is based. I am grateful to the following individuals for their help and encouragement: John Lawrence Abbott, Judith Briggs, Gwen Crane, Margaret Anne Doody, Richard Kroll, Roger Lonsdale, Judith Luna, Bruce Redford, Florian Stuber, and Sarah Zimmerman.

Almoran and Hamet

sir,

AMIDST the congratulations and praises of a free, a joyful, and now united people, who are ambitious to express their duty and their wishes in their various classes; I think myself happy to have Your Majesty's most gracious permission to approach You, and, after the manner of the people whose character I have assumed, to bring an humble offering in my hand.*

As some part of my subject led me to consider the advantages of our excellent constitution in comparison of others, my thoughts were naturally turned to Your Majesty, as its warmest friend and most powerful protector: and as the whole is intended, to recommend the practice of virtue, as the means of happiness; to whom could I address it with so much propriety, as to a Prince, who illustrates and enforces the precepts of the moralist by his life.

I am,

    May it please Your Majesty,

                Your Majesty's

          Most faithful, most obliged,

             And most obedient

              Subject and Servant,

                    John Hawkesworth

VOLUME I

CHAPTER I

Who is he among the children of the earth, that repines at the power of the wicked? and who is he, that would change the lot of the righteous? He, who has appointed to each his portion, is God; the Omniscient and the Almighty, who fills eternity, and whose existence is from Himself! but he who murmurs, is man, who yesterday was not, and who to-morrow shall be forgotten: let him listen in silence to the voice of knowledge, and hide the blushes of confusion in the dust.*

Solyman,* the mighty and the wise, who, in the one hundred and second year of the Hegyra*, sat upon the throne of Persia, had two sons, Almoran and Hamet, and they were twins. Almoran was the first born, but Solyman divided his affection equally between them: they were both lodged in the same part of the seraglio,* both were attended by the same servants, and both received instructions from the same teacher.

One of the first things that Almoran learnt, was the prerogative of his birth; and he was taught very early to set a high value upon it, by the terms in which those about him expressed their sense of the power, the splendor, and the delights of royalty. As his mind gradually opened, he naturally considered these as the objects of universal desire, and the means of supreme felicity: he was often reminded, that the time was coming, when the sole possession of sovereign power would enable him to fulfil all his wishes, to determine the fate of dependent nations with a nod, and dispense life and death, and happiness and misery, at his will: he was flattered by those who hoped to draw wealth and dignity from his favour; and interest prompted all who approached him, to administer to his pleasures with a zeal and assiduity, which had the appearance of reverence to his merit, and affection to his person.

Hamet, on the contrary, soon became sensible of a subordinate station: he was not, indeed, neglected; but he was not much caressed. When the gratification of Hamet came in competition with that of Almoran, he was always obliged to give it up, except when Solyman interposed: his mind was, therefore, naturally led to seek for happiness in objects very different from those which had fixed the attention of Almoran. As he knew not to how narrow a sphere caprice or jealousy might confine him, he considered what pleasures were least dependent upon external advantages; and as the first popular commotion which should happen after his brother's accession to the throne, might probably cost him his life, he was very inquisitive about the state into which his spirit would be dismissed by the Angel of Death*, and very diligent to do whatever might secure him a share of the permanent and unchangeable felicity of Paradise.*

This difference in the situation of Almoran and Hamet, produced great dissimilarity in their dispositions, habits, and characters; to which, perhaps, nature might also in some degree contribute. Almoran was haughty, vain, and voluptuous;* Hamet was gentle, courteous, and temperate: Almoran was volatile, impetuous, and irascible; Hamet was thoughtful, patient, and forbearing. Upon the heart of Hamet also were written the instructions of the Prophet;* to his mind futurity was present by habitual anticipation; his pleasure, his pain, his hopes, and his fears, were perpetually referred to the Invisible and Almighty Father of Life, by sentiments of gratitude or resignation, complacency or confidence; so that his devotion was not periodical but constant.

But the views of Almoran were terminated by nearer objects: his mind was perpetually busied in the anticipation of pleasures and honours, which he supposed to be neither uncertain nor remote; these excited his hopes, with a power sufficient to fix his attention; he did not look beyond them for other objects, nor enquire how enjoyments more distant were to be acquired; and as he supposed these to be already secured to him by his birth, there was nothing he was solicitous to obtain as the reward of merit, nor any thing that he considered himself to possess as the bounty of Heaven. If the sublime and disinterested rectitude that produces and rewards itself, dwells indeed with man, it dwelt not with Almoran: with respect to God, therefore, he was not impressed with a sense either of duty or dependence; he felt neither reverence nor love, gratitude nor resignation: in abstaining from evil, he was not intentionally good; he practised the externals of morality without virtue, and performed the rituals of devotion without piety.

Such were Almoran and Hamet, when Solyman their father, full of days and full of honour, slept in peace the sleep of death. With this event they were immediately acquainted. The emotions of Almoran were such as it was impossible to conceal: the joy that he felt in secret was so great, that the mere dread of disappointment for a moment suspended his belief of what he heard: when his fears and his doubts gave way, his cheeks were suffused with sudden blushes, and his eyes sparkled with exultation and impatience: he looked eagerly about him, as if in haste to act; yet his looks were embarrassed, and his gestures irresolute, because he knew not what to do: he uttered some incoherent sentences, which discovered at once the joy that he felt, and his sense of its impropriety; and his whole deportment expressed the utmost tumult and perturbation of mind.

Upon Hamet, the death of his father produced a very different effect: as soon as he heard it, his lips trembled and his countenance grew pale; he stood motionless a moment, like a pilgrim transfixed by lightning in the desert; he then smote his breast, and looking upward, his eyes by degrees overflowed with tears, and they fell, like dew distilling from the mountain, in a calm and silent shower. As his grief was thus mingled with devotion, his mind in a short time recovered its tranquility, though not its chearfulness, and he desired to be conducted to his brother.

He found him surrounded by the lords of his court, his eye still restless and ardent, and his deportment elate and assuming. Hamet pressed hastily through the circle, and prostrated himself before him: Almoran received the homage with a tumultuous pleasure; but at length raised him from the ground, and assured him of his protection, though without any expressions either of kindness or of sorrow. 'Hamet,' says he, 'if I have no cause to complain of you as a subject, you shall have no cause to complain of me as a king.' Hamet, whose heart was again pierced by the cold and distant behaviour of his brother, suppressed the sigh that struggled in his bosom, and secretly wiped away the tear that started to his eye: he retired, with his looks fixed upon the ground, to a remote corner of the apartment; and though his heart yearned to embrace his brother, his modest diffidence restrained him from intruding upon the king.

In this situation were Almoran and Hamet, when Omar entered the apartment. Omar, upon whose head the hand of time became heavy, had from his youth acquainted himself with wisdom: to him nature had revealed herself in the silence of the night, when his lamp was burning alone, and his eyes only were open: to him was known the power of the Seal of Solomon;* and to him the knowledge of things invisible had been revealed. Nor was the virtue of Omar inferior to his knowledge; his heart was a fountain of good, which though it flowed through innumerable streams was never dry: yet was the virtue of Omar cloathed with humility; and he was still pressing nearer to perfection, by a devotion which though elevated was rational, and though regular was warm. From the council of Omar, Solyman had derived glory and strength; and to him he had committed the education of his children.

When he entered the apartment, the croud, touched at once with reverence and love, drew back; every eye was cast downward, and every tongue was silent. The full of days approached the king, and kneeling before him he put into his hand a sealed paper: the king received it with impatience, seeing it superscribed with the hand of his father; and Omar looking round, and perceiving Hamet, beckoned him to come forward. Hamet, whose obedience to Omar had been so long habitual that it was now almost spontaneous, instantly drew near, though with a slow and irresolute pace; and Almoran, having broken the seal of the paper, began to read it to himself, with a look that expressed the utmost anxiety and impatience. Omar kept his eye fixed upon him, and soon perceived that his countenance was disfigured by confusion and trouble, and that he seemed preparing to put up the paper in his bosom: he then produced another paper from under his robe, and gave it to Hamet: 'This,' says he, 'is a copy of the will of Solyman, your father; the original is in the hand of Almoran: read it, and you will find that he has bequeathed his kingdom between you.'

The eyes of all present were now turned upon Hamet, who stood silent and motionless with amazement, but was soon roused to attention by the homage that was paid him. In the mean time, Almoran's confusion increased every moment: his disappointment was aggravated by the sudden attention of those who were present to his brother; and his jealousy made him think himself neglected, while those acts of duty were performed to Hamet, which were now known to be his right; and which he had himself received before him.

Hamet, however, regarded but little what so much excited the envy of Almoran; his mind was employed upon superior objects, and agitated by nobler passions: the coldness of his brother's behaviour, though it had grieved had not quenched his affection; and as he was now no longer restrained by the deference due from a subject to his king, he ran to him, and catching him to his breast attempted to speak; but his heart was too full, and he could express his affection and joy only by his tears. Almoran rather suffered than received the embrace; and after a few ceremonies, to which neither of them could much attend, they retired to separate apartments.

CHAPTER II

WHEN Almoran was alone, he immediately locked the door; and throwing himself upon a sofa* in an agony of vexation and disappointment, of which he was unwilling there should be any witness, he revolved in his mind all the pleasures and honours of supreme dominion which had now suddenly been snatched from him, with a degree of anguish and regret, not proportioned to their real, but their imaginary value. Of future good, that which we obtain is found to be less than our expectations; but that of which we are disappointed, we suppose would have been more: thus do the children of hope extract evil, both from what they gain, and from what they lose. But Almoran, after the first tumult of his mind had subsided, began to consider as well what was left him, as what had been taken away. He was still without a superior, though he had an equal; he was still a king, though he did not govern alone: and with respect to every individual in his dominions, except one, his will would now be a law; though with respect to the public, the concurrence of his brother would be necessary to give it force. 'Let me then,' says he, 'make the most of the power that is now put into my hand, and wait till some favourable opportunity shall offer to increase it. Let me dissemble my jealousy and disappointment, that I may not alarm suspicion, or put the virtues of Hamet upon their guard against me; and let me contrive to give our joint administration such a form, as may best favour my design.'

Such were the reflections, with which Almoran soothed the anguish of his mind; while Hamet was busied in speculations of a very different kind. If he was pleased at reflecting, that he was raised from a subject to a prince; he was pleased still more, when he considered his elevation as a test of his father's affection to his person, and approbation of his conduct: he was also delighted with the thought, that his brother was associated with him in the arduous task which he was now called to perform. 'If I had been appointed to govern alone,' said he, 'I should have had no equal; and he who has no equal, though he may have faithful servants, can have no friend: there cannot be that union of interests, that equal participation of good, that unrestrained intercourse of mind, and that mutual dependence, which constitutes the pure and exalted happiness of friendship. With Almoran, I shall share the supreme delight of wresting the innocent and the helpless from the iron hand of oppression; of animating merit by reward, and restraining the unworthy by fear: I shall share, with Almoran, the pleasures of governing a numerous, a powerful, and a happy people; pleasures which, however great, are, like all others, increased by participation.'

While Hamet was thus enjoying the happiness, which his virtue derived from the same source, from which the vices of Almoran had filled his breast with anguish and discontent; Omar was contriving in what manner their joint government could best be carried into execution.

He knew that Solyman, having considered the dispositions of his sons, was of opinion, that if they had been blended in one person, they would have produced a character more fit to govern in his stead, than either of them alone: Almoran, he thought, was too volatile and warm; but he suspected, that Hamet would sink into inactivity for want of spirit: he feared alike Almoran's love of enterprize, and Hamet's fondness for retirement: he observed, in Hamet, a placid easiness of temper, which might suffer the reins of government to lie too loose; and, in Almoran, a quickness of resentment, and jealousy of command, which might hold them too tight: he hoped, therefore, that by leaving them a joint dominion, he should blend their dispositions, at least in their effects, in every act of government that should take place; or that, however they should agree to administer their government, the public would derive benefit from the virtues of both, without danger of suffering from their imperfections, as their imperfections would only operate against each other, while, in whatever was right, their minds would naturally concur, as the coincidence of rectitude with rectitude is necessary and eternal. But he did not consider, that different dispositions operating separately upon two different wills, would appear in effects very unlike those, which they would concur to produce in one: that two wills, under the direction of dispositions so different, would seldom be brought to coincide; and that more mischiefs would probably arise from the contest, than from the imperfections of either alone.

But Solyman had so long applauded himself for his project before he revealed it to Omar, that Omar found him too much displeased with any objection, to consider its weight: and knowing that peculiar notions are more rarely given up, than opinions received from others, and made our own only by adoption, he at length acquiesced, lest he should by farther opposition lose his influence, which on other occasions he might still employ to the advantage of the public; and took a solemn oath, that he would, as far as was in his power, see the will carried into execution.

To this, indeed, he consented without much reluctance, as he had little less reason to fear the sole government of Almoran, than a joint administration; and if a struggle for superiority should happen, he hoped the virtues of Hamet would obtain the suffrages of the people in his favour, and establish him upon the throne alone. But as change is itself an evil, and as changes in government are seldom produced without great confusion and calamity, he applied himself to consider in what manner the government of Almoran and Hamet could be administered, so as most effectually to blend their characters in their administration, and prevent the conduct of one from exciting jealousy in the other.

After much thought, he determined that a system of laws* should be prepared, which the sons of Solyman should examine and alter till they perfectly approved, and to which they should then give the sanction of their joint authority: that when any addition or alteration should be thought necessary, it should be made in the same manner; and that when any insuperable difference of sentiment happened, either in this or in any act of prerogative independent of the laws for regulating the manners of the people, the kings should refer it to some person of approved integrity and wisdom, and abide by his determination. Omar easily foresaw, that when the opinion of Almoran and Hamet should differ, the opinion of Almoran would be established; for there were many causes that would render Almoran inflexible, and Hamet yielding: Almoran was naturally confident and assuming, Hamet diffident and modest; Almoran was impatient of contradiction, Hamet was attentive to argument, and solicitous only for the discovery of truth. Almoran also conceived, that by the will of his father, he had suffered wrong; Hamet, that he had received a favour: Almoran, therefore, was disposed to resent the first appearance of opposition; and Hamet, on the contrary, to acquiesce, as in his share of government, whatever it might be, he had more than was his right by birth, and his brother had less. Thus, therefore, the will of Almoran would probably predominate in the state: but as the same cause which conferred this superiority, would often prevent contention, Omar considered it, upon the whole, rather as good than evil.

When he had prepared his plan, therefore, he sent a copy of it, by different messengers at the same time, both to Almoran and Hamet, inclosed in a letter, in which he expresst his sense of obligation to their father, and his zeal and affection for them: he mentioned the promise he had

made, to devote himself to their service; and the oath he
had taken, to propose whatever he thought might facilitate
the accomplishment of their father's design, with honour to
them and happiness to their people: these motives, which
he could not resist without impiety, he hoped would absolve
him from presumption; and trusting in the rectitude of his
intentions, he left the issue to God.

CHAPTER III

THE receipt of this letter threw Almoran into another agony of indignation: he felt again the loss of his prerogative; the offer of advice he disdained as an insult, to which he had been injuriously subjected by the will of his father; and he was disposed to reject whatever was suggested by Omar, even before his proposal was known. With this temper of mind he began to read, and at every paragraph he took new offence; he determined, however, not to admit Omar to the honour of a conference upon the subject, but to settle a plan of government with his brother, without the least regard to his advice.

A supercilious attention to minute formalities, is a certain indication of a little mind, conscious to the want of innate dignity, and solicitous to derive from others what it cannot supply to itself: as the scrupulous exaction of every trifling tribute discovers the weakness of the tyrant, who fears his claim should be disputed; while the prince, who is conscious of superior and indisputable power, and knows that the states he has subjugated do not dare to revolt, scarce enquires whether such testimonies of allegiance are given or not.

Thus, the jealousy of Almoran already enslaved him to the punctilios of state; and the most trifling circumstances involved him in perplexity, or fired him with resentment: the friendship and fidelity of Omar stung him with rage, as insolent and intrusive; and though it determined him to an immediate interview with his brother, yet he was embarrassed how to procure it. At first he rose, and was about to go to him, but he stopped short with disdain, upon reflecting, that it was an act of condescension which might be deemed an acknowledgement of superiority: he then thought of sending for Hamet to come to him; but this he feared might provoke him, as implying a denial of his equality: at length he determined to propose a meeting in the chamber of council, and was just dispatching an officer with the message, when Hamet entered the apartment.

The countenance of Hamet was flushed with joy, and his heart was warmed with the pleasing sensations of affection and confidence, by the same letter, from which Almoran had extracted the bitterness of jealousy and resentment; and as he had no idea that an act of courtesy to his brother could derogate from his own dignity or importance, he indulged the honest impatience of his heart to communicate the pleasure with which it overflowed: he was, indeed, somewhat disappointed, to find no traces of satisfaction in the countenance of Almoran, when he saw the same paper in his hand, which had impressed so much upon his own.

He waited some time after the first salutations, without mentioning the scheme of government he was come to concert; because having observed that Almoran was embarrassed and displeased, he expected that he would communicate the cause, and pleased himself with the hope that he might remove it: finding, however, that this expectation was disappointed, he addressed him to this effect:

'How happy are we, my dear brother, in the wisdom and fidelity of Omar! how excellent is the system of government that he has proposed! how easy and honourable will it be to us that govern, and how advantageous to the people that obey!'

'The advantages,' said Almoran, 'which you seem to have discovered, are not evident to me: tell me, then, what you imagine they are, and I will afterwards give you my opinion.'

'By establishing a system of laws as the rule of government,' said Hamet, 'many evils will be avoided, and many benefits procured. If the law is the will only of the sovereign, it can never certainly be known to the people: many, therefore, may violate that rule of right, which the hand of the Almighty has written upon the living tablets of the heart, in the presumptuous hope, that it will not subject them to punishment; and those, by whom that rule is fulfilled, will not enjoy that consciousness of security, which they would derive from the protection of a prescribed law, which they have never broken. Neither will those who are inclined to do evil, be equally restrained by the fear of punishment if neither the offence is ascertained, nor the punishment prescribed. One motive to probity, therefore, will be wanting; which ought to be supplied, as well for the sake of those who may be tempted to offend, as of those who may suffer by the offence. Besides, he who governs not by a written and a public law, must either administer that government in person, or by others: if in person, he will sink under a labour which no man is able to sustain; and if by others, the inferiority of their rank must subject them to temptations which it cannot be hoped they will always resist, and to prejudices which it will perhaps be impossible for them to surmount. But to administer government by a law which ascertains the offence, and directs the punishment, integrity alone will be sufficient; and as the perversion of justice will in this case be notorious, and depend not upon opinion but fact, it will seldom be practised, because it will be easily punished.'

Almoran, who had heard the opinions of Hamet with impatience and scorn, now started from his seat with a proud and contemptuous aspect: he first glanced his eyes upon his brother; and then looking disdainfully downward, he threw back his robe, and stretching out his hand from him, 'Shall the son of Solyman,' said he, 'upon whose will the fate of nations was suspended, whose smiles and frowns were alone the criterions of right and wrong, before whom the voice of wisdom itself was silent, and the pride even of virtue humbled in the dust; shall the son of Solyman be harnessed, like a mule, in the trammels of law? shall he become a mere instrument to execute what others have devised? shall he only declare the determinations of a statute, and shall his ear be affronted by claims of right? It is the glory of a prince, to punish for what and whom he will; to be the sovereign, not only of property, but of life; and to govern alike without prescription or appeal.'

Hamet, who was struck with astonishment at this declaration, and the vehemence with which it was uttered, after a short recollection made this reply: 'It is the glory of a prince, to govern others, as he is governed by Him, who is alone most merciful and almighty! It is his glory to prevent crimes, rather than to display his power in punishment; to diffuse happiness, rather than inforce subjection; and rather to animate with love, than depress by fear. Has not He that shall judge us, given us a rule of life by which we shall be judged? is not our reward and punishment already set before us? are not His promises and threatenings, motives to obedience? and have we not confidence and joy, when we have obeyed? To God, His own divine perfections are a law; and these He has transcribed as a law to us. Let us, then, govern, as we are governed; let us seek our happiness in the happiness that we bestow, and our honour in emulating the benevolence of Heaven.'

As Almoran feared, that to proceed farther in this argument would too far disclose his sentiments, and put Hamet too much upon his guard; he determined for the present to dissemble: and as he perceived, that Hamet's opinion, and an administration founded upon it, would render him extreamly popular, and at length possibly establish him alone; he was now solicitous only to withdraw him from public notice, and persuade him to leave the government, whatever form it should receive, to be administered by others: returning therefore, to his seat, and assuming an appearance of complacence and tranquillity, with which he could not form his language perfectly to agree; 'Let us then,' said he, 'if a law must be set up in our stead, leave the law to be executed by our slaves: and as nothing will be left for us to do, that is worthy of us, let us devote ourselves to the pleasures of ease; and if there are any enjoyments peculiar to royalty, let us secure them as our only distinction from the multitude.'

'Not so,' says Hamet, 'for there is yet much for a prince to do, after the best system of laws has been established: the government of a nation as a whole, the regulation and extent of its trade, the establishment of manufactories, the encouragement of genius, the application of the revenues, and whatever can improve the arts of peace, and secure superiority in war, is the proper object of a king's attention.'

'But in these,' said Almoran, 'it will be difficult for two minds to concur; let us, then, agree to leave these also to the care of some other, whom we can continue as long as we approve, and displace when we approve no longer: we shall, by this expedient, be able to avert the odium of any unpopular measure; and by the sacrifice of a slave, we can always satisfy the people, and silence public discontent.'

'To trust implicitly to another,' says Hamet, 'is to give up a prerogative, which is at once our highest duty and interest to keep; it is to betray our trust, and to sacrifice our honour to another. The prince, who leaves the government of his people implicitly to a subject, leaves it to one, who has many more temptations to betray their interest than himself: a vicegerent is in a subordinate station; he has, therefore, much to fear, and much to hope; he may also acquire the power of obtaining what he hopes, and averting what he fears, at the public expence; he may stand in need of dependents, and may be able no otherwise to procure them, than by conniving at the fraud or the violence which they commit: he may receive, in bribes, an equivalent for his share, as an individual, in the public prosperity; for his interest is not essentially connected with that of the state; he has a separate interest; but the interest of the state, and of the king, are one: he may even be corrupted to betray the councils, and give up the interests of the nation, to a foreign power; but this is impossible to the king; for nothing equivalent to what he would give up, could be offered him. But as a king has not equal temptations to do wrong, neither is he equally exposed to opposition, when he does right: the measures of a substitute are frequently opposed, merely from interest; because the leader of a faction against him, hopes, that if he can remove him by popular clamour, he shall succeed to his power; but it can be no man's interest to oppose the measures of a king, if his measures are good, because no man can hope to supplant him. Are not these the precepts of the Prophet, whose wisdom was from above?—"Let not the eye of expectation be raised to another, for that which thyself only should bestow: suffer not thy own shadow to obscure thee; nor be content to derive that glory, which it is thy prerogative to impart"'.*

'But is the prince,' said Almoran, 'always the wisest man in his dominions? Can we not find, in another, abilities and experience, which we do not possess? and is it not the duty of him who presides in the ship to place the helm in that hand which can best steer it?'

'A prince,' said Hamet, 'who sincerely intends the good of his people, can scarce fail to effect it; all the wisdom of the nation will be at once turned to that object: whatever is his principal aim, will be that of all who are admitted to his council; for to concur with his principal aim, must be the surest recommendation to his favour. Let us, then, hear others; but let us act ourselves.'

As Almoran now perceived, that the longer this conversation continued, the more he should be embarrassed; he put an end to it, by appearing to acquiesce in what Hamet had proposed. Hamet withdrew, charmed with the candour and flexibility which he imagined he had discovered in his brother; and not without some exultation in his own rhetoric, which he supposed had gained no inconsiderable victory. Almoran, in the mean time, applauded himself for having thus far practised the arts of dissimulation with success; fortified himself in the resolutions he had before taken; and conceived new malevolence and jealousy against Hamet.

CHAPTER IV

WHILE Hamet was exulting in his conquest, and his heart was overflowing at once with self-complacency, and affection to his brother; he was told, that Omar was waiting without, and desired admittance. Hamet ordered that he should be immediately introduced; and when Omar entered, and would have prostrated himself before him, he catched him in his arms in a transport of affection and esteem; and having ordered that none should interrupt them, compelled him to sit down on a sofa.

He then related, with all the joy of a youthful and an ardent mind, the conversation he had had with Almoran, intermixed with expressions of the highest praise and the most cordial esteem. Omar was not without suspicion, that the sentiments which Almoran had first expressed with such vehemence of passion, were still predominant in his mind: but of these suspicions he did not give the least hint to Hamet; not only because to communicate suspicions is to accuse without proof, but because he did not think himself at liberty to make an ill report of another, though he knew it to be true. He approved the sentiments of Hamet, as they had indeed been infused by his own instructions; and some precepts and cautions were now added, which the accession of Hamet to a share of the imperial power made particularly necessary.

'Remember,' said Omar, 'that the most effectual way of promoting virtue, is to prevent occasions of vice. There are, perhaps, particular situations, in which human virtue has always failed: at least, temptation often repeated, and long continued, has seldom been finally resisted. In a government so constituted as to leave the people exposed to perpetual seduction, by opportunities of dissolute pleasure or iniquitous gain, the multiplication of penal laws will only tend to depopulate the kingdom, and disgrace the state; to devote to the scymitar and the bow-string,* those who might have been useful to society, and to leave the rest dissolute, turbulent and factious. If the streets not only abound with women, who inflame the passenger by their appearance, their gesture, and their solicitations; but with houses, in which every desire which they kindle may be gratified with secrecy and convenience; it is vain that "the feet of the prostitute go down to death, and that her steps take hold on hell:"* what then can be hoped from any punishment, which the laws of man can superadd to disease and want, to rottenness and perdition? If you permit opium to be publickly sold at a low rate; it will be folly to hope, that the dread of punishment will render idleness and drunkenness strangers to the poor. If a tax is so collected, as to leave opportunities to procure the commodity, without paying it; the hope of gain will always surmount the fear of punishment. If, when the veteran has served you at the risque of life, you withold his hire; it will be in vain to threaten usury and extortion with imprisonment and fines. If, in your armies, you suffer it to be any man's interest, rather to preserve the life of a horse than a man; be assured, that your own sword is drawn for your enemy: for there will always be some, in whom interest is stronger than humanity and honour. Put no man's interest, therefore, in the ballance against his duty; nor hope that good can often be produced, but by preventing opportunities of evil.'

To these precepts of Omar, Hamet listened as to the instructions of a father; and having promised to keep them as the treasure of life, he dismissed him from his presence. The heart of Hamet was now expanded with the most pleasing expectations; but Almoran was pining with solicitude, jealousy, and distrust: he took every opportunity to avoid both Omar and Hamet; but Hamet still retained his confidence, and Omar his suspicions.

CHAPTER V

In the mean time, the system of government was established which had been proposed by Omar, and in which Hamet concurred from principle, and Almoran from policy. The views of Almoran terminated in the gratification of his own appetites and passions; those of Hamet, in the discharge of his duty: Hamet, therefore, was indefatigable in the business of the state; and as his sense of honour, and his love of the public, made this the employment of his choice, it was to him the perpetual source of a generous and sublime felicity. Almoran also was equally diligent, but from another motive: he was actuated, not by love of the public, but by jealousy of his brother; he performed his task as the drudge of necessity, with reluctance and ill will; so that to him it produced pain and anxiety, weariness and impatience.

To atone for this waste of time, he determined to crowd all that remained with delight: his gardens were an epitome of all nature, and on his palace were exhausted all the treasures of art; his seraglio was filled with beauties of every nation, and his table supplied with dainties from the remotest corners of his dominions. In the songs that were repeated in his presence, he listened at once to the voice of adulation and music; he breathed the perfumes of Arabia,* and he tasted the forbidden pleasure of wine.* But as every appetite is soon satiated by excess, his eagerness to accumulate pleasure deprived him of enjoyment. Among the variety of beauty that surrounded him, the passion, which, to be luxurious, must be delicate and refined, was degraded to a mere instinct, and exhausted in endless dissipation; the caress was unendeared by a consciousness of reciprocal delight, and was immediately succeeded by indifference or disgust. By the dainties that perpetually urged him to intemperance, that appetite, which alone could make even dainties tasteful, was destroyed. The splendor of his palace and the beauty of his gardens, became at length so familiar to his eye, that they were frequently before him, without being seen. Even flattery and music lost their power, by too frequent a repetition: and the broken slumbers of the night, and the languor of the morning, were more than equivalent to the transient hilarity that was inspired by wine. Thus passed the time of Almoran, divided between painful labours which he did not dare to shun, and the search of pleasure which he could never find.

Hamet, on the contrary, did not seek pleasure, but pleasure seemed to seek him: he had a perpetual complacence and serenity of mind, which rendered him constantly susceptible of pleasing impressions; every thing that was prepared to refresh or entertain him in his seasons of retirement and relaxation, added something to the delight which was continually springing in his breast, when he reviewed the past, or looked forward to the future. Thus, the pleasures of sense were heightened by those of his mind, and the pleasures of the mind by those of sense: he had, indeed, as yet no wife; for as yet no woman had fixed his attention, or determined his choice.

Among the ambassadors whom the monarchs of Asia sent to congratulate the sons of Solyman upon their accession to the throne, there was a native of Circassia,* whose name was Abdallah. Abdallah had only one child, a daughter, in whom all his happiness and affection centered; he was unwilling to leave her behind, and therefore brought her to the court of Persia. Her mother died while she was yet an infant; she was now in the sixteenth year of her age, and her name was Almeida. She was beautiful as the daughters of Paradise,* and gentle as the breezes of the spring; her mind was without stain, and her manners were without art.

She was lodged with her father in a palace that joined to the gardens of the seraglio; and it happened that a lamp which had one night been left burning in a lower apartment, by some accident set fire to the net-work of cotton that surrounded a sopha, and the whole room was soon after in a flame. Almoran, who had been passing the afternoon in riot and debauchery, had been removed from his banquet-ting room asleep; but Hamet was still in his closet, where he had been regulating some papers that were to be used the next day. The windows of this room opened towards the inner apartments of the house in which Abdallah resided; and Hamet, having by accident looked that way, was alarmed by the appearance of an unusual light, and starting up to see whence it proceeded, he discovered what had happened.

Having hastily ordered the guard of the night to assist in quenching the flame, and removing the furniture, he ran himself into the garden. As soon as he was come up to the house, he was alarmed by the shrieks of a female voice; and the next moment, Almeida appeared at the window of an apartment directly over that which was on fire. Almeida he had till now never seen, nor did he so much as know that Abdallah had a daughter: but though her person was unknown, he was strongly interested in her danger, and called out to her to throw herself into his arms. At the sound of his voice she ran back into the room, such is the force of inviolate modesty, though the smoke was then rising in curling spires from the windows: she was, how-ever, soon driven back; and part of the floor at the same instant giving way, she wrapt her veil round her, and leaped into the garden. Hamet caught her in his arms; but though he broke her fall, he sunk down with her weight: he did not, however, quit his charge; but perceiving she had fainted, he made haste with her into his apartment, to afford her such assistance as he could procure.

She was covered only with the light and loose robe in

which she slept, and her veil had dropped off by the way.*
The moment he entered his closet, the light discovered to
him such beauty as before he had never seen: she now
began to revive; and before her senses returned, she pressed
the prince with an involuntary embrace, which he returned
by straining her closer to his breast, in a tumult of delight,
confusion, and anxiety, which he could scarce sustain. As
he still held her in his arms, and gazed silently upon her,
she opened her eyes, and instantly relinquishing her hold,
shrieked out, and threw herself from him. As there were no
women nearer than that wing of the palace in which his
brother resided, and as he had many reasons not to leave
her in their charge; he was in the utmost perplexity what to
do. He assured her, in some hasty and incoherent words, of
her security; he told her, that she was in the royal palace,
and that he who had conveyed her thither was Hamet. The
habitual reverence of sovereign power, now surmounted all
other passions in the bosom of Almeida: she was instantly
covered with new confusion; and hiding her face with her
hands, threw herself at his feet: he raised her with a
trepidation almost equal to her own, and endeavoured to
sooth her into confidence and tranquillity.

Hitherto her memory had been wholly suspended by
violent passions, which had crowded upon her in a rapid
and uninterrupted succession, and the first gleam of recollection threw her into a new agony; and having been silent
a few moments, she suddenly smote her hands together,
and bursting into tears, cried out, 'Abdallah! my father! my
father!'—Hamet not only knew but felt all the meaning of
the exclamation, and immediately ran again into the garden:
he had advanced but a few paces, before he discerned an
old man sitting upon the ground, and looking upward in
silent anguish, as if he had exhausted the power of complaint. Hamet, upon a nearer approach, perceived by the
light of the flame that it was Abdallah; and instantly calling
him by his name, told him, that his daughter was safe. At

the name of his daughter, Abdallah suddenly started up, as if he had been roused by the voice of an angel from the sleep of death: Hamet again repeated, that his daughter was in safety; and Abdallah looking wistfully at him, knew him to be the king. He was then struck with an awe that restrained him from enquiry: but Hamet directing him where he might find her, went forward, that he might not lessen the pleasure of their interview, nor restrain the first transports of duty and affection by his presence. He soon met with other fugitives from the fire, which had opened a communication between the gardens and the street; and among them some women belonging to Almeida, whom he conducted himself to their mistress. He immediately allotted to her and to her father, an apartment in his division of the palace; and the fire being now nearly extinguished, he retired to rest.

CHAPTER VI

THOUGH the night was far advanced, yet the eyes of
Hamet were strangers to sleep: his fancy incessantly
repeated the events that had just happened; the image of
Almeida was ever before him; and his breast throbbed with
a disquietude, which, though it prevented rest, he did not
wish to lose.

Almoran, in the mean time, was slumbering away the
effects of his intemperance; and in the morning, when he
was told what had happened, he expressed no passion but
curiosity: he went hastily into the garden; but when he had
gazed upon the ruins, and enquired how the fire began, and
what it had consumed, he thought of it no more.

But Hamet suffered nothing that regarded himself, to
exclude others from his attention: he went again to the
ruins, not to gratify his curiosity, but to see what might yet
be done to alleviate the misery of the sufferers, and secure
for their use what had been preserved from the flames. He
found that no life had been lost, but that many persons had
been hurt; to these he sent the physicians of his own
houshold: and having rewarded those who had assisted
them in their distress, not forgetting even the soldiers who
had only fulfilled his own orders, he returned, and applied
himself to dispatch the public business in the chamber of
council, with the same patient and diligent attention as if
nothing had happened. He had, indeed, ordered enquiry to
be made after Almeida; and when he returned to his
apartment, he found Abdallah waiting to express his gratitude for the obligations he had received.

Hamet accepted his acknowledgements with a peculiar
pleasure, for they had some connexion with Almeida; after

whom he again enquired, with an ardour uncommon even to the benevolence of Hamet. When all his questions had been asked and answered, he appeared still unwilling to dismiss Abdallah, though he seemed at a loss how to detain him; he wanted to know, whether his daughter had yet received an offer of marriage, though he was unwilling to discover his desire by a direct enquiry: but he soon found, that nothing could be known, which was not directly asked, from a man whom reverence and humility kept silent before him, except when something was said which amounted to a command to speak. At length, however, he said, not without some hesitation, 'Is there no one, Abdallah, who will thank me for the preservation of thy daughter, with a zeal equal to thy own?' 'Yes,' replied Abdallah, 'that daughter whom thou hast preserved.' This reply, though it was unexpected, was pleasing: for Hamet was not only gratified to hear, that Almeida had expressed herself warmly in his behalf, at least as a benefactor; but he judged, that if any man had been interested in her life as a lover, the answer which Abdallah had given him would not so readily have occurred to his mind.

As this reflection kept Hamet a few moments silent, Abdallah withdrew; and Hamet, as he observed some marks of haste and confusion in his countenance, was unwilling longer to continue him in a situation, which he had now reason to think gave him pain. But Abdallah, who had conceived a sudden thought that Hamet's question was an indirect reproach of Almeida, for not having herself solicited admission to his presence; went in haste to her apartment, and ordered her immediately to make ready to attend him to the king.

Almeida, from whose mind the image of Hamet had not been absent a moment since she first saw him, received this order with a mixture of pain and pleasure; of wishes, hopes, and apprehensions, that filled her bosom with emotion, and covered her face with blushes. She had not courage to ask

the reason of the command, which she instantly prepared
to obey; but the tenderness of Abdallah, who perceived and
pitied her distress, anticipated her wish. In a short time,
therefore, he returned to the chamber of presence, and
having received permission, he entered with Almeida in his
hand. Hamet rose in haste to receive her, with a glow of
pleasure and impatience in his countenance: and having
raised her from the ground, supported her in his arms,
waiting to hear her voice; but though she made many
attempts, she could not speak. Hamet, who knew not to
what he owed this sudden and unexpected interview,
which, though he wished, he could contrive no means to
obtain; imagined that Almeida had some request, and
therefore urged her tenderly to make it: but as she still
remained silent, he looked at Abdallah, as expecting to hear
it from him. 'We have no wish,' said Abdallah, 'but to
atone for our offence; nor any request, but that my lord
would now accept the thanks of Almeida for the life which
he has preserved, and impute the delay, not to ingratitude,
but inadvertence: let me now take her back, as thy gift; and
let the light of thy favour be upon us.' 'Take her then,' said
Hamet; 'for I would give her only to thee.'

These words of Hamet did not escape the notice either of
Abdallah or Almeida; but neither of them mentioned their
conjectures to the other. Almeida, who was inclined to
judge of Hamet's situation by her own, and who recollected
many little incidents, known only to herself, which
favoured her wishes; indulged the hope, that she should
again hear of Hamet, with more confidence than her father;
nor were her expectations disappointed. Hamet reflected
with pleasure, that he had prepared the way for a more
explicit declaration; and as his impatience increased with
his passion every hour, he sent for Abdallah the next
morning, and told him, that he wished to be more
acquainted with his daughter, with a view to make her his
wife: 'As neither you nor your daughter are my subjects,'

says Hamet, 'I cannot command you; and if you were, upon this occasion, I would not. I do not want a slave, but a friend; not merely a woman, but a wife. If I find Almeida such as my fancy has feigned her; if her mind corresponds with her form; and if I have reason to think, that she can give her heart to Hamet, and not merely her hand to the king; I shall be happy.' To this declaration, Abdallah replied with expressions of the profoundest submission and gratitude; and Hamet dismissed him, to prepare Almeida to receive him in the afternoon of the same day.

CHAPTER VII

As eight moons only had passed since the death of Solyman, and as the reverence of Hamet for the memory of his
father would not suffer him to marry till the year should be
completed;* he determined not to mention Almeida to his
brother, till the time when he could marry her was near.
The fierce and haughty deportment of Almoran had now
left Hamet no room to doubt of his character: and though
he had no apprehension that he would make any attempts
upon Almeida, after she should be his wife; yet he did not
know how much might justly be feared from his passion, if
he should see her and become enamoured of her, while she
was yet a virgin in the house of her father.

Almeida had not only unsullied purity of mind, but
principles of refined and exalted virtue, and as the life of
Hamet was an example of all that was either great or good,
Abdallah felt no anxiety upon leaving them together, except
what arose from his fears, that his daughter would not be
able to secure the conquest she had made.

As it was impossible for Hamet to have such an acquaintance with Almeida as he desired, till he could enter into
conversation with her upon terms of equality; it was his
first care to sooth her into confidence and familiarity, and
by degrees he succeeded: he soon found, in the free
intercourse of mind with mind, which he established
instead of the implicit submission which only echoed his
own voice, how little of the pleasure that women were
formed to give can be enjoyed, when they are considered
merely as slaves to a tyrant's will, the passive subjects of
transient dalliance and casual enjoyment. The pleasure
which he took in the youthful beauty of Almeida, was now

endeared, exalted, and refined, by the tender sensibility of her heart, and by the reflexion of his own felicity from her eyes: when he admired the gracefulness of her motion, the elegance of her figure, the symmetry of her features, and the bloom of her complexion, he considered them as the decorations only of a mind, capable of mixing with his own in the most exquisite delight, of reciprocating all his ideas, and catching new pleasure from his pleasure. Desire was no longer appetite; it was imagination, it was reason; it included remembrance of the past, and anticipation of the future; and its object was not the sex, but Almeida.

As Hamet never witheld any pleasure that it was in his power to impart, he soon acquainted Abdallah, that he waited only for a proper time to place Almeida upon the throne; but that he had some reasons for keeping a resolution, which he thought himself obliged to communicate to him, concealed from others.

It happened, however, that some of the women who attended upon Almeida, met with some female slaves belonging to the seraglio of Almoran, at the public baths,* and related to them all the particulars of Almeida's preservation by Hamet; that he had first conveyed her to his own apartments, and had since been frequently with her in that which he had assigned her in his palace: they were also lavish in the praise of her beauty, and free in their conjectures what might be the issue of her intercourse with Hamet.

Thus the situation of Hamet and Almeida became the subject of conversation in the seraglio of Almoran, who learnt it himself in a short time from one of his women.

He had hitherto professed great affection for Hamet, and Hamet was deceived by his professions; for notwithstanding the irregularities of his life, he did not think him capable of concealed malice; or of offering injury to another, except when he was urged by impetuous passions to immediate pleasure. As there was, therefore, an appearance of mutual affection between them, Almoran, though the report of

Almeida's beauty had fired his imagination and fixed him in a resolution to see her, did not think proper to attempt it without asking Hamet's consent, and being introduced by his order; as he made no doubt of there being a connexion between them which would make him resent a contrary conduct.

He took an opportunity, therefore, when they were alone in a summer pavilion that was built on a lake behind the palace,* to reproach him, with an air of mirth, for having concealed a beauty near his apartments, though he pretended to have no seraglio. Hamet instantly discovered his surprize and emotion by a blush, which the next moment left his countenance paler than the light clouds that pass by night over the moon. Almoran took no notice of his confusion; but that he might more effectually conceal his sentiments and prevent suspicion, he suddenly adverted to another subject, while Hamet was hesitating what to reply. By this artifice Hamet was deceived; and concluded, that whatever Almoran had heard of Almeida, had passed slightly over his mind, and was remembered but by chance; he, therefore, quickly recovered that ease and chearfulness, which always distinguished his conversation.

Almoran observing the success of his artifice, soon after, as if by a sudden and casual recollection, again mentioned the lady; and told him, he would congratulate Abdallah upon having resigned her to his bed. As Hamet could not bear to think of Almoran's mentioning Almeida to her father as his mistress, he replied, that he had no such intimacy with Almeida as he supposed; and that he had so high an opinion of her virtue, as to believe that if he should propose it she would not consent. The imagination of Almoran caught new fire from beauties which he found were yet unenjoyed, and virtue which stamped them with superior value by rendering them more difficult of access; and as Hamet had renounced a connection with her as a mistress, he wanted only to know whether he intended her for a wife.

This secret he was contriving to discover, when Hamet, having reflected, that if he concealed this particular, Almoran might think himself at liberty to make what attempts he should think fit upon Almeida, without being accountable to him, or giving him just cause of offence, put an end to his doubts, by telling him, he had such a design; but that it would be some time before he should carry it into execution. This declaration increased Almoran's impatience: still, however, he concealed his interest in the conversation, which he now suffered to drop.

He parted from his brother, without any farther mention of Almeida; but while he was yet near him, turned hastily back, and, as if merely to gratify his curiosity, told him with a smile, that he must indulge him with a sight of his Circassian; and desired he might accompany him in his next visit, or at some more convenient time: with this request, Hamet, as he knew not how to refuse it, complied; but it filled his mind with anxiety and trouble.

He went immediately to Almeida, and told her all that had happened; and as she saw that he was not without apprehensions of mischief from his brother's visit, she gently reproached him for doubting the fidelity of her affection, as she supposed no power could be exerted by Almoran to injure him, who in power was his equal. Hamet, in a transport of tenderness, assured her that he doubted neither her constancy nor her love: but as to interrupt the comfort of her mind, would only double his own distress, he did not tell her whence his apprehensions proceeded; nor indeed had they any determinate object, but arose in general from the character of his brother, and the probability of his becoming a competitor, for what was essential to the happiness of his life.

But if the happiness of Hamet was lessened, the infelicity of Almoran was increased. All the enjoyments that were in his power he neglected, his attention being wholly fixed upon that which was beyond his reach; he was impatient to see the beauty, who had taken intire possession of his mind; and the probability that he would be obliged to resign her to Hamet, tormented him with jealousy, envy, and indignation.

Hamet, however, did not long delay to fulfil his promise to his brother; but having prepared Almeida to receive him, he conducted him to her apartment. The idea which Almoran had formed in his imagination, was exceeded by the reality, and his passion was proportionately increased; yet, he found means not only to conceal it from Hamet, but from Almeida, by affecting an air of levity and merriment, which is not less incompatible with the pleasures than the pains of love. After they had been regaled with coffee and sherbet,* they parted; and Hamet congratulated himself, that his apprehensions of finding in Almoran a rival for Almeida's love, were now at an end.

But Almoran, whose passions were become more violent by restraint, was in a state of mind little better than distraction: one moment he determined to seize upon the person of Almeida in the night, and secrete her in some place accessible only to himself; and the next to assassinate his brother, that he might at once destroy a rival both in empire and in love. But these designs were no sooner formed by his wishes, than they were rejected by his fears: he was not ignorant, that in any contest between him and Hamet, the voice of the public would be against him; especially in a contest, in which it would appear, that Hamet had suffered wrong.

Many other projects, equally rash, violent, and injurious, were by turns conceived and rejected: and he came at last to no other determination, than still carefully to conceal his passion, till he should think of some expedient to gratify it; lest Hamet should have a just reason for refusing to let him see the lady again, and remove her to some place which he might never be able to discover.

CHAPTER VIII

IN the mean time, Omar, to whom Hamet had from time to time disclosed the minutest particulars of his situation and design, kept his eye almost continually upon Almoran; and observed him with an attention and sagacity, which it was difficult either to elude or deceive. He perceived, that he was more than usual restless and turbulent; that in the presence of Hamet he frequently changed countenance; that his behaviour was artificial and inconsistent, frequently shifting from gloomy discontent and furious agitation, to forced laughter and noisy merriment. He had also remarked, that he seemed most discomposed after he had been with Hamet to Almeida, which happened generally once in a week; that he was become fond of solitude, and was absent several days together from the apartment of his women.

Omar, who from this conduct of Almoran had begun to suspect his principles, determined to introduce such topics of discourse, as might lead him to discover the state of his mind; and enable him to enforce and confirm the principles he had taught him, by new proofs and illustrations.

Almoran, who, since the death of his father, had nothing to apprehend from the discovery of sentiments which before he had been careful to conceal; now urged his objections against religion, when Omar gave him opportunity, without reserve. 'You tell me,' says he, 'of beings that are immortal, because they are immaterial; beings which do not consist of parts, and which, therefore, can admit no solution, the only natural cause of corruption and decay: but that which is not material, can have no extension; and what has no extension, possesses no space; and of such beings, the mind itself, which you pretend to be such a being, has no conception.'

'If the mind,' says Omar, 'can perceive that there is in itself any single property of such a being, it has irrefragable evidence that it is such a being; though its mode of existence, as distinct from matter, cannot now be comprehended.' 'And what property of such a being,' said Almoran, 'does the mind of man perceive in itself?' 'That of *acting*,' said Omar, 'without *motion*. You have no idea, that a material substance can act, but in proportion as it moves: yet to *think*, is to *act*; and with the idea of thinking, the idea of motion is never connected: on the contrary, we always conceive the mind to be fixed, in proportion to the degree of ardour and intenseness with which the power of thinking is exerted. Now, if that which is material cannot act without motion; and if man is conscious, that to think, is to act and not to move; it follows, that there is, in man, somewhat that is not matter; somewhat that has no extension, and that possesses no space; somewhat which, having no contexture or parts that can be dissolved or separated, is exempted from all the natural causes of decay.'

Omar paused; and Almoran having stood some moments without reply, he seized this opportunity to impress him with an awful sense of the power and presence of the Supreme and Eternal Being, from whom his own existence was derived: 'Let us remember,' said he, 'that to every act of this immaterial and immortal part, the Father of spirits, from whom it proceeds, is present: when I behold the busy multitudes that crowd the metropolis of Persia, in the persuit of business and projects infinitely complicated and various; and consider that every idea which passes over their minds, every conclusion and every purpose, with all that they remember of the past, and all that they imagine of the future, is at once known to the Almighty, who without labour or confusion weighs every thought of every mind in His balance, and reserves it to the day of retribution; my

follies cover me with confusion, and my soul is humbled in
the dust.'

Almoran, though he appeared to listen with attention,
and offered nothing against the reasoning of Omar, yet
secretly despised it as sophistry, which cunning only had
rendered specious; and which he was unable to confute,
merely because it was subtil, and not because it was true:
he had been led, by his passions, first to love, and then to
adopt different opinions; and as every man is inclined to
judge of others by himself, he doubted, whether the
principles which Omar had thus laboured to establish, were
believed even by Omar himself.

Thus was the mind of Almoran to the instructions of
Omar, as a rock slightly covered with earth, is to the waters
of heaven: the craggs are left bare by the rain that washes
them; and the same showers that fertilize the field, can only
discover the sterility of the rock.

Omar, however, did not yet disclose his suspicions to
Hamet, because he did not yet see that it could answer any
purpose. To remove Almeida from her apartment, would
be to shew a distrust, for which there would not appear to
be any cause; and to refuse Almoran access to her when he
desired it, might precipitate such measures as he might
meditate, and engage him in some desperate attempt: he,
therefore, contented himself with advising Hamet, to conceal the time of his marriage till the evening before he
intended it should take place, without assigning the reason
on which his advice was founded.

To the council of Omar, Hamet was implicitly obedient,
as to the revelations of the Prophet; but, like his instructions, it was neglected by Almoran, who became every
moment more wretched. He had a graceful person, and a
vigorous mind; he was in the bloom of youth, and had a
constitution that promised him length of days; he had
power which princes were emulous to obey, and wealth by
which whatever could administer to luxury might be

bought; for every passion, and every appetite, it was easy for him to procure a perpetual succession of new objects: yet was Almoran, not only without enjoyment, but without peace; he was by turns pining with discontent, and raving with indignation; his vices had extracted bitter from every sweet; and having exhausted nature for delight in vain, he was repining at the bounds in which he was confined, and regretting the want of other powers as the cause of his misery.

Thus the year of mourning for Solyman was compleated, without any act of violence on the part of Almoran, or of caution on the part of Hamet: but on the evening of the last day, Hamet, having secretly prepared every thing for performing the solemnity in a private manner, acquainted Almoran by a letter, which Omar undertook to deliver, that he should celebrate his marriage on the morrow. Almoran, who never doubted but he should have notice of this event much longer before it was to happen, read the letter with a perturbation that it was impossible to conceal: he was alone in his private apartment, and taking his eye hastily from the paper, he crushed it together in his hand, and thrusting it into his bosom, turned from Omar without speaking; and Omar, thinking himself dismissed, withdrew.

The passions which Almoran could no longer suppress, now burst out in a torrent of exclamation: 'Am I then,' said he, 'blasted for ever with a double curse, divided empire and disappointed love! What is dominion, if it is not possessed alone? and what is power, which the dread of rival power perpetually controuls? Is it for me to listen in silence to the wrangling of slaves, that I may at last apportion to them what, with a clamorous insolence, they demand as their due! as well may the sun linger in his course, and the world mourn in darkness for the day, that the glowworm may still be seen to glimmer upon the earth, and the owls and bats that haunt the sepulchres of the dead enjoy a longer night. Yet this have I done, because this has been done by Hamet: and my heart sickens in vain with the desire of beauty, because my power extends not to Almeida. With dominion undivided and Almeida, I should be Almoran; but without them, I am less than nothing.'

Omar, who, before he had passed the pavilion, heard a sound which he knew to be the voice of Almoran returned hastily to the chamber in which he left him, believing he had withdrawn too soon, and that the king, as he knew no other was present, was speaking to him: he soon drew near enough to hear what was said; and while he was standing torpid in suspense, dreading to be discovered, and not knowing how to retire, Almoran turned about.

At first, both stood motionless with confusion and amazement; but Almoran's pride soon surmounted his other passions, and his disdain of Omar gave his guilt the firmness of virtue.

'It is true,' said he, 'that thou hast stolen the secret of my heart; but do not think, that I fear it should be known: though my poignard* could take it back with thy life, I leave it with thee. To reproach, or curse thee, would do thee honour, and lift thee into an importance which otherwise thou canst never reach.' Almoran then turned from him with a contemptuous frown: but Omar caught him by the robe; and prostrating himself upon the ground, intreated to be heard. His importunity at length prevailed; and he attempted to exculpate himself, from the charge of having insiduously intruded upon the privacy of his prince; but Almoran sternly interrupted him: 'And what art thou,' said he, 'that I should care, whether thou art innocent or guilty?' 'If not for my sake,' said Omar, 'listen for thy own; and though my duty is despised, let my affection be heard. That thou art not happy, I know; and I now know the cause. Let my lord pardon the presumption of his slave: he that seeks to satisfy all his wishes, must be wretched; he only can be happy, by whom some are suppressed.' At these words Almoran snatched his robe from the hand of

Omar, and spurned him in a transport of rage and indignation: 'The suppression of desire,' said he, 'is such happiness, as that of the deaf who do not remember to have heard. If it is virtue, know, that, as virtue, I despise it; for though it may secure the obedience of the slave, it can only degrade the prerogative of a prince. I cast off all restraint, as I do thee: begone, therefore, to Hamet, and see me no more.'

Omar obeyed without reply; and Almoran being again alone, the conflict in his mind was renewed with greater violence than before. He felt all that he had disguised to Omar, with the keenest sensibility; and anticipated the effects of his detection, with unutterable anguish and regret. He walked backward and forward with a hasty but interrupted pace; sometimes stopping short, and pressing his hand hard upon his brow; and sometimes by violent gestures showing the agitation of his mind: he sometimes stood silent with his eyes fixed upon the ground, and his arms folded together; and sometimes a sudden agony of thought forced him into loud and tumultuous exclamations: he cursed the impotence of mind that had suffered his thoughts to escape from him unawares, without reflecting that he was even then repeating the folly; and while he felt himself the victim of vice, he could not suppress his contempt of virtue: 'If I must perish,' said he, 'I will at least perish unsubdued: I will quench no wish that nature kindles in my bosom; nor shall my lips utter any prayer, but for new powers to feed the flame.'

As he uttered this expression, he felt the palace shake; he heard a rushing, like a blast in the desart; and a being of more than human appearance stood before him. Almoran, though he was terrified, was not humbled; and he stood expecting the event, whether evil or good, rather with obduracy than courage.

'Thou seest,' says the Appearance, 'a Genius,* whom the daring purpose of thy mind has convoked from the middle

region, where he was appointed to wait the signal; and who
is now permitted to act in concert with thy will. Is not this
the language of thy heart?—"Whatever pleasure I can
snatch from the hand of time, as he passes by me, I will
secure for myself: my passions shall be strong, that my
enjoyments may be great; for what is the portion allotted to
man, but the joyful madness that prolongs the hours of
festivity, the fierce delight that is extorted from injury by
revenge, and the sweet succession of varied pleasures which
the wish that is ever changing prepares for love?"'

'Whatever thou art,' said Almoran, 'whose voice has thus
disclosed the secret of my soul, accept my homage; for I
will worship thee: and be thou henceforth my wisdom and
my strength.'

'Arise,' said the Genius, 'for therefore am I sent. To thy
own powers, mine shall be superadded: and if, as weak
only, thou hast been wretched; henceforth thou shalt be
happy. Take no thought for to-morrow; to-morrow, my
power shall be employed in thy behalf. Be not affrighted at
any prodigy; but put thy confidence in me.' While he was
yet speaking and the eyes of Almoran were fixed upon him,
a cloud gathered round him; and the next moment dissolv-
ing again into air, he disappeared.

CHAPTER IX

ALMORAN, when he recovered from his astonishment, and had reflected upon the prodigy, determined to wait the issue, and refer all his hopes to the interposition of the Genius, without attempting any thing to retard the marriage; at which he resolved to be present, that he might improve any supernatural event which might be produced in his favour.

Hamet, in the mean time, was anticipating the morrow with a mixture of anxiety and pleasure; and though he had no reason to think any thing could prevent his marriage, yet he wished it was over, with an impatience that was considerably increased by fear.

Though the anticipation of the great event that was now so near, kept him waking the greatest part of the night, yet he rose early in the morning; and while he waited till Almeida should be ready to see him, he was told that Omar was without, and desired admittance. When he came in, Hamet, who always watched his countenance as a mariner the stars of heaven, perceived that it was obscured with perplexity and grief. 'Tell me,' said Hamet, 'whence is the sorrow that I discover in thy face?' 'I am sorrowful,' said Omar, 'not for myself, but for thee.' At these words Hamet stept backward, and fixed his eyes upon Omar, without power to speak. 'Consider,' said Omar, 'that thou art not a man only, but a prince: consider also, that immortality is before thee; and that thy felicity, during the endless ages of immortality, depends upon thyself: fear not, therefore, what thou canst suffer from others; the evil and the good of life are transient as the morning dew, and over these only the hand of others can prevail.'

Hamet, whose attachment to life was strong, and whose expectations of immediate enjoyment were high, did not feel the force of what Omar had said, though he assented to its truth. 'Tell me,' said he, 'at once, what thou fearest for me; deliver me from the torments of suspense, and trust my own fortitude to save me from despair.' 'Know then,' said Omar, 'that thou art hated by Almoran, and that he loves Almeida.' At this declaration, the astonishment of Hamet was equal to his concern; and he was in doubt whether to believe or disbelieve what he heard: but the moment he recollected the wisdom and integrity of Omar, his doubts were at an end; and having recovered from his surprize, he was about to make such enquiries as might gratify the anxious and tumultuous curiosity which was excited in his breast, when Omar, lifting up his hand, and beginning again to speak, Hamet remained silent.

'Thou knowest,' said Omar, 'that when my cheeks were yet ruddy with youth, and my limbs were braced by vigour, that mine eye was guided to knowledge by the lamp that is kindled at midnight; and much of what is hidden in the innermost recesses of nature, was discovered to me: my prayer ascended in secret to Him, with whom there is wisdom from everlasting to everlasting, and He illuminated my darkness with His light. I know, by such sensations as the world either feels not at all, or feels unnoticed without knowledge of their use, when the powers that are invisible are permitted to mingle in the walks of men; and well I know, that some being, who is more than mortal, has joined with Almoran against thee, since the veil of night was last spread upon the earth.'

Hamet, whose blood was chilled with horror, and whose nerves were no longer obedient to his will, after several ineffectual attempts to speak, looked up at Omar; and striking his hand upon his breast, cried out, in an earnest, but faultering voice, 'What shall I do?' 'Thou must do,' said Omar, 'that which is RIGHT. Let not thy foot be drawn by any terror, from the path of virtue. While thou art there, thou art in safety: and though the world should unite against thee, by the united world thou canst not be hurt.'

'But what friendly power,' said Hamet, 'shall guard even the path of virtue from grief and pain; from the silent shaft of disappointed love, or the sounding scourge of outrageous jealousy? These, surely, have overtaken the foot of perseverance; and by these, though I should persevere, may my feet be overtaken.' 'What thou sayest,' replied Omar, 'is true; and it is true also, that the tempest which roots up the forest, is driven over the mountain with unabated rage: but from the mountain, what can it take more than the vegetable dust, which the hand of nature has scattered upon the moss that covers it? As the dust is to the mountain, so is all that the storms of life can take from virtue, to the sum of good which the Omnipotent has appointed for its reward.' Hamet, whose eye now expressed a kind of doubtful confidence, a hope that was repressed by fear, remained still silent; and Omar, perceiving the state of his mind, proceeded to fortify it by new precepts: 'If heaven,' said he, 'should vanish like a vapour, and this firm orb of earth should crumble into dust, the virtuous mind would stand unmoved amidst the ruins of nature: for He, who has appointed the heavens and the earth to fail, has said to virtue, "Fear not; for thou canst neither perish, nor be wretched."* Call up thy strength, therefore, to the fight in which thou art sure of conquest: do thou only that which is RIGHT, and leave the event to Heaven.'

Hamet, in this conference with Omar, having gradually recovered his fortitude; and the time being now near, when he was to conduct Almeida to the court of the palace, where the marriage ceremony was to be performed; they parted with mutual benedictions, each recommending the other to the protection of the Most High.

At the appointed hour, the princes of the court being assembled, the mufti and the imans* being ready, and

Almoran seated upon his throne; Hamet and Almeida came forward, and were placed one on the right hand, and the other on the left. The mufti was then advancing, to hear and to record the mutual promise which was to unite them;* Almoran was execrating the appearance of the Genius, as a delusive dream, in all the tumults of anguish and despair; and Hamet began to hope, that the suspicions of Omar had been ill founded; when a stroke of thunder shook the palace to its foundations, and a cloud rose from the ground, like a thick smoke, between Hamet and Almeida.

Almoran, who was inspired with new confidence and hope, by that which had struck the rest of the assembly with terror, started from his seat with an ardent and furious look; and at the same moment, a voice, that issued from the cloud, pronounced with a loud but hollow tone,

'Fate has decreed, to Almoran, Almeida.'

At these words, Almoran rushed forward, and placing himself by the side of Almeida, the cloud disappeared; and he cried out, 'Let me now proclaim to the world the secret, which to this moment I have hidden in my bosom: I love Almeida. The being who alone knew my love, has now by miracle approved it. Let his decree be accomplished.' He then commanded that the ceremony should proceed; and seizing the hand of the lady, began to repeat that part of it which was to have been repeated by Hamet. But Almeida instantly drew her hand from him in an agony of distress; and Hamet, who till then had stood motionless with amazement and horror, started from his trance, and springing forward rushed between them. Almoran turned fiercely upon him; but Hamet, who having been warned by Omar, knew the prodigy to be effected by some evil being whom it was virtue to resist, laid his hand upon his scymitar, and, with a frown of indignation and defiance, commanded him to stand off: 'I now know thee,' said he, 'as a man; and, therefore, as a brother I know thee not.'

Almoran reflecting, that the foundation of this reproach was unknown to all who were present, and that to them he would therefore appear to be injured; looked round with an affected smile of wonder and compassion, as appealing to them from a charge that was thus fiercely and injuriously brought against him, and imputing it to the violence of sudden passions by which truth and reason were overborne. The eye of Hamet at once detected the artifice, which he disdained to expose; he, therefore, commanded the guard that attended to carry off Almeida to her apartment. The guard was preparing to obey, when Almoran, who thought he had now such an opportunity to get her into his own power as would never return, ordered them to see her safely lodged in his own seraglio.

The men, who thus received opposite commands from persons to whom they owed equal obedience, stood still in suspense, not knowing which to prefer: Almoran then reproached them with want of obedience, not to him, but to God, appealing to the prodigy for the justification of his claim. Hamet, on the contrary, repeated his order, with a look and emphasis scarce less commanding than the thunder and the voice. But the priests interposing in favour of Almoran, upon presumption that his right had been decided by a superior power; the guard rushed between Hamet and Almeida, and with looks that expressed the utmost reluctance and regret, attempted to separate their hands, which were clasped in each other. She was affrighted at the violence, but yet more at the apprehension of what was to follow; she, therefore, turned her eyes upon Hamet, conjuring him not to leave her, in a tone of tenderness and distress which it is impossible to describe: he replied with a vehemence that was worthy of his passion, 'I will not leave thee,' and immediately drew his sabre. At the same moment they forced her from him; and a party having interposed to cover those that were carrying her off, Hamet lifted up his weapon to force his passage through them; but was prevented by Omar, who, having pressed through the crowd, presented himself before him. 'Stop me not,' said Hamet, 'it is for Almeida.' 'If thou wouldst save Almeida,' said Omar, 'and thyself, do that only which is RIGHT. What have these done who oppose thee, more than they ought? and what end can their destruction answer, but to stain thy hands with unavailing murder? Thou canst only take the life of a few faithful slaves, who will not lift up their hands against thee: thou canst not rescue Almeida from thy brother; but thou canst preserve thyself from guilt.'

These words of Omar suspended the rage of Hamet, like a charm; and returning his scymitar into its sheath, 'Let me then,' said he, 'suffer, and be guiltless. It is true, that against these ranks my single arm must be ineffectual; but if my wrongs can rouse a nation to repress the tyranny, that will shortly extend over it the injuries that now reach only to me, justice shall be done to Hamet.' Then turning to Almoran, 'Henceforth,' said he, 'the kingdom shall be mine or thine. To govern in concert with thee, is to associate with the powers of hell. The beings that are superior to evil, are the friends of Hamet; and if these are thy enemies, what shall be thy defence?' Almoran replied only by a contemptuous smile; and the assembly being dismissed he retired to his apartment: and Hamet and Omar went out to the people, who had gathered in an incredible multitude about the palace.

CHAPTER X

A RUMOUR of what had happened within had reached them, which some believed, and some doubted: but when they saw Omar and Hamet return together, and observed that their looks were full of resentment and trouble, they became silent with attention in a moment; which Omar observing, addressed them with an eloquence of which they had often acknowledged the force, and of which they never repented the effect.

He told them the tender connexion between Hamet and Almeida, and disclosed the subtil hypocrisy of Almoran: he expatiated upon the folly of supposing, that the power that was supreme in goodness and truth, should command a violation of vows that had been mutually interchanged, and often repeated; and devote to Almoran the beauties, which could only be voluntarily surrendered to Hamet. They heard him with a vacant countenance of surprize and wonder; and while he waited for their reply, they agreed among themselves, that no man could avoid the destiny that was written upon his head; and that if Almeida had thus been taken from Hamet, and given to Almoran, it was an event that by an unchangeable decree was appointed to happen; and that, therefore, it was their duty to acquiesce. Omar then beckoned with his hand for audience a second time; and told them, that Almoran had not only practised the arts of sorcery to deprive Hamet of Almeida, but that he meditated a design to usurp the sole dominion, and deprive him of the share of the government to which he had a right by the will of Solyman his father. This also they heard with the same sentiments of wonder and acquiescence: If it is decreed, said they, that Almoran shall be king alone, who can prevent it? and if it is not, who can bring it to pass? 'But know ye not,' said Omar, 'that when the end is appointed, the means are appointed also. If it is decreed that one of you shall this night die by poison, is it not decreed also that he shall drink it?'

The crowd now gazed upon each other, without reply, for some minutes: and at last they only said, that no effort of theirs could change the universal appointment of all things; that if Almoran was to be king alone, he would be so notwithstanding all opposition; and that if he was not to be king alone, no attempt of his own, however supported, could make him so. 'I will not,' said Omar, 'contradict your opinion; I will only tell you what I have heard, and leave you to suffer the calamities which threaten you, with a fortitude and resignation that are suitable to your principles; having no consolation to offer you, but that Hamet, whose destiny it was not to make you happy, will suffer with you the evils, that neither he nor you could prevent: the mournful comfort of this fellowship, he will not be denied; for he loves you too well, to wish even to be happy alone.' The crowd fixed their eyes upon Hamet, for whom their affection was now strongly moved, with looks of much greater intelligence and sensibility; a confused murmur, like the fall of the pebbles upon the beach when the surge retires from the shore, expressed their gratitude to Hamet, and their apprehensions for themselves.

Omar waited till they were again silent, and then improved the advantage he had gained. 'Almoran,' said he, 'considers you as the slaves of his power; Hamet as the objects of his benevolence: your lives and your properties, in the opinion of Almoran, are below his notice; but Hamet considers his own interest as connected with yours. When Almoran, therefore, shall be unchecked by the influence of Hamet; he will leave you to the mercy of some delegated tyrant, whose whole power will be exerted to oppress you, that he may enrich himself.'

A new fire was now kindled in their eyes, and their cheeks glowed with indignation at the wrongs that threatened them; they were no longer disposed to act upon the principles of fatality, as they had perversely understood them; and they argued at once like reasonable and free beings, whose actions were in their choice, and who had no doubt but that their actions would produce adequate effects. They recollected that Omar had, in the reign of Solyman, often rescued them from such oppression, as now threatened them; and that the power of Hamet had since interposed in their behalf, when Almoran would have stretched his prerogative to their hurt, or have left them a prey to the farmer of a tax. 'Shall Hamet,' said they, 'be deprived of the power, that he employs only for our benefit, and shall it center on Almoran, who will abuse it to our ruin? Shall we rather support Almoran in the wrong he has done to Hamet, than Hamet to obtain justice of Almoran? Hamet is our king; let him command us, and we will obey.' This was uttered with a shout that echoed from the mountains beyond the city, and continued near a full hour. In the mean time, the multitude was increasing every moment; and the troops that lay in and near the city having taken arms, fell in with the stream: they were secretly attached to Hamet, under whose eye they had been formed, and of whose bounty they had often partaken; and their fear being removed by the general cry, which left them no room to apprehend an opposition in favour of Almoran, they were now at full liberty to follow their inclinations.

In the mean time, Almoran, who had retired to the innermost court of the palace, had heard the tumult, and was alarmed for his safety: he ran from room to room, confused and terrified, without attempting or directing any thing either for his defence or escape; yet he sent every moment to know the state of the insurrection, and to what end its force would be directed.

Among those whom accident rather than choice had

attached to the interest of Almoran, were Osmyn and Caled: they were both distinguished by his favour; and each had conceived hopes that, if he should possess the throne alone, he would delegate his authority to him. Almoran now ordered them to take the command of the troops, that were appointed to attend his person as their peculiar duty, with as many others as had not declared for Hamet, and to secure all the avenues that led to his seraglio.

Omar and Hamet were now on horseback, and had begun to form the troops that had joined them, and as many others as were armed, which were before mingled together in a confused multitude. An account of this was brought to Almoran by Osmyn; and threw him into a perturbation and perplexity, that disgraced his character, and confounded his attendants. He urged Osmyn, in whom he most confided, to dispatch, without giving him any orders to execute; then turning from him, he uttered, in a low and inarticulate voice, the most passionate exclamations of distress and terror, being struck with the thought that his guard might betray him: when he recollected himself, and perceived that Osmyn was still present, he burst into a rage, and snatching out his poignard, he swore by the soul of the Prophet, that if he did not instantly attempt something, he would stab him to the heart. Osmyn drew back trembling and confused; but having yet received no orders, he would have spoken, but Almoran drove him from his presence with menaces and execrations.

The moment that Osmyn left him, his rage subsided in his fears, and his fears were mingled with remorse: 'Which way soever I turn,' said he, 'I see myself surrounded by destruction. I have incensed Osmyn by unreasonable displeasure, and causeless menaces. He must regard me at once with abhorrence and contempt: and it is impossible, but he should revolt to Hamet.'

In this agony, the terrors of futurity rushed upon his mind with all their force; and he started as if at the bite of a scorpion: 'To me,' said he, 'death, that now approaches, will be but the beginning of sorrow. I shall be cut off at once from enjoyment, and from hope; and the dreadful moment is now at hand.' While he was speaking, the palace again shook, and he stood again in the presence of the Genius.

'Almoran,' said the inhabitant of the unapparent world, 'the evil which thou fearest, shall not be upon thee. Make haste, and shew thyself from the gallery unto the people, and the tumult of faction shall be still before thee: tell them, that their rebellion is not against thee only, but against Him by whom thou reignest: appeal boldly to that power for a confirmation of thy words, and rely for the attesting sign upon me.' Almoran, who had stooped with his face to the ground, now looked upward, and found himself alone: he hasted, therefore, to follow the directions he had received; and hope was again kindled in his bosom.

Osmyn, in the mean time, made a proper disposition of the troops now under his command; and had directed a select company to remain near the person of the king, that they might at least make good his retreat. While he was waiting at his post, and revolving in his mind the total disappointment of his hopes, and considering what he should do if Hamet should establish himself alone, he was joined by Caled.

Caled had a secret enmity against Osmyn, as his rival in the favour of Almoran; but as he had concealed his own pretensions from Osmyn; Osmyn had no ill will against Caled. As they were now likely to be involved in one common calamity, by the ruin of the prince whose party they had espoused; Caled's enmity subsided, and the indifference of Osmyn was warmed into kindness: mutual distress produced mutual confidence; and Caled, after condoling with Osmyn on their present hopeless situation, proposed that they should draw off their forces, and revolt to Hamet. This proposition Osmyn rejected, not only from principle, but from interest: 'Now we have accepted of a trust,' said he, 'we ought not to betray it. If we had gone over to Hamet, when he first declared against his brother, he would have received us with joy, and probably have rewarded our service; but I know, that his virtue will abhor us for treachery, though practised in his favour: treachery, under the dominion of Hamet, will not only cover us with dishonour, but will probably devote us to death.'

In this reasoning, Caled could not but acquiesce; he felt himself secretly but forcibly reproved, by the superior virtue of Osmyn: and while he regretted his having made a proposal, which had been rejected not only as imprudent but infamous; he concluded, that Osmyn would ever after suspect and despise him; and he, therefore, from a new cause, conceived new enmity against him. They parted, however, without any appearance of suspicion or disgust; and, in a short time, they were in circumstances very different from their expectations.

END OF VOL. I

VOLUME II

CHAPTER XI

ALMORAN had now reached the gallery; and when the multitude saw him, they shouted as in triumph, and demanded that he should surrender. Hamet, who also perceived him at a distance, and was unwilling that any violence should be offered to his person, pressed forward, and when he was come near, commanded silence. At this moment Almoran, with a loud voice, reproached them with impiety and folly; and appealing to the power, whom in his person they had offended, the air suddenly grew dark, a flood of lightning descended from the sky, and a peal of thunder was articulated into these words:

> Divided sway, the God who reigns alone
> Abhors; and gives to Almoran the throne.

The multitude stood aghast at the prodigy; and hiding their faces with their hands, every one departed in silence and confusion, and Hamet and Omar were left alone. Omar was taken by some of the soldiers who had adhered to Almoran, but Hamet made his escape.

Almoran, whose wishes were thus far accomplished by the intervention of a power superior to his own, exulted in the anticipation of that happiness which he now supposed to be secured; and was fortified in his opinion, that he had been wretched only because he had been weak, and that to multiply and not to suppress his wishes was the way to acquire felicity.

As he was returning from the gallery, he was met by Osmyn and Caled, who had heard the supernatural declaration in his behalf, and learned its effects. Almoran, in that hasty flow of unbounded but capricious favour, which, in contracted minds, is the effect only of unexpected good fortune, raised Osmyn from his feet to his bosom: 'As in the trial,' said he, 'thou hast been faithful, I now invest thee with a superior trust. The toils of state shall from this moment devolve upon thee; and from this moment, the delights of empire unallayed shall be mine: I will recline at ease, remote from every eye but those that reflect my own felicity; the felicity that I shall taste in secret, surrounded by the smiles of beauty, and the gaities of youth. Like heaven, I will reign unseen; and like heaven, though unseen, I will be adored.' Osmyn received this delegation of power with a tumultuous pleasure, that was expressed only by silence and confusion. Almoran remarked it; and exulting in the pride of power, he suddenly changed his aspect, and regarding Osmyn, who was yet blushing, and whose eyes were swimming in tears of gratitude, with a stern and ardent countenance; 'Let me, however,' said he, 'warn thee to be watchful in thy trust: beware, that no rude commotion violate my peace by thy fault; lest my anger sweep thee in a moment to destruction.' He then directed his eye to Caled: 'And thou too,' said he, 'hast been faithful; be thou next in honour and in power to Osmyn. Guard both of you my paradise from dread and care; fulfill the duty that I have assigned you, and live.'

He was then informed by a messenger, that Hamet had escaped, and that Omar was taken. As he now despised the power both of Hamet and Omar, he expressed neither concern nor anger that Hamet had fled; but he ordered Omar to be brought before him.

When Omar appeared bound and disarmed, he regarded him with a smile of insult and derision; and asked him, what he had now to hope. 'I have, indeed,' said Omar, 'much less to hope, than thou hast to fear.' 'Thy insolence,' said Almoran, 'is equal to thy folly: what power on earth is there, that I should fear?' 'Thy own,' said Omar. 'I have not leisure now,' replied Almoran, 'to hear the paradoxes of thy philosophy explained: but to shew thee, that I fear not thy power, thou shalt live. I will leave thee to hopeless regret; to wiles that have been scorned and defeated; to the unheeded petulance of dotage; to the fondness that is repayed with neglect; to restless wishes, to credulous hopes, and to derided command: to the slow and complicated torture of despised old age; and that, when thou shalt long have abhorred thy being, shall destroy it.' 'The misery,' said Omar, 'which thou hast menaced, it is not in thy power to inflict. As thou hast taken from me all that I possessed by the bounty of thy father, it is true that I am poor; it is true also, that my knees are now feeble, and bend with the weight of years that is upon me. I am, as thou art, a man; and therefore I have erred: but I have still kept the narrow path in view with a faithful vigilance, and to that I have soon returned: the past, therefore, I do not regret; and the future I have no cause to fear. In Him who is most merciful, I have hope; and in that hope even now I rejoice before thee. My portion in the present hour, is adversity: but I receive it, not only with humility, but thankfulness; for I know, that whatever is ordained is best.'

Almoran, in whose heart there were no traces of Omar's virtue, and therefore no foundation for his confidence; sustained himself against their force, by treating them as hypocrisy and affectation: 'I know,' says he, 'that thou hast long learned to echo the specious and pompous sounds, by which hypocrites conceal their wretchedness, and excite the admiration of folly and the contempt of wisdom: yet thy walk in this place, shall be still unrestrained. Here the splendor of my felicity shall fill thy heart with envy, and cover thy face with confusion; and from thee shall the world be instructed, that the enemies of Almoran can move no passion in his breast but contempt, and that most to punish them is to permit them to live.'

Omar, whose eye had till now been fixed upon the ground, regarded Almoran with a calm but steady countenance: 'Here then,' said he, 'will I follow thee, constant as thy shadow; tho', as thy shadow, unnoticed or neglected: here shall mine eye watch those evils, that were appointed from everlasting to attend upon guilt: and here shall my voice warn thee of their approach. From thy breast may they be averted by righteousness! for without this, though all the worlds that roll above thee should, to aid thee, unite all their power, that power can aid thee only to be wretched.'

Almoran, in all the pride of gratified ambition, invested with dominion that had no limits, and allied with powers that were more than mortal; was overawed by this address, and his countenance grew pale. But the next moment, disdaining to be thus controuled by the voice of a slave, his cheeks were suffused with the blushes of indignation: he turned from Omar, in scorn, anger, and confusion, without reply; and Omar departed with the calm dignity of a benevolent and superior being, to whom the smiles and frowns of terrestrial tyranny were alike indifferent, and in whom abhorrence of the turpitude of vice was mingled with compassion for its folly.

CHAPTER XII

In the mean time, Almeida, who had been conveyed to an apartment in Almoran's seraglio, and delivered to the care of those who attended upon his women, suffered all that grief and terror could inflict upon a generous, a tender, and a delicate mind; yet in this complicated distress, her attention was principally fixed upon Hamet. The disappointment of his hope, and the violation of his right, were the chief objects of her regret and her fears, in all that had already happened, and in all that was still to come; every insult that might be offered to herself, she considered as an injury to him. Yet the thoughts of all that he might suffer in her person, gave way to her apprehensions of what might befall him in his own: in his situation, every calamity that her imagination could conceive, was possible; her thoughts were, therefore, bewildered amidst an endless variety of dreadful images, which started up before them which way soever they were turned; and it was impossible that she could gain any certain intelligence of his fate, as the splendid prison in which she was now confined, was surrounded by mutes and eunuchs,* of whom nothing could be learned, or in whose report no confidence could be placed.

While her mind was in this state of agitation and distress, she perceived the door open, and the next moment Almoran entered the apartment. When she saw him, she turned from him with a look of unutterable anguish; and hiding her face in her veil, she burst into tears. The tyrant was moved with her distress; for unfeeling obduracy is the vice only of the old, whose sensibility has been worn away by the habitual perpetration of reiterated wrongs.

He approached her with looks of kindness, and his voice was involuntarily modulated to pity; she was, however, too much absorbed in her own sorrows, to reply. He gazed upon her with tenderness and admiration; and taking her hand into his own, he pressed it ardently to his bosom: his compassion soon kindled into desire, and from soothing her distress, he began to solicit her love. This instantly roused her attention, and resentment now suspended her grief: she turned from him with a firm and haughty step, and instead of answering his professions, reproached him with her wrongs. Almoran, that he might at once address her virtue and her passions, observed, that though he had loved her from the first moment he had seen her, yet he had concealed his passion even from her, till it had received the sanction of an invisible and superior power; that he came, therefore, the messenger of heaven; and that he offered her unrivalled empire and everlasting love. To this she answered only by an impatient and fond enquiry after Hamet. 'Think not of Hamet,' said Almoran; 'for why should he who is rejected of Heaven, be still the favourite of Almeida?' 'If thy hand,' said Almeida, 'could quench in everlasting darkness, that vital spark of intellectual fire, which the word of the Almighty has kindled in my breast to burn for ever, then might Almeida cease to think of Hamet; but while that shall live, whatever form it shall inhabit, or in whatever world it shall reside, his image shall be for ever present, and to him shall my love be for ever true.' This glowing declaration of her love for Hamet, was immediately succeeded by a tender anxiety for his safety; and a sudden reflection upon the probability of his death, and the danger of his situation if alive, threw her again into tears.

Almoran, whom the ardour and impetuosity of her passions kept sometimes silent, and sometimes threw into confusion, again attempted to sooth and comfort her: she often urged him to tell her what was become of his brother, and he as often evaded the question. As she was about to renew her enquiry, and reflected that it had already been often made, and had not yet been answered, she thought that Almoran had already put him to death: this threw her into a new agony, of which he did not immediately discover the cause; but as he soon learned it from her reproaches and exclamations, he perceived that he could not hope to be heard, while she was in doubt about the safety of Hamet. In order, therefore, to sooth her mind, and prevent its being longer possessed with an image that excluded every other; he assumed a look of concern and astonishment at the imputation of a crime, which was at once so horrid and so unnecessary. After a solemn deprecation of such enormous guilt, he observed, that as it was now impossible for Hamet to succeed as his rival, either in empire or in love, without the breach of a command, which he knew his virtue would implicitly obey; he had no motive either to desire his death, or to restrain his liberty: 'His walk,' says he, 'is still uncircumscribed in Persia; and except this chamber, there is no part of the palace to which he is not admitted.'

To this declaration Almeida listened, as to the music of paradise; and it suspended for a while every passion, but her love: the sudden ease of her mind made her regardless of all about her, and she had in this interval suffered Almoran to remove her veil, without reflecting upon what he was doing. The moment she recollected herself, she made a gentle effort to recover it, with some confusion, but without anger. The pleasure that was expressed in her eyes, the blush that glowed upon her cheek, and the contest about the veil, which, to an amorous imagination had an air of dalliance, concurred to heighten the passion of Almoran almost to phrensy: she perceived her danger in his looks, and her spirits instantly took the alarm. He seized her hand, and gazing ardently upon her, he conjured her, with a tone and emphasis that strongly expressed the tumultuous vehemence of his wishes, that she would renounce the rites which had been forbidden above, and that she would receive him to whom by miracle she had been alloted.

Almeida, whom the manner and voice of Almoran had terrified into silence, answered him at first only with a look that expressed aversion and disdain, over-awed by fear. 'Wilt thou not,' said Almoran, 'fulfill the decrees of Heaven? I conjure thee, by Heaven, to answer.' From this solemn reference to Heaven, Almeida derived new fortitude: she instantly recollected, that she stood in the presence of Him, by whose permission only every other power, whether visible or invisible, can dispense evil or good: 'Urge no more,' said she, 'as the decree of Heaven, that which is inconsistent with Divine perfection. Can He, in whose hand my heart is, command me to wed the man whom he has not enabled me to love? Can the Pure, the Just, the Merciful, have ordained that I should suffer embraces which I loath, and violate vows which His laws permitted me to make? Can He have ordained a perfidious, a loveless, and a joyless prostitution? What if a thousand prodigies should concur to enforce it a thousand times, the deed itself would be a stronger proof that those prodigies were the works of darkness, than those prodigies that the deed was commanded by the Father of light.'

Almoran, whose hopes were now blasted to the root, who perceived that the virtue of Almeida could neither be deceived nor overborne; that she at once contemned his power, and abhorred his love; gave way to all the furies of his mind, which now slumbered no more: his countenance expressed at once anger, indignation, and despair; his gesture became furious, and his voice was lost in menaces and execrations. Almeida beheld him with an earnest yet steady countenance, till he vowed to revenge the indignity he had suffered, upon Hamet. At the name of Hamet, her fortitude forsook her; the pride of virtue gave way to the softness of love; her cheeks became pale, her lips trembled, and taking hold of the robe of Almoran, she threw herself at his feet. His fury was at first suspended by hope and expectation; but when from her words, which grief and terror had rendered scarce articulate, he could learn only that she was pleading for Hamet, he burst from her in an extasy of rage; and forcing his robe from her hand, with a violence that dragged her after it, he rushed out of the chamber, and left her prostrate upon the ground.

As he passed through the gallery with a hasty and disordered pace, he was seen by Omar; who knowing that he was returned from an interview with Almeida, and conjecturing from his appearance what had happened, judged that he ought not to neglect this opportunity to warn him once more of the delusive phantoms, which, under the appearance of pleasure, were leading him to destruction: he, therefore, followed him unperceived, till he had reached the apartment in which he had been used to retire alone, and heard again the loud and tumultuous exclamations, which were wrung from his heart by the anguish of disappointment: 'What have I gained,' said he, 'by absolute dominion! The slave who, secluded from the gales of life and from the light of Heaven, toils without hope in the darkness of the mine, riots in the delights of paradise compared with me. By the caprice of one woman, I am robbed not only of enjoyment but of peace, and condemned for ever to the torment of unsatisfied desire.'

Omar, who was impatient to apprize him that he was not alone, and to prevent his disclosing sentiments which he wished to conceal, now threw himself upon the ground at his feet. 'Presumptuous slave!' said Almoran, 'from whence, and wherefore art thou come?' 'I am come,' said Omar, 'to tell thee that not the caprice of a woman, but the wishes of Almoran, have made Almoran wretched.' The king, stung with the reproach, drew back, and with a furious look laid his hand upon his poignard; but was immediately restrained from drawing it, by his pride. 'I am come,' said Omar, 'to repeat that truth, upon which, great

as thou art, thy fate is suspended. Thy power extends not
to the mind of another; exert it, therefore, upon thy own:
suppress the wishes, which thou canst not fulfill; and secure
the happiness that is within thy reach.'

Almoran, who could bear no longer to hear the precepts
which he disdained to practise, sternly commanded Omar
to depart: 'Be gone,' said he, 'lest I crush thee like a
noisome reptile, which men cannot but abhor, though it is
too contemptible to be feared.' 'I go,' said Omar, 'that my
warning voice may yet again recall thee to the path of
wisdom and of peace, if yet again I shall behold thee while
it is to be found.'

CHAPTER XIII

ALMORAN was now left alone; and throwing himself upon a sofa, he sat some time motionless and silent, as if all his faculties had been suspended in the stupefaction of despair. He revolved in his mind the wishes that had been gratified, and the happiness of which he had been disappointed: 'I desired,' said he, 'the pomp and power of undivided dominion; and Hamet was driven from the throne which he shared with me, by a voice from heaven: I desired to break off his marriage with Almeida; and it was broken off by a prodigy, when no human power could have accomplished my desire. It was my wish also to have the person of Almeida in my power, and this wish also has been gratified; yet I am still wretched. But I am wretched, only because the means have not been adequate to the end: what I have hitherto obtained, I have not desired for itself; and of that, for which I desired it, I am not possessed: I am, therefore, still wretched, because I am weak. With the soul of Almoran, I should have the form of Hamet: then my wishes would indeed be filled; then would Almeida bless me with consenting beauty, and the splendor of my power should distinguish only the intervals of my love; my enjoyments would then be certain and permanent, neither blasted by disappointment, nor withered by satiety.' When he had uttered these reflections with the utmost vehemence and agitation, his face was again obscured by gloom and despair; his posture was again fixed; and he was falling back into his former state of silent abstraction, when he was suddenly roused by the appearance of the Genius, the sincerity of whose friendship he began to distrust.

'Almoran,' said the Genius, 'if thou art not yet happy,

know that my powers are not yet exhausted: fear me not, but let thine ear be attentive to my voice.' The Genius then stretched out his hand towards him, in which there was an emerald of great lustre, cut into a figure that had four and twenty sides, on each of which was engraven a different letter.* 'Thou seest,' said he, 'this talisman: on each side of it is engraven one of those mysterious characters, of which are formed all the words of all the languages that are spoken by angels, genii, and men. This shall enable thee to change thy figure: and what, under the form of Almoran, thou canst not accomplish; thou shalt still be able to effect, if it can be effected by thee, in the form of any other. Point only to the letters that compose the name of him whose appearance thou wouldst assume, and it is done. Remember only, that upon him, whose appearance thou shalt assume, thine shalt be imprest, till thou restorest his own. Hide the charm in thy bosom, and avail thyself of its power.' Almoran received the talisman in a transport of gratitude and joy, and the Genius immediately disappeared.

The use of this talisman was so obvious, that it was impossible to overlook it. Almoran instantly conceived the design with which it was given, and determined instantly to put it in execution: 'I will now,' said he, 'assume the figure of Hamet; and my love, in all its ardour, shall be returned by Almeida. As his fancy kindled at the anticipation of his happiness, he stood musing in a pleasing suspense, and indulged himself in the contemplation of the several gradations, by which he should ascend to the summit of his wishes.

Just at this moment, Osmyn, whom he had commanded to attend him at this hour, approached his apartment: Almoran was roused by the sound of his foot, and supposed it to be Omar, who had again intruded upon his privacy; he was enraged at the interruption which had broken a series of imaginations so flattering and luxurious; he snatched out his poignard, and lifting up his arm for the stroke, hastily turned round to have stabbed him; but seeing Osmyn, he discovered his mistake just in time to prevent the blow.

Osmyn, who was not conscious of any crime, nor indeed of any act that could have given occasion of offence; started back terrified and amazed, and stood trembling in suspense whether to remain or to withdraw. Almoran, in the mean time, sheathed the instrument of death, and bid him fear nothing, for he should not be hurt. He then turned about; and putting his hand to his forehead, stood again silent in a musing posture: he recollected, that if he assumed the figure of Hamet, it was necessary he should give orders for Hamet to be admitted to Almeida, as he would otherwise be excluded by the delegates of his own authority; turning, therefore, to Osmyn, 'Remember,' he said, 'that whenever Hamet shall return, it is my command, that he be admitted to Almeida.'

Osmyn, who was pleased with an opportunity of recommending himself to Almoran, was praising an act of generous virtue which he supposed him now to exert in favour of his brother, received the command with a look, that expressed not only approbation but joy: 'Let the sword of destruction,' said he, 'be the guard of the tyrant; the strength of my lord shall be the bonds of love: those, who honour thee as Almoran, shall rejoice in thee as the friend of Hamet.' To Almoran, who was conscious to no kindness for his brother, the praise of Osmyn was a reproach: he was offended at the joy which he saw kindled in his countenance, by a command to shew favour to Hamet; and was fired with sudden rage at that condemnation of his real conduct, which was implied by an encomium on the generosity of which he assumed the appearance for a malevolent and perfidious purpose: his brow was contracted; his lip quivered; and the hilt of his dagger was again grasped in his hand. Osmyn was again overwhelmed with terror and confusion; he had again offended, but knew not his offence. In the mean time, Almoran recollecting that to express displeasure against Osmyn was to betray his own secret, endeavoured to suppress his anger; but his anger was succeeded by remorse, regret, and disappointment. The anguish of his mind broke out in imperfect murmurs: 'What I am,' said he, 'is, to this wretch, the object not only of hatred but of scorn; and he commends only what I am not, in what to him I would seem to be.'

These sounds, which, tho' not articulate, were yet uttered with great emotion, were still mistaken by Osmyn for the overflowings of capricious and causeless anger: 'My life,' says he to himself, 'is even now suspended in a doubtful balance. Whenever I approach this tyrant, I tread the borders of destruction: like a hood-winked* wretch, who is left to wander near the brink of a precipice, I know my danger; but which way soever I turn, I know not whether I shall incur or avoid it.'

In these reflections, did the sovereign and the slave pass those moments, in which the sovereign intended to render the slave subservient to his pleasure or his security, and the slave intended to express a zeal which he really felt, and a homage which his heart had already paid. Osmyn was at length, however, dismissed with an assurance, that all was well; and Almoran was again left to reflect with anguish upon the past, to regret the present, and to anticipate the future with solicitude, anxiety, and perturbation.

He was, however, determined to assume the figure of his brother, by the talisman which had been put into his power by the Genius: but just as he was about to form the spell, he recollected, that by the same act he would impress his own likeness upon Hamet, who would consequently be invested with his power, and might use it to his destruction. This held him some time in suspense: but reflecting that Hamet might not, perhaps, be apprized of his advantage, till it was too late to improve it; that he was now a fugitive, and probably alone, leaving Persia behind him with all the speed he could make; and that, at the worst, if he should be still near, if he should know the transformation as soon as it should be made, and should instantly take the most effectual measures to improve it; yet as he could dissolve the charm in a moment, whenever it should be necessary for his safety, no formidable danger could be incurred by the experiment, to which he, therefore, proceeded without delay.

CHAPTER XIV

In the mean time, Hamet, to whom his own safety was of no importance but for the sake of Almeida, resolved, if possible, to conceal himself near the city. Having, therefore, reached the confines of the desert, by which it was bounded on the east, he quitted his horse, and determined to remain there till the multitude was dispersed, and the darkness of the evening might conceal his return, when in less than an hour he could reach the palace.

He sat down at the foot of the mountain Kabessed,* without considering, that in this place he was most likely to be found, as those who travel the desert seldom fail to enter the cave that winds its way under the mountain, to drink of the water that issues there from a clear and copious spring.

He reviewed the scenes of the day that was now nearly passed, with a mixture of astonishment and distress, to which no description can be equal. The sudden and amazing change that a few hours had made in his situation, appeared like a wild and distressful dream, from which he almost doubted whether he should not wake to the power and the felicity that he had lost. He sat for some time bewildered in the hurry and multiplicity of his thoughts, and at length burst out into passionate exclamations: 'What,' says he, 'and where am I? Am I, indeed, Hamet; that son of Solyman who divided the dominion of Persia with his brother, and who possessed the love of Almeida alone? Dreadful vicissitude! I am now an outcast, friendless and forlorn; without an associate, and without a dwelling: for me the cup of adversity overflows, and the last dregs of sorrow have been wrung out for my portion: the powers not only of the earth, but of the air, have combined against me;

and how can I stand alone before them? But is there no power that will interpose in my behalf? If He, who is supreme, is good, I shall not perish. But wherefore am I thus? Why should the desires of vice be accomplished by superior powers; and why should superior powers be permitted to disappoint the expectations of virtue? Yet let me not rashly question the ways of Him, in whose balance the world is weighed: by Him, every evil is rendered subservient to good; and by His wisdom, the happiness of the whole is secured. Yet I am but a part only, and for a part only I can feel. To me, what is that goodness of which I do not partake? In my cup the gall is unmixed; and have I not, therefore, a right to complain? But what have I said? Let not the gloom that surrounds me, hide from me the prospect of immortality. Shall not eternity atone for time? Eternity, to which the duration of ages is but as an atom to a world! Shall I not, when this momentary separation is past, again meet Almeida to part no more? and shall not a purer flame than burns upon the earth, unite us? Even at this moment, her mind, which not the frauds of sorcery can taint or alienate, is mine: that pleasure which she reserved for me, cannot be taken by force; it is in the consent alone that it subsists; and from the joy that she feels, and from that only, proceeds the joy she can bestow.'

With these reflections he soothed the anguish of his mind, till the dreadful moment arrived, in which the power of the talisman took place, and the figure of Almoran was changed into that of Hamet, and the figure of Hamet into that of Almoran.

At the moment of transformation, Hamet was seized with a sudden languor, and his faculties were suspended as by the stroke of death. When he recovered, his limbs still trembled, and his lips were parched with thirst: he rose, therefore, and entering the cavern, at the mouth of which he had been sitting, he stooped over the well to drink; but glancing his eyes upon the water, he saw, with astonishment and horror, that it reflected, not his own countenance, but that of his brother. He started back from the prodigy; and supporting himself against the side of the rock, he stood some time like a statue, without the power of recollection: but at length the thought suddenly rushed into his mind, that the same sorcery which had suspended his marriage, and driven him from the throne, was still practised against him; and that the change of his figure to that of Almoran, was the effect of Almoran's having assumed his likeness, to obtain, in this disguise, whatever Almeida could bestow. This thought, like a whirlwind of the desert, totally subverted his mind; his fortitude was borne down, and his hopes were rooted up; no principles remained to regulate his conduct, but all was phrensy, confusion, and despair. He rushed out of the cave with a furious and distracted look; and went in haste towards the city, without having formed any design, or considered any consequence that might follow.

The shadows of the mountains were now lengthened by the declining sun; and the approach of evening had invited Omar to meditate in a grove, that was adjacent to the gardens of the palace. From this place he was seen at some distance by Hamet, who came up to him with a hasty and disordered pace; and Omar drew back with a cold and distant reverence, which the power and the character of Almoran concurred to excite. Hamet, not reflecting upon the cause of this behaviour, was offended, and reproached him with the want of that friendship he had so often professed: the vehemence of his expression and demeanor, suited well with the appearance of Almoran; and Omar, as the best proof of that friendship which had been impeached, took this opportunity to repeat his admonitions in the behalf of Hamet: 'What ever evil,' said he, 'thou canst bring upon Hamet, will be doubled to thyself: to his virtues, the Power that fills infinitude is a friend, and he can be afflicted only till they are perfect; but thy sufferings will be the punishment of vice, and as long as thou art vicious they must increase.'

Hamet, who instantly recollected for whom he was mistaken, and the anguish of whose mind was for a moment suspended by this testimony of esteem and kindness, which could not possibly be feigned, and which was paid him at the risque of life, when it could not be known that he received it; ran forward to embrace the hoary sage, who had been the guide of his youth, and cried out, in a voice that was broken by contending passions, 'The face is the face of Almoran; but the heart is the heart of Hamet.'

Omar was struck dumb with astonishment; and Hamet, who was impatient to be longer mistaken, related all the circumstances of his transformation, and reminded him of some particulars which could be known only to themselves: 'Canst thou not yet believe,' said he, 'that I am Hamet? when thou hast this day seen me banished from my kingdom; when thou hast now met me a fugitive returning from the desert; and when I learnt from thee, since the sun was risen which is not yet set, that more than mortal powers were combined against me.' 'I now believe,' said Omar, 'that thou, indeed, art Hamet.' 'Stay me not then,' said Hamet; 'but come with me to revenge.' 'Beware,' said Omar, 'lest thou endanger the loss of more than empire and Almeida.' 'If not to revenge,' said Hamet, 'I may at least be permitted to punish.' 'Thy mind,' says Omar, 'is now in such a state, that to punish the crimes by which thou hast been wronged, will dip thee in the guilt of blood. Why else are we forbidden to take vengeance for ourselves? and why is it reserved as the prerogative of the Most High? In Him, and in Him alone, it is goodness guided by wisdom: He approves the means, only as necessary to the end; He wounds only to heal, and destroys only to save; He has complacence, not in the evil, but in the good only which it is appointed to produce. Remember, therefore, that he, to whom the punishment of another is sweet; though his act may be just with respect to others, with respect to himself it is a deed of darkness, and abhorred by the Almighty.' Hamet, who had stood abstracted in the contemplation of the new injury he had suffered, while Omar was persuading him not to revenge it, started from his posture in all the wildness of distraction; and bursting away from Omar, with an ardent and furious look hasted toward the palace, and was soon out of sight.

CHAPTER XV

IN the mean time, Almoran, after having effected the transformation, was met, as he was going to the apartment of Almeida, by Osmyn. Osmyn had already experienced the misery of dependent greatness, that kept him continually under the eye of a capricious tyrant, whose temper was various as the gales of summer, and whose anger was sudden as the bolt of heaven; whose purpose and passions were dark and impetuous as the midnight storm, and at whose command death was inevitable as the approach of time. When he saw Almoran, therefore, in the likeness of Hamet, he felt a secret desire to apprize him of his situation, and offer him his friendship.

Almoran, who with the form assumed the manners of Hamet, addressed Osmyn with a mild though mournful countenance: 'At length,' said he, 'the will of Almoran alone is law; does it permit me to hold a private rank in this place, without molestation?' 'It permits,' said Osmyn, 'yet more; he has commanded, that you should have admittance to Almeida.' Almoran, whose vanity betrayed him to flatter his own power in the person of Hamet, replied with a smile: 'I know, that Almoran, who presides like a God in silent and distant state, reveals the secrets of his will to thee; I know that thou art'—'I am,' said Osmyn, 'of all thou seest, most wretched.' At this declaration, Almoran turned short, and fixed his eyes upon Osmyn with a look of surprize and anger: 'Does not the favour of Almoran,' said he, 'whose smile is power, and wealth, and honour, shine upon thee?' 'My lord,' said Osmyn, 'I know so well the severity of thy virtue, that if I should, even for thy sake, become perfidious to thy brother'——Almoran, who was unable to preserve the character of Hamet with propriety, interrupted him with a fierce and haughty tone: 'How!' said he, 'perfidious to my brother! to Almoran perfidious!'

Osmyn, who had now gone too far to recede, and who still saw before him the figure of Hamet, proceeded in his purpose: 'I knew,' said he, 'that in thy judgment I should be condemned; and yet, the preservation of life is the strongest principle of nature, and the love of virtue is her proudest boast.' 'Explain thyself,' said Almoran, 'for I cannot comprehend thee.' 'I mean,' said Osmyn, 'that he, whose life depends upon the caprice of a tyrant, is like the wretch whose sentence is already pronounced; and who, if the wind does but rush by his dungeon, imagines that it is the bow-string and the mute.'* 'Fear not,' said Almoran, who now affected to be again calm; 'be still faithful, and thou shalt still be safe.' 'Alas!' said Osmyn, 'there is no diligence, no toil, no faith, that can secure the slave from the sudden phrensy of passion, from the causeless rage either of drunkenness or lust. I am that slave; the slave of a tyrant whom I hate.' The confusion of Almoran was now too great to be concealed, and he stood silent with rage, fear, and indignation. Osmyn, supposing that his wonder suspended his belief of what he had heard, confirmed his declaration by an oath.

Whoever thou art, to whose mind Almoran, the mighty and the proud, is present; before whom, the lord of absolute dominion stands trembling and rebuked; who seest the possessor of power by which nature is controuled, pale and silent with anguish and disappointment: if, in the fury of thy wrath, thou hast aggravated weakness into guilt; if thou hast chilled the glow of affection, when it flushed the cheek in thy presence, with the frown of displeasure, or repressed the ardour of friendship with indifference or neglect; now, let thy heart smite thee: for, in thy folly, thou hast cast away that gem, which is the light of life; which power can never seize, and which gold can never buy!

The tyrant fell at once from his pride, like a star from Heaven; and Osmyn, still addressing him as Hamet, at once increased his misery and his fears: 'O,' said he, 'that the throne of Persia was thine! then should innocence enjoy her birth-right of peace, and hope should bid honest industry look upward. There is not one to whom Almoran has delegated power, nor one on whom his transient favour has bestowed any gift, who does not already feel his heart throb with the pangs of boding terror. Nor is there one who, if he did not fear the displeasure of the invisible power by whom the throne has been given to thy brother, would not immediately revolt to thee.'

Almoran, who had hitherto remained silent, now burst into a passionate exclamation of self pity: 'What can I do?' said he; 'and whither can I turn?' Osmyn, who mistook the cause of his distress, and supposed that he deplored only his want of power to avail himself of the general disposition in his favour, endeavoured to fortify his mind against despair: 'Your state,' said he, 'indeed is distressful, but not hopeless.' The king who, though addressed as Hamet, was still betrayed by his confusion to answer as Almoran, smote his breast, and replied in an agony, 'It is hopeless!' Osmyn remarked his emotion and despair, with a concern and astonishment that Almoran observed, and at once recollected his situation. He endeavoured to retract such expressions of trouble and despondency, as did not suit the character he had assumed; and telling Osmyn, that he thanked him for his friendship, and would improve the advantages it offered him, he directed him to acquaint the eunuchs that they were to admit him to Almeida. When he was left alone, his doubts and perplexity held him long in suspense; a thousand expedients occurred to his mind by turns, and by turns were rejected.

His first thought was to put Osmyn to death: but he considered, that by this he would gain no advantage, as he would be in equal danger from whoever should succeed him: he considered also, that against Osmyn he was upon his guard; and that he might at any time learn, from him, whatever design might be formed in favour of Hamet, by assuming Hamet's appearance: that he would thus be the confident of every secret, in which his own safety was concerned; and might disconcert the best contrived project at the very moment of its execution, when it would be too late for other measures to be taken: he determined, therefore, to let Osmyn live; at least, till it became more necessary to cut him off. Having in some degree soothed and fortified his mind by these reflections, he entered the apartment of Almeida.

His hope was not founded upon a design to marry her under the appearance of Hamet; for that would be impossible, as the ceremony must have been performed by the priests who supposed the marriage with Hamet to have been forbidden by a divine command; and who, therefore, would not have consented, even supposing they would otherwise have ventured, at the request of Hamet, to perform a ceremony which they know would be displeasing to Almoran: but he hoped to take advantage of her tenderness for his brother, and the particular circumstances of her situation, which made the solemnities of marriage impossible, to seduce her to gratify his desires, without the sanction which alone rendered the gratification of them lawful: if he succeeded in this design, he had reason to expect, either that his love would be extinguished by enjoyment; or that, if he should still desire to marry Almeida, he might, by disclosing to her the artifice by which he had effected his purpose, prevail upon her to consent, as her connexion with Hamet, the chief obstacle to her marriage with him, would then be broken for ever; and as she might, perhaps, wish to sanctify the pleasure which she might be not unwilling to repeat, or at least to make that lawful which it would not be in her power to prevent.

In this disposition, and with this design, he was admitted

to Almeida; who, without suspicion of her danger, was exposed to the severest trial, in which every passion concurred to oppose her virtue: she was solicited by all the powers of subtilty and desire, under the appearance of a lover whose tenderness and fidelity had been long tried, and whose passion she returned with equal constancy and ardour; and she was thus solicited, when the rites which alone could consecrate their union, were impossible, and were rendered impossible by the guilty designs of a rival, in whose power she was, and from whom no other expedient offered her a deliverance. Thus deceived and betrayed, she received him with an excess of tenderness and joy, which flattered all his hopes, and for a moment suspended his misery. She enquired, with a fond and gentle solicitude, by what means he had gained admittance, and how he had provided for his retreat. He received and returned her caresses with a vehemence, in which, to less partial eyes, desire would have been more apparent than love; and in the tumult of his passion, he almost neglected her enquiries: finding, however, that she would be answered, he told her, that being by the permission of Almoran admitted to every part of the palace, except that of the women, he had found means to bribe the eunuch who kept the door; who was not in danger of detection, because Almoran, wearied with the tumult and fatigue of the day, had retired to sleep, and given order to be called at a certain hour. She then complained of the solicitations to which she was exposed, expressed her dread of the consequences she had reason to expect from some sudden sally of the tyrant's rage, and related with tears the brutal outrage she had suffered when he last left her: 'Though I abhorred him,' said she, 'I yet kneeled before him for thee. Let me bend in reverence to that Power, at whose look the whirlwinds are silent, and the seas are calm, that his fury has hitherto been restrained from hurting thee!'

At these words, the face of Almoran was again covered

with the blushes of confusion: to be still beloved only as Hamet, and as Almoran to be still hated; to be thus reproached without anger, and wounded by those who knew not that they struck him; was a species of misery peculiar to himself, and had been incurred only by the acquisition of new powers, which he had requested and received as necessary to obtain that felicity, which the parsimony of nature had placed beyond his reach. His emotions, however, as by Almeida they were supposed to be the emotions of Hamet, she imputed to a different cause: 'As Heaven,' says she, 'has preserved thee from death; so has it, for thy sake, preserved me from violation.' Almoran, whose passion had in this interval again surmounted his remorse, gazed eagerly upon her, and catching her to his bosom; 'Let us at least,' says he, 'secure the happiness that is now offered; let not these inestimable moments pass by us unimproved; but to shew that we deserve them, let them be devoted to love.' 'Let us then,' said Almeida, 'escape together.' 'To escape with thee,' said Almoran, 'is impossible. I shall retire, and, like the shaft of Arabia, leave no mark behind me;* but the flight of Almeida will at once be traced to him by whom I was admitted, and I shall thus retaliate his friendship with destruction.' 'Let him then,' said Almeida, 'be the partner of our flight.' 'Urge it not now,' said Almoran; 'but trust to my prudence and my love, to select some hour that will be more favourable to our purpose. And yet,' said he, 'even then, we shall, as now, sigh in vain for the completion of our wishes: by whom shall our hands be joined, when in the opinion of the priests it has been forbidden from above?' 'Save thyself then,' said Almeida, 'and leave me to my fate.' 'Not so,' said Almoran. 'What else,' replied Almeida, 'is in our power?' 'It is in our power,' said Almoran, 'to seize that joy, to which a public form can give us no new claim; for the public form can only declare that right by which I claim it now.'

As they were now reclining upon a sofa, he threw his arm

round her; but she suddenly sprung up, and burst from him: the tear started to her eye, and she gazed upon him with an earnest but yet tender look: 'Is it?' says she—'No sure, it is not the voice of Hamet!' 'O! yes,' said Almoran, 'what other voice should call thee to cancel at once the wrongs of Hamet and Almeida; to secure the treasures of thy love from the hand of the robber; to hide the joys, which if now we lose we may lose for ever, in the sacred and inviolable stores of the past, and place them beyond the power not of Almoran only but of fate?' With this wild effusion of desire, he caught her again to his breast, and finding no resistance his heart exulted in his success; but the next moment, to the total disappointment of his hopes, he perceived that she had fainted in his arms. When she recovered, she once more disengaged herself from him, and turning away her face, she burst into tears. When her voice could be heard, she covered herself with her veil, and turning again towards him, 'All but this,' said she, 'I had learnt to bear; and how has this been deserved by Almeida of Hamet? You were my only solace in distress; and when the tears have stolen from my eyes in silence and in solitude, I thought on thee; I thought upon the chaste ardour of thy sacred friendship, which was softened, refined, and exalted into love. This was my hoarded treasure; and the thoughts of possessing this, soothed all my anguish with a miser's happiness, who, blest in the consciousness of hidden wealth, despises cold and hunger, and rejoices in the midst of all miseries that make poverty dreadful: this was my last retreat; but I am now desolate and forlorn, and my soul looks round, with terror, for that refuge which it can never find.' 'Find that refuge,' said Almoran, 'in me.' 'Alas!' said Almeida, 'can he afford me refuge from my sorrows, who, for the guilty pleasures of a transient moment, would for ever sully the purity of my mind, and aggravate misfortune by the consciousness of guilt?'

As Almoran now perceived, that it was impossible, by

any importunity, to induce her to violate her principles; he
had nothing more to attempt, but to subvert them. 'When,'
said he, 'shall Almeida awake, and these dreams of folly
and superstition vanish? That only is virtue, by which
happiness is produced; and whatever produces happiness,
is therefore virtue; and the forms, and words, and rites,
which priests have pretended to be required by Heaven, are
the fraudful arts only by which they govern mankind.'

Almeida, by this impious insult, was roused from grief to
indignation: 'As thou hast now dared,' said she, 'to deride
the laws, which thou wouldst first have broken; so hast
thou broken for ever the tender bonds, by which my soul
was united to thine. Such as I fondly believed thee, thou
art not; and what thou art, I have never loved. I have loved
a delusive phantom only, which, while I strove to grasp it,
has vanished from me.' Almoran attempted to reply; but on
such a subject, neither her virtue nor her wisdom would
permit debate. 'That prodigy,' said she, 'which I thought
was the sleight of cunning, or the work of sorcery, I now
revere as the voice of Heaven; which, as it knew thy heart,
has in mercy saved me from thy arms. To the will of
Heaven shall my will be obedient; and my voice also shall
pronounce, to Almoran Almeida.'

Almoran, whose whole soul was now suspended in attention, conceived new hopes of success; and foresaw the
certain accomplishment of his purpose, though by an effect
directly contrary to that which he had laboured to produce.
Thus to have incurred the hatred of Almeida in the form of
Hamet, was more fortunate than to have taken advantage
of her love; the path that led to his wishes was now clear
and open; and his marriage with Almeida in his own person,
waited only till he could resume it. He, therefore, instead
of soothing, provoked her resentment: 'If thou hast loved a
phantom,' said he, 'which existed only in imagination; on
such a phantom my love also has been fixed: thou hast,
indeed, only the form of what I called Almeida; my love

thou hast rejected, because thou hast never loved; the object of thy passion was not Hamet, but a throne; and thou hast made the observance of rituals, in which folly only can suppose there is good or ill, a pretence to violate thy faith, that thou mayst still gratify thy ambition.'

To this injurious reproach, Almeida made no reply; and Almoran immediately quitted her apartment, that he might reassume his own figure, and take advantage of the disposition which, under the appearance of Hamet, he had produced in favour of himself: But Osmyn, who supposing him to be Hamet, had intercepted and detained him as he was going to Almeida, now intercepted him a second time at his return, having placed himself near the door of his apartment for that purpose.

Osmyn was by no means satisfied with the issue of their last interview: he had perceived a perturbation in the mind of Almoran, for which, imagining him to be Hamet, he could not account; and which seemed more extraordinary upon a review, than when it happened; he, therefore, again entered into conversation with him, in which he farther disclosed his sentiments and designs. Almoran, notwithstanding the impatience natural to his temper and situation, was thus long detained listening to Osmyn, by the united influence of his curiosity and his fears; his enquiries still alarmed him with new terrors, by discovering new objects of distrust, and new instances of disaffection: still, however, he resolved, not yet to remove Osmyn from his post, that he might give no alarm by any appearance of suspicion, and consequently learn with more ease, and detect with more certainty, any project that might be formed against him.

CHAPTER XVI

ALMEIDA, as soon as she was left alone, began to review the scene that had just past; and was every moment affected with new wonder, grief, and resentment. She now deplored her own misfortune; and now conceived a design to punish the author of it, from whose face she supposed the hand of adversity had torn the mask under which he had deceived her: it appeared to her very easy, to take a severe revenge upon Hamet for the indignity which she supposed he had offered her, by complaining of it to Almoran; and telling him, that he had gained admittance to her by bribing the eunuch who kept the door. The thought of thus giving him up, was one moment rejected, as arising from a vindictive spirit; and the next indulged, as an act of justice to Almoran, and a punishment due to the hypocrisy of Hamet: to the first she inclined, when her grief, which was still mingled with a tender remembrance of the man she loved, was predominant; and to the last, when her grief gave way to indignation.

Thus are we inclined to consider the same action, either as a virtue, or a vice, by the influence of different passions, which prompt us either to perform or to avoid it. Almeida, from deliberating whether she should accuse Hamet to Almoran, or conceal his fault, was led to consider what punishment he would either incur or escape in consequence of her determination; and the images that rushed into her mind, the moment this became the object of her thoughts, at once determined her to be silent: 'Could I bear to see,' said she, 'that hand, which has so often trembled with delight when it enfolded mine, convulsed and black! those eyes, that as often as they gazed upon me were dissolved in tears of tenderness and love, start from the sockets! and those lips that breathed the softest sighs of elegant desire, distorted and gasping in the convulsions of death!'

From this image, her mind recoiled in an agony of terror and pity; her heart sunk within her; her limbs trembled; she sunk down upon the sofa, and burst into tears.

By this time, Hamet, on whose form the likeness of Almoran was still impressed, had reached the palace. He went instantly towards the apartment of the women. Instead of that chearful alacrity, that mixture of zeal and reverence and affection, which his eye had been used to find wherever it was turned, he now observed confusion, anxiety and terror; whoever he met, made haste to prostrate themselves before him, and feared to look up till he was past. He went on, however, with a hasty pace: and coming up to the eunuch's guard, he said with an impatient tone; 'To Almeida.' The slave immediately made way before him, and conducted him to the door of the apartment, which he would not otherwise have been able to find, and for which he could not directly enquire.

When he entered, his countenance expressed all the passions that his situation had roused in his mind. He first looked sternly round him, to see whether Almoran was not present; and then fetching a deep sigh he turned his eyes, with a look of mournful tenderness, upon Almeida. His first view was to discover, whether Almoran had already supplanted him; and for this purpose he collected the whole strength of his mind: he considered that he appeared now, not as Hamet, but as Almoran; and that he was to question Almeida concerning Almoran, while she had mistaken him for Hamet; he was therefore to maintain the character, at whatever expence, till his doubts were resolved, and his fears either removed or confirmed: he was so firmly persuaded that Almoran had been there before him, that he did not ask the question, but supposed the fact; he restrained alike both his tenderness and his fears; and looking earnestly upon Almeida, who had risen up in his presence with blushes and confusion, 'To me,' says he, 'is Almeida still cold? and has she lavished all her love upon Hamet?'

At the name of Hamet, the blushes and confusion of Almeida increased: her mind was still full of the images, which had risen from the thought of what Hamet might suffer, if Almoran should know that he had been with her; and though she feared that their interview was discovered, yet she hoped it might be only suspected, and in that case the removal or confirmation of the suspicions, on which the fate of Hamet depended, would devolve upon her.

In this situation, she, who had but a few moments before doubted, whether she should not voluntarily give him up, when nothing more was necessary for his safety than to be silent; now determined, with whatever reluctance, to secure him, though it could not be done without dissimulation, and though it was probable that in this dissimulation she would be detected. Instead, therefore, of answering the question, she repeated it: 'On whom said my lord, on Hamet?' Hamet, whose suspicions were increased by the evasion, replied with great emotion, 'Aye, on Hamet; did he not this moment leave you?' 'Leave me this moment?' said Almeida, with yet greater confusion, and deeper blushes. Hamet, in the impatience of his jealousy, concluded, that the passions which he saw expressed in her countenance, and which arose from the struggle between her regard to truth and her tenderness for Hamet, proceeded from the consciousness of what he had most reason to dread, and she to conceal, a breach of virtue, to which she had been betrayed by his own appearance united with the vices of his brother: he, therefore, drew back from her with a look of inexpressible anguish, and stood some time silent. She observed, that in his countenance there was more expression of trouble, than rage; she, therefore, hoped to divert him from persuing his enquiries, by at once removing his jealousy; which she supposed would be at an end, as soon as she should disclose the resolution she had taken in his favour. Addressing him, therefore, as Almoran, with a voice which though it was gentle and soothing, was yet mournful and tremulous; 'Do not turn from me,' said she, 'with those unfriendly and frowning looks; give me now that love which so lately you offered, and with all the future I will atone the past.'

Upon Hamet, whose heart involuntarily answered to the voice of Almeida, these words had irresistible and instantaneous force; but recollecting, in a moment, whose form he bore, and to whom they were addressed, they struck him with new astonishment, and increased the torments of his mind. Supposing what he at first feared had happened, and that Almoran had seduced her as Hamet; he could not account for her now addressing him, as Almoran, with words of favour and compliance: he, therefore, renewed his enquiries concerning himself, with apprehensions of a different kind. She, who was still solicitous to put an end to the enquiry, as well for the sake of Hamet, as to prevent her own embarrassment, replied with a sigh, 'Let not thy peace be interrupted by one thought of Hamet; for of Hamet Almeida shall think no more.' Hamet, who, though he had fortified himself against whatever might have happened to her person, could not bear the alienation of her mind, cried out, with looks of distraction and a voice scarcely human, 'Not think of Hamet!' Almeida, whose astonishment was every moment increasing, replied, with a tender and interesting enquiry, 'Is Almoran then offended, that Almeida should think of Hamet no more?' Hamet, being thus addressed by the name of his brother, again recollected his situation; and now first conceived the idea, that the alteration of Almeida's sentiments with respect to himself, might be the effect of some violence offered her by Almoran in his likeness; he, therefore, recurred to his first purpose, and determined, by a direct enquiry, to discover, whether she had seen him under that appearance. This enquiry he urged with the utmost solemnity and ardour, in terms suitable to his present appearance and situation: 'Tell me,' said he, 'have these doors been open to Hamet? Has he obtained possession of that treasure, which, by the voice of Heaven, has been allotted to me?'

To this double question, Almeida answered by a single negative; and her answer, therefore, was both false and true: it was true that her person was still inviolate, and it was true also that Hamet had not been admitted to her; yet her denial of it was false, for she believed the contrary; Almoran only had been admitted, but she had received him as his brother. Hamet, however, was satisfied with the answer, and did not discover its fallacy. He looked up to Heaven, with an expression of gratitude and joy; and then turning to Almeida, 'Swear then,' said he, 'that thou hast granted to Hamet, no pledge of thy love which should be reserved for me.' Almeida, who now thought nothing more than the asseveration necessary to quiet his mind, immediately complied: 'I swear,' said she, 'that to Hamet I have given nothing, which thou wouldst wish me to with-hold: the power that has devoted my person to thee, has disunited my heart from Hamet, whom I renounce in thy presence for ever.'

Hamet, whose fortitude and recollection were again overborne, was thrown into an agitation of mind, which discovered itself by looks and gestures very different from those which Almeida had expected, and overwhelmed her with new confusion and disappointment: that he, who had so lately solicited her love with all the vehemence of a desire impatient to be gratified, should now receive a declaration that she was ready to comply, with marks of distress and anger, was a mystery which she could not solve. In the mean time, the struggle in his breast became every moment more violent: 'Where then,' said he, 'is the constancy which you vowed to Hamet; and for what instance of his love is he now forsaken?'

Almeida was now more embarrassed than before; she felt all the force of the reproof, supposing it to have been given by Almoran; and she could be justified only be relating the particular, which at the expence of her sincerity she had determined to conceal. Almoran was now exalted in her opinion, while his form was animated by the spirit of Hamet; as much as Hamet had been degraded, while his form was animated by the spirit of Almoran. In his resentment of her perfidy to his rival, though it favoured his fondest and most ardent wishes, there was an abhorrence of vice, and a generosity of mind, which she supposed to have been incompatible with his character. To his reproach, she could reply only by complaint; and could no otherwise evade his question, than by observing the inconsistency of his own behaviour: 'Your words,' said she, 'are daggers to my heart. You condemn me for a compliance with your own wishes; and for obedience to that voice, which you supposed to have revealed the will of Heaven. Has the caprice of desire already wandered to a new object? and do you now seek a pretence to refuse, when it is freely offered, what so lately you would have taken by force?'

Hamet, who was now fired with resentment against Almeida, whom yet he could not behold without desire; and who, at the same moment, was impatient to revenge his wrongs upon Almoran; was suddenly prompted to satisfy all his passions, by taking advantage of the wiles of Almoran, and the perfidy of Almeida, to defeat the one and to punish the other. It was now in his power instantly to consummate his marriage, as a priest might be procured without a moment's delay, and as Almeida's consent was already given; he would then obtain the possession of her person, by the very act in which she perfidiously resigned it to his rival; to whom he would then leave the beauties he had already possessed, and cast from him in disdain, as united with a mind that he could never love. As his imagination was fired with the first conception of this design, he caught her to his breast with a fury, in which all the passions in all their rage were at once concentered: 'Let the priest,' said he, 'instantly unite us. Let us comprize, in one moment, in this instant, NOW, our whole of being, and exclude alike the future and the past!' Then grasping her still in his arms, he looked up to heaven: 'Ye powers,' said he, 'invisible but yet present, who mould my changing and unresisting form; prolong, but for one hour, that mysterious charm, that is now upon me, and I will be ever after subservient to your will!'

Almeida, who was terrified at the furious ardor of this unintelligible address, shrunk from his embrace, pale and trembling, without power to reply. Hamet gazed tenderly upon her; and recollecting the purity and tenderness with which he had loved her, his virtues suddenly recovered their force; he dismissed her from his embrace; and turning from her, he dropped in silence the tear that started to his eye, and expressed, in a low and faultering voice, the thoughts that rushed upon his mind: 'No,' said he; 'Hamet shall still disdain the joy, which is at once sordid and transient: in the breast of Hamet, lust shall not be the pander of revenge. Shall I, who have languished for the pure delight which can arise only from the interchange of soul with soul, and is endeared by mutual confidence and complacency; shall I snatch under this disguise, which belies my features and degrades my virtue, a casual possession of faithless beauty, which I despise and hate? Let this be the portion of those, that hate me without a cause; but let this be far from me!' At this thought, he felt a sudden elation of mind; and the conscious dignity of virtue, that in such a conflict was victorious, rendered him, in this glorious moment, superior to misfortune: his gesture became calm, and his countenance sedate; he considered the wrongs he suffered, not as a sufferer, but as a judge; and he determined at once to discover himself to Almeida, and to reproach her with her crime. He remarked her confusion without pity, as the effect not of grief but of guilt; and fixing his eyes upon her, with the calm severity of a superior and offended being, 'Such,' said he, 'is the benevolence of the Almighty to the children of the dust, that our misfortunes are, like poisons, antidotes to each other.'

Almeida, whose faculties were now suspended by wonder and expectation, looked earnestly at him, but continued silent. 'Thy looks,' said Hamet, 'are full of wonder; but as yet thy wonder has no cause, in comparison of that which shall be revealed. Thou knowest the prodigy, which so lately parted Hamet and Almeida: I am that Hamet, thou art that Almeida.' Almeida would now have interrupted him; but Hamet raised his voice, and demanded to be heard: 'At that moment,' said he, 'wretched as I am, the child of error and disobedience, my heart repined in secret at the destiny which had been written upon my head; for I then thought thee faithful and constant: but if our hands had been then united, I should have been more wretched than I am; for I now know that thou art fickle and false. To know thee, though it has pierced my soul with sorrow, has yet healed the wound which was inflicted when I lost thee: and though I am now compelled to wear the form of Almoran, whose vices are this moment disgracing mine, yet in the balance I shall be weighed as Hamet, and I shall suffer only as I am found wanting.'

Almeida, whose mind was now in a tumult that bordered upon distraction, bewildered in a labyrinth of doubt and wonder, and alike dreading the consequence of what she heard, whether it was false or true, was yet impatient to confute or confirm it; and as soon as she had recovered her speech, urged him for some token of the prodigy he asserted, which he might easily have given, by relating any of the incidents which themselves only could know. But just at this moment, Almoran, having at last disengaged himself from Osmyn, by whom he had been long detained, resumed his own figure: and while the eyes of Almeida were fixed upon Hamet, his powers were suddenly taken from him, and restored in an instant; and she beheld the features of Almoran vanish, and gazed with astonishment upon his own: 'Thy features change!' said she, 'and thou indeed art Hamet.' 'The sudden trance,' said he, 'has restored me to myself; and from my wrongs where shalt thou be hidden?' This reproach was more than she could sustain; but he caught her as she was falling, and supported her in his arms. This incident renewed in a moment all the tenderness of his love: while he beheld her distress, and pressed her by the embrace that sustained her to his bosom, he forgot every injury which he supposed she had done him; and perceived her recover with a pleasure, that for a moment suspended the sense of his misfortunes.

Her first reflection was upon the snare, in which she had been taken; and her first sensation was joy that she had escaped: she saw at once the whole complication of events that had deceived and distressed her; and nothing more was now necessary, than to explain them to Hamet; which, however, she could not do, without discovering the insincerity of her answers to the enquiries which he had made, while she mistook him for his brother: 'If in my heart,' says she, 'thou hast found any virtue, let it incline thee to pity the vice that is mingled with it: by the vice I have been ensnared, but I have been delivered by the virtue. Almoran, for now I know that it was not thee, Almoran, when he possessed thy form, was with me: he prophaned thy love, by attempts to supplant my virtue; I resisted his importunity, and escaped perdition; but the guilt of Almoran drew my resentment upon Hamet. I thought the vices which, under thy form, I discovered in his bosom, were thine; and in the anguish of grief, indignation, and disappointment, my heart renounced thee: yet, as I could not give thee up to death, I could not discover to Almoran the attempt which

I imputed to thee; when you questioned me, therefore, as Almoran, I was betrayed to dissimulation, by the tenderness which still melted my heart for Hamet.' 'I believe thee,' said Hamet, catching her in a transport to his breast: 'I love thee for thy virtue; and may the pure and exalted beings, who are superior to the passions that now throb in my heart, forgive me, if I love thee also for thy fault. Yet, let the danger to which it betrayed thee, teach us still to walk in the strait path, and commit the keeping of our peace to the Almighty; for he that wanders in the maze of falsehood, shall pass by the good that he would meet, and shall meet the evil that he would shun. I also was tempted; but I was strengthened to resist: if I had used the power, which I derived from the arts that have been practised against me, to return evil for evil; if I had not disdained a secret and unavowed revenge, and the unhallowed pleasures of a brutal appetite; I might have possessed thee in the form of Almoran, and have wronged irreparably myself and thee: for how could I have been admitted, as Hamet, to the beauties which I had enjoyed as Almoran? and how couldst thou have given, to Almoran, what in reality had been appropriated by Hamet?'

CHAPTER XVII

BUT while Almeida and Hamet were thus congratulating each other upon the evils which they had escaped, they were threatened by others, which, however obvious, they had overlooked.

Almoran, who was now exulting in the prospect of success that had exceeded his hopes, and who supposed the possession of Almeida before the end of the next hour, was as certain as that the next hour would arrive, suddenly entered the apartment; but upon discovering Hamet, he started back astonished and disappointed. Hamet stood unmoved; and regarded him with a fixed and steady look, that at once reproached and confounded him. 'What treachery,' said Almoran, 'has been practised against me? What has brought thee to this place; and how hast thou gained admittance?' 'Against thy peace,' said Hamet, 'no treachery has been practised, but by thyself. By those arts in which thy vices have employed the powers of darkness, I have been brought hither; and by those arts I have gained admittance: thy form which they have imposed upon me was my passport; and by the restoration of my own, I have detected and disappointed the fraud, which the double change was produced to execute. Almeida, whom, as Hamet, thou couldst teach to hate thee, it is now impossible that, as Almoran, thou shouldst teach to love.'

Almeida, who perceived the storm to be gathering which the next moment would burst upon the head of Hamet, interposed between them, and addressed each of them by turns; urging Hamet to be silent, and conjuring Almoran to be merciful. Almoran, however, without regarding Almeida, or making any reply to Hamet, struck the ground with his foot, and the messengers of death, to whom the signal was familiar, appeared at the door. Almoran then commanded them to seize his brother, with a countenance pale and livid, and a voice that was broken by rage. Hamet was still unmoved; but Almeida threw herself at the feet of Almoran, and embracing his knees was about to speak, but he broke from her with sudden fury: 'If the world should sue,' said he, 'I would spurn it off. There is no pang that cunning can invent, which he shall not suffer: and when death at length shall disappoint my vengeance, his mangled limbs shall be cast out unburied, to feed the beasts of the desert and the fowls of heaven.' During this menace, Almeida sunk down without signs of life; and Hamet struggling in vain for liberty to raise her from the ground, she was carried off by some women who were called to her assistance.

In this awful crisis, Hamet, who felt his own fortitude give way, looked up; and though he conceived no words, a prayer ascended from his heart to heaven, and was accepted by Him, to whom our thoughts are known while they are yet afar off. For Hamet, the fountain of strength was opened from above; his eye sparkled with confidence, and his breast was dilated by hope. He commanded the guard that were leading him away to stop, and they implicitly obeyed; he then stretched out his hand towards Almoran, whose spirit was rebuked before him: 'Hear me,' said he, 'thou tyrant! for it is thy genius that speaks by my voice. What has been the fruit of all thy guilt, but accumulated misery? What joy hast thou derived from undivided empire? what joy from the prohibition of my marriage with Almeida? what good from that power, which some evil dæmon has added to thy own? what, at this moment, is thy portion, but rage and anguish, disappointment, and despair? Even I, whom thou seest the captive of thy power, whom thou hast wronged of empire, and yet more of love; even I am happy, in comparison of thee. I know that my

sufferings, however multiplied, are short; for they shall end
with life, and no life is long: then shall the everlasting ages
commence; and through everlasting ages thy sufferings
shall increase. The moment is now near, when thou shalt
tread that line which alone is the path to heaven, the narrow
path that is stretched over the pit, which smokes for ever,
and for ever! When thine aking eye shall look forward to
the end that is far distant, and when behind thou shalt find
no retreat; when thy steps shall faulter, and thou shalt
tremble at the depth beneath, which thought itself is not
able to fathom; then shall the angel of distribution lift his
inexorable hand against thee: from the irremeable* way
shall thy feet be smitten; thou shalt plunge in the burning
flood; and though thou shalt live for ever, thou shalt rise no
more.'

As the words of Hamet struck Almoran with terror, and
over-awed him by an influence which he could not surmount; Hamet was forced from his presence, before any
other orders had been given about him, than were implied
in the menace that was addressed to Almeida: no violence,
therefore, was yet offered him; but he was secured, till the
king's pleasure should be known, in a dungeon not far from
the palace, to which he was conducted by a subterranean
passage; and the door being closed upon him, he was left in
silence, darkness, and solitude, such as may be imagined
before the voice of the Almighty produced light and life.

When Almoran was sufficiently recollected to consider
his situation, he despaired of prevailing upon Almeida to
gratify his wishes, till her attachment to Hamet was irreparably broken; and he, therefore, resolved to put him to
death. With this view, he repeated the signal, which
convened the ministers of death to his presence; but the
sound was lost in a peal of thunder that instantly followed
it, and the Genius, from whom he received the talisman,
again stood before him.

'Almoran,' said the Genius, 'I am now compelled into

thy presence by the command of a superior power; whom, if I should dare to disobey, the energy of his will might drive me, in a moment, beyond the limits of nature and the reach of thought, to spend eternity alone, without comfort, and without hope.' 'And what,' said Almoran, 'is the will of this mighty and tremendous being?' 'His will,' said the Genius, 'I will reveal to thee. Hitherto, thou hast been enabled to lift the rod of adversity against thy brother, by powers which nature has not entrusted to man: as these powers, and these only, have put him into thy hand, thou art forbidden to lift it against his life; if thou hadst prevailed against him by thy own power, thy own power would not have been restrained: to afflict him thou art still free; but thou art not permitted to destroy. At the moment, in which thou shalt conceive a thought to cut him off by violence, the punishment of thy disobedience shall commence, and the pangs of death shall be upon thee.' 'If then,' said Almoran, 'this awful power is the friend of Hamet; what yet remains, in the stores of thy wisdom, for me? 'Till he dies, I am at once precluded from peace, and safety, and enjoyment.' 'Look up,' said the Genius, 'for the iron hand of despair is not yet upon thee. Thou canst be happy, only by his death; and his life thou art forbidden to take away: yet mayst thou still arm him against himself; and if he dies by his own hand, thy wishes will be full.' 'O name,' said Almoran, 'but the means, and it shall this moment be accomplished!' 'Select,' said the Genius, 'some friend—

At the name of friend, Almoran started and looked round in despair. He recollected the perfidy of Osmyn and he suspected that, from the same cause, all were perfidious: 'While Hamet has yet life,' said he, 'I fear the face of man, as of a savage that is prowling for his prey.' 'Relinquish not yet thy hopes,' said the Genius; 'for one, in whom thou wilt joyfully confide, may be found. Let him secretly obtain admittance to Hamet, as if by stealth; let him profess an abhorrence of thy reign, and compassion for his misfor-

tunes; let him pretend that the rack is even now preparing
for him; that death is inevitable, but that torment may be
avoided: let him then give him a poignard, as the instrument of deliverance; and, perhaps, his own hand may strike
the blow, that shall give thee peace.' 'But who,' said
Almoran, 'shall go upon this important errand?' 'Who,'
replied the Genius, 'but thyself? Hast thou not the power
to assume the form of whomsoever thou wouldst have sent?'
'I would have sent Osmyn,' said Almoran, 'but that I know
him to be a traitor.' 'Let the form of Osmyn, then,' said
the Genius, 'be thine. The shadows of the evening have
now stretched themselves upon the earth: command Osmyn
to attend thee alone in the grove, where Solyman, thy
father, was used to meditate by night; and when thy form
shall be impressed upon him, I will there seal his eyes in
sleep, till the charm shall be broken; so shall no evil be
attempted against thee, and the transformation shall be
known only to thyself.'

Almoran, whose breast was again illuminated by hope,
was about to express his gratitude and joy; but the Genius
suddenly disappeared. He began, therefore, immediately to
follow the instructions that he had received: he commanded
Osmyn to attend him in the grove, and forbad every other
to approach; by the power of the talisman he assumed his
appearance, and saw him sink down in the supernatural
slumber before him: he then quitted the place, and prepared to visit Hamet in the prison.

CHAPTER XVIII

THE officer who commanded the guard that kept the gate of the prison, was Caled. He was now next in trust and power to Osmyn: but as he had proposed a revolt to Hamet, in which Osmyn had refused to concur, he knew that his life was now in his power; he dreaded lest, for some slight offence, or in some fit of causeless displeasure, he should disclose the secret to Almoran, who would then certainly condemn him to death. To secure this fatal secret, and put an end to his inquietude, he resolved, from the moment that Almoran was established upon the throne, to find some opportunity secretly to destroy Osmyn: in this resolution, he was confirmed by the enmity, which inferior minds never fail to conceive against that merit, which they cannot but envy without spirit to emulate, and by which they feel themselves disgraced without an effort to acquire equal honour; it was confirmed also by the hope which Caled had conceived, that, upon the death of Osmyn, he should succeed to his post: his apprehensions likewise were increased, by the gloom which he remarked in the countenance of Osmyn; and which not knowing that it arose from fear, he imputed to jealousy and malevolence.

When Almoran, who had now assumed the appearance of Osmyn, had passed the subterranean avenue to the dungeon in which Hamet was confined, he was met by Caled; of whom he demanded admittance to the prince, and produced his own signet, as a testimony that he came with the authority of the king. As it was Caled's interest to secure the favour of Osmyn till an opportunity should offer to cut him off, he received him with every possible mark of respect and reverence; and when he was gone into the dungeon, he commanded a beverage to be prepared for him against he should return, in which such spices were infused, as might expel the malignity which, in that place, might be received with the breath of life; and taking himself the key of the prison, he waited at the door.

When Almoran entered the dungeon, with a lamp which he had received from Caled, he found Hamet sitting upon the ground: his countenance was impressed with the characters of grief; but it retained no marks either of anger or fear. When he looked up, and saw the features of Osmyn, he judged that the mutes were behind him; and, therefore, rose up, to prepare himself for death. Almoran beheld his calmness and fortitude with the involuntary praise of admiration; yet persisted in his purpose without remorse. 'I am come,' said he, 'by the command of Almoran, to denounce that fate, the bitterness of which I will enable thee to avoid.' 'And what is there,' said Hamet, 'in my fortunes, that has prompted thee to the danger of this attempt?' 'The utmost that I can give thee,' said Almoran, 'I can give thee without danger to myself: but though I have been placed, by the hand of fortune, near the person of the tyrant, yet has my heart in secret been thy friend. If I am the messenger of evil, impute it to him only by whom it is devised. The rack is now preparing to receive thee; and every art of ingenious cruelty will be exhausted to protract and to increase the agonies of death.' 'And what,' said Hamet, 'can thy friendship offer me?' 'I can offer thee,' said Almoran, 'that which will at once dismiss thee to those regions, where the wicked cease from troubling, and the weary rest for ever.' He then produced the poignard from his bosom; and presenting it to Hamet, 'Take this,' said he, 'and sleep in peace.'

Hamet, whose heart was touched with sudden joy at the sight of so unexpected a remedy for every evil, did not immediately reflect, that he was not at liberty to apply it: he snatched it in a transport from the hand of Almoran, and expressed his sense of the obligation by clasping him in his arms, and shedding tears of gratitude in his breast. 'Be quick,' said Almoran: 'this moment I must leave thee; and in the next, perhaps, the messengers of destruction may bind thee to the rack.' 'I will be quick,' said Hamet, 'and the sigh that shall last linger upon my lips, shall bless thee.' They then bid each other farewell: Almoran retired from the dungeon, and the door was again closed upon Hamet.

Caled, who waited at the door till the supposed Osmyn should return, presented him with the beverage which he had prepared, of which he recounted the virtues; and Almoran received it with pleasure, and having eagerly drank it off, returned to the palace. As soon as he was alone, he resumed his own figure, and sate, with a confident and impatient expectation, that in a short time a messenger would be dispatched to acquaint him with the death of Hamet. Hamet, in the mean time, having grasped the dagger in his hand, and raised his arm for the blow, 'This,' said he, 'is my passport to the realms of peace, the immediate and only object of my hope!' But at these words, his mind instantly took the alarm: 'Let me reflect,' said he, 'a moment: from what can I derive hope in death?—from that patient and persevering virtue, and from that alone, by which we fulfill the task that is assigned us upon the earth. Is it not our duty, to suffer, as well as to act? If my own hand consigns me to the grave, what can it do but perpetuate that misery, which, by disobedience, I would shun? what can it do, but cut off my life and hope together?' With this reflection he threw the dagger from him; and stretching himself again upon the ground, resigned himself to the disposal of the Father of man, most Merciful and Almighty.

Almoran, who had now resolved to send for the intelligence which he longed to hear, was dispatching a messenger to the prison, when he was told that Caled desired admittance to his presence. At the name of Caled, he started up in an extasy of joy; and not doubting but that Hamet was dead, he ordered him to be instantly admitted. When he came in, Almoran made no enquiry about Hamet, because he would not appear to expect the event, which yet he supposed he had brought about; he, therefore, asked him only upon what business he came. 'I come, my lord,' said he, 'to apprize thee of the treachery of Osmyn.' 'I know,' said Almoran, 'that Osmyn is a traitor; but of what dost thou accuse him?' 'As I was but now,' said he, 'changing the guard which is set upon Hamet, Osmyn came up to the door of the prison, and producing the royal signet demanded admittance. As the command which I received, when he was delivered to my custody, was absolute, that no foot should enter, I doubted whether the token had not been obtained, by fraud, for some other purpose; yet, as he required admittance only, I complied: but that if any treachery had been contrived, I might detect it; and that no artifice might be practised to favour an escape; I waited myself at the door, and listening to their discourse I overheard the treason that I suspected.' 'What then,' said Almoran, 'didst thou hear?' 'A part of what was said,' replied Caled, 'escaped me: but I heard Osmyn, like a perfidious and presumptuous slave, call Almoran a tyrant; I heard him profess an inviolable friendship for Hamet, and assure him of deliverance. What were the means, I know not; but he talked of speed, and supposed that the effect was certain.'

Almoran, though he was still impatient to hear of Hamet, and discovered, that if he was dead, his death was unknown to Caled; was yet notwithstanding rejoiced at what he heard: and as he knew what Caled told him to be true, as the conversation he related had passed between himself and Hamet, he exulted in the pleasing confidence that he had yet a friend; the glooms of suspicion, which had involved his mind, were dissipated, and his countenance brightened with complacency and joy. He had delayed to put Osmyn to death, only because he could appoint no man to succeed him, of whom his fears did not render him equally suspicious: but having now found, in Caled, a friend, whose fidelity had been approved when there had been no intention to try it; and being impatient to reward his zeal, and to invest his fidelity with that power, which would render his services most important; he took a ring from his own finger, and putting it upon that of Caled, 'Take this,' said he, 'as a pledge, that to-morrow Osmyn shall lose his head; and that, from this moment, thou art invested with his power.'

Caled having, in the conversation between Almoran and Hamet, discerned indubitable treachery, which he imputed to Osmyn whose appearance Almoran had then assumed, eagerly seized the opportunity to destroy him; he, therefore, not trusting to the event of his accusation, had mingled poison in the bowl which he presented to Almoran when he came out from Hamet; this, however, at first he had resolved to conceal.

In consequence of his accusation, he supposed Osmyn would be questioned upon the rack; he supposed also, that the accusation, as it was true, would be confirmed by his confession; that what ever he should then say to the prejudice of his accuser, would be disbelieved; and that when after a few hours the poison should take effect, no inquisition would be made into the death of a criminal, whom the bow-string or the scimitar would otherwise have been employed to destroy. But he now hoped to derive new merit from an act of zeal, which Almoran had approved before it was known, by condemning his rival to die, whose death he had already insured: 'May the wishes of my lord,' said he, 'be always anticipated; and may it be found, that whatever he ordains is already done: may he accept the zeal of his servant, whom he has delighted to honour; for, before the light of the morning shall return, the eyes of Osmyn shall close in everlasting darkness.'

At these words, the countenance of Almoran changed; his cheeks became pale, and his lips trembled: 'What then,' said he, 'hast thou done?' Caled, who was terrified and astonished, threw himself upon the ground, and was unable to reply. Almoran, who now, by the utmost effort of his mind, restrained his confusion and his fear, that he might learn the truth from Caled without dissimulation or disguise, raised him from the ground and repeated his enquiry. 'If I have erred,' said Caled, 'impute it not: when I had detected the treachery of Osmyn, I was transported by my zeal for thee. For proof that he is guilty, I appeal now to himself; for he yet lives: but that he might not escape the hand of justice, I mingled, in the bowl I gave him, the drugs of death.'

At these words, Almoran, striking his hands together, looked upward in an agony of despair and horror, and fell back upon a sofa that was behind him. Caled, whose astonishment was equal to his disappointment and his fears, approached him with a trembling though hasty pace; but as he stooped to support him, Almoran suddenly drew his dagger and stabbed him to the heart; and repeated the blow with reproaches and execrations, till his strength failed him.

In this dreadful moment, the Genius once more appeared before him; at the sight of whom he waved his hand, but was unable to speak: 'Nothing,' said the Genius, 'that has happened to Almoran is hidden from me. Thy peace has been destroyed alike by the defection of Osmyn, and by the zeal of Caled: thy life may yet be preserved; but it can be preserved only by a charm, which Hamet must apply.' Almoran, who had raised his eyes, and conceived some languid hope, when he heard that he might yet live; cast them again down in despair, when he heard that he could receive life only from Hamet. 'From Hamet,' said he, 'I have already taken the power to save me; I have, by thy counsel, given him the instrument of death, which, by thy counsel also, I urged him to use: he received it with joy, and he is now doubtless numbered with the dead.' 'Hamet,' said the Genius, 'is not dead; but from the fountain of virtue he drinks life and peace. If what I shall propose, he refuses to perform, not all the powers of earth, and sea, and air, if they should combine, can give thee life: but if he complies, the death, that is now suspended over thee, shall fall upon his head; and thy life shall be again delivered to the hand of time.' 'Make haste then,' said Almoran, 'and I will here wait the event.' 'The event,' said the Genius, 'is not distant; and it is the last experiment which my power can make, either upon him or thee: when the star of the night, that is now near the horizon, shall set, I will be with him.'

When Almoran was alone, he reflected, that every act of supernatural power which the Genius had enabled him to perform, had brought upon him some new calamity, though it always promised him some new advantage. As he would not impute this disappointment to the purposes for which he employed the power that he had received, he indulged a suspicion, that it proceeded from the perfidy of the Being by whom it was bestowed; in his mind, therefore, he thus reasoned with himself: 'The Genius, who has pretended to be the friend of Almoran, has been secretly in confederacy with Hamet: why else do I yet sigh in vain for Almeida? and why else did not Hamet perish, when his life was in my power? By his counsel, I persuaded Hamet to destroy himself; and, in the very act, I was betrayed to drink the potion, by which I shall be destroyed: I have been led on, from misery to misery, by ineffectual expedients, and fallacious hopes. In this crisis of my fate, I will not trust, with implicit confidence, in another: I will be present at the interview of this powerful, but suspected Being, with Hamet; and who can tell, but that if I detect a fraud, I may be able to disappoint it: however powerful, he is not omniscient; I may, therefore, be present, unknown and unsuspected even by him, in a form that I can chuse by a thought, to which he cannot be conscious.'

CHAPTER XIX

IN consequence of this resolution, Almoran, having commanded one of the soldiers of the guard that attended upon Hamet into an inner room of the palace, he ordered him to wait there till his return: then making fast the door, he assumed his figure, and went immediately to the dungeon; where producing his signet, he said, he had received orders from the king to remain with the prisoner, till the watch expired.

As he entered without speaking, and without a light, Hamet continued stretched upon the ground, with his face towards the earth; and Almoran, having silently retired to a remote corner of the place, waited for the appearance of the Genius.

The dawn of the morning now broke; and, in a few minutes, the prison shook, and the Genius appeared. He was visible by a lambent light that played around him; and Hamet starting from the ground, turned to the vision with reverence and wonder: but as the Omnipotent was ever present to his mind, to whom all beings in all worlds are obedient, and on whom alone he relied for protection, he was neither confused nor afraid. 'Hamet,' said the Genius, 'the crisis of thy fate is near.' 'Who art thou,' said Hamet, 'and for what purpose art thou come?' 'I am,' replied the Genius, 'an inhabitant of the world above thee; and to the will of thy brother, my powers have been obedient: upon him they have not conferred happiness, but they have brought evil upon thee. It was my voice, that forbad thy marriage with Almeida; and my voice, that decreed the throne to Almoran: I gave him the power to assume thy form; and, by me, the hand of oppression is now heavy upon thee. Yet I have not decreed, that he should be happy, nor that thou shouldst be wretched: darkness as yet rests upon my purpose; but my heart in secret is thy friend.' 'If thou art, indeed my friend,' said Hamet, 'deliver me from this prison; and preserve Hamet for Almeida.' 'Thy deliverance,' said the Genius, 'must depend upon thyself. There is a charm, of which the power is great; but it is by thy will only, that this power can be exerted.'

The Genius then held out towards him a scroll, on which the seal of seven powers was impressed. 'Take,' said he, 'this scroll, in which the mysterious name of Orosmades* is written. Invoke the spirits, that reside westward from the rising of the sun; and northward, in the regions of cold and darkness: then stretch out thy hand, and a lamp of sulphur, self kindled, shall burn before thee. In the fire of this lamp, consume that which I now give thee; and as the smoke, into which it changes, shall mix with the air, a mighty charm shall be formed, which shall defend thee from all mischief: from that instant, no poison, however potent, can hurt thee; nor shall any prison confine: in one moment, thou shalt be restored to the throne, and to Almeida; and the Angel of death, shall lay his hand upon thy brother; to whom, if I had confided this last best effort of my power, he would have secured the good to himself, and have transferred the evil to thee.'

Almoran, who had listened unseen to this address of the Genius to Hamet, was now confirmed in his suspicions, that evil had been ultimately intended against him, and that he had been entangled in the toils of perfidy, while he believed himself to be assisted by the efforts of friendship: he was also convinced, that by the Genius he was not known to be present. Hamet, however, stood still doubtful, and Almoran was kept silent by his fears. 'Whoever thou art,' said Hamet, 'the condition of the advantages which thou hast offered me, is such as it is not lawful to fulfill: these horrid rites, and this commerce with unholy powers, are prohibited to mortals in the Law of life.' 'See thou to that,' said the Genius: 'Good and evil are before thee; that which I now offer thee, I will offer no more.'

Hamet, who had not fortitude to give up at once the possibility of securing the advantages that had been offered, and who was seduced by human frailty to deliberate at least upon the choice; stretched out his hand, and receiving the scroll, the Genius instantly disappeared. That which had been proposed as a trial of his virtue, Almoran believed indeed to be an offer of advantage; he had no hope, therefore, but that Hamet would refuse the conditions, and that he should be able to obtain the talisman, and fulfill them himself: he judged that the mind of Hamet was in suspense, and was doubtful to which side it might finally incline; he, therefore, instantly assumed the voice and the person of Omar, that by the influence of his council he might be able to turn the scale.

When the change was effected, he called Hamet by his name; and Hamet, who knew the voice, answered him in a transport of joy and wonder: 'My friend,' said he, 'my father! in this dreary solitude, in this hour of trial, thou art welcome to my soul as liberty and life! Guide me to thee by thy voice; and tell me, while I hold thee to my bosom, how and wherefore thou art come?' 'Do not now ask me,' said Almoran: 'it is enough that I am here; and that I am permitted to warn thee of the precipice, on which thou standest. It is enough, that concealed in this darkness, I have overheard the specious guile, which some evil demon had practised upon thee.' 'Is it then certain,' said Hamet, 'that this being is evil?' 'Is not that being evil,' said Almoran, 'who proposes evil, as the condition of good?' 'Shall I then,' said Hamet, 'renounce my liberty and life? The rack is now ready; and, perhaps, the next moment, its tortures will be inevitable.' 'Let me ask thee then,' said Almoran, 'to preserve thy life, wilt thou destroy thy soul?' 'O! stay,' said Hamet—'Let me not be tried too far! Let the strength of Him who is Almighty, be manifest in my weakness!' Hamet then paused a few moments; but he was no longer in doubt: and Almoran, who disbelieved and despised the arguments, by which he intended to persuade him to renounce what, upon the same condition, he was impatient to secure for himself, conceived hopes that he should succeed; and those hopes were instantly confirmed.' 'Take then,' said Hamet, 'this unholy charm; and remove it far from me, as the sands of Alai from the trees of Oman;* lest, in some dreadful hour, my virtue may fail me, and thy counsel may be wanting!' 'Give it me, then,' said Almoran; and feeling for the hands of each other, he snatched it from him in an extasy of joy, and instantly resuming his own voice and figure, he cried out, 'At length I have prevailed: and life and love, dominion and revenge, are now at once in my hand!'

Hamet heard and knew the voice of his brother, with astonishment; but it was too late to wish that he had withheld the charm, which his virtue would not permit him to use. 'Yet a few moments pass,' said Almoran, 'and thou art nothing.' Hamet, who doubted not of the power of the talisman, and knew that Almoran had no principles which would restrain him from using it to his destruction, resigned himself to death, with a sacred joy that he had escaped from guilt. Almoran then, with an elation of mind that sparkled in his eyes, and glowed upon his cheek, stretched out his hand, in which he held the scroll; and a lamp of burning sulphur was immediately suspended in the air before him: he held the mysterious writing in the flame; and as it began to burn, the place shook with reiterated thunder, of which every peal was more terrible and more loud. Hamet, wrapping his robe round him, cried out, 'In the Fountain of Life that flows for ever, let my life be mingled! Let me not be, as if I had never been; but still conscious of my being, let me still glorify Him from whom it is derived, and be still happy in his love!'

Almoran, who was absorbed in the anticipation of his own felicity, heard the thunder without dread, as the proclamation of his triumph: 'Let thy hopes,' said he, 'be thy portion; and the pleasures that I have secured, shall be mine.' As he pronounced these words, he started as at a sudden pang; his eyes became fixed, and his posture immoveable; yet his senses still remained, and he perceived the Genius once more to stand before him. 'Almoran,' said he, 'to the last sounds which thou shalt hear, let thine ear be attentive! Of the spirits that rejoice to fulfill the purpose of the Almighty, I am one. To Hamet, and to Almoran, I have been commissioned from above: I have been appointed to perfect virtue, by adversity; and in the folly of her own projects, to entangle vice. The charm, which could be formed only by guilt, has power only to produce misery: of every good, which thou, Almoran, wouldst have secured by disobedience, the opposite evil is thy portion; and of every evil, which thou, Hamet, wast, by obedience, willing to incur, the opposite good is bestowed upon thee. To thee, Hamet, are now given the throne of thy father, and Almeida. And thou, Almoran, who, while I speak, art incorporating with the earth, shalt remain, through all generations, a memorial of the truths which thy life has taught!'

At the words of the Genius, the earth trembled beneath, and above the walls of the prison disappeared: the figure of Almoran, which was hardened into stone, expanded by degrees; and a rock, by which his form and attitude are still rudely expressed, became at once a monument of his punishment and his guilt.*

Such are the events recorded by Acmet, the descendant of the Prophet, and the preacher of righteousness! for, to Acmet, that which passed in secret was revealed by the Angel of instruction,* that the world might know, that, to the wicked, increase of power is increase of wretchedness;

and that those who condemn the folly of an attempt to defeat the purpose of a Genius, might no longer hope to elude the appointment of the Most High.

FINIS

The History of Nourjahad

SCHEMZEDDIN* was in his two and twentieth year when he mounted the throne of Persia. His great wisdom and extraordinary endowments rendered him the delight of his people, and filled them with expectations of a glorious and happy reign. Amongst the number of persons who stood candidates for the young sultan's favour, in the new administration, which was now going to take place, none seemed so likely to succeed, as Nourjahad the son of Namarand. This young man was about the age of Schemzeddin, and had been bred up with him from his infancy. To a very engaging person was added a sweetness of temper, a liveliness of fancy, and a certain agreeable manner of address, that engaged every one's affections who approached him. The sultan loved him, and every one looked on Nourjahad as the rising star of the Persian court, whom his master's partial fondness would elevate to the highest pinnacle of honour. Schemzeddin indeed was desirous of promoting his favourite, yet notwithstanding his attachment to him, he was not blind to his faults; but they appeared to him only such as are almost inseparable from youth and inexperience; and he made no doubt but that Nourjahad, when time had a little more subdued his youthful passions, and matured his judgment, would be able to fill the place of his first minister, with abilities equal to any of his predecessors. He would not, however, even in his own private thoughts, resolve on so important a step, without first consulting with some old lords of his court, who had been the constant friends and counsellors of the late sultan his father. Accordingly having called them into his closet one day, he proposed the matter to them, and desired their opinion. But before they delivered it, he could easily discover by the countenances of these grave and prudent men, that they disapproved his choice. What have you to object to Nourjahad, said the sultan, finding that they all continued silent, looking at each other? His youth, replied the eldest of the counsellors. That objection, answered Schemzeddin, will grow lighter every day. His avarice, cried the second. Thou art not just, said the sultan, in charging him with that; he has no support but from my bounty, nor did he ever yet take advantage of that interest which he knows he has in me, to desire an encrease of it. What I have charged him with, is in his nature notwithstanding, replied the old lord. What hast thou to urge, cried the sultan, to his third adviser? His love of pleasure, answered he. That, cried Schemzeddin, is as groundless an accusation as the other; I have known him from his childhood, and think few men of his years are so temperate. Yet would he indulge to excess, if it were in his power, replied the old man. The sultan now addressed the fourth: What fault hast thou to object to him, cried he? His irreligion, answered the sage. Thou art even more severe, replied the sultan, than the rest of thy brethren, and I believe Nourjahad as good a Mussulman* as thyself. He dismissed them coldly from his closet; and the four counsellors saw how impolitic a thing it was to oppose the will of their sovereign.

Though Schemzeddin seemed displeased with the remonstrances of the old men, they nevertheless had some weight with him. It is the interest of Nourjahad, said he, to conceal his faults from me; the age and experience of these men doubtless has furnished them with more sagacity than my youth can boast of; and he may be in reality what they have represented him. This thought disquieted the sultan, for he loved Nourjahad as his brother. Yet who knows, cried he, but it may be envy in these old men? they may be provoked at having a youth raised to that honour to which each of them perhaps in his own heart aspires. We can sometimes form a better judgment of a man's real disposition, from an unguarded sally of his own lips, than from a close observation of years, where the person, conscious of being observed, is watchful and cautious of every look and expression that falls from him. I will sound Nourjahad when he least suspects that I have any such design, and from his own mouth will I judge him.

It was not long before the sultan had an opportunity of executing his purpose. Having past the evening with his favourite at a banquet, where they had both indulged pretty freely, he invited Nourjahad to a walk by moon-light in the gardens of the seraglio.* Schemzeddin leaned on his shoulder as they rambled from one delicious scene to another; scenes rendered still more enchanting by the silence of the night, the mild lustre of the moon now at full, and the exhalations which arose from a thousand odoriferous shrubs. The spirits of Nourjahad were exhilerated by the mirth and festivity in which he had passed the day. The sultan's favour intoxicated him; his thoughts were dissipated by a variety of agreeable sensations, and his whole soul as it were rapt in a kind of pleasing delirium. Such was the frame of Nourjahad's mind, when the sultan, with an assumed levity, throwing himself down on a bank of violets,* and familiarly drawing his favourite to sit by him, said, *Tell me, Nourjahad, and tell me truly, what would satisfy thy wishes, if thou wert certain of possessing whatsoever thou shouldst desire?* Nourjahad remaining silent for some time, the sultan, smiling, repeated his question. My wishes, answered the favourite, are so boundless, that it is impossible for me to tell you directly; but in two words, I should desire to be possessed of inexhaustible riches, and to enable me to enjoy them to the utmost, to have my life prolonged to eternity. Wouldst thou then, said Schemzeddin, forego thy hopes of paradise? I would, answered the favourite, make a paradise of this earthly globe, whilst it lasted, and take my chance for the other afterwards.

The sultan, at hearing these words, started up from his seat, and knitting his brow, Be gone, said he, sternly, thou art no longer worthy of my love or my confidence: I thought to have promoted thee to the highest honours, but such a wretch does not deserve to live. Ambition, though a vice, is yet the vice of great minds; but avarice, and an insatiable thirst for pleasure, degrades a man below the brutes.

Saying this, he turned his back on Nourjahad, and was about to leave him; when the favourite catching him by the robe, and falling on his knees, Let not my lord's indignation, said he, be kindled against his slave, for a few light words, which fell from him only in sport: I swear to thee, my prince, by our holy prophet,* that what I said is far from being the sentiments of my heart; my desire for wealth extends not farther than to be enabled to procure the sober enjoyments of life; and for length of years, let not mine be prolonged a day, beyond that, in which I can be serviceable to my prince and my country.

It is not, replied the sultan, with a mildness chastened with gravity, it is not for mortal eyes to penetrate into the close recesses of the human heart; thou hast attested thy innocence by an oath; it is all that can be required from man to man; but remember thou hast called our great prophet to witness; him thou canst not deceive, though me thou mayest.

Schemzeddin left him without waiting for his reply; and Nourjahad, exceedingly mortified that his unguarded declaration had so much lessened him in his master's esteem, retired to his own house, which immediately joined the sultan's palace.

He passed the rest of the night in traversing his chamber, being unable to take any rest. He dreaded the thoughts of losing the sultan's favour, on which alone he depended for his future advancement; and tormenting himself all night with apprehensions of his disgrace, he found himself so indisposed in the morning, that he was unable to leave his chamber. He spent the day in gloomy reflections without suffering any one to come near him, or taking any repast: and when night came, wearied with painful thoughts, and want of sleep, he threw himself on his bed. But his slumbers were disturbed by perplexing dreams. What had been the subject of his anxiety when awake, served now to imbitter and distract his rest: his fancy represented the sultan to him as he had last seen him in the garden, his looks severe, and his words menacing. 'Go wretch,' 'he thought he heard him cry, go seek thy bread in a remote country, thou hast nothing to expect from me but contempt.'

Nourjahad awoke in agonies: Oh heaven, cried he aloud, that I could now inherit the secret wish I was fool enough to disclose to thee, how little should I regard thy threats! And thou shalt, Oh Nourjahad, replied a voice, possess the utmost wishes of thy soul! Nourjahad started up in his bed, and rubbed his eyes, doubting whether he was really awake, or whether it was not his troubled imagination which cheated him with this delusive promise; when behold! to his unutterable astonishment, he saw a refulgent light in his chamber, and at his bed's side stood a youth of more than mortal beauty. The lustre of his white robes dazzled his eyes; his long and shining hair was incircled with a wreath of flowers that breathed the odours of paradise.

Nourjahad gazed at him, but had not power to open his mouth. Be not afraid, said the divine youth, with a voice of ineffable sweetness; I am thy guardian genius,* who have carefully watched over thee from thy infancy, though never till this hour have I been permitted to make myself visible to thee. I was present at thy conversation in the garden with Schemzeddin, I was a witness to thy unguarded declaration, but found thee afterwards awed by his frowns to retract what thou hadst said: I saw too the rigour of the sultan's looks as he departed from thee, and know that they proceeded from his doubting thy truth. I, though an immortal spirit, am not omniscient; to God only are the secrets of the heart revealed; speak boldly then, thou highly favoured of our prophet, and know that I have power from Mahomet to grant thy request, be it what it will. Wouldst thou be restored to the favour and confidence of thy master, and receive from his friendship and generosity the reward of thy long attachment to him, or dost thou really desire the accomplishment of that extravagant wish, which thou didst in the openness of thy heart avow to him last night?

Nourjahad, a little recovered from his amazement, and encouraged by the condescension of his celestial visitant, bowed his head low in token of adoration.

Disguise to thee, Oh son of paradise, replied he, were vain and fruitless; if I dissembled to Schemzeddin it was in order to reinstate myself in his good opinion, the only means in my power to secure my future prospects: from thee I can have no reason to conceal my thoughts; and since the care of my happiness is consigned to thee my guardian angel; let me possess that wish, extravagant as it may seem, which I first declared.

Rash mortal, replied the shining vision, reflect once more, before you receive the fatal boon; for once granted, you will wish perhaps, and wish in vain, to have it recalled. What have I to fear, answered Nourjahad, possessed of endless riches and of immortality? Your own passions, said the heavenly youth. I will submit to all the evils arising from them, replied Nourjahad, give me but the power of gratifying them in their full extent. Take thy wish then, cried the genius, with a look of discontent. The contents of this viol will confer immortality on thee, and to-morrow's sun shall behold thee richer than all the kings of the East. Nourjahad stretched his hands out eagerly to receive a vessel of gold, enriched with precious stones, which the angel took from under his mantle. Stop, cried the aerial being, and hear the condition, with which thou must accept the wondrous gift I am now about to bestow. Know then, that your existence here shall equal the date of this sublunary globe; yet to enjoy life all that while, is not in my power to grant. Nourjahad was going to interrupt the celestial, to desire him to explain this, when he prevented him, by proceeding thus: Your life, said he, will be frequently interrupted by the temporary death of sleep. Doubtless, replied Nourjahad, nature would languish without that sovereign balm. Thou misunderstandest me, cried the genius; I do not mean that ordinary repose which nature requires: The sleep thou must be subject to, at certain periods, will last for months, years, nay, for a whole revolution of Saturn at a time, or perhaps for a century. Frightful! cried Nourjahad, with an emotion that made him forget the respect which was due to the presence of his guardian angel. He seemed suspended, while the radiant youth proceeded; It is worth considering, resolve not too hastily. If the frame of man, replied Nourjahad, in the usual course of things, requires for the support of that short span of life which is allotted to him, a constant and regular portion of sleep, which includes at least one third of his existence; my life, perhaps, stretched so much beyond its natural date, may require a still greater proportion of rest, to preserve my body in due health and vigour. If this be the case, I submit to the conditions; for what is thirty or fifty years out of eternity? Thou art mistaken, replied the genius; and though thy reasoning is not unphilosophical, yet is it far from reaching the true cause of these mysterious conditions which are offered thee; know that these are contingencies which depend entirely on thyself. Let me beseech you, said Nourjahad, to explain this. If thou walkest, said the genius, in the paths of virtue, thy days will be crowned with gladness, and the even tenor of thy life undisturbed by any evil; but if, on the contrary, thou pervertest the good which is in thy power, and settest thy heart on iniquity, thou wilt thus be occasionally punished

by a total privation of thy faculties. If this be all, cried
Nourjahad, then am I sure I shall never incur the penalty;
for though I mean to enjoy all the pleasures that life can
bestow, yet am I a stranger to my own heart, if it ever lead
me to the wilful commission of a crime. The genius sighed.
Vouchsafe then, proceeded Nourjahad, vouchsafe, I conjure you, most adorable and benign spirit, to fulfil your
promise, and keep me not longer in suspence. Saying this,
he again reached forth his hand for the golden vessel, which
the genius no longer with-held from him. Hold thy nostrils
over that viol, said he, and let the fumes of the liquor which
it contains ascend to thy brain. Nourjahad opened the
vessel, out of which a vapour issued of a most exquisite
fragrance; it formed a thick atmosphere about his head, and
sent out such volatile and sharp effluvia, as made his eyes
smart exceedingly, and he was obliged to shut them whilst
he snuffed up the essence. He remained not long in this
situation, for the subtle spirit quickly evaporating, the
effects instantly ceased, and he opened his eyes; but the
apparition was vanished, and his apartment in total darkness. Had not he still found the viol in his hands, which
contained the precious liquor, he would have looked on all
this as a dream; but so substantial a proof of the reality of
what had happened, leaving no room for doubts, he
returned thanks to his guardian genius, whom he concluded, though invisible, to be still within hearing, and
putting the golden vessel under his pillow, filled as he was
with the most delightful ideas, composed himself to sleep.

The sun was at his meridian height when he awoke next
day; and the vision of the preceding night immediately
recurring to his memory, he sprung hastily from his bed;
but how great was his surprize, how high his transports, at
seeing the accomplishment of the genius's promise! His
chamber was surrounded with several large urns of polished
brass, some of which were filled with gold coin of different

value and impressions; others with ingots of fine gold; and others with precious stones of prodigious size and lustre.

Amazed, enraptured at the sight, he greedily examined his treasures, and looking into each of the urns one after the other, in one of them he found a scroll of paper, with these words written on it.

'I have fulfilled my promise to thee, Oh Nourjahad. Thy days are without number, thy riches inexhaustible, yet cannot I exempt thee from the evils to which all the sons of Adam are subject. I cannot screen thee from the machinations of envy, nor the rapaciousness of power: thy own prudence must henceforth be thy guard. There is a subterraneous cave in thy garden where thou mayst conceal thy treasure: I have marked the place, and thou wilt easily find it. Farewel, my charge is at an end.'

And well hast thou acquitted thyself of this charge, most munificent and benevolent genius, cried Nourjahad; ten thousand thanks to thee for this last friendly warning; I should be a fool indeed if I had not sagacity enough to preserve myself against rapaciousness or envy; I will prevent the effects of the first, by concealing thee, my precious treasure, thou source of all felicity, where no mortal shall discover thee; and for the other, my bounty shall disarm it of its sting. Enjoy thyself, Nourjahad, riot in luxurious delights, and laugh at Schemzeddin's impotent resentment.

He hastened down into his garden, in order to find the cave, of which he was not long in search. In a remote corner, stood the ruins of a small temple, which in former days, before the true religion prevailed in Persia, had been dedicated to the worship of the Gentiles.* The vestiges of this little building were so curious, that they were suffered to remain, as an ornament, where they stood. It was raised on a mount, and according to the custom of idolaters, surrounded with shady trees. On a branch of one of these, Nourjahad perceived hanging a scarf of fine white taffety,* to which was suspended a large key of burnished steel.

Nourjahad's eager curiosity, soon rendered his diligence successful, in finding the door, to which this belonged; it was within-side the walls of the temple, and under what formerly seemed to have been the altar. He descended by a few steps into a pretty spacious cavern, and by groping about, for there was scarce any light, he judged it large enough to contain his treasures.

Whether his guardian genius had contrived it purely for his use, or whether it had been originally made for some other purpose, he did not trouble himself to enquire; but glad to have found so safe a place, in which to deposite his wealth, he returned to his house; and having given orders that no visitors should approach him, he shut himself up in his chamber for the rest of the day, in order to contemplate his own happiness, and without interruption, to lay down plans of various pleasures and delights for ages to come.

Whilst Nourjahad was rich only in speculation, he really thought that he should be able to keep his word with the genius. That the employing his wealth to noble and generous purposes, would have constituted great part of his happiness; and that without plunging into guilt, he could have gratified the utmost of his wishes. But he soon found that his heart had deceived him, and that there is a wide difference between the fancied and actual possession of wealth. He was immediately absorbed in selfishness, and thought of nothing but the indulgence of his own appetites. My temper, said he, as he lay stretched at length on a sopha, does not much incline me to take any trouble; I shall therefore never aspire at high employments, nor would I be the sultan of Persia, if I might; for what addition would that make to my happiness? None at all; it would only disturb my breast with cares, from which I am now exempt. And which of the real, substantial delights of life, could I then possess, that are not now within my power? I will have a magnificent house in town, and others in the country, with delicious parks and gardens. What does it signify whether or not they are dignified with the names of palaces? or whether I am attended by princes or slaves? The latter will do my business as well, and be more subservient to my will. There are three particulars indeed, in which I will exceed my master. In the beauties of my seraglio; the delicacies of my table; and the excellence of my musicians. In the former of these especially, King Solomon himself shall be outdone.* All parts of the earth shall be explored for women of the most exquisite beauty; art and nature shall combine their utmost efforts, to furnish the boundless variety and elegance of my repasts; the sultan's frigid temperance shall not be a pattern to me. Then no fear of surfeits; I may riot to excess, and bid defiance to death. Here he started, on recollection that he had not requested the genius to secure him against the attacks of pain or sickness. I shall not however be impaired by age, said he, and this too perhaps is included in his gift. But no matter; since I cannot die, a little temporary pain will make me the more relish my returning health. Then, added he, I will enjoy the charms of music in its utmost perfection. I will have the universe searched for performers of both sexes, whose exquisite skill both in instrumental and vocal harmony, shall ravish all hearts. I shall see the line of my posterity past numeration, and all the while enjoy a constant succession of new delights. What more is there wanting to consummate happiness, and who would ever wish to change such an existence, for one of which we are entirely ignorant? Here he paused. But are there not, he proceeded, some things called intellectual pleasures? Such as Schemzeddin used to talk of to me, and for which, when I was poor, I fancied I had a sort of relish. They may have their charms, and we will not leave them quite out of our plan. I will certainly do abundance of good; besides, I will retain in my family half a score of wise and learned men, to entertain my leisure hours with their discourse. Then when I am weary of living in this country, I will set out with some chosen companions to make a tour through the whole earth. There shall not be a spot of the habitable world, which contains any thing worthy of my curiosity, that I will not visit; residing longest in those places which I like best: and by this means I may pass through two or three centuries, even before I have exhausted the variety of my prospects: after that I must content myself with such local enjoyments, as may fall in my way.

With such thoughts as these he entertained himself, waiting for the hour when his slaves should be retired to rest, as he had resolved to take that opportunity of burying his treasure.

He had tried the weight of the urns one by one; those which contained the gold he found so extreamly heavy that it was impossible for him to lift them. Those which held the jewels, he could easily carry. Accordingly, when every one in his house was asleep, he loaded himself with his pleasing burdens; and having from each of the repositories which held the gold, filled several large purses for his immediate expences, he conveyed the rest by many journeys to and from the cave, all safe to his subterranean treasury; where having locked them up securely, he retired to his apartment, and went to bed.

For the three succeeding days his thoughts were so perplexed and divided, that he knew not which of his favourite schemes he should first enter upon. Satisfied with having the means in his power, he neglected those ends for which he was so desirous of them. Shall I, said he, purchase or set about building for myself a magnificent palace? Shall I dispatch emissaries in search of the most beautiful virgins that can be obtained? and others, at the same time, to procure for me the rarest musicians? My household, meanwhile, may be established, and put on a footing suitable to the grandeur in which I purpose to live. I will directly hire a number of domestics, amongst which shall be a dozen of the best cooks in Persia, that my table at least may be immediately better supplied than that of the sultan. I am bewildered with such a multiplicity of business, and must find out some person, who, without giving me any trouble, will undertake to regulate the œconomy of all my domestic concerns.

In these thoughts he was so immersed, that he entirely forgot to pay his court to Schemzeddin; and without any other enjoyment of his riches, than the pleasure of thinking of them, he sat for whole days alone, alternately improving on, or rejecting, such systems of happiness as arose in his mind.

The sultan, mean time, offended at his absenting himself, without offering any excuse for it, especially as their last parting had been a cold one; was so disgusted at his behaviour, that he sent one of his officers to forbid him his presence, and charge him never more to appear at court. Tell him, however, said he, that I have not so far forgot my former friendship for him, as to see him want a decent support; that house, therefore, in which he now lives, I freely bestow on him; and shall moreover allow him a pension of a thousand crowns yearly.* Bid him remember that this is sufficient to supply him with all the sober enjoyments of life. These being his favourite's own words, the sultan thought proper to remind him of them.

Nourjahad received this message with the utmost indifference; but without daring to shew any mark of disrespect. Tell my lord the sultan, said he, that I would not have been thus long without prostrating myself at his feet, but that I was hastily sent for to visit a kinsman, whose dwelling was some leagues from Ormuz;* and who in his last hours was desirous of seeing me. He died very rich, and has made me his heir. The thousand crowns a year therefore, my royal master may please to bestow on some one who wants them more, and is more deserving of his bounty, than I; wretch that I am, to have forfeited my prince's favour! The house that his goodness bestows on me, with all gratitude I

thankfully accept, as it will daily remind me that Schemzeddin does not utterly detest his slave. Saying this, he
presented the officer with a handsome diamond, which he
took from his finger, and begged him to accept of it as a
token of his respect for him, and submission to the sultan's
pleasure.

Though Nourjahad had given such a turn to his acceptance of the house, his true reason was, that having his
treasure buried in the garden, he thought he could not
without great difficulty, and the hazard of a discovery,
remove it. Thus had he already, in two instances, been
obliged to depart from truth, in consequence of his ill
judged and pernicious choice.

The house which the sultan had given him, was handsome and commodious; and he thought by enlarging and
furnishing it magnificently, it would sufficiently answer the
purpose of his town residence; besides, as it was a royal
grant, he was sure of remaining unmolested in the possession of it.

He now bent his thoughts on nothing but in giving a
loose to his appetites, and indulging without controul in
every delight which his passions or imagination could
suggest to him. As he was not of an active temper, he put
the conduct of his pleasures into the hands of one, whom
he had lately received into his service. This man, whose
name was Hasem, he found had good sense, and a quickness
of parts, which he thought qualified him for the trust he
reposed in him. To him he committed the care of regulating
his family, and appointed him the director of his household.
In short, under Hasem's inspection, who on this occasion
displayed an admirable taste, his house was soon furnished
with every thing that could charm the senses, or captivate
the fancy. Costly furniture, magnificent habits, sumptuous
equipages, and a grand retinue, fully gratified his vanity.
By Hasem's diligence his seraglio was soon adorned with a
number of the most beautiful female slaves, of almost every

nation, whom he purchased at a vast expence. By Hasem's care, his board was replenished with the most delicious products of every climate; and by Hasem's management he had a chosen band of the most skilful musicians of the age; and by Hasem's judgement and address, he had retained in his house some of the most learned and ingenious men of all Persia, skilled in every art and science. These were received into his family for the instruction and entertainment of his hours of reflection, if he should chance to be visited with any such.

Behold him now arrived at the height of human felicity; for, to render his happiness incapable of addition, he had distinguished amongst the beauties of his seraglio, a young maid, so exquisitely charming and accomplished, that he gave her the intire possession of his heart; and preferring her to the rest of his women, past whole days in her apartment. By Mandana he found himself equally beloved; a felicity very rare amongst Eastern husbands; and longing to unbosom himself to one, on whose tenderness and fidelity he could rely, to her he disclosed the marvellous story of his destiny. His mind thus disburthened of this important secret, which he had often longed to divulge, but could find none whom he dared to trust with the discovery, he had not one anxious thought remaining. He gave himself up to pleasures, he threw off all restraint, he plunged at once into a tide of luxurious enjoyments; he forgot his duty towards God, and neglected all the laws of his prophet. He grew lazy and effeminate; and had not his pride now and then urged him to display to the wondering eyes of the public, the magnificence of his state, he would seldom have been inclined to go out of his house.

Thus possessed of every thing that his soul could wish, he continued for the space of three moons, without any interruption, to wallow in voluptuousness: When one morning just as he was preparing to set out for a beautiful villa, which Hasem had recommended to him for his rural retirement, and which he purposed to buy if it answered his description, he was prevented by a messenger from the sultan. It was the same person who once before had been sent to him, to forbid him the court. I am sorry, my lord, said he, on entering Nourjahad's apartment, to be a second time the bearer of unwelcome tidings; but Schemzeddin, hearing of the extraordinary grandeur and magnificence in which you live, a magnificence indeed equal to that of the sultan himself, would needs know whence you derive your wealth, which seems so much to surpass that of any of his subjects; and has commanded me to conduct you to his presence, in order to give an account of it.

Nourjahad was exceedingly startled at this unexpected summons; but it was in vain to dispute the sultan's orders, and he was forced, though with great reluctance, to accompany the officer to the palace of Schemzeddin.

He entered it trembling, fearful to declare a falsehood to his sovereign, yet still more unwilling to confess the truth.

In this suspence the officer left him, to acquaint the sultan of his arrival. He waited not long before he was admitted to the royal presence.

Whence is it, Nourjahad, said the sultan, that thy imprudence hath drawn on thee the attention of my whole empire, insomuch that the representations made to me of thy pomp and luxury, now renders it necessary to enquire into thy riches. They seem indeed to be immense. Who was that relation that bequeathed them to thee, and wherein do they consist?

Though Nourjahad had endeavoured to prepare himself with proper answers to all those questions, which he naturally expected would be asked on the occasion, he was nevertheless confounded; he could not utter the lies he had framed with the unabashed look of sincerity; his speech faltered, and his colour changed. Schemzeddin saw his confusion. I perceive, said he, there is some mystery in this affair which thou hast no mind to discover; I pray heaven that thou hast used no sinister means to come at the great wealth which I am told thou possessest! Confess the truth, and beware of prevaricating with thy prince.

Nourjahad, frightened at the difficulties he found himself involved in, fell at the sultan's feet. If my lord, said he, will give me a patient hearing, and forgive the presumption of his servant, I will unfold such wonders as will amaze him, and at the same time utter nothing but the strictest truth. The sultan turned coldly towards him; but by seeming to attend to his explanation, encouraged him to proceed.

He then gave a faithful relation of the vision he had seen, with all the consequences of that miraculous event. Schemzeddin suffered him to conclude his narration without interruption; but instead of shewing any marks of surprize, or appearing to credit what he said, looking at him with the utmost indignation, Audacious wretch, cried he, how darest thou presume thus to abuse my patience, and affront my understanding with the relation of so ridiculous a forgery? Go tell thy incredible tales to fools and children, but dare not to insult thy sovereign with such outrageous falsehoods.

Though Nourjahad was terrified at the sultan's anger, he nevertheless persisted in his declaration, confirming all he had said by the most solemn oaths. The sultan commanded him to be silent. Thou art mad, said he: I perceive now that the riches thou hast acquired, let the means be what they may, have turned thy brain; and I am now more than ever convinced of the sordidness of thy mind, when the unexpected acquisition of a little wealth could thus pervert thy judgment, and teach thee to impose on thy master for truth, the monstrous chimeras of thy wild fancy. Thy folly be on thy head; for a little, a very little time must, with the unbounded extravagance of which thou art guilty, dissipate what thy friend hath left thee; and when thou art again reduced to thy former state, thou wilt be glad to sue to my bounty for that which thou didst lately with so much arrogance reject. Go, unhappy Nourjahad, continued he, (his voice a little softened) the remembrance of what thou once wert to me, will not permit me to see thee fall a victim to thy own desperate folly. Should it be publickly known that thou hast thus endeavoured by lies and profanation to abuse the credulity of thy prince, thou wouldst find that thy boasted immortality would not be proof against that death, which he should think himself obliged, in justice to his own honour and dignity, to inflict on so bold an impostor. Hence, miserable man, pursued he, retire to thy house; and if thou art not quite abandoned, endeavour by a sober and regular conduct to expiate thy offences against heaven and thy sovereign; but as a punishment for thy crime, presume not, without my leave, to stir beyond the limits of thy own habitation, on pain of a more rigorous and lasting confinement.

Nourjahad, thunder-struck at this unexpected sentence, was unable to reply; and the sultan having ordered the captain of his guards to be called, committed his prisoner to his hands; telling him if he suffered Nourjahad to escape, his head should answer it.

Filled with resentment and discontent, Nourjahad was conducted back to his own house; at all the avenues of which he had the mortification to see guards posted, agreeably to the charge given by the sultan.

He retired pensively to his closet, where, shutting himself up, he now for the first time repented of his indiscretion in the choice he had made.

Unfortunate that I am, cried he, what will riches or length of days avail me, if I am thus to be miserably immured within the walls of my own dwelling? Would it not have been better for me to have requested the genius to restore me to the favour of my prince? Schemzeddin always loved me, and would not fail to have promoted me to wealth and honours; mean while I should have enjoyed my liberty, which now methinks, as I am debarred of it, appears to me a greater blessing than any I possess. Unhappy Nourjahad, what is become of all thy schemes of felicity! He was even weak enough to shed tears, and gave himself up to vexation for the remainder of the day.

His mind, however, was by pleasure rendered too volatile to suffer any thing to make a lasting impression on him; and he had still too many resources of happiness in his power, to give himself up to despair. It is true, said he, I am debarred of my liberty, but have I not still a thousand delights in my possession? The incredulous sultan, satisfied with punishing me, will give himself no farther concern about me, provided I do not attempt to escape; and thus withdrawn from the public eye, envy will not endeavour to penetrate into the recesses of a private dwelling. I will secure the fidelity of my servants, by my liberality towards them. Schemzeddin's resentment will not last; or if it should, even as long as he lives, what is his life, the scanty portion of years allotted to common men, to my promised immortality?

Having thus reconciled his thoughts to his present situation, he resolved, in order to make himself amends for the restraint on his person, to indulge himself with an unbounded freedom in his most voluptuous wishes. He commanded a banquet to be prepared for him that night, which exceeded in luxury and profusion any of the preceding. He ordered all his women, of which he had a great number, adorned with jewels and dressed in their richest habits, to attend on him whilst he was at supper, permitting none but Mandana the favour to sit down with him. The magnificence of his apartments was heightened by a splendid illumination of a thousand torches, composed of odoriferous gums, which cast a blaze of light that vied with the glories of the sun. His musicians, both vocal and instrumental, were ordered to exert the utmost stretch of their art, and to sooth his mind with all the enchanting powers of harmony. Himself attired in robes, such as the kings of

Persia were used to wear, was seated under a canopy of silver tissue, which he had put up for the purpose; and assuming the pomp of an Eastern monarch, suffered the illusion to take such possession of his mind, that if he were not before mad, he now seemed to be very near distraction.

Intoxicated with pleasure, the historian who writes his life, affirms that this night Nourjahad for the first time got drunk.*

Be that as it may, it is certain that having retired to rest, he slept sounder and longer than usual; for on his awaking, and missing Mandana from his side, whom he had made the partner of his bed, he called out to the slave who always attended in his antichamber, in order to enquire for her, resolving to chide her tenderly for leaving him.

He called loud and often, but nobody answering him, as he was naturally choleric, he jumped out of bed, and stepping hastily into the outer chamber, he found that none of the slaves were in waiting. Enraged at this neglect, he called several of his domestics by their names, one after another; when at length, after he was almost out of breath with passion, a female slave appeared, who was one of those appointed to wait on Mandana.

The damsel no sooner perceived him, than giving a loud shriek, she was about to run away; when Nourjahad, provoked at her behaviour, catching her roughly by the arm, Where is thy mistress, said he, and whence arises that terror and amazement in thy countenance? Alas! my lord, answered the slave, pardon my surprize, which is occasioned by my seeing you so unexpectedly. Nourjahad now perceiving that in his hurry he had forgot to put on his cloaths, concluded that it was that circumstance which had alarmed the damsel, and turning from her, Foolish woman, said he, go tell Mandana that I desire to see her. Ah, my lord, replied the maid, I would she were in a condition to come to you. Why, what is the matter, said Nourjahad, no ill I hope has befallen the dear light of my life? Is she sick?

Methinks she went to bed last night in perfect health. Last night! my lord, replied the slave, and shook her head. Trifler, cried Nourjahad, what means that motion? Where is thy mistress? Speak! She is, I hope, said the slave, gone to receive the reward of her goodness! Here she began to weep. Oh Heaven, cried Nourjahad, is my dear Mandana dead? She is, answered the damsel, redoubling her tears, and I shall never have so kind a mistress.

Alas! replied Nourjahad, by what fatal accident am I thus suddenly deprived of the adorable creature?

It was not suddenly, my lord, replied the slave, Mandana died in childbed. Ah traitress, cried Nourjahad, how darest thou thus mock the sorrow of thy master, and traduce the chastity of my beloved. Thou knowest it is not more than three moons since I received her a virgin to my arms, and doest thou presume to impose so ridiculous a story on me as that of her having died in childbed? My lord, answered the slave, it is more than three years since Mandana died. Audacious wretch, cried Nourjahad, wouldst thou persuade me out of my senses? With this he pinched the slave so hard by the arm, that she screamed out.

The noise she made brought several of the servants into the room, who, on seeing Nourjahad, all shewed manifest tokens of fear and surprize. What is the reason of all this, cried he out in a rage, are ye all leagued in combination against me? Be quick and explain to me the cause of this distraction which appears amongst you.

Hasem, who had run in amongst the other domestics, took upon him to answer for the rest. It is not to be wondered at, my lord, said he, that your slaves seem surprised at seeing you thus as it were raised from the dead; but if they are amazed, their joy doubtless is equal to their wonder; mine I am sure is unutterable, to behold my lord once more restored to his faithful servants, after we had almost despaired of your ever more unclosing your eyes.

You talk strangely, said Nourjahad, a little staggered at

what he saw and heard. He just then recollected the terms on which he had received the important gift from the genius; and began to suspect that he had endured one of those preternatural slumbers, to which he had subjected himself. How long may I have slept, said he? Four years and twenty days exactly, answered Hasem; I have reason to know, for I counted the melancholy hours as they passed, and seldom quitted your bed-side. It may be so, said Nourjahad, I have been subject to these trances from a boy, but this has lasted rather longer than usual. He then commanded all his slaves to withdraw, retaining only Hasem, with whom he wanted to have some discourse.

Tell me now, said he, (when they were alone) and tell me truly, is all I have heard real, and is Mandana actually dead? Too true, my lord, replied Hasem, Mandana died in childbed, and dying left her infant son to my care. Is my child alive, said Nourjahad eagerly? He is, my lord, answered Hasem, and you shall see him presently: Mandana called me to her, continued he, when she found herself dying.

Hasem, said she, be careful of your lord; Heaven will one day restore him to you again. See that you manage his household with the same prudence and regularity that you would if he himself were to inspect into your conduct; for be assured he will sooner or later exact a just account of your proceedings. Here are the keys of his coffers. I ventured to take them from under his pillow, where I knew he kept them. I have husbanded his fortune with œconomy, and have hitherto kept order and harmony in his family: On you it rests to preserve it in the same condition. Nourjahad will not fail to reward your diligence and fidelity. It is not expedient that any one should know the condition to which he is reduced. His life is governed by a strange fatality. You have nothing to do therefore, but to give out that he is seized with a lingering distemper, which confines him to his bed. Let no impertinent enquirers see him, and all curiosity about him will soon cease. These, proceeded Hasem, were almost the last words that my beloved mistress spoke. I have punctually complied with her orders. Your condition has been kept a profound secret from every one but your own family, and they all love you too well to betray their trust. Your women are all immured within the sacred walls of your seraglio, and though they murmur at their situation, they fail not to offer up their daily prayers that Heaven would restore you to them. I will now, continued he, present your son to you; it will be some consolation to you to see that charming pledge of Mandana's love. Saying this, he withdrew, but soon returned leading in the child, who was as beautiful as a little cherub.

Nourjahad melted into tears at the sight of him, and renewed his complaints for the loss of his adored Mandana. He saw that the child's age seemed to agree exactly with the account he had received; and now fully convinced of the truth of his misfortune, Oh Heaven, cried he, clasping the young boy to his bosom, what would I give that my dear Mandana were now here to partake of the pleasure I feel in this infant's caresses; gladly would I consent to have three ages cut off from the number of my years, to have her more precious life restored. But my felicity would then be too great, and I must submit to the destiny which I myself have chosen. Prudent Hasem, said he, observing he looked surprised, thou dost wonder at the words which thou hast heard me speak, but I will not conceal from thee the marvellous story of my life. Thy fidelity and zeal deserve this confidence; besides, it is requisite that I should trust some discreet person with my important secret, since Mandana, on whose tenderness and loyalty I could depend, is no more.

Nourjahad then acquainted Hasem with the wonderful mystery of his life. He did not, however, divulge the circumstance of his concealed treasure; he judged from his own heart, that it would not be altogether advisable to lay

such a tempting bait in the way even of the most virtuous
and steady mind; but contented himself with telling him
that his genius constantly supplied him with riches, as his
occasions required. Hasem listened to him with astonishment; but assured him, after what had already past, he
doubted not a tittle of the truth of what he had been told,
amazing and almost incredible as it appeared.

My lord, said he, you may securely rely on my zeal and
diligence, so long as you are pleased to entertain me in your
service. That I shall do during your life, interrupted
Nourjahad: But, replied Hasem, what if one of those
unmerciful long trances should continue for a length of
time much beyond that from which you are but now
awakened, and that I should happen to die before you
recover your senses, who knows in that case what might be
the consequences? It is an accident exceedingly to be
dreaded, replied Nourjahad; Heaven knows to what indig-
nities I might be exposed, perhaps to be buried alive, and
condemned to pass a century or two in a dismal sepulchre.
The thought makes me shudder, and I almost repent of
having accepted life on such conditions. As I have no
warning, continued he, when those fatal slumbers will
overpower me, (for who can always be guarded against the
starts of passion, or what man is so attentive to that
impertinent monitor within, as to hear his whispers amidst
the hurry of tumultuous pleasures?) As I know not, I say,
when I am to be condemned to that state of insensibility, or
how long I shall continue in it, I can only conjure thee if I
should happen to be seized with another trance during thy
life, (which, considering my disposition, is not impossible)
that thou wilt observe the same conduct which thou hast
lately done; and if the angel of death should summon thee
away before my senses are loosed from their mysterious
bands, that thou wilt with thy dying breath, commit the
secret to some one faithful person of my family, whom thou
thinkest most fit to be relied on, for a punctual discharge of

their duty. As I shall never part with any of my servants, till the inevitable stroke of death separates them from me, and shall constantly supply their places with the worthiest persons that can be found, I think I cannot fail of a succession of people, from amongst whom, one at least may always be found, in whose secrecy and truth I may safely confide.

Without doubt, my lord, answered Hasem, you may by such wise measures as these, be always guarded against the worst that may befal you.

Though Nourjahad had, by thus providing against evil events, exceedingly relieved his mind from the fears by which it was agitated, lest any ill should happen to him during his slumbers; yet was his heart far from being at ease. The loss of Mandana preyed upon his spirits. He had no relish for the charms of his other women. Mandana's superior loveliness was always present to his eyes: The delicacies of his table grew tasteless; Mandana's sprightly wit was wanting to give a relish to the feast. The melodious concerts of music with which he was wont to be so delighted, now only served to overwhelm him with melancholy: Mandana's enchanting voice was not heard, which used to swell his heart to rapture.

In short, for a time he took pleasure in nothing but the caresses and innocent prattle of his little son, whom by his tenderness and endearments he had taught to love him.

I am unhappy, my dear Hasem, would he often say; the loss of Mandana imbitters all my joys, and methinks I begin to look forward with disgust.

My lord, said Hasem, there is nothing which has befallen you but what is common to all. Every one may naturally expect to see the death of some person or other whom they love; but you who are endowed with so miraculous a life must needs look to drop a tear over a thousand graves.

Melancholy reflection, said Nourjahad! it occurred not to me in this light when I made my choice. I knew indeed I must of necessity bury hundreds of succeeding generations; but said I to myself, I shall insensibly contract new amities, as I perceive the old ones are likely to be dissolved by the hand of time. My heart, said I, shall never feel a vacuity, for want of fit objects of desire. A new beauty will naturally take place of her whose charms begin to decline; thus the ardors of love will be supplied with perpetual fewel; and upon the same principle will the social joys of friendship be unremitting. I considered the world as a flower garden, the product of which was to delight my senses for a certain season. The bloom is not made to last, thought I, but it will be succeeded by a fresh blow,* whose sweetness and variety will equal the former, and intirely obliterate them from my memory. I thought not, alas, that before the spring ended, a cruel blast might suddenly destroy my fairest flower.

Would you, my lord, said Hasem, if it were in your power, absolve your genius from his promise, seeing your life must be perpetually subject to such misfortunes?

Not so neither, answered Nourjahad; time is a never-failing remedy for grief; I shall get over this, and be better prepared against the next assault of evil.

In effect, Nourjahad kept his word, and soon returned to his former way of living.

He had the mortification, however, to find himself still a prisoner. Hasem told him that the sultan had not yet taken off the restraint, under which he had formerly laid him; and whether it was through forgetfulness or design, the guards still maintained their posts about his house. This Nourjahad was himself convinced of, by seeing them from his windows.

It is strange, said he, that Schemzeddin should retain his resentment against me for so long a time; especially as he might have been convinced of the truth of what I asserted, by the extraordinary state in which I have lain all this while. You forget, my lord, said Hasem, that this was an absolute secret, no one from under your own roof knowing a word of the matter. Such were Mandana's last injunctions, and your faithful servants never divulged a tittle of it.

Did not my friends come to visit me, said Nourjahad, during that interval in which I slept? Those whom you called your friends, answered Hasem, came as usual, during the first month of your dormant state; but being refused admittance, under pretence that your health was so much declined, that you were not in a condition to receive them, they soon desisted from their visits; and finding they could no more be entertained with feasting and jollity, they have never since inquired after you.

Ungrateful wretches, said Nourjahad! I cast them off for ever. Yet it is an irksome thing to live without friends. You Hasem are a prudent and honest man, but still you are my servant; I cannot therefore consider you on that footing of equality which friendship requires. There is one man, said Hasem, who has shewn himself grateful and compassionate; and those two virtues never come alone, but are ever found attended with many others. Oh name him, said Nourjahad. It is Zamgrad, replied Hasem, that officer of the sultan's whom you once obliged by a trifling present of a ring; he never fails sending every day to enquire after your welfare. Nay, he has often called himself, and expressed an honest sorrow for the ill state of health to which I told him you were reduced; tenderly blaming the sultan for his rigorous confinement of you.

Worthy Zamgrad, said Nourjahad, thou, thou alone shalt be the chosen friend of my heart; the rest of my worthless acquaintance I from this minute discard.

I will write to Schemzeddin, pursued he; perhaps he may now relent and restore me to my liberty. I long to shift the scene, and remove to some place where Mandana's image may not be so often revived in my memory. Wert thou not, Hasem, about to procure for me a noble seat in the country, which I was going to take a view of that day on which the

good Zamgrad came to carry me before the sultan? If I
might but retire thither, I should think myself happy.

Alas, my lord, replied Hasem, that fine seat cannot now
be yours. You may remember I made only a conditional
agreement with the owner of it, depending on your approbation of the place after your having seen it. I recollect it,
said Nourjahad, but may it not still be mine? By no means,
answered Hasem; the owner has long since disposed of it to
another.

That is unlucky, said Nourjahad; but we can easily find
another. Be it your care to look out for one, whilst I
endeavour to move the sultan in my favour.

Hasem was not slow in executing his master's orders. In
three days he told him he had seen a villa, which seemed to
him to surpass all the descriptions of Eden in its primary
state of beauty. It is but at the distance of ten leagues from
Ormuz, said he. The house and gardens are in compleat
order, and you may purchase the whole for fifty thousand
pieces of gold. The sultan himself hath not in his possession
any thing more delightful. I will have it, said Nourjahad:
Get the money ready, you have the keys of my coffers, and
they contain more than that sum.

My lord, answered Hasem, when you last saw them they
did contain much more; but you will be pleased to recollect
that it is above four years since, and that your household
has been maintained during that time; which, notwithstanding I have used the utmost œconomy, must needs have
somewhat diminished your treasury. I had forgot, replied
Nourjahad, but I will soon supply you with the gold you
want.

Accordingly he paid a visit to the subterraneous cave that
very night; where finding every thing as he had left it, he
loaded himself with a quantity of gold, sufficient to prevent
the necessity of drawing from his hidden store of wealth for
a considerable time.

Intent now on the pursuit of his pleasures, he neglected

not applying to the sultan for a repeal, or at least a mitigation of his sentence. He writ to Schemzeddin a letter in terms full of humility; thinking if he could remove his incredulity by convincing him that the extraordinary fact he had related, was nothing more than the truth, that the sultan would no longer deny him his liberty. He scrupled not to acquaint him, that he had been for more than four years in a profound sleep, for the confirmation of which fact, strange as it might seem to his majesty, he desired leave to appeal to every one of his own household, and conjured the sultan to take the trouble of informing himself more fully from some of his people, whom he might cause to be brought into his presence and privately examined, as he confessed he did not wish to have so uncommon an event divulged.

Nourjahad from this expedient had great hopes of obtaining his desire; but the event turned out contrary to his expectations.

Zamgrad two days after brought him an answer from the sultan in writing: Nourjahad laid the paper on his head, then kissing the seals, he broke them open,* and read as follows.

'I have not been unmindful of thy motions, and I was pleased to hear from time to time, that for these four years past, order and decency have been preserved in thy dwelling. I flattered myself that this was owing to thy having returned to a sense of thy duty. But my hope deceived me, when I found that Nourjahad was by a violent malady which seized him (doubtless the effects of his intemperance) disqualified from indulging in those excesses in which he was wont to riot.

'This visitation from heaven, I thought would have produced salutary effects on thy mind, and hoped if the angel of health were again to revisit thy pillow, that thou wouldst make a different use of thy recovered strength. How must my indignation then be roused against thee, abandoned as thou art to perdition, to find thou persistest in thy enormous folly and wickedness; and continuest to abuse the patience of thy benefactor and sovereign master, with such unparalleled falsehoods. A prince less merciful than myself, would no longer delay to punish thee with death: But I give thee thy wretched life. Spend it if thou canst in penitence. Nay, I will so far indulge thee, as to permit thee, for the more perfect recovery of thy health, to retire to thy house in the country; but at the peril of thy head presume not to stir beyond the bounds of thy own habitation.'

Nourjahad now too late found his error in endeavouring to force belief of a thing which appeared so incredible, and wished he had rather availed himself of the sultan's prepossessions in favour of the story propagated by his servants, as he found that would have been the wiser course.

What a world is this, said he to Zamgrad, (after having read the letter) where he who ought to be the rewarder of truth, and the dispenser of justice, shuts his ears against conviction, and condemns an innocent man for endeavouring to set him right? But I will not involve you in the punishment imposed on my imaginary guilt, by requiring your belief of what I have in vain endeavoured to convince the incredulous Schemzeddin.

I know not, my lord, replied Zamgrad, what has passed between the sultan and you; of this only I am certain, that he seems exceedingly enraged against you. I would it were in my power, from the respect I bear you, to mitigate his resentment.

I thank thee, gentle Zamgrad, said Nourjahad; I find thou, of all my numerous acquaintance, art the only man who has shewn any attachment to me. If the friendship of one labouring under the displeasure of his prince, be worth thy accepting, I offer thee mine, and conjure thee to grant me yours in return. The base ingratitude I have already experienced from the rest of my pretended friends, has determined me to disclaim all society with them: if thou wilt sometimes visit me in my retirement, thou wilt find Nourjahad not undeserving of thy kindness.

Zamgrad promised to see him as often as he could, and took his leave.

However vexed Nourjahad was at his disappointment, in finding himself, by being still debarred of his liberty, deprived for a time at least from executing one of his favourite purposes, that of travelling all over the world, he yet contented himself with the reflection, that this project was only postponed to another opportunity; and that he should have time enough for executing his design, after Schemzeddin, and many of his posterity were in their graves. I will not waste my hours, said he, in fruitless languishment for what I cannot at present attain, but make the most of the good which now offers itself to my acceptance.

He ordered Hasem to pay down the money forthwith, for that fine seat: I will remove thither, said he, immediately; and make myself some recompence by all the means that art can devise, for that cruel long trance, which over-powered me so unseasonably: I hope I shall not be visited by another for these fifty or sixty years at least.

Hasem's diligence kept pace with his lord's impatience: He got every thing in readiness for his reception at his rural mansion: and to avoid the notice which might be taken of so numerous a seraglio, and such a train of domestics, the prudent Hasem advised that they should set out and travel by night. This precaution, said he, will prevent the malice of your enemies from making ill-natured representations of your conduct to the sultan; and as you yourself are supposed by every body in Ormuz to have laboured under a long and painful illness, I think, to give colour to this report, it would be most advisable for you to be carried in a litter. As Nourjahad loved his ease, he readily enough consented to this proposal, and in this manner suffered himself to be conveyed to his new habitation.

On his arrival he found Hasem had not exaggerated in his description of this place. The house, or rather palace, for such it might be called, infinitely exceeded his expectations; but above all, the gardens were so delicious, that his senses were ravished with delight. He declared that those mansions of joy prepared for the reception of the faithful,* could not exceed them; and forgetting that this paradise was to be his prison, he ordered that a pavilion of light brocade should be reared for him in the midst of his garden, where he purposed to enjoy the cool hours of the evening, amidst the noise of falling waters, and the wild notes of innumerable birds, who had taken up their residence in this terrestrial paradise.

Behold him now once more, in the possession of every thing, for which the heart of man in the wildest wishes of Epicurean phrenzy,* could pant. He gave the reins to his passions; he again became the slave of voluptuous appetites: He submitted a second time to the power of beauty; he invented new modes of luxury; and his delightful abode became the scene of every licentious pleasure.

The delicacies and profusion in which he himself wallowed, made him forget that there were wants or miseries amongst his fellow-creatures; and as he had but little intercourse with mankind, except with those who flattered his follies, or administered to his loose pleasures, he became hardened to all the social affections. He ceased to relieve the poor, because they never came in his way; and with a heart naturally generous and benevolent, he lived only for himself.

Immersed in sensual gratifications, he lost all relish for any others. The poets and sages whom he entertained in his house, began to grow irksome to him. He derided the wisdom and philosophy of the latter; and if they attempted to entertain him with learned or grave discourses, he laughed at them; and at length thinking their company tedious, he turned them out of his house.

His bards would have shared the same fate, if they had not by a timely address rendered their art subservient to his depraved inclinations. They composed nothing but pieces filled with adulation on himself, or light verses in praise of one or other of his mistresses; these were set to melting airs, and sung accompanied by the lute.

Thus did Nourjahad pass his days. Every rising sun beheld some fresh outrage on the laws of temperance and decency; and the shades of every night descended on his unatoned offences.

The delightful season of the year, winged with pleasures, was now almost fled, when one of the most extravagant projects came into the head of Nourjahad, that ever entered the imagination of man.

As the gardens of his palace were exceedingly delicious, he vainly fancied that they must be very like the regions of aradise (where all good Musselmen are received after death) and that in order to make the resemblance perfectly complete, he would cause the women of his seraglio to personate the Houriis; those beautiful virgins who are given as a reward to all true believers.* He himself would needs represent Mahomet; and one of his mistresses whom he loved best, and who was indeed the handsomest of them, he would have to appear under the name and character of Cadiga, the favourite wife of the great Prophet.*

The idea, wild and profane as it was, was notwithstanding readily adopted by all the people about him, no one presuming to dispute his will. Nor were the women on this occasion much inclined to do so, as it served them for a very agreeable amusement.

Some debates however arose amongst them on account of the dresses proper to be worn on this occasion; as none of them remembered to have read in the Koran what sort of habits the Houriis wore; and some of the ladies gave it as their opinion that those beauties went naked.

After many disputes on the subject, however, they struck a sort of medium, and agreed to be attired in loose robes of the thinnest Persian gauze, with chaplets of flowers on their heads.

Nourjahad approved of the invention, and gave orders to Hasem to prepare for this celestial masquerade, with all possible diligence; charging him to leave nothing out, that could render the entertainment worthy of Mahomet himself.

Neither art nor expence were spared on this extraordinary occasion. He gave commandment that the fountains which adorned his garden should be so contrived, that instead of water, they should pour forth milk and wine; that the seasons should be anticipated, and the early fragrance of the spring should be united with the more vivid colours of the glowing summer. In short, that fruits, blossoms, and flowers, should at once unite their various beauties, to imbellish this terrestrial paradise.

The diligence of Hasem was so active, that every thing was got in readiness, even sooner than Nourjahad expected. He descended into his garden to take a survey of these wondrous preparations; and finding all exactly to his mind, he gave orders to his women to hold themselves prepared to act their parts; telling them that on that very evening he would give them a foretaste of the ravishing pleasures they were to enjoy, in the happy regions of light.

The weather was extremely hot, and Nourjahad, in order to take a view of the magnificent decorations, having fatigued himself with wandering through his elysium, retired to his apartment, and threw himself down on a sopha, with intent to take a short repose, the better to prepare himself for the excesses of the night: leaving orders with Hasem and Cadiga to awake him from sleep before sunset.

Nourjahad, however, opened his eyes without any one's having roused him from his slumbers; when perceiving that the day was almost closed, and finding that his commands had been neglected, he flew into a violent passion, suspecting that his women had prevailed on Hasem, to grant them this opportunity whilst he slept, of indulging themselves in liberties without that restraint to which they were accustomed in his presence.

Enraged at the thought, he resolved to have them called before him, and after severely reprimanding them, and punishing Hasem proportionally to his fault, to have his women all locked up, and postpone his festivity till he was in a better humour to relish it.

Impatient, and even furious at his disappointment, he stamped on the floor with his foot; when immediately a black eunuch presented himself at the door. Go, said he, his words almost choaked with indignation, go and bid my women one and all hasten directly into my presence.

The slave retired in respectful silence; and presently after all the ladies of his seraglio entered his apartment. They were, according to the custom, covered with vails, but on appearing in their lord's presence, they threw them off. But, Oh Heaven! what was Nourjahad's anger and astonishment, when instead of the beautiful Houriis whom he expected to see, to behold a train of wrinkled and deformed old hags.

Amazement and rage for a while suspended the power of speech: When the foremost of the old women approaching, and offering to embrace him, he thrust her rudely from him: Detestable fiend, said he, whence this presumption? where are my slaves? Where is Hasem? and the women of my seraglio? The traitoresses! they shall pay dearly for thus abusing my indulgence.

The old women at this all fell upon their faces to the ground; but the first who had advanced addressing herself to speak, Avaunt! cried Nourjahad, begone wretches, and rid my sight of such hideous aspects.

Alas, my lord, replied the old woman, have you intirely forgot me? has time left no traces to remind you of your once beloved Cadiga? Cadiga? thou Cadiga? do not provoke me, said Nourjahad, or by Allah I'll spurn thee with my foot.

The old women now all set up a lamentable cry, Miserable wretches that we are, said they, beating their withered breasts, it had been happy for us if we had all died in our youth, rather than have thus out-lived our lord's affections!

Evil betide ye, said Nourjahad, who in the name of deformity are ye all? Hereupon the beldames cried out with one voice, Your mistresses! the once admired and loved partners of your bed, but the relentless hand of time has made such cruel ravage on our charms, that we do not wonder thou shouldst find it impossible to recollect us.

Nourjahad now began to suspect that he had been overpowered by a second trance. Why, how long, in the devil's name, have I then slept, said he?

Forty years and eleven moons, answered the lady who called herself Cadiga. Thou liest, I am sure, said Nourjahad, for it appears to me but as yesterday since I ordered thee (if thou really art Cadiga) to awake me at a certain hour, that I might enjoy the glorious entertainment prepared for me in the gardens of the Houriis.

I do remember it, said Cadiga, and we your faithful slaves were to personate those beautiful virgins. Alas, alas, we are not now fit to represent those daughters of paradise! Thou art fitter, said Nourjahad, to represent the furies.* I tell thee again, it cannot be many hours since I first fell into a slumber.

It may well seem so, answered Cadiga, buried as your senses have been in forgetfulness, and every faculty consigned to oblivion, that the interval of time so past must be quite annihilated; yet it is most certain that you have slept as long as I tell you.

Nourjahad upon this examined the faces of the old women one after the other, but finding them so totally different from what they once were, he swore that he did not believe a word they said. Thou Cadiga! said he, the black-browed Cadiga, whose enchanting smiles beguiled all hearts; thou art wonderously like her I confess!

Yet that I am that identical fair one, answered she, I shall be able to convince you, from a remarkable signature which I bear on my bosom, and which still remains, though the rest of my person is so entirely changed.

Saying this, she uncovered her breast, on which the figure of a rose-bud was delineated by the hand of nature. Nourjahad well remembered the mark; he had once thought it a beauty, and made it the subject of an amorous sonnet, when the bosom of the fair Cadiga was as white and as smooth as alabaster.

Convinced by this proof, that these women were really what they pretended to be, Nourjahad could not conceal his vexation. By the Temple of Mecca,* said he, this genius of mine is no better than he should be, and I begin to suspect he is little less than an evil spirit, or he could not thus take delight in persecuting me for nothing.

Ah, my lord, said Cadiga, I am not ignorant of the strange fate by which your life is governed. Hasem, your faithful Hasem, communicated the secret to me with his dying breath. Is Hasem dead, cried Nourjahad? He is, my lord, answered Cadiga, and so is the worthy Zamgrad. What is become of my son, said Nourjahad? I hope he has not shared the same fate. It were better that he had, replied Cadiga, for it is now some five and twenty years since he ran away from the governor in whose hands the wise Hasem had placed him for his education; and having in vain endeavoured to prevail on that honest man to bury you, that giving out you were deceased, he might take possession of all your wealth, finding he could not succeed in his unnatural design, he took an opportunity of breaking open your cabinet, and securing all the treasure he could find, stole secretly away, and has never been heard of since.

Ungrateful viper! exclaimed Nourjahad; and thou cruel genius, thus to imbitter a life, which was thy own voluntary gift; for thou camest to me unasked.

Had not, proceeded Cadiga, myself and the rest of your women consented to give up all our jewels to Hasem, who turned them into money, we must long ere this have been reduced to want; for your unworthy son stripped you of all your wealth; but Hasem conducted every thing with the same regularity and care as if you had been awake, discharging such of your domestics as he thought unnecessary, and replacing such as died in your service; and it is not many days since the good old man was himself summoned away by the angel of death.

Tell me, said Nourjahad, does Schemzeddin still live?

He does, replied Cadiga, but bending under the weight of age and infirmities, he is become so intolerably peevish that no one dares speak to him. Indeed he is at times so fantastical and perverse, that it is secretly whispered he is not perfectly in his senses. It may very well be, said Nourjahad, that he is doating by this time, for he cannot be much less than seventy years old. The genius has in this article been faithful to his promise; for I, though nearly of the same age, find myself as vigorous and healthy as ever, but I give him little thanks for this, seeing he has defrauded me of such an unconscionable portion of my life.

My lord, said Cadiga, there is one circumstance which may in some measure reconcile you to what has already happened. You know, by the severity of the sultan, you have been the greatest part of your days a prisoner; which condition, however it might have been alleviated by the pleasures which surrounded you, must nevertheless have by this time grown exceedingly irksome, had you all the while been sensible of your restraint; and you would not probably have been so palled with the repetition of the same enjoyments, that I know not whether your good genius, has not, instead of cruelty, shewn an extreme indulgence, in rendering you for such a number of years unconscious of your misfortune; especially as the sultan, by what I learnt from Hasem, has, notwithstanding the length of time since he first deprived you of your liberty, never reversed the barbarous sentence.

What thou hast said, has some colour, replied Nourjahad, and I am very much inclined to think thou hast hit upon the truth. Sage Cadiga, pursued he, what thou hast lost in beauty, thou hast gained in wisdom; and though I can no longer regard thee with tenderness, I will still retain thee in my service, and constitute thee governess over my female slaves; for I must have my seraglio supplied with a new race of beauties. For the rest of those hags, as I do not know of any thing they are now good for, I desire to see them no more. Be gone, said he to them, I shall give orders to Cadiga concerning you.

When Nourjahad was left alone, he began seriously to reflect on his condition. How unhappy I am, said he, thus to find myself at once deprived of every thing that was dear to me; my two faithful friends, Hasem and Zamgrad, all the blooming beauties of my seraglio, who used to delight my eyes; but above all, my son, whose ingratitude and cruelty pierces me more deeply than all my other losses; and that rigid spirit who presides over my life, to take advantage of those hours of insensibility, to deprive me of all my comforts! Yet why do I reproach my protector for that? the same ills might have befallen me, had the progress of my life been conducted by the common laws of nature. I must have seen the death of my friends, and they might possibly have been snatched from me in a manner equally sudden and surprising as their loss now appears.

My women, had I seen them every day, must necessarily

by this time have grown old and disgustful to me; and I should certainly before now, have discarded two or three generations of beauties. My son too, would, in his heart, have been the same thankless and perfidious creature that he has now shewn himself, had the eye of watchful authority been constantly open on his conduct; and there is only this difference perhaps, between me and every other parent, that I have lived to see my offspring trampling on filial duty, riotously seizing on my wealth, leaving my family to poverty, and not so much as bestowing a grateful thought on him who gave him being, and by whose spoils he is enriched; whilst other fathers, deceived by a specious outside, in the full persuasion of the piety, justice, and affection of their children, have descended to the grave in peace, whilst their heirs, with as little remorse as my graceless child, have laughed at their memories.

I see it is in vain, proceeded he, to escape the miseries that are allotted to human life. Fool that I was to subject myself to them more by ten thousand fold than any other can possibly experience! But stop, Nourjahad, how weak are thy complaints? thou knowest the conditions of thy existence, and that thou must of necessity behold the decay and dissolution of every thing that is mortal; take comfort then, and do not imbitter thy days by melancholy reflections, but resolve for the future to let no events disturb thy peace, seize every fleeting joy as it passes, and let variety be thy heaven, for thou seest there is nothing permanent.

As Nourjahad was never used, but on occasions of distress, to make use of his reason or philosophy, he no sooner found an alleviation of the evil, than he put them both to flight, as impertinent intruders. He did not therefore long disturb himself with disagreeable reflections, but resolved as soon as possible to return to those pleasures which he thought constituted the felicity of man's life.

He gave himself but little concern about those treasures of which his son had robbed him, knowing he had an inexhaustible fund of wealth, of which, agreeably to the genius's promise, he could not be deprived.

From Cadiga he learnt that his house at Ormuz was in the same condition he had left it; Hasem having taken care to place a diligent and faithful servant there, on whom he might rely with equal security as on himself; and he had the farther precaution, added Cadiga, not long before his death, to solicit, through Zamgrad's means, the sultan's permission for your return thither. This, said he, may be necessary in case our lord awakes before Schemzeddin's decease, and should have a desire to quit this place, he may do it without the trouble of a fresh application.

And has the sultan granted this, cried Nourjahad?

He has, answered Cadiga, as a matter of great indulgence: for having, as he said, heard that your profusion was unbounded, finding there were no hopes of reclaiming you, he had determined to confine you for the remainder of your life, with this liberty however, that you might make choice either of this palace or your house at Ormuz for your prison.

Fool, cried Nourjahad, he little imagines how impotent are his threats, when he speaks of confining me for life! I would however *he* were dead, that I might be rid of this irksome restraint; but it cannot last much longer, for the days of Schemzeddin must needs draw towards a period. I will not, mean while, bestow any farther thought on him, but avail myself of that liberty which he has allowed me, and return to Ormuz; for I am weary of this solitude, seeing I have lost every thing that could render my retirement agreeable.

Do thou, said he, see that every thing is prepared for my reception. I would have my seraglio filled once more, otherwise my house, when I enter it, will appear a desert to me, and I shall be at a loss how to divert the tedious hours which may yet remain of my confinement. I will depend on thy experience and skill in beauty, to make choice of such

virgins, as you think will well supply the place of those I
have lost.

I have a friend, said Cadiga, a merchant, who deals in
female slaves; and he has always such a number, that it will
be easy to select from amongst them some whose charms
cannot fail to please you. I will order him to repair to your
house, and bring with him a collection of the rarest beauties
he has in his possession; you may then chuse for yourself.

Be it so, said Nourjahad, I leave the conduct of every
thing to thee; if I approve of the damsels, I shall not scruple
at any price for their purchase.

The day being come for his return to Ormuz, full of
pleasing eagerness to behold the divine creatures which he
was told waited his arrival, he set out with a splendid
equipage, but had the mortification to behold his chariot
surrounded by a party of the sultan's guards, with drawn
sabres in their hands, to repress the curiosity of those who
might approach the chariot, to gaze at the person who was
conducted in so unusual a manner.

I could well excuse this part of my retinue, said Nourjahad, as he passed along, but there is no resisting the
commands of this whimsical old fellow Schemzeddin. Being
thus conducted to his house, the guards as before posted
themselves round it.

However chagrined Nourjahad was at this circumstance,
he was resolved it should not interrupt his pleasures.

He found the young slaves whom Cadiga had prepared
all waiting his arrival. They were richly cloathed, and
standing together in a row, in a long gallery through which
he was to pass. On his entering, the merchant to whom
they belonged, ordered the women to unvail.

Nourjahad examined them one after the other, but none
of them pleased him. One had features too large, and
another's were too small; the complexion of this was not
brilliant, and the air of that wanted softness; this damsel
was too tall, and the next was ill proportioned.

Dost thou call these beauties, said Nourjahad, angrily? By my life they are a pack of as awkward damsels as ever I beheld.

Surely, my lord, cried the merchant, you do not speak as you think. These young maids are allowed by all good judges to be the most perfect beauties that ever were seen in Persia: The sultan himself has none equal to them in his seraglio.

I tell thee, man, said Nourjahad, they are not worthy even to wait on those of whom I myself was formerly master. I know not that, my lord, answered the merchant, but this I am sure of, that I can have any sum which I shall demand for their purchase. Then thou must carry them to some other market, cried Nourjahad, for to me they appear fit for nothing but slaves.

Cadiga, who was present, now taking Nourjahad aside, said, These, my lord, these damsels are less charming than those of which you were formerly possessed, but the taste for beauty is quite altered since that time: You may assure yourself that none will be offered to your acceptance that will exceed these. Were I and my companions, whom you once so much admired, to be restored to our youth again, we should not now be looked upon; such is the fantastic turn of the age.

If this be so, said Nourjahad, I shall be very unfashionable in my amours; for the present, however, I shall content myself with some of the most tolerable of these maidens, till I have time and opportunity of supplying myself with better.

Saying this, he selected half a dozen of those young slaves, whom he thought the most agreeable, and having paid the merchant what he demanded for them, dismissed the rest.

Nourjahad having now once more established his household, and perceiving that these damsels upon a longer acquaintance were really amiable, expected to find himself

restored to his former contentment and alacrity of spirits.
But in this he was deceived. He was seized with a lassitude
that rendered his days tiresome. The vacancy he found in
his heart was insupportable. Surrounded by new faces, he
saw nobody for whom he could entertain either love or
friendship. This is a comfortless life, would he exclaim to
himself, yet how often, during the date of my existence,
must this situation, melancholy as it is, recur to me. A
friend shall no sooner be endeared to me by long experience
of kindness and fidelity, without which it is impossible I
should regard him; than death will deprive me of him, as it
has already done of Hasem and Zamgrad; and how many
bright eyes am I doomed to see for ever closed, or what is
as mortifying to behold, their faded lustre. There is but one
way, said he, to guard against those evils: I will no more
contract friendships amongst men, nor ever again suffer my
mind to be subdued by female charms. I will confound all
distinction by variety, nor permit one woman to engross
my heart; for I find by sad experience, even after such an
amazing length of time, that the bare idea of my dear
Mandana, inspires me with more tenderness, than ever I
experienced from the fondest blandishments of all the
beauties I have since possessed.

Nourjahad endeavoured to banish those melancholy
thoughts by others more agreeable; but he had no resources
within himself. He had nothing to reflect on, from which
he could derive any satisfaction. My life, said he, appears
like a dream of pleasure, that has passed away without
leaving any substantial effects: and I am even already weary
of it, though in fact, notwithstanding my advanced age, I
have enjoyed it but a short time, dating from that period
whence my immortality commenced.

He tried to read to divert his distempered thoughts; but
from books he could receive no entertainment. If he turned
over the pages of philosophers, moralists, or expounders of
the mysteries of his religion, What have I to do with thy

tedious lessons, or dry precepts, said he? Thou writest to
men like thyself, subject to mortality; thou teachest them
how to live, that they may learn how to die; but what is this
to me? as I am not subject to the latter, thy advice can be
of little use to me in regard to the former.

He had next recourse to the poets; but their works gave
him as little pleasure as the others. Absorbed as he had
been in the grosser pleasures of sense, he had lost those fine
feelings, which constitute that delicate and pleasing percep-
tion we have, of such images, as are addressed to the heart.
He knew the fallacy and even essence of all sensual enjoyments; and to the most warm descriptions of love, and the
most pathetic pictures of grief he was equally insensible.

Poor wretches, said he, on reading a fine elegy written by
a lover on the death of his mistress, doomed as thou wert to
a short span of life, and a narrow circle of enjoyments, thou
magnifiest every thing within thy confined sphere. One
single object having engrossed thy whole heart, and inspired
thee with transports, thou dost immortalize her charms.
Her death (despairing to supply her place) filled thy eyes
with tears, and taught thee to record thy own sorrows with
her praises. I partake not of thy pleasures or thy pains;
none but such as are liable to the same fate can be affected
by thy sentiments.

When he read of the death of heroes and kings, and the
destruction of cities, or the revolution of empires, How
circumscribed, said he, is the knowledge of a paltry historian! Who is at the pains of collecting the scanty materials
which a life of forty or fifty years perhaps affords him, and
then he makes a mighty parade of learning, with the poor
pittance for which he has been drudging all his days. How
infinitely superior will my fund of information be, who
shall myself be an eye-witness to events as extraordinary as
these, and numbered a thousand times over; for doubtless
the same things which have happened, will happen again.
What curiosity can you incite in me, who shall infallibly see

the same chain of causes and effects take place over and over again, in the vast round of eternity.

The accounts of travellers, descriptions of the manners and customs of various countries, and books of geography, afforded him a little more entertainment. All these places, said he, I shall visit in my own proper person, and shall then be able to judge whether these accounts are just.

Whilst he endeavoured to fill up the vacuity he found in his mind, his time was spent at best but in a sort of insipid tranquillity. The voluptuary has no taste for mental pleasures.

He every now and then returned to his former excesses, but he had not the same relish for them as before. Satiety succeeded every enjoyment. In vain did his slaves torture their invention to procure new delights for him. The powers of luxury were exhausted, and his appetites palled with abundance.

He grew peevish, morose, tyrannical; cruelty took possession of his breast; he abused his women and beat his slaves, and seemed to enjoy no satisfaction but that of tormenting others.

In vain did the prudent Cadiga, who had still some little influence over him, expostulate with him on the enormity of his behaviour.

How darest thou, said he, presume to dictate to thy master, or to censure his conduct! To whom am I accountable for my actions? To God and our prophet, answered Cadiga, with a boldness that provoked Nourjahad's wrath. Thou liest, said he, as I am exempt from death, I never can be brought to judgment, what then have I to fear from the resentment, or hope from the favour of the powers whom thou namest?

But hast thou no regard, said Cadiga, for the laws of society, nor pity for the sufferings of thy fellow creatures, whom thou makest to groan every day under thy cruelty?

Foolish woman, said Nourjahad, dost thou talk to me of

laws, who think myself bound by none. Civil and religious laws are so interwoven, that you cannot pluck out a single thread without spoiling the whole texture, and if I cut the woof, thinkest thou that I will spare the weft, when I can do it with impunity? The privilege of immortality which I enjoy, would be bestowed on me to little purpose, if I were to suffer the weak prejudices of religion, in which I am no way concerned, to check me in any of my pursuits. And what can the feeble laws of man do? My life they cannot reach. Yet thou art a prisoner notwithstanding, answered Cadiga. True, replied Nourjahad, but even in my confinements I have surfeited with delights. Schemzeddin's death must soon give me that liberty, which considering the race of uncontrouled freedom I have before me, I do not now think worth attempting. I shall then expatiate freely all over the globe; mean while I tell thee, woman, I am weary of the dull round of reiterated enjoyments which are provided for me; my sensual appetites are cloyed, I have no taste for intellectual pleasures, and I must have recourse to those which gratify the malevolent passions.

Thou art not fit to live, cried Cadiga, with a warmth of which she had cause to repent; for Nourjahad, enraged at her reply, plucked a poniard from his girdle, Go tell thy prophet so, said he, and plunged it into the side of the unfortunate slave, who fell at his feet weltering in blood.

The brutal Nourjahad, so far from being moved with this spectacle, turned from her with indifference, and quitting the chamber, entered the apartments of his women, to whom with barbarous mirth he related what he had done.

Though he had now lost all relish for delicate pleasures, or even for the more gross enjoyments of sense, he nevertheless indulged himself in them to excess; and knowing he was not accountable to any one for the death of his slave, he thought no more of Cadiga; but after a day spent in extravagant debauchery sunk to repose.

But his eyes were opened to a different scene from that

on which he had closed them. He no sooner awoke than he perceived a man sitting at his bed's-foot, who seemed to be plunged in sorrow; he leaned pensively on his arm, holding a handkerchief before his eyes.

What mockery is this, said Nourjahad, didst thou suppose me dead, and art thou come to mourn over me?

Not so, my lord, replied the man, I knew that you still lived; but the sultan is dead, the good Schemzeddin is no more! I am glad of it, replied Nourjahad, I shall now obtain my liberty. Who then is to reign in Ormuz? Doubtless, my lord, answered the man, the prince Schemerzad, the eldest son of Schemzeddin. Thou ravest, cried Nourjahad, Schemzeddin has no son. Pardon me, my lord, said the man, the sultana Nourmahal was delivered of this prince the very hour on which the unfortunate Cadiga died by your hand. Thou art insolent, replied Nourjahad, to mention that circumstance; but if so, we have indeed got a very young successor to the throne. My lord, answered the man, Schemerzad is allowed to be one of the most accomplished and wise young princes in all Persia. That is marvellous, cried Nourjahad, bursting into a fit of laughter, a sultan of four and twenty hours old must needs be wonderously wise and accomplished. Nay, my lord, replied the man, the prince is this day exactly twenty years of age.

(Nourjahad, on hearing this, looked in the face of the man, whom, from his dress, supposing he had been one of his slaves, he had not regarded before, but now perceived he was a stranger.) Twenty years old! cried he, starting up, thou dost not tell me so! Most certain, said the man. Schemzeddin was so far advanced in years before the birth of the prince, that he despaired of ever having a child; yet had the righteous monarch the satisfaction to see his beloved son arrive at manhood, and adorned with such virtues as made him worthy to fill his father's throne. When did the old sultan die, cried Nourjahad? His funeral obsequies were performed last night, answered the man, and

the people of Ormuz have not yet wiped the tears from
their eyes. It should seem then, said Nourjahad, that I have
slept about twenty years! if so, prithee, who art thou? for I
do not remember ever to have seen thy face before.

My name, answered the stranger, is Cozro, and I am the
brother of Cadiga, that faithful creature whom thy ungoverned fury deprived of life. How darest thou mention her
again, cried Nourjahad, art thou not afraid to share the
same fate thyself for thy presumption?

I do not value my life, answered Cozro; having acquitted
myself well of my duty here, I am sure of my reward in
those blessed mansions, where avarice, luxury, cruelty and
pride, can never enter. Strike then, Nourjahad, if thou
darest; dismiss me to endless and uninterrupted joys, and
live thyself a prey to remorse and disappointment, the slave
of passions never to be gratified, and a sport to the
vicissitudes of fortune.

Nourjahad was confounded at the undaunted air with
which Cozro pronounced these words; he trembled with
indignation, but had not courage to strike the unarmed man
who thus insulted him; wherefore, dissembling his anger, I
see, said he, that thou partakest of thy sister Cadiga's spirit;
but answer me, How camest thou hither, and in what
condition are the rest of my family? I will tell thee,
answered Cozro. When Cadiga found herself dying, she
sent for me: I was then a page to one of the emirs of
Schemzeddin's court.* She made me kneel by her bed-side
and take a solemn oath, to perform with fidelity and secrecy
what she should enjoin me. She then told me the secret of
your life, and conjured me to watch and attend you
carefully. I have hitherto, said she, had the conduct of his
house; do you supply my place, and do not let Nourjahad,
when he awakes from his trance, be sensible of the loss of
the unfortunate Cadiga.

She then called in your principal slaves, and delivering to
me in their presence the keys with which you had entrusted

her, she told them they were henceforth to obey me, as they had done her. Tell my lord, said she to me, that I forgive him the death which his cruelty inflicted on a woman who loved him to the latest minute of her life. In pronouncing these words, she expired.

I knew not till then, pursued Cozro, that thou hadst been the murderer of my sister; but she was no sooner dead, than the slaves informed me of the manner of her death. My resentment against thee was proportioned to the horror of thy guilt; and had I thrown myself at the feet of Schemzeddin, and implored justice on thy crimes, neither thy riches nor thy immortality would have availed thee, but thou wouldst have been condemned by a perpetual decree, to have languished out thy wretched existence in a vile dungeon.

And what hindered thee, cried Nourjahad, from pursuing thy revenge, seeing I was not in a condition to resist thee? My reverence for the oath I had taken, answered Cozro, and fear of offending the Almighty!

Nourjahad, at this reply, was struck with a secret awe which he could not repel; he remained silent whilst Cozro proceeded.

I obtained permission of the master whom I served, to leave him, and entered immediately on my new employment; but I found I had undertaken a difficult task. Thou hadst rendered thyself so odious to thy women, that not one of them retained the smallest degree of love or fidelity towards thee. In spite of my vigilance they made thy hated seraglio the scene of their unlawful pleasures; and at length having bribed the eunuchs who guarded them, they all in one night fled from thy detested walls, taking with them the slaves who had assisted them in their purpose. Pernicious spirit, exclaimed Nourjahad, are these the fruits I am to reap from thy fatal indulgence! The rest of your servants, pursued Cozro, I endeavoured to keep within the bounds of their duty. And how didst thou succeed, cried Nourjahad? But ill, replied Cozro; they all declared that nothing could have induced them to stay so long with a master of so capricious and tyrannical a humour, but the luxury and idleness in which thou permittedst them to live; and finding I managed your affairs with œconomy, they one after the other left your house; neither promises nor threats having power to prevent those who stayed longest in thy service, from following the example of the first who deserted thee; so that I alone of all thy numerous household have remained faithful to thee: I, who of all others, had the most reason to abhor thee! But I have now acquitted myself of the trust which was reposed in me, and I leave thee as one condemned to wander in an unknown land, where he is to seek out for new associates, and to endeavour by the power of gold, to bribe that regard from men, which his own worth cannot procure for him.

Unfortunate wretch that I am, cried Nourjahad, pierced to the quick with what he had just been told, what benefit have I hitherto received from my long life, but that of feeling by miserable experience, the ingratitude and frailty of man's nature. How transitory have been all my pleasures! the recollection of them dies on my memory, like the departing colours of the rainbow, which fades under the eye of the beholder, and leaves not a trace behind. Whilst on the other hand, every affliction with which I have been visited, has imprinted a deep and lasting wound on my heart, which not even the hand of time itself has been able to heal.

What have thy misfortunes been, said Cozro, that are not common to all the race of man? Oh, I have had innumerable griefs, said Nourjahad. After a short enjoyment (during my fatal slumbers) the grave robbed me of Mandana, whilst she was yet in the bloom of youth and beauty. I lamented her death, tears and heaviness of heart were my portion for many days. Yet remembering that sorrow would not recall the dead, I suffered myself to be comforted, and sought for consolation in the society of my other women, and the fond and innocent caresses of an infant son, whom Mandana left me. Joy and tranquillity revisited my dwelling, and new pleasures courted my acceptance; but they again eluded my grasp, and in one night (for so it appeared to me) my son like an unnatural viper, forgetting all my tenderness, plundered and deserted me. The two faithful friends in whom I most confided, had closed their eyes for ever; and the beauties of my seraglio, whom I had last beheld fresh and charming as the lillies of the field, I now saw deformed with wrinkles and bending under the infirmities of age.

Yet these afflictions I surmounted; and resolved once more to be happy. And wert thou so, interrupted Cozro? No, replied Nourjahad, the treacherous joys deceived me; yet I still looked forward with hope, but now awake to fresh disappointment. I find myself abandoned by those whose false professions of love had lulled me into security, and I rouse myself like a savage beast in the desert, whose paths are shunned by all the children of men.

Nourjahad could not conclude this speech without a groan, that seemed to rend his heart.

As thou art, said Cozro, exempt from punishment hereafter, dost thou think also to escape the miseries of this life? Mistaken man, know, that the righteous Being, whose ordinances thou defyest, will even here take vengeance on thy crimes. And if thou wilt look back on thy past life, thou wilt find (for I have heard thy story) that every one of those several ills of which thou complainest, were sent as scourges to remind thee of thy duty, and inflicted immediately after the commission of some notorious breach of it.

The death of Mandana was preceded by a brutal fit of drunkenness, by which, contrary to the laws of our prophet, thou sufferedst thyself to be overtaken. Then it was thy good genius, to punish thee, plunged thee into that temporary death, from which thou didst awake to grief and disappointment: But thou madest no use of the admonition, but didst permit thyself to be again swallowed up by intemperance; and not content to tread the ordinary paths of vice, thou turnedst out of the road, to the commission of a crime, to which thou couldst have no temptation, but the pride and licentiousness of thy heart. Thy profanation of our holy religion, in presuming to personate our great prophet, and make thy concubines represent the virgins of paradise, was immediately chastised as it deserved, by a second time depriving thee of those faculties, which thou didst prostitute to such vile purposes.

The ills with which thou foundest thyself surrounded on awaking from thy trance, served to no other purpose than to stir up thy resentment against the power who governed thy life. And instead of reforming thy wickedness, thou soughtest out new ways of rendering thyself still more obnoxious to the wrath of Heaven. In the wantonness of thy cruelty, thou stainedst thy hand in blood; and that same night, were thy eyelids sealed up by the avenging hand of thy watchful genius, and thy depraved senses consigned for twenty years to oblivion! See then, continued Cozro, if a life which is to be a continued round of crimes and punishments in alternate succession, is a gift worthy to be desired by a wise man? for assure thyself, Oh Nourjahad, that by the immutable laws of heaven one is to be a constant concomitant of the other, and that either in this world or the next, vice will meet its just reward.

Alas, replied Nourjahad, thou hast awakened in me a remorse of which I was never sensible before; I look back with shame on the detested use I have made of those extraordinary gifts vouchsafed me by my guardian spirit.

What shall I do, Oh Cozro, to expiate the offences I have committed? For though I have no dread of punishment hereafter, yet does that ætherial spark within, inspire me with such horror for my former crimes, that all the vain delights which this world can afford me, will not restore my mind to peace, till by a series of good actions I have atoned for my past offences.

If thou art sincere in thy resolutions, replied Cozro, the means, thou knowest, are amply in thy power. Thy riches will enable thee to diffuse blessings amongst mankind, and thou wilt find more true luxury in that, than in all the gratifications wherewith thou hast indulged thy appetites.

It shall be so, replied Nourjahad; my treasures shall be open to thee, thou venerable old man, and do thou make it thy business to find out proper objects, whereon charity and benevolence may exert their utmost powers.

Enquire out every family in Ormuz whom calamity hath overtaken, and provided they did not bring on their distresses by their own wilful misconduct, restore them to prosperity. Seek out the helpless and the innocent; and by a timely supply of their wants, secure them against the attacks of poverty, or temptations of vice. Search for such as you think have talents which will render them useful to society; but who, for want of the goods of fortune, are condemned to obscurity; relieve their necessities, and enable them to answer the purposes for which nature designed them. Find out merit wherever it lies concealed, whether with-held from the light by diffidence, chained down and clogged by adversity, obscured by malice, or overborn by power; lift it up from the dust, and let it shine conspicuous to the world.

Glorious talk! cried Cozro; happy am I in being the chosen instrument of Nourjahad's bounty, and still more happy shall he be in seeing the accomplishment of his good designs.

We must not stop here, said Nourjahad; I will have hospitals built for the reception of the aged and the sick; and my tables shall be spread for the refreshment of the weary traveller. No virtuous action shall pass by me unrewarded, and no breach of the laws of temperance, justice, or mercy, shall escape unreproved. My own example, so far as it can influence, shall henceforth countenance the one, and discourage the other.

Blessed be the purpose of thy heart, said Cozro, and prosperous be the days of thy life!

Nourjahad now found the anxiety under which he had but a little before laboured, exceedingly relieved. My mind, said he, is much more at ease than it was; let us not delay to put our design in execution. I will lead you to the place where my treasure is concealed, which I never yet discovered to any one. Saying this, he took Cozro by the hand, and conducted him to the cave.

Thou seest here, said he, riches which can never be exhausted; thou mayest perceive that I have not yet sunk a third part of one of these urns which contain my wealth; yet have I with monstrous profusion lavished away immense sums. Five more such urns as these are yet untouched. Those six which thou seest on the right hand, contain wedges of the finest gold, which must be equal in value to the others. These six, which are ranged on the left, are filled with precious stones, whose worth must be inestimable: The wealth of Ormuz would not purchase a single handful. Judge then, my friend, if I need be sparing in my liberality.

Cozro expressed his astonishment at the sight of these wonders. If thou wouldst be advised by me, said he, thou wouldst secretly remove from Ormuz, and carry thy treasures with thee. Thou mayest deposit part of them in each of the different countries through which thou passest in thy progress all over the earth. By this means thou mayest have it in thy power to distribute with more ease thy bounty wherever thou goest; and be always provided with riches in what part soever of the world thou shalt chuse for a time to take up thy residence. Thy long abode in this city will draw observations on thee sooner or later; and thy person's not having undergone any change from length of time, will bring on thee the suspicion of magic; for tradition will not fail to inform posterity of thy strange history.

You counsel well, replied Nourjahad; as I am now at liberty, I will retire from Ormuz. You, my dear Cozro, shall accompany me; your prudent counsel shall be my guide; and when I shall be deprived of you by death, I will still endeavour to follow your wise precepts.

Come, continued he, I am in haste to enter on my new course of life, let us both go into the city and try to find out proper objects on which to exert our charity. I shall pass without observation, and unknown, as few of my contemporaries can now be living, and I will not leave the country which gave me birth, without first making it feel the effects of that beneficence which thou hast awakened in my heart.

Deserving of praise as thou art, said Cozro, thou for the present must suppress thy ardor to do good; for though by the death of Schemzeddin thou art no longer a prisoner, thou art not nevertheless yet at liberty to leave thy house. Why not? answered Nourjahad, who is there now to prevent me?

The young sultan, replied Cozro, deeply afflicted for the death of his father, and out of a pious regard to his memory, has given strict commandment, that all his subjects should observe a solemn mourning for him, during the space of twenty days;* in which time all the shops, and places of public resort (except the mosques) are to be shut up, and no business of any kind transacted; nor are any persons to be seen in the streets, excepting those who visit the sick, and the slaves who must necessarily be employed to carry provisions, on pain of the sultan's heavy displeasure.

This edict was published yesterday, and the people of Ormuz all love the memory of Schemzeddin, and the person of their present sultan too well, not to pay an exact obedience to it.

If so, said Nourjahad, I will not by my example encourage others to infringe their duty; yet as the relieving of the

poor is in itself meritorious, I would not wish to be with-
held from doing it so long as twenty days; How many
virtuous people may be during that time pining for want!
more especially as this prohibition must cut off all intercourse between man and man, and deprive many poor
wretches of the charitable succour they might otherwise
receive. I think therefore that thou, Cozro, in thy slave's
habit,* mayst go forth unsuspected; and by privately seeking out, and alleviating the miseries of our fellow citizens,
do an act of more real benefit, than can result from the
strictest conformity to this pageant of sorrow, which many
in their hearts I am sure must condemn.

Cozro approving of these sentiments, readily agreed to
the expedient, and taking a large purse of gold with him to
distribute as occasion might serve, immediately set out in
order to execute his lord's commands.

Nourjahad now entered on a total reformation in his way
of living. He rose at day break, and spent the morning in
study or meditation. Luxury and intemperance were banished from his board; his table was spread with the plainest
dishes, and he wholly abstained from excess in wine. His
slumbers were sweet, and he found his health more
vigorous.

I will no more, said he, enslave myself to the power of
beauty. I have lived to see the decay of a whole seraglio of
the fairest faces in Persia, and have sighed for the ingratitude of the next generation that succeeded them. I will not
then seek out for those destroyers of my quiet, for whose
death or infidelity I must for ever complain. Mandana was
the only woman who ever really deserved my love; could I
recal her from the grave, and endue her with the same
privilege of which I am myself possessed, I would confine
myself to her arms alone; but since that is impossible, I will
devote myself to the charms of virtue, which of all things
she most resembled.

Whilst Nourjahad was thus resolving to correct the errors

of his past life, his virtue was not merely in speculation. He never laid him down to rest, without the satisfaction of having made some one the better for him. Cozro, who constantly spent the day in enquiring out and relieving the distressed, failed not to return every night to give an account of his charitable mission, and to infuse into his master's bosom, the (till now unfelt) joy which springs from righteous deeds.

The heart of Nourjahad was expanded, and glowed with compassion for those sufferings which Cozro feelingly described as the lot of so many of his fellow creatures. As charity and benevolence rose in his breast, he found his pride subside. He was conscious of his own unworthiness. He kneeled, he prayed, he humbled himself before the Almighty, and returned thanks to God for enabling him to succour the unfortunate.

In this happy frame of mind he continued for eighteen days; there wanted but two more to the expiration of the mourning for the sultan, when Nourjahad was to be at full liberty to pursue in his own person the dictates of his reformed, and now truly generous and benevolent heart.

He was sitting alone in his apartment, waiting the arrival of Cozro, in the pleasing expectation of receiving some fresh opportunity of doing good. The hour of his usual return was already past, and Nourjahad began to fear some accident had happened to him; but he little knew that a black cloud hung over him, which was ready to pour down all its malignity on his own head.

As he mused on what might be the occasion of Cozro's long stay, he heard a loud knocking at his door. It was immediately opened by one of his slaves, and a man, who by his habit he knew to be one of the cady's officers,* rudely entered his chamber.

How comes it, said the stranger, that thou hast had the temerity, in contempt of our sovereign lord's commands, to employ thy emissary about the city at a time when thou knowest that so strict an injunction has been laid on all people to keep within their houses, none being permitted to stir abroad but for the absolute necessities of life, or in cases of imminent danger?

Far be it from me, replied Nourjahad, to disobey our mighty sultan's orders; but I understood that slaves had permission to go unquestioned on their master's business. And what business, answered the man, can thy slave have from morning to night in so many different quarters of the city?

Nourjahad, who did not care to be himself the trumpeter of his own good deeds, hesitated to give an answer.

Ha, ha, cried the stranger, I see plainly there is something dangerous in thy mystery, and that the money which thy slave has been distributing amongst such a variety of people, is for a purpose very different from that which he pretends. A likely matter it is indeed that a private man should bestow in charity such sums as Cozro acknowledges he has within these few days distributed!

Yet nothing is more certain, replied Nourjahad, than that Cozro has spoke the truth. We shall see that, replied the officer, in a tone of insolence; Cozro is already in prison, and my orders are to conduct thee to him.

Nourjahad, exceedingly troubled at hearing this, replied, He was ready to go with him; and the officer led him out of his house.

It was now late at night; they passed along the streets without meeting any one, and soon reached the place wherein Cozro was confined. It was the prison where such persons were shut up as were accused of treason against the state.

Here he found the unfortunate Cozro in a dungeon. Alas, cried he, as soon as his master entered, why do I see thee here? Say rather, my dear Cozro, replied Nourjahad, what strange fatality has brought *thee* to this dismal place?

I can give no other account, answered Cozro, but that in

returning home this night, I was seized on in the street by some of those soldiers who were employed to patrol about the city, to see that the sultan's orders were punctually observed; and being questioned concerning my business, I told them that I had been relieving the wants of indigent people, and saving even from perishing, some poor wretches who had not wherewithal to buy food.

That is an idle errand, replied one of them, and might have been deferred till the term of mourning was expired; however, if you will give me a piece of gold, I will let you pass for this time, otherwise both you and your employer may happen to repent of having transgressed the sultan's commands. I made no scruple, pursued Cozro, to take out my purse, in which there were ten sequins* left. I gave one of them to the soldier, but the rapacious wretches seeing I had more money, were not content with this, but insisted on my giving the whole amongst them. I refused; some angry words ensued; one of the miscreants struck me, and I returned the blow. Enraged at this, they hurried me before the cady, to whom they accused me of having disobeyed the edict, and assaulted the sultan's officers in the discharge of their duty. I was not heard in my defence, having four witnesses against me, but was immediately dragged to this horrid prison; and the sultan himself, they say, is to take cognizance of my offence.

Oh, Heaven, cried Nourjahad, to what mischiefs does not the love of gold expose us! See, my friend, into what misfortunes thou art plunged by the sordid avarice of those vile soldiers. But why, why didst thou hesitate to give up that paltry sum which thou hadst in thy purse, to obtain thy liberty? I do not repent what I have done, answered Cozro, and shall contentedly suffer the penalty I have incurred, since it was in so good a cause.

If the sultan is just, replied Nourjahad, the punishment ought only to fall on me, who alone am guilty, since what thou didst was by my command.

Here the officer who had conducted Nourjahad to prison, and who was present at this discourse, interposed, and addressing himself to Nourjahad, Thou hast not as yet been accused to the sultan, said he, and it is not too late to extricate even thy slave from this troublesome affair; it is but making a handsome present to the cady, and I will undertake this matter will go no farther. I am willing to do so, replied Nourjahad, eagerly; name your demand, and you shall have it. Provided I am allowed to go home to my own house, I will fetch the money; and if you are afraid of my escaping, you yourself may bear me company.

I will not consent to it, replied Cozro; neither liberty nor life are worth purchasing on base conditions. I will submit my cause to Schemerzad's justice; the cause of uprightness and truth; my own innocence shall be my support, and I will dare the worst that fraud and malice can suggest against me.

In vain did Nourjahad urge him to accept the profered terms; he remained inflexible to all the arguments he could use to persuade him; wherefore, finding him determined, he was obliged to desist; and Cozro, after passing the remainder of the night in quiet and profound sleep, though without any other bed than the bare earth, was at dawn of day called forth to appear before the sultan.

The reflections Nourjahad made on the resolute behaviour of Cozro, served not a little to fortify his mind. How noble must this man's soul be, said he, which sets him thus above the reach of adversity? and with what contempt he looks down on the glorious prospects he has before him, when put in the balance with his integrity. Surely it is not in this life he places his happiness, since he is so ready to forego the pleasures he might enjoy with me, in that participation of wealth and liberty which I have promised him. How superior is my servant to me, who but for his example, should now sink under my fears; but he has resources which I have not. Alas, why did I barter my hopes of paradise for the vain, the transitory, the fallacious joys which this vile world bestows! Already I have tried them; what do they inspire but satiety and disgust. I never experienced true contentment, but during the time, short as it is, since I abjured those follies in which I once delighted: And I am now persuaded, that after having past a few, a very few years more in the enjoyment of such gratifications as I have not yet had an opportunity of tasting, that I shall grow even weary of the light, and wish to be dismissed to that place, where we are told no sorrows can approach.

Nourjahad was buried in these reflections, when he was roused by the return of Cozro. The glimmering light which a lamp afforded, struck full on the face of his friend (for he no longer considered him as a servant) and he rejoiced to see Cozro's chearful countenance, by which he judged that he had nothing to fear.

I am come, said Cozro, approaching Nourjahad, and kissing his hand, to bid thee adieu, for from this day, we are to be for ever divided! It is that thought only which makes our separation grievous: Had I hopes of ever beholding thy face in the mansions of light, I should go to death with the same alacrity with which I close my eyes in slumber.

Good Heaven, cried Nourjahad, doest thou talk of death? Can it be, is it possible that thy life is in danger?

What is the life, about which thou art anxious? replied Cozro; our being here is but a shadow; that only is real existence which the blessed enjoy after their short travel here. And know, Oh Nourjahad, I would not yield up my expectations of the humblest place in paradise for the sovereign rule of the whole earth, though my days were to be extended to the date of thy life, and every wish of my soul gratified to the utmost. Think then, with how little reluctance I shall leave a world, wherein I am sure of meeting nothing but oppression, treachery, and disappointment, where mercy is construed into treason, and charity is called sedition!

And art thou then doomed to die? said Nourjahad, pale and trembling at the thought, though convinced it was a predicament in which he could never stand.

I am, answered Cozro, my offence was found capital. Disobedience to the sultan's edict alone, incurred a heavy punishment; but my crime was, by the malice of my accusers, so highly aggravated, that the penalty became death. They charged me with having distributed money for evil purposes, amongst persons disaffected to the state, and with having beat and abused those officers who first detected me. In vain did I offer all the pleas that truth could suggest; my enemies, exasperated at losing the sum which they hoped to have extorted from you, swore to the facts of which I was accused, and the rigid sultan condemned me to death. What thy fate is to be, I know not; but since it is thy misfortune to be doomed to perpetual life, better purchase thy freedom on any terms, than be condemned to languish for years in a prison, for such probably will be thy lot.

Oh that I could die with thee! said Nourjahad, miserable that I am, thus to be deprived of thy counsel and friendship, at a time when I so much stood in need of them; but wherefore, my friend, why should we submit to the tyranny of the sultan? though thou art condemned, there may yet be found means to deliver thee. The keeper of the prison will gladly set a price on thy liberty; a hundred thousand pieces of gold shall be thy ransom; and I shall think myself rich by the purchase! And what is to become of thee, replied Cozro? I will buy my own freedom at the same rate, answered Nourjahad, and we will both fly from Ormuz together. And leave your treasures behind you, cried Cozro, for it will be impossible to convey from hence such a vast mass of riches without discovery.

I value them no longer, said Nourjahad; they can never

yield me any permanent enjoyment. The saving thy life is the only good turn I now expect from them. That once accomplished, I shall desire to retain no more of them than what will support me above want, and I will leave the rest to be for ever hid in the bosom of the earth, where they now lie, that they may never more become a snare to others as they have been to me.

Praised be our holy prophet, said Cozro, that has at length endued the heart of Nourjahad with wisdom. Pursue the purposes of thy soul; effect thy own freedom as soon as possible, since no comfort can visit thee in the gloom of this frightful prison; but tempt not Cozro back to a life which he despises. I tell thee again, there is nothing in this world to be put in competition with the glories I have in prospect in that state to which I am now hastening. Why then, Nourjahad, wouldst thou retard my felicity, or wish me to hazard, for the sake of delusive pleasures, those transcendent joys which await the virtuous.

The energy with which Cozro delivered himself, pierced Nourjahad to the inmost soul. A holy ardor was kindled in his breast, which he had never felt before; he found his faculties enlarged, his mind was transported above this world; he felt as it were unimbodied, and an involuntary adjuration burst from his lips. 'Oh, holy prophet,' said he, 'take, take back the gift, that I in the ignorance and presumption of my heart so vainly sought, and which too late I find a punishment instead of a blessing! I contemn riches, and for ever cast them from me; suffer me then to yield up my life; for there can be no true happiness but in beholding thee, Oh Mahomet, face to face, in the never-fading fields of paradise!'

Saying this, he prostrated himself on the ground, and continued for some time in mental prayer.

Cozro observed an awful silence whilst he continued in this posture. When Nourjahad arose from the earth, May our great prophet, said Cozro, hear your prayers; and were he even now to grant them, all the favours he has already bestowed on you would be poor and contemptible to this last best boon. Farewel, said he, I must now leave thee, I was only permitted to come and bid thee adieu. May the Supreme grant thy petition, then shall we again meet in the mansions of happy spirits. Nourjahad embraced him, and Cozro withdrew.

Being now left at liberty to his own thoughts, he made bitter reflections on the strangeness of his fate. Fool, fool that I was, cried he aloud, beating his breast, to prefer so rash, so impious a petition to the prophet, as to desire the everlasting laws of nature to be overturned, to gratify my mad luxurious wishes. I thought the life of man too short for the enjoyment of those various and unbounded pleasures which wealth could procure; but it is long since I have found my error. Well did my guardian spirit say I should repent of the gift I had implored, when it should be too late. I do indeed repent; but Oh, thou benign intelligence, if thou hast remaining any favour for thy inconsiderate unhappy charge, descend once more to my relief, and if possible restore me to that state, for which I was designed by my creator; a poor mortal, liable to, and now longing for the friendly stroke of death.

He had scarce pronounced these words, when his prison doors flew open; a refulgent light flashed in, which illuminated the whole dungeon, and he beheld his guardian genius standing before him, exactly as he had appeared to him before. Thy prayers are heard, said he, Oh son of frailty, and thy penitence is accepted in the sight of the Most High. I am sent down again by our prophet to reassume that gift which thou art now satisfied must make thee miserable. Yet examine thy heart once more before I pronounce thy irrevocable doom; say, art thou willing again to become subject to the common lot of mortals?

Most willing, replied Nourjahad; yet I wonder not, my seraphic guide, that thou shouldst doubt the stability of my mind; but in this last purpose of it I am sure I shall remain unshaken.

If so, replied the shining vision, thy guardian angel consigns thee to the arms of death, with much more joy than he conferred on thee riches and immortality. Thou hast nothing more to do, than to prostrate thyself with thy face to the earth. Remain this evening in fervent prayer, and await what shall befal thee to-morrow.

Nourjahad made no reply, but falling with his face to the ground, he soon found the dungeon restored to its former gloom, the light and the guardian spirit vanishing together in an instant.

He continued in devout prayer till night; when the keeper of the prison entered his dungeon to bring him some refreshment.

The sultan, said he, purposes to examine you to-morrow, and much I fear you will have as rigorous a sentence passed on you, as that which has been already executed on Cozro. Is he then dead, cried Nourjahad, mournfully? He is, replied the keeper; it is but an hour since I saw him deprived of breath; but he received the blow with such an heroic firmness, that thou wouldst have thought he rather enjoyed a triumph, than suffered an ignominious death.

Happy, happy Cozro! cried Nourjahad; thou art now beyond the reach of misfortune, whilst I, perhaps, may be doomed to sustain for years a wretched life.

Thy life, said the keeper, may be nearer a period than thou art aware of. The sultan is covetous, and surrounded by needy favourites, whom the report of your immense wealth has made eager for your destruction; for you cannot be ignorant, that should you die, involved as it is said you are, in Cozro's guilt, your treasures would be confiscated to the sultan. From this circumstance I have heard it whispered, your head is already devoted; and this perhaps was the true cause of Cozro's death, and will give the better colour to yours. It is not, however, added he, even yet too late to prevent the danger; had not your slave been obstinate, he might now have been alive, and out of the reach of harm. You have the same means of preservation in regard to your own person, still in your power; and if you will make it worth my while to run the risque, I will this night set you at liberty.

And dost thou think, said Nourjahad, that I have profited so little by the example of my noble friend, as to accept of thy offer, sordid and treacherous as thou art? If thou art base enough to betray thy trust for gold, know that the mind of Nourjahad is above receiving a favour from such a wretch. As for my wealth, let the sultan take it; my only wish is to part with that and my life also.

That wish may speedily be accomplished, said the keeper, in an angry tone, and to-morrow perhaps you may repent of your folly, when you find yourself condemned to follow your noble friend to the other world. Nourjahad made no reply; and the keeper sullenly departed.

Nourjahad spent the night in prayers and meditation; he found peace and tranquillity restored to his breast, and perfectly resigned to the will of the prophet, he waited the event of the next day with the utmost composure.

In the morning the keeper of the prison entered to him. Follow me, said he; thou art going to appear before the sultan, who himself is to be thy judge; a rigorous one thou wilt find him, but thy folly be on thy own head, who didst proudly refuse the profer I made thee of liberty and life.

Lead on, said Nourjahad, it is not for such men as thou art, to censure a conduct, to which thou dost not know the motive.

He was now carried out of the dungeon, and ordered to ascend a chariot, in which the captain of the sultan's guards was already placed, to receive his prisoner. The chariot was surrounded by soldiers; and in this manner he was conducted to the presence of the sultan.

Schemerzad was seated on a throne, in the hall of his

palace, wherein he was used to distribute justice. The emirs, and great officers of his court, were standing round him.

Nourjahad stood before him with his eyes bent to the ground; and however awed he might be at the presence of his royal master, and the august assembly which surrounded him, yet the dignity of conscious innocence, and the perfect reliance he had on the Supreme Judge of *his* judge, rendered him superior to every thing. His deportment was modest and respectful, yet did he discover no symptom of fear.

The sultan made a sign for every one present to withdraw, but one person who stood on the lower step of his throne, and whom Nourjahad judged to be his prime visier.*

What hast thou to say, presumptuous man, said Schemerzad, in a stern voice, what excuse canst thou offer for daring, in contempt of my edict, to employ thy agent (during the time set apart for mourning) in going about the city from day to day; ostentatiously displaying thy ill-timed liberality amongst my subjects; endeavouring, as I am informed, to conciliate their affections, for purposes dangerous to me, and the safety of my crown. What hast thou to offer in answer to this charge?

Nourjahad prostrated himself to the ground. Mighty sultan, said he, I have nothing to offer in extenuation of my fault, with regard to the first part of the charge. I acknowlege that I distributed money amongst your majesty's subjects, and that at a time too when every act (but those of absolute necessity) was interdicted. I offer not to palliate this breach of my duty.—

Audacious wretch, interrupted the sultan, to what end was thy profusion employed?

To obtain a blessing from heaven, answered Nourjahad; and by relieving the wants and afflictions of others, to make some atonement for my own riotous and intemperate abuse of that wealth, which ought to have been employed to better purposes.

Wouldst thou persuade me then, cried Schemerzad, that charity was thy motive! It was, illustrious sultan, replied Nourjahad; I have spoke the truth, and to convince your majesty that I have no sinister designs against the ever sacred person of my sovereign, I will now voluntarily yield up that treasure to thee, which had I been vile enough to have so employed, would have bought the fidelity of more than half thy subjects, though every man of them had stood near the heart, and throne of Schemerzad.

The undaunted manner in which Nourjahad spoke these words, made Schemerzad shake on his imperial seat; but quickly reassuming the majesty of his station, Do then as thou hast spoken, said he, and I will believe thee.

If your majesty will permit me, said Nourjahad, to go to my house, and will send a proper person with me, I will deliver up into his hands all my wealth, requesting no more than will supply my wants so long as heaven permits me to live.

I will not trust thee out of my sight, said Schemerzad; thou mayest as well instruct some one in my presence where to find the riches of which I hear thou art possessed, and I will send for them.

Nourjahad then informed the sultan of the subterraneous cave in his garden; and delivering him the key, told him he would there find all the wealth of which he was master.

Schemerzad immediately dispatched his visier, ordering him to have the riches he should find, immediately conveyed to his treasury. He then commanded Nourjahad to retire into a saloon,* that was separated from the hall only by a curtain, and there wait the return of the visier; before whom, the sultan said he had some farther questions to put to him.

As the gardens of Nourjahad joined to those belonging to the royal palace, the visier was not long in going and returning. Nourjahad heard him talk to Schemerzad, and straight he was called on to come forth, and stand before the sultan: But Schemerzad now accosted him in a voice like thunder. Perfidious and insolent slave, said he, art thou not afraid of instant death falling on thee, for daring thus to falsify before thy sovereign lord and master? Say, before thou art cut off by torture from the face of the earth, where thou hast concealed thy wealth! for well thou knowest, there is nothing contained in that cave, which thou pretendest with so much care to lock up.

Nothing! replied Nourjahad, in amazement. By the head of our prophet, when I last was there, it contained more than would purchase thy whole empire a thousand times over. It was but the very day on which I was dragged to prison, that I saw it; the key has never since been out of my pocket; who then could possibly have conveyed away my treasure?

As Nourjahad applied himself to the visier whilst he spoke, that minister thinking himself reflected on by his words, replied scornfully, Thou thinkest perhaps it is I who have robbed thee, and that I have framed this story to deceive the sultan, and ruin thee. I do not say so, answered Nourjahad; but this I am sure of, that no human being but thyself knew where to find my treasure. Some dæmon, perhaps, replied the visier, with an air of contempt, has removed it thence.

Nourjahad now recollecting suddenly, that his guardian spirit had probably reclaimed this, as well as the other gift, replied coolly, It is not at all unlikely; a certain genius, who watches over my motions, has undoubtedly carried away my wealth.

Do not think, said the sultan, that affecting to be out of thy senses, shall preserve thee from my wrath.

Your majesty, said the visier, had best order that his head be instantly struck off, for daring to impose on your credulity, and abuse your clemency in suffering him to outlive that slave, who obstinately persisted in refusing to discover his master's riches.

Did Cozro do so? cried Nourjahad: He did, answered the visier; but we will see whether thou wilt persevere in the denial, and to the latest minute of thy life preserve the firmness of thy slave.

And who is it that thou callest a slave, thou minister of cruelty? said Nourjahad boldly: The soul of Cozro raised him infinitely more above thee, than the rank of the sultan of Persia lifts him above the meanest of his subjects.—My lord, pursued he, throwing himself at Schemerzad's feet, I have no other plea to offer for my life; I call Heaven to witness I have spoken nothing but the truth; the severest tortures you can inflict on me will extort no more. I was willing to make a voluntary sacrifice of my riches: I am now as ready to yield my life.

Art thou not then afraid to die? said Schemerzad.

No, mighty sultan, answered Nourjahad, I look upon death to a virtuous man, as the greatest good the Almighty can bestow!

The sultan, instead of making any reply, clapped his hands; and Nourjahad supposing it was a signal to have him seized and carried to execution, rose up, and stood with an intrepidity in his looks, that shewed how little he was affected with the near prospect of death.

But instead of the slaves whom he expected to see coming to lay hold on him, he beheld standing close to the throne of Schemerzad, his guardian genius, just in the same celestial form in which he had twice before appeared to him!

Awed and amazed, Nourjahad started back, and gazed at the heavenly vision. Not daring to trust his senses, he remained mute, and motionless, for some minutes; but he was roused from his deep attention, by a loud burst of laughter, which broke at once from the sultan, the visier, and the guardian genius.

This new and extraordinary incident threw Nourjahad into fresh astonishment; when, without giving him time to recover himself, the angelic youth, snatching from his head a circlet of flowers intermixed with precious stones, which encompassed his brows, and shaded a great part of his forehead; and at the same time throwing off a head of artificial hair which flowed in golden ringlets down his shoulders; a fine fall of brown hair which was concealed under it succeeded, dropping in light curls on his neck and blushing cheeks; and Nourjahad, in the person of his seraphic guide, discovered his beloved and beautiful Mandana!

Whatever transports the sight of her would at another time have inspired in the breast of Nourjahad, his faculties were now too much absorbed in wonder, to leave room for any other passion. Wherefore, not daring to approach her, the sultan, willing to put an end to his suspence, cried out, Look up, Nourjahad, raise thy eyes to thy master's face, no longer the angry Schemerzad, thy offended prince, but the real Schemzeddin, thy friend and kind protector.

Nourjahad, who before, out of respect and awful distance, had not ventured to look in the sultan's face, now fixed his eyes earnestly upon him. By the life of Schemerzad, said he, if I were not certain that all this is illusion, and that thy illustrious father, my royal and once beloved master, is dead, thou art so very like him, that I should swear that thou wert the real sultan Schemzeddin himself; such at thy years was his countenance and features.

The sultan at this burst into a second fit of laughter. And for whom, said the visier, (who had by this time taken off his turban, and a false beard which he wore) for whom wouldst thou take me?

By Mahomet, cried Nourjahad, falling back a step or two, I should take thee for my old friend Hasem, if I were not convinced that the good man died above twenty years ago.

It is time, said the sultan, descending from his throne, and taking Nourjahad by the hand, it is now time to undeceive thee, and explain to thee the mystery of all those extraordinary events, which seem to have bewildered thy senses.

Know then, Nourjahad, that the adventure of thy guardian genius was all a deception, and a piece of machinery of my contrivance. You are now convinced, by the evidence of your own eyes, that your celestial intelligence was no other than this young damsel.

I had a mind to make trial of thy heart, and for this purpose made choice of this charming virgin, for whom I own I had entertained a passion, but found I could not gain her affections. She had seen you from the windows of the womens apartments, walking with me in the gardens of the seraglio, and had conceived a tenderness for you, which she frankly confessed to me, declaring at the same time, she would never give her love to any other. Though she was my slave, I would not put a constraint upon her inclinations; but told her, if she would assist me faithfully in a design I had formed, I would reward her, by bestowing her on you.

She readily assented to my proposal, and having previously prepared every thing for my purpose, I equipped her as you see.

It was not difficult for me to introduce her into your chamber, by a private door which you know communicates between your apartments, and certain lodgings in my palace.

I myself stood at the door, whilst she entered as you slept, and contrived to throw that light into your chamber, which disclosed to you the wonderful vision. I overheard all your discourse, and could scarce contain my laughter, when you so greedily received that marvellous essence from Mandana; which you supposed would confer immortality; but which was in reality nothing more than a soporific drug, of so potent a nature, that the fumes of it alone, were capable of throwing the person who smelt to them into a profound sleep. It had quickly this effect on you; and I took that opportunity of conveying into your chamber those coffers which you thought contained such immense treasures; but which in truth were as great counterfeits as your guardian angel. The supposed precious stones, were nothing more than false gems, which I procured from a skilful lapidary, who had given them such an extraordinary polish and lustre, that they might well pass for jewels of inestimable value, on one better skilled in those matters than you were.

The ingots of gold were all base metal, which I got from the same artist. Nothing, in short, was real, but the money, part of which I was very willing to sacrifice to my experiment; though, as I have managed it, the largest sums which thou in thy extravagance hast expended, were returned into my coffers.

As I naturally supposed, that so long as the money lasted you would not have recourse to the other treasures, I was not afraid of having the fraud detected. The cave, which was an accidental circumstance, but of which I had long known, was by my contrivance made the repository of thy riches.

When thou wert settled in the full possession of thy imaginary felicity, thou mayst remember that Hasem was first recommended to thy service; Mandana too was amongst other slaves presented to thy view. No wonder that her charms captivated thy heart. Her love to thee was as pure as it was fervent; but thy boundless wishes were not to be restrained; and forgetting all the rational principles that thou didst at first lay down to regulate thy conduct, thou gavest thyself up to all manner of vile excesses, and didst shew the depravity of the human heart, when unrestrained by divine laws.

It was now time, I thought, to punish thee, and to shew thee the vanity of all earthly enjoyments. By opiates infused

into thy wine that night on which thou didst debase thyself
by drunkenness, I threw thee into a sound sleep; and
though it lasted not much longer than the usual term of
ordinary repose, it yet gave me an opportunity of making
such farther dispositions, as I thought necessary for the
carrying on of my design.

I laid hold of this juncture to withdraw Mandana from
thy arms, promising however to restore her to thee, if I
found thee ever worthy of her.

I believe it is needless to inform you, that the confinement
I laid you under was for no other end than to cut off all
intercourse between you and any others than those of your
own household, every one of whom were of my placing
about you, even to the ladies of your seraglio, who were no
others than the prettiest slaves I could find, amongst those
who attended on my own women.

Every one entrusted with my secret, were tied down by
the most solemn oaths to keep it inviolably; and this with a
promise of reward, served, as the event has shewn, to
secure their fidelity.

There was not an action of thy life but I was made
acquainted with; and whilst thou didst triumph in the joys
of my successful illusion, I sometimes pitied thy weakness,
and sometimes laughed at thy extravagance.

That magnificent palace of which thou thoughtest thyself
master, was one which I had borrowed for the purpose
from an emir who was in my secret, and who was himself
often present in disguise amongst your slaves, a witness to
your extravagancies. I will not encrease thy confusion by
reminding thee of the inordinate excesses thou wert guilty
of in thy retirement. Thou canst not have forgot the project
of creating for thyself an earthly paradise. This was the
second crisis I laid hold on to punish thee; and by tearing
thee from thy impious pleasures, to remind thee that crimes
cannot be committed with impunity. A second sleep,
procured as the former was, but of somewhat a longer

duration, gave me full opportunity to make a total change in the face of thy affairs. Hasem (whom thou didst suppose to be dead) remained still secretly concealed in thy house, to be as it were the grand spring to move all the rest of thy domestics. The hags whom thou hadst imposed upon thee for the decayed beauties of thy seraglio, were really a set of notable old dames, whom he had tutored for the purpose: Thy former mistresses, who were insignificant slaves, were dismissed. She who personated the feigned Cadiga, acted her part to admiration, and with the artful contrivance of having a rose-bud painted on her breast, a mark which your young favourite really bore from nature, she had cunning and address enough to impose herself on you for the very Cadiga whom you formerly loved.

I believe, proceeded the sultan, you are by this time convinced, that there was nothing supernatural in the several events of your life, and that you were in reality nothing more than the dupe of your own folly and avarice.

Thou mayst remember after this period, that, sated with voluptuousness, thy licentious heart began to grow hardened; and from rioting without controul in pleasures, which, however criminal in themselves, carry at least with them the excuse of temptation, thou wantonly didst stir up, and indulge the latent cruelty of thy nature. Thy ungoverned passions led thee to an act of blood! thou piercedst with thy poniard the honest creature who remonstrated with thee on thy evil works; but Heaven did not, however, permit thee to deprive her of life.

See, Nourjahad, of what the heart of man is capable, when he shuts his eyes against the precepts of our holy prophet. Thou stoodst as it were alone in the creation, and self-dependent for thy own happiness or misery, thou lookedst not for rewards or punishments in that invisible world, from which thou thoughtest thyself by thy own voluntary act excluded.

This last barbarous deed, however, called aloud for

chastisement; and thou wast for the third time deceived with a belief that thou hadst slept a number of years, in which many mortifying revolutions had happened in thy family.

I was now resolved to be myself an eye-witness of thy behaviour, and to try if there was any spark of virtue remaining in thy soul which could possibly be rekindled.

I disguised myself in the habit of a slave; and having altered my face, and my voice, I presented myself to thee under the name of Cozro. Thou knowest what passed between us on thy first awaking from thy compelled slumbers, and that I heard and saw with what indifference thou receivedst the news of my supposed death. But I will not reproach thee with ingratitude—let the memory of *that* be buried with the rest of thy errors.

I had soon the satisfaction to find that thou wast as it were a new man. The natural goodness of thy disposition, thy reason, thy experience of the deceitfulness of worldly enjoyments, joined to the remorse which thou couldst not help feeling, for a series of vice and folly, at length rouzed thee to a just sense of what thou owedst to the dignity of thy own nature, and to the duties incumbent on thee towards the rest of thy fellow-creatures.

I now discovered, with joy, that thou hadst intirely divested thyself of that insatiable love of pleasure, to which thou hadst before addicted thyself, and that thou no longer didst regard wealth, but as it enabled thee to do good. There was but one trial more remained. If, said I, his repentance be sincere, and he has that heroism of mind which is inseparable from the truly virtuous, he will not shrink at death; but, on the contrary, will look upon it as the only means by which he can obtain those refined enjoyments suited to the divine part of his nature, and which are as much superior in their essence, as they are in their duration to all the pleasures of sense.

I made the trial—The glorious victory, Oh Nourjahad, is

thine! By thy contempt of riches, thou hast proved how well thou deservedst them; and thy readiness to die, shews how fit thou art to live.—

In the space of fourteen moons (for it is no longer since I first imposed on thy credulity the belief of thy miraculous state) thou hast had the experience of four times so many years. Such assuredly would be the vicissitudes of thy life, hadst thou in reality possessed what thou didst in imagination. Let this dream of existence then be a lesson to thee for the future, never to suppose that riches can ensure happiness; that the gratification of our passions can satisfy the human heart; or that the immortal part of our nature, will suffer us to taste unmixed felicity, in a world which was never meant for our final place of abode. Take thy amiable Mandana to thee for a wife, and receive the fixed confidence and love of Schemzeddin.

The history says that Nourjahad was from that minute raised to be the first man in power next to the sultan; that his wisdom and virtue proved an ornament and support to the throne of Persia during the course of a long and prosperous life; and that his name was famous throughout the Eastern world.

FINIS

The History of Charoba, Queen of Ægypt

CHAROBA, was the only daughter and heir of Totis king of Ægypt; who was likewise called Pharaon, and Pheron, by other nations.*

In the reign of Totis, Abraham the beloved of God came into Ægypt; and it is written, that he would have corrupted Sarah the wife of Abraham, but God punished the king, and delivered his servants.* Afterwards Totis shewed them great respect, and offered them gold and treasures, but they refused them. Then he recommended Sarah to his daughter Charoba, and desired her to shew her some tokens of respect. Charoba was a young and blooming Virgin, handsome, ingenious, and of a generous spirit, she took Sarah into her friendship, shewed her all kinds of honour, and sent her many rich presents.—Sarah brought them all to Abraham, and asked his advice concerning them; he ordered her to restore them, and to say that they had no need of them.—Sarah therefore returned them all to Charoba, who was surprised, and acquainted her father with all that had passed, which increased his admiration of them; seeing they refused all those things, which others the most eagerly sought, and used every means to obtain. And he said unto his daughter,—'These are persons of high estimation, who are full of holiness and sincerity, and are not covetous of perishable goods;—Charoba do whatever you can to shew them honour, that they may leave their blessing with us when they depart our country.'

After this, Charoba gave Hagar unto Sarah, who was in due time the mother of our father Ishmael* (God's peace be with him!)—Hagar was a beautiful young maiden, a Coptess by nation.* When she was presented to Sarah, Charoba said—'Behold thy recompence,' therefore Sarah called her Agar.*

When Abraham had resolved to return out of Ægypt into Syria, Charoba provided many baskets of provision of all kinds, with preserved fruits and many excellent things to eat by the way; saying 'these things are only for your accommodation by the way, and not to enrich you.'

Sarah told Abraham of this, and he permitted her to accept this present, saying, 'there was no harm in receiving it from the generous princess.' Totis requested of Abraham that he would pray to God for his benediction of his country.—Abraham therefore prayed to God for Ægypt and its inhabitants.—He also gave his benediction to the Nile, and told Totis that his family should reign there for many ages.—Likewise he gave his benediction to Charoba, and Sarah gave her the hand of friendship, and they departed out of Ægypt.

Charoba caused mules to be loaden with her provisions, and sent her own people to conduct them till they were gotten quite out of Ægypt.

Being got a good way on their journey, Abraham said unto Sarah, 'Give us to eat some of those provisions which the princess of Ægypt gave unto you.' Then Sarah ordered the baskets to be set before them, and they, and their companions also, eat of the provisions.—And they did so many days.—But when they came to the last basket, they found it full of precious jewels, and curious things, and changes of garments.—Whereupon Abraham said, 'this princess hath deceived us, and obliged us to accept of her treasures.—Great God give her subtilty to deceive her enemies, and to vanquish all those who shall arise to do her harm, and to strive with her for her land!—Bless her in her country, and in her river, and make that country a place of plenty, safety, and prosperity!'

When the beloved of God was come into the land of Syria, he spent those gifts in pious works,—in lodging and feeding pilgrims, and in making many wells, which he ordered to be common. He also bought flocks and herds, which he set apart for all travellers,—for the poor and needy,—for the lame and the blind: and God gave him his benediction, and caused his riches to increase and multiply. Also God gave him children after a long time, and in his old age:—first Hagar bore him a son which was our father Ishmael; and after some years Sarah likewise bare a son,*— And Hagar and her son left Syria and went into Arabia.— And Hagar sent a messenger to Charoba, to acquaint her that she had borne a son,—whereat Charoba rejoiced, and sent her abundance of gold, and jewels, and fine Ægyptian linen,* to dress her son withal. Out of these treasures Hagar provided ornaments for the square temple at Mecca,* and she also established a porter in the same temple.

Totis king of Ægypt, lived till after that time, and Hagar sent him word that she had a strong and valiant son; but that they lived in a barren land, and prayed him to supply them with provisions.

To this end, Totis caused a channel to be made on the Eastern side of Ægypt, and brought into it the water of the Nile, so that it carried vessels into the salt sea, which is the channel of the red Sea.—By this way he caused Wheat to be sent to Hagar and her son, and many other presents.— They went by water as far as Gedde,* and from thence were carried to Mecca on the backs of beasts.—By these means God preserved the inhabitants of Mecca, and relieved their wants;—therefore the Arabians spoke well of Totis, and called him the just, as having performed the promises he made them, and given proofs of his good will to them.— Nevertheless, Totis was more feared than beloved in his own Country, for he did many unjust and cruel actions. Moreover he put many people to death, and particularly those of his own family, even his nearest relations; and this he did out of jealousy of them, lest they should deprive his daughter of the crown after his death:but Charoba was —

of a mild and gentle disposition, always endeavouring to prevent the shedding of blood. She was also of a great capacity and ingenuity:—she concealed a near kinsman from the King's cruelty, and preserved him and his family; one of which she afterwards appointed to succeed her on the throne, as we shall shew hereafter.

Totis in his old age, was hated and feared by all the nobility; and even Charoba dreaded his cruelty. She also suspected that they would take away the Crown from his posterity; therefore, it was surmised, that she connived at the conspiracy against his life; for he was poisoned, but no man knew by what means, or by what persons.*

After Totis was dead, the people could not, at first, agree about a successor:—Some said they would have the race of Abribus, one of their ancient princes—others would have a new family called to the throne:—most of them objected to the government of a woman.—While they were thus undetermined, one of the Viziers rose up, and spoke thus to them.

'My friends,—Charoba is a woman of great understanding, she is likewise of a mild and merciful disposition;—there is no reason why she should be excluded from the succession:—moreover the good man that came from Syria and his wife have given her their benedictions:—she is beloved by all that are acquainted with her noble qualities, and if you take the crown from her and give it to another, you will certainly have cause to repent of your precipitation.'

The people on better consideration, inclined to this good advice, and the grandees of the kingdom by degrees came into it: so they deputed this Vizier to go to Charoba, and in their name, intreat her to fill the vacant throne. So that Vizier placed Charoba, in the royal seat.—The first time she sate on the royal throne, she gave great sums away to the people; shewing great liberality, and promising much happiness to all her subjects,—she doubled the pay of the soldiers,—she honoured the priests and sages, and the chiefs of the nobility.—She likewise countenanced the magicians and their fraternity,—she caused the temples to be repaired and enlarged, and built many public edifices. She reigned many years wisely and happily; and she remembered the benediction of Abraham, and believed that by the protection of his God, she subdued all her enemies, and was respected by her people.

After a long time, it happened that Gebirus the Metaphequian* heard of her fame; and he was minded to pay her a visit, and oblige her to marry him.—Gebirus was of a gigantic stature, and descended from the race of the Gadites,—and when he sat on the ground seemed as high as the tallest men,—he was strong of body, and fierce of disposition,—he had a distemper in his body that gave him constant pain;—his physicians advised him to seek out another country, the soil of which, with the air and water were more suitable to his temperament.

They gave him such an account of the land of Ægypt, that he resolved to go and take up his abode there.—He called together all his people,—he distributed money and arms among them, and then declared to them his design of taking possession of the land of Ægypt; and flattered them with the hopes of victory, reward, and a settlement, in a country that was the garden of the world.—Soon after he began his march, and took with him five thousand Gadites, men of great stature and strength; every one of which carried a large stone upon his head, and was completely armed. He travelled till he came to the borders of Ægypt, and then sent a message to the Queen, desiring to know in what place she chose he should enter Ægypt; for he was unwilling to oppose her in any thing, but would appear to be obedient to all her commands.—His design was to marry her, and make himself King of Ægypt; or, in case she refused him, to dam up the course of the Nile, with the stones his people brought upon their heads,—to turn the

channel into another country and so make the Ægyptians
die of famine, and to ruin their country. He sent a splendid
Embassy to Charoba, bragging of his strength and riches,
and offering himself to be her husband.

Charoba had a woman servant, who had been her
nurse,—an artful, subtle, contriving woman, and a great
Enchantress.—Charoba consulted her in all affairs, and
advised with her on this emergency.—She gave her advice
to this effect.—'It seems to me that there is no probability
of defeating these huge bodies by fighting, we must rather
subdue them by stratagem; And to this end, we must
manage our business so, that they may neither do harm to
you, nor your subjects.—I will therefore, with your permission, go myself to him and give an answer to his embassy in
your name.'

The Queen bade her do what seemed best to her. She
ordered many of her servants to wait upon the nurse, to do
her honour in the sight of the Prince, and to shew that she
was highly esteemed by her mistress.

The nurse took with her, presents of the most valuable
things in Ægypt,—precious stones, carved works, preserved fruits, costly garments, perfumes, arms, fine tempered swords, etc.—She presented all these rarities to
Gebirus, which he willingly receieved, and afterwards
enquired what answer she brought to his suit.—'Great
King,' said she, 'My mistress is sensible of your valour and
merit, and is far from refusing so advantageous an offer;
but she must wait for a proper time, before she can reward
your love according to your deserts.—The nobility are
jealous of a foreign prince; and she must manage with them
so as to bring them to agree, and to receive you as their
sovereign lord; in the mean time you must shew readiness
to obey all her commands;—to reside where she shall
appoint, and to do what she shall require, and she will take
care to provide for you and your servants.' He returned for
answer.—'If she will receive me for her husband, I am

ready to obey her commands in all things; and if the nobility refuse to accept me for a King, let her call upon me, and I will compel them to her will:—and tell her for a marriage gift, I will bring her whatever she pleases to ask of me.'—'My Queen,' replied this cunning ambassadress, 'needs not any thing of yours, seeing, that all the riches on both sides, will henceforward be in common between you: but while she is employed in promoting your interest and happiness, she desires that instead of a marriage present, you will cause a city to be built on that side next the great sea, that it may be an honorable mark of your affection to her even to the end of the world.—And that it may be a discovery of your great power, and strength, she would have you employ in this work, those great stones and pillars, which she is informed you brought to dam up the channel of the Nile;—by this you will give proof of your good intentions towards the inhabitants of Ægypt, and you will gain their love and duty towards you.—Moreover when this work is finished, she will over-rule all other difficulties, and make you her husband before all the world.'

The King was exceeding glad at this proposal, and granted her request,—And so it was agreed between them that he should enter Ægypt on the west side, and that he should found a city there; which was in the same place where Alexandria now standeth.* So he encamped his army on the sea-side, and Charoba sent provisions for him and his people.

Now there were the ruins of a city in that place, which city was founded by Sedad, the son of Gad,* who was a great King, and purposed to bring thither whatever was rare and precious in all parts of the world. But the destroyer of castles prevented him, even Death, which none can escape or avoid.—There were many remains of this ancient city, and Gebirus caused to be brought thither, all the stones and the pillars he had brought into Ægypt. And he assembled the engineers and the artists from all those parts, and they made a model for the new city; and Charoba sent him a thousand workmen. Now the nurse who was Charoba's confident, by her orders consulted the magicians; and they by their arts, employed certain demons of the sea, to obstruct the buildings; so that Gebirus spent a long time in building, and yet the city advanced very little: for whenever the buildings were nearly finished; while the workmen took their rest by night, the demons of the sea came and pulled down the buildings, and destroyed them; at which Gebirus was greatly troubled and afflicted, until he understood the reason, by means of a strange adventure that befel him.

Charoba had sent a thousand goats and sheep, which were milked every day for the King's kitchen. They were kept by a young shepherd to whom Gebirus gave the charge of them,—he had other shepherds under him, and they led their flocks out to graze every day by the sea-side.

Now the chief shepherd was a beautiful person and of a good stature and aspect. One day when he had committed his flocks to the other shepherds, and wandered far away from them, he saw a fair young lady rising out of the sea, who walked towards him and saluted him graciously.—He returned her salutation and she began to converse with him.—'Young man,'—said she, 'will you wrestle with me for a wager that I shall lay against you?'—'What will you lay, fair lady,' said the shepherd, 'and what can I take against you?'—'If you give me a fall,' said the lady, 'I will be yours and at your disposal,—and if I give you a fall, you shall give me a beast, out of your flock.'—'I am content,'—said the shepherd,—so he went towards her, and she met him, and wrestled with him, and presently gave him a fall. She then took a beast out of the flock, and carried it away with her into the sea.

She came every evening afterwards, and did the same, until the shepherd was desperately in love with her:—so the flock was diminished, and the shepherd was pining away with love and grief.

One day King Gebirus, passing by the shepherd, found him sitting very pensively by the flocks: so he came near and spoke to him.—'What misfortune hath befallen thee, shepherd?—why are thou so altered and dejected?—thy flock also diminishes, and gives less milk every day.'— Upon this the shepherd took courage, and told the King all that had befallen him with the lady of the sea.—Which when Gebirus heard he was astonished, and in doubt whether to believe him.—'At what time,' said he, 'does this lady visit thee?'—'Every evening,' reply'd the shepherd, 'when the sun is just ready to set.'—'Take off thy upper garment,' said the King, 'and thy bonnet also,—give them to me, and retire thyself a little way out of sight.'—And the shepherd did so. So the King put on the shepherd's upper garment and his bonnet, and sat down in his place.

At the accustomed time, the young lady came out of the sea, and saluted the King, who returned her salutation.— 'Wilt thou wrestle any more with me upon the same terms?' said she.—'Yes with all my heart,' said the King. So he came towards her, and gave her a fall presently, and crush'd her very much.—She cried out to him to spare her, saying, 'you are not my ordinary match.'—'No,' said the King, 'I am his master.'—'Then,' said she, 'put me into his hands, since I am taken; for he has treated me courteously, and I have tormented his heart with love and grief:—mean time he hath captivated me, as I have him, and I will at last reward his love.—If thou wilt resign me to thy shepherd, I will in requital, teach thee how to compleat thy buildings, and the city which thou hast begun.' He then promised to give her to the shepherd, upon condition, that she would tell him from whence came the misfortunes that happened to his buildings, and the means whereby he might finish them.—'Know then, Oh King!' said she, 'that this land of Ægypt, is full of magicians and enchanters; and that the sea is full of demons and spirits, which assist them to carry on their affairs,—to build, and to destroy. These are they who pull down thy buildings, and obstruct thy city.'—'And what must I do to prevent them?'—said the King.

So she taught him to make certain statues of copper, and stone, and earth, and wood, and set them along by the sea-side, and she taught him to set spells upon them; so that when the demons of the sea came up to destroy the buildings, they saw the statues and returned back into the sea.

So she went and abode with the shepherd every day, but every night she returned into the sea.

From this time, the buildings of Gebirus advanced, and he compleated many structures as he had desired. Then Gebirus had another conference with the lady of the sea, and he spoke thus to her.

'Behold I have expended all the money that I brought hither, and the city is not yet finished; and I have no more money. Canst not thou discover to me any hidden treasures in this land, whereby I may finish my city, and not leave off my work to my disgrace and sorrow.'—The lady replied—'There is much treasure in this ruined city, and I will instruct thee how to find it.—On the north side of your buildings there is a round place,—on the outside are seven pillars, with a brazen* statue on the top of each of them.— Thou shalt sacrifice a fat bull to every one of those statues, and cause the pillar under it to be rubb'd with the blood of the bull; then perfume it with the hair of his tail, and shavings of his horns and hoofs. Then thou shalt say unto it,—"Behold the offering I make to thee,—let me have that which is under thee, and about thee."—Having said and done thus to every one of them, measure from every pillar, on that side the face of the statue is turned towards, fifty cubits.—Then let thy people dig there.—You shall do all this when the moon is at the full.—After you have digged thirty cubits, you will find a great door; cause it to rubb'd with the gall of the bulls, and then take it away.—You shall then descend into a cave, fifty cubits in length. In it you will find a storehouse made fast with a lock, and the Key will be under the threshold of the door; take it and rub the door with the remainder of the bulls galls, and perfume it with shavings of the horns and hoofs, and the hair of the tails, and then the door shall open.—You shall then wait a while, till the winds that are enclosed within get vent; and when they are calmed, you may enter. At the entrance, you will meet with a statue of brass, having about its neck, a plate of the same metal; on which is written a catalogue of all the treasures in these storehouses, of which you may take what you please. You shall make no stay before a dead person, whom you shall see there, laid upon a bed with regal ornaments. Let not what is about him, of jewels and precious things, excite your envy or covetousness; but, having taken away what is sufficient for your occasions, depart immediately; making fast the doors, and covering the place with earth as you found it.—Know also that there are storehouses under every pillar and its statue; for they are the tombs of seven Kings, who are buried there with all their treasures.'

Gebirus, was extremely satisfied with this account which the nymph gave him; he thanked her much, and went immediately, and did all things that she had ordered; and he found immense wealth and treasures, and many rare and admirable things.—By these means he completed the buildings of his city.

When Charoba heard that the city was almost finished, she was afflicted, and fell into great perturbation of mind: for she meant only to weary out the King, and to reduce him to an impossibility.

After the city was finished, Gebirus sent some of his chief men, with the tidings to Charoba; and invited her to come and see it.—She was almost overwhelmed with grief and apprehension, that she should now be compelled to marry:—but her nurse comforted her with these words.— 'Do not yet despair, my royal mistress!—give not yourself further trouble concerning this audacious man.—Leave him to me, and I will shortly put it out of his power to give you any further concern, or to do you mischief.'

She returned with the messengers to Gebirus, and carried with her fine tapestry of great value, as a present from her mistress.—'Let this be put over the seat on which the King sitteth,' said she, 'then let him divide his people into three parties, and send them forward to meet the Queen, who will give them such treatment as they deserve. When the first party shall be about a third part of the way, you shall send away the second; and when the second are got to their station, you shall send away the third:—thus they shall be dispersed about the country for the Queen's safety, and she shall have no cause to fear the designs of her enemies,—she will be attended by the King's servants only, and when they return she will come with them.'

So Gebirus sent away his servants, according to her instructions, and she continued sending him rich presents every day, till such time as she knew that the first party were arrived at their station.

Then by her orders there were tables set before them covered with refreshments of all kinds; but they were all poisoned meats.—And while they sat down to eat, the Queen's men and maid-servants stood all around them, with umbrellas and fans to keep them cool;—also their liquors were cooled. So while they sat at the tables they all died from the first to the last.—Then the Queen's servants went forwards to meet the second party, which they treated in the same manner.—Then they removed to the third party, and served them as they had done the others.—So the Queen's servants went forward; and a part of the Queen's army followed them, and they buried all the dead bodies.

Then the Queen, sent a message to the King, that she had left his army in and about her own city of Masar,* and that she was coming to meet him speedily.—So she set forward with many attendants, and her nurse met her, and accompanied her to the city of the King.

When she drew near the palace, the King rose up, and went forward to meet her. Then the nurse threw over his shoulders a regal garment, which was poisoned, and which she had prepared for that purpose;* afterwards she blew a fume into his face, which almost deprived him of his senses;—then she sprinkled him with a water that loosened all his joints, and deprived him of his strength; so that he fell down in a swoon at the feet of Charoba.—The attendants raised him up and seated him in a chair of state, and the nurse said unto him—'Is the King well to night?'—He replied,—'A mischief on your coming hither!—may you be treated by others as you have treated me!—this only grieves me, that a man of strength and valour should be overcome by the subtilty of a woman.'—'Is there any thing you would ask of me before you taste of death?' said the Queen—'I would only intreat,' said he, 'that the words I shall utter may be engraven on one of the pillars of this palace which I have builded.'

Then said Charoba, 'I give thee my promise that it shall be done; and I also will cause to be engraven on another pillar—"This is the fate of such men as would compel Queens to marry them, and kingdoms to receive them for their Kings."—Tell us now thy last words.'

Then the King said—'I Gebirus, the Metaphequian, the son of Gevirus, that have caused marbles to be polished,—both the red and the green stone to be wrought curiously; who was possessed of gold, and jewels, and various treasures; who have raised armies; built cities; erected palaces;—who have cut my way through mountains; have stopped rivers; and done many great and wonderful actions;—with all this my power, and my strength, and my valour, and my riches: I have been circumvented by the wiles of a woman; weak, impotent, and deceitful; who hath deprived me of my strength and understanding; and finally hath taken away my life:—Wherefore, whoever is desirous to be great and to prosper; (though there is no certainty of long success in this world,)—yet, let him put no trust in a woman; but let him, at all times, beware of the craft and subtilty of a woman.'

After saying these words, he fainted away, and they supposed him dead; but after some time he revived again.—Charoba comforted him, and renewed her promise to him.—Being at the point of death, he said,—'Oh Charoba!—triumph not in my death!—for there shall come upon thee a day like unto this, and the time is not very far distant.—Then shalt thou reflect on the vicissitudes of fortune, and the certainty of death.'—

Soon after this he expired.—Charoba ordered his body to be honorably interred in the city which he had builded:—Afterwards, she built an high tower in the same city; and caused to be engraven upon it her own name, and that of Gebirus: and an history of all that she had done unto him; and also those his last words.—So her fame went forth, and came to the ears of many Kings, and they feared and respected her. And she received many offers of friendship and alliance; but Charoba remained a virgin to the end of her life.

Now it happened about three years after the death of Gebirus, that Charoba having embarked on board a small vessel, in which she was wont to take her pleasure upon the Nile by moon-light, went on shore with some of her attendants.

As they were returning to the ship, with great mirth and jollity, it so happened that the Queen trod upon a serpent; which turned again, and stung her in the heel; the pain whereof, took away her sight.—Her women comforted her,—saying, it would be nothing.—'You are deceived,' said she.—'The day is come with which Gebirus threatened me:—a day which all the great ones of the earth must meet and submit to.—Carry me home immediately, that I may die there.'

The day following Charoba died;—having first appointed Dalica, her kinswoman to succeed her.—She was the daughter of that kinsman, whom Charoba preserved from the cruelty of her father Totis.

So died Charoba, Queen of Ægypt; but her name died not with her, for it remaineth, and is honoured unto this day.

Queen Dalica, was endowed with beauty and wisdom.— She followed the example of her predecessor, and governed her kingdom with great prudence.—She did many great works in Ægypt,—and caused many castles to be erected on the frontiers of the kingdom, to repel her enemies on whatever side they should be attacked. She caused the body of Charoba, to be embalmed with camphire and spices;* and it was carried into the city of Gebirus: for Charoba had caused her tomb to be prepared there in her lifetime, and embellished it with regal ornaments, and appointed priests to attend on it.

Queen Dalica solemnized the funeral of Charoba with great magnificence. She made her subjects rich and happy by her wise government; and, after reigning seventy years in Ægypt, died also a virgin, and was succeeded by her sister's son, Ablinos, whose posterity wore the crown of Ægypt for many generations.

FINIS

Murad the Unlucky

CHAPTER I

Credulity is always the Cause of Misery.

IT is well known that the Grand Seignior amuses himself
by going at night, in disguise, through the streets of
Constantinople; as the Caliph, Haroun Alraschid, used
formerly to do in Bagdad.*

One moon-light night, accompanied by his grand-vizier,
he traversed several of the principal streets of the city,
without seeing any thing remarkable. At length, as they
were passing a rope-maker's, the Sultan recollected the
Arabian story of Cogia-Hassan, Alhabal, the rope-maker,
and his two friends, Saad and Saadi, who differed so much
in their opinion concerning the influence of fortune over
human affairs.*

'What is your opinion on this subject,' said the Grand
Seignior to his vizier.

'I am inclined, please your majesty,' replied the vizier,
'to think that success in the world, depends more upon
prudence than upon what is called luck, or fortune.'

'And I,' said the sultan, 'am persuaded that fortune does
more for men than prudence. Do you not every day hear of
persons who are said to be fortunate, or unfortunate? How
comes it that this opinion should prevail amongst men, if it
be not justified by experience?'

'It is not for me to dispute with your majesty,' replied
the prudent vizier.

'Speak your mind freely; I desire and command it,' said
the sultan.

'Then I am of opinion,' answered the vizier, 'that people
are often led to believe others fortunate, or unfortunate,
merely because they only know the general outline of their

histories; and are ignorant of the incidents and events in which they have shewn prudence, or imprudence. I have heard, for instance, that there are at present, in this city, two men who are remarkable for their good and bad fortune—one is called *Murad, the Unlucky*, and the other *Saladin, the Lucky*.* Now I am inclined to think, if we could hear their stories, we should find that one is a prudent and the other an imprudent character.'

'Where do these men live?' interrupted the sultan. 'I will hear their histories, from their own lips, before I sleep.'

'Murad, the Unlucky, lives in the next square,' said the vizier.

The sultan desired to go thither immediately. Scarcely had they entered the square, when they heard the cry of loud lamentations. They followed the sound till they came to a house, of which the door was open; and where there was a man tearing his turban, and weeping bitterly. They asked the cause of his distress, and he pointed to the fragments of a china vase, which lay on the pavement at his door.

'This seems undoubtedly to be beautiful china,' said the sultan, taking up one of the broken pieces; 'but can the loss of a china vase be the cause of such violent grief and despair?'

'Ah, gentlemen,' said the owner of the vase, suspending his lamentations, and looking at the dress of the pretended merchants, 'I see that you are strangers: you do not know how much cause I have for grief and despair! You do not know that you are speaking to Murad the Unlucky! Were you to hear all the unfortunate accidents that happened to me, from the time I was born till this instant, you would perhaps pity me, and acknowledge I have just cause for despair.'

Curiosity was strongly expressed by the sultan; and the hope of obtaining sympathy inclined Murad to gratify it, by the recital of his adventures. 'Gentlemen,' said he, 'I scarcely dare invite you into the house of such an unlucky being as I am; but, if you will venture to take a night's lodging under my roof, you shall hear at your leisure the story of my misfortunes.'

The sultan and the vizier excused themselves from spending the night with Murad; saying that they were obliged to proceed to their khan,* where they should be expected by their companions: but they begged permission to repose themselves for half an hour in his house, and besought him to relate the history of his life, if it would not renew his grief too much to recollect his misfortunes.

Few men are so miserable as not to like to talk of their misfortunes, where they have, or where they think they have, any chance of obtaining compassion. As soon as the pretended merchants were seated, Murad began his story in the following manner:

'My father was a merchant of this city. The night before I was born, he dreamed that I came into the world with the head of a dog, and the tail of a dragon; and that, in haste to conceal my deformity, he rolled me up in a piece of linen, which unluckily proved to be the Grand Seignior's turban; who, enraged at his insolence in touching his turban, commanded that his head should be struck off.*

'My father wakened before he lost his head; but not before he had half lost his wits, from the terror of his dream. Being a firm believer in predestination, he was persuaded that I should be the cause of some great evil to him; and he took an aversion to me even before I was born. He considered his dream as a warning, sent from above, and consequently determined to avoid the sight of me. He would not stay to see whether I should really be born with the head of a dog, and the tail of a dragon; but he set out, the next morning, on a voyage to Aleppo.*

'He was absent for upwards of five years; and, during that time, my education was totally neglected. One day, I enquired, from my mother, why I had been named Murad, the Unlucky? She told me that this name was given to me in consequence of my father's dream; but she added that, perhaps, it might be forgotten, if I proved fortunate in my future life. My nurse, a very old woman, who was present, shook her head, with a look which I never shall forget, and whispered to my mother loud enough for me to hear, "Unlucky he was, and is, and ever will be. Those that are born to ill luck cannot help themselves: nor could any, but the great prophet, Mahomet himself, do any thing for them. It is a folly for an unlucky person to strive with their fate: it is better to yield to it at once."

'This speech made a terrible impression upon me, young as I then was; and every accident that happened to me afterwards confirmed my belief in my nurse's prognostic. I was in my eighth year when my father returned from abroad. The year after he came home my brother Saladin was born, who was named Saladin, the Lucky, because, the day he was born, a vessel, freighted with rich merchandize for my father, arrived safely in port.

'I will not weary you with a relation of all the little instances of good fortune, by which my brother Saladin was distinguished, even during his childhood. As he grew up, his success, in every thing he undertook, was as remarkable as my ill luck, in all that I attempted. From the time the rich vessel arrived, we lived in splendour; and the supposed prosperous state of my father's affairs was, of course, attributed to the influence of my brother Saladin's happy destiny.

'When Saladin was about twenty, my father was taken dangerously ill; and, as he felt that he should not recover, he sent for my brother to the side of his bed, and, to his great surprize, informed him that the magnificence, in which we had lived, had exhausted all his wealth; that his affairs were in the greatest disorder; for, having trusted to the hope of continual success, he had embarked in projects beyond his powers.

'The sequel was, he had nothing remaining, to leave to his children, but two large china vases, remarkable for their beauty, but still more valuable on account of certain verses, inscribed upon them in an unknown character, which were supposed to operate as a talisman, or charm, in favour of their possessors.

'Both these vases my father bequeathed to my brother Saladin; declaring he could not venture to leave either of them to me, because I was so unlucky that I should inevitably break it. After his death, however, my brother Saladin, who was blessed with a generous temper, gave me my choice of the two vases; and endeavoured to raise my spirits by repeating, frequently, that he had no faith either in good fortune or ill-fortune.

'I could not be of his opinion; though I felt and acknowledged his kindness, in trying to persuade me out of my settled melancholy. I knew it was in vain for me to exert myself, because I was sure that, do what I would, I should still be Murad, the Unlucky. My brother, on the contrary, was no ways cast down, even by the poverty in which my father left us: he said he was sure he should find some means of maintaining himself, and so he did.

'On examining our china vases, he found in them a powder of a bright scarlet colour; and it occurred to him that it would make a fine dye. He tried it; and, after some trouble, it succeeded to admiration.

'During my father's life-time, my mother had been supplied with rich dresses, by one of the merchants who was employed by the ladies of the Grand Seignior's seraglio.* My brother had done this merchant some trifling favours; and, upon application to him, he readily engaged to recommend the new scarlet dye. Indeed it was so beautiful that, the moment it was seen, it was preferred to every other colour. Saladin's shop was soon crowded with customers; and his winning manners, and pleasant conversation, were almost as advantageous to him as his scarlet dye. On the contrary, I observed that the first glance, at my melancholy countenance, was sufficient to disgust every one who saw me. I perceived this plainly; and it only confirmed me the more in my belief in my own evil destiny.

'It happened one day that a lady, richly apparelled and attended by two female slaves, came to my brother's house, to make some purchases. He was out, and I alone was left to attend the shop. After she had looked over some goods, she chanced to see my china vase, which was in the room. She took a prodigious fancy to it, and offered me any price, if I would part with it: but this I declined doing, because I believed that I should draw down upon my head some dreadful calamity, if I voluntary relinquished the talisman. Irritated by my refusal, the lady, according to the custom of her sex, became more resolute in her purpose; but neither entreaties nor money could change my determination. Provoked beyond measure at my obstinacy, as she called it, she left the house.

'On my brother's return, I related to him what had happened, and expected that he would have praised me for my prudence: but, on the contrary, he blamed me for the superstitious value I set upon the verses on my vase; and observed that it would be the height of folly to lose a certain means of advancing my fortune, for the uncertain hope of magical protection. I could not bring myself to be of his opinion; I had not the courage to follow the advice he gave. The next day the lady returned, and my brother sold his vase to her for ten thousand pieces of gold. This money he laid out in the most advantageous manner, by purchasing a new stock of merchandise. I repented, when it was too late; but, I believe, it is part of the fatality attending certain persons, that they cannot decide rightly at the proper moment. When the opportunity has been lost, I have always regretted that I did not do exactly the contrary to what I had previously determined upon. Often, whilst I was hesitating, the favourable moment passed.[1] Now this is what I call being unlucky. But to proceed with my story.

'The lady, who bought my brother Saladin's vase, was the favourite of the Sultana, and all-powerful in the Seraglio. Her dislike to me, in consequence of my opposition to her wishes, was so violent that she refused to return to my brother's house, whilst I remained there. He was unwilling to part with me; but I could not bear to be the ruin of so good a brother. Without telling him my design, I left his house, careless of what should become of me. Hunger, however, soon compelled me to think of some immediate mode of obtaining relief. I sat down upon a stone, before the door of a baker's shop: the smell of hot bread tempted me in, and with a feeble voice I demanded charity.

'The master baker gave me as much bread as I could eat, upon condition that I should change dresses with him, and carry the rolls for him through the city this day. To this I readily consented; but I had soon reason to repent of my compliance. Indeed, if my ill luck had not, as usual, deprived me at the critical moment of memory and judgment, I should never have complied with the baker's treacherous proposal. For some time before, the people of Constantinople had been much dissatisfied with the weight and quality of the bread, furnished by the bakers.* This species of discontent has often been the sure forerunner of an insurrection; and, in these disturbances, the master bakers frequently lose their lives. All these circumstances I knew; but they did not occur to my memory, when they might have been useful.

'I changed dresses with the baker; but scarcely had I proceeded through the adjoining street, with my rolls, before the mob began to gather round me, with reproaches and execrations. The crowd pursued me even to the gates

---

[1] 'Whom the Gods wish to destroy, they first deprive of understanding.'*

of the Grand Seignior's palace; and the Grand Vizier, alarmed at their violence, sent out an order to have my head struck off: the usual remedy, in such cases, being to strike off the baker's head.

'I now fell upon my knees, and protested I was not the baker for whom they took me; that I had no connection with him; and that I had never furnished the people of Constantinople with bread that was not weight. I declared I had merely changed clothes with a master baker, for this day; and that I should not have done so, but for the evil destiny which governs all my actions. Some of the mob exclaimed that I deserved to lose my head for my folly: but others took pity on me, and, whilst the officer, who was sent to execute the vizier's order, turned to speak to some of the noisy rioters, those who were touched by my misfortune opened a passage for me through the crowd, and thus favoured I effected my escape.

CHAPTER II

Folly has always an Excuse for itself.

'I QUITTED Constantinople: my vase I had left in the care of my brother. At some miles distance from the city, I overtook a party of soldiers. I joined them; and, learning that they were going to embark with the rest of the Grand Seignior's army for Egypt, I resolved to accompany them.* If it be, thought I, the will of Mahomet that I should perish, the sooner I meet my fate the better. The despondency, into which I was sunk, was attended by so great a degree of indolence that I scarcely would take the necessary means to preserve my existence. During our passage to Egypt, I sat all day long upon the deck of the vessel, smoking my pipe: and I am convinced that, if a storm had arisen, as I expected, I should not have taken my pipe from my mouth: nor should I have handled a rope, to save myself from destruction. Such is the effect of that species of resignation or torpor, whichever you please to call it, to which my strong belief in *fatality* had reduced my mind.

'We landed however safely, contrary to my melancholy forebodings. By a trifling accident, not worth relating, I was detained longer than any of my companions in the vessel, when we disembarked; and I did not arrive at the camp, at El Arish,* till late at night. It was moonlight, and I could see the whole scene distinctly. There was a vast number of small tents scattered over a desert of white sand; a few date trees were visible at a distance; all was gloomy, and all still; no sound was to be heard but that of the camels, feeding near the tents; and, as I walked on, I met with no human creature.

'My pipe was now out, and I quickened my pace a little

towards a fire, which I saw near one of the tents. As I proceeded, my eye was caught by something sparkling in the sand: it was a ring. I picked it up, and put it on my finger; resolving to give it to the public crier the next morning, who might find out its rightful owner: but, by ill luck, I put it on my little finger, for which it was much too large; and, as I hastened towards the fire to light my pipe, I dropped the ring. I stooped to search for it amongst the provender, on which a mule was feeding; and the cursed animal gave me so violent a kick, on the head, that I could not help roaring aloud.

'My cries awakened those who slept in the tent, near which the mule was feeding. Provoked at being disturbed, the soldiers were ready enough to think ill of me; and they took it for granted that I was a thief, who had stolen the ring I pretended to have just found. The ring was taken from me by force; and the next day I was bastinadoed* for having found it; the officer persisting in the belief that stripes would make me confess where I had concealed certain other articles of value, which had lately been missed in the camp. All this was the consequence of my being in a hurry to light my pipe, and of my having put the ring on a finger that was too little for it; which no one but Murad, the Unlucky, would have done.

'When I was able to walk again after my wounds were healed, I went into one of the tents distinguished by a red flag, having been told that these were coffee-houses. Whilst I was drinking coffee, I heard a stranger near me complaining that he had not been able to recover a valuable ring he had lost; although he had caused his loss to be published for three days by the public crier, offering a reward of two hundred sequins to whoever should restore it. I guessed that this was the very ring which I had unfortunately found. I addressed myself to the stranger, and promised to point out to him the person who had forced it from me. The stranger recovered his ring; and, being convinced that I had acted honestly, he made me a present of two hundred sequins,* as some amends for the punishment which I had unjustly suffered, on his account.

'Now you would imagine that this purse of gold was advantageous to me: far the contrary: it was the cause of new misfortunes.

'One night, when I thought that the soldiers who were in the same tent with me were all fast asleep, I indulged myself in the pleasure of counting my treasure. The next day, I was invited by my companions to drink sherbet with them.* What they mixed with the sherbet, which I drank, I know not; but I could not resist the drowsiness it brought on. I fell into a profound slumber; and, when I awoke, I found myself lying under a date tree, at some distance from the camp.

'The first thing I thought of, when I came to my recollection, was my purse of sequins. The purse I found still safe in my girdle; but, on opening it, I perceived that it was filled with pebbles, and not a single sequin was left. I had no doubt that I had been robbed by the soldiers with whom I had drunk sherbet; and I am certain that some of them must have been awake, the night I counted my money: otherwise, as I had never trusted the secret of my riches to any one, they could not have suspected me of possessing any property; for, ever since I kept company with them, I had appeared to be in great indigence.

'I applied in vain to the superior officers for redress: the soldiers protested they were innocent; no positive proof appeared against them, and I gained nothing by my complaint but ridicule and ill-will. I called myself, in the first transport of my grief, by that name which, since my arrival in Egypt, I had avoided to pronounce: I called myself Murad, the Unlucky! The name and the story ran through the camp; and I was accosted afterwards, very frequently, by this appellation. Some indeed varied their wit, by calling me Murad with the purse of pebbles.

'All that I had yet suffered is nothing, compared to my
succeeding misfortunes.

'It was the custom at this time, in the Turkish camp, for
the soldiers to amuse themselves with firing at a mark. The
superior officers remonstrated against this dangerous practice,[1] but ineffectually. Sometimes a party of soldiers would
stop firing for a few minutes, after a message was brought
them from their commanders; and then they would begin
again, in defiance of all orders. Such was the want of
discipline, in our army, that this disobedience went unpun-
ished. In the mean time, the frequency of the danger made
most men totally regardless of it. I have seen tents pierced
with bullets, in which parties were quietly seated, smoking
their pipes; whilst those without were preparing to take
fresh aim at the red flag on the top.

'This apathy proceeded, in some, from unconquerable
indolence of body; in others, from the intoxication produced by the fumes of tobacco and of opium; but, in most
of my brother Turks, it arose from the confidence the belief
in predestination inspired. When a bullet killed one of their
companions, they only observed, scarcely taking the pipes
from their mouths, "Our hour is not come: it is not the will
of Mahomet that we should fall."

'I own that this rash security appeared to me, at first,
surprizing; but it soon ceased to strike me with wonder;
and it even tended to confirm my favourite opinion, that
some were born to good and some to evil fortune. I became
almost as careless as my companions, from following the
same course of reasoning. It is not, thought I, in the power
of human prudence to avert the stroke of destiny. I shall
perhaps die to-morrow; let me therefore enjoy to-day.

'I now made it my study, every day, to procure as much
amusement as possible. My poverty, as you will imagine,
restricted me from indulgence and excess; but I soon found

---

[1] Antes's *Observations on the Manners and Customs of the Egyptians.**

means to spend what did not actually belong to me. There were certain Jews, who were followers of the camp, and who, calculating on the probability of victory for our troops, advanced money to the soldiers; for which they engaged to pay these usurers exorbitant interest.* The Jew, to whom I applied, traded with me also upon the belief that my brother Saladin, with whose character and circumstances he was acquainted, would pay my debts, if I should fall. With the money I raised from the Jew I continually bought coffee and opium, of which I grew immoderately fond. In the delirium it created, I forgot all my past misfortunes, and all fear of the future.

'One day, when I had raised my spirits by an unusual quantity of opium, I was strolling through the camp, sometimes singing, sometimes dancing, like a madman, and repeating that I was not now Murad, the Unlucky. Whilst these words were on my lips, a friendly spectator, who was in possession of his sober senses, caught me by the arm, and attempted to drag me from the place where I was exposing myself. "Do you not see," said he, "those soldiers, who are firing at a mark? I saw one of them, just now, deliberately taking aim at your turban; and, observe, he is now re-loading his piece." My ill-luck prevailed even at the instant, the only instant in my life, when I defied its power. I struggled with my adviser, repeating, "I am not the wretch you take me for; I am not Murad, the Unlucky." He fled from the danger himself: I remained, and in a few seconds afterwards a ball reached me, and I fell senseless on the sand.

'The ball was cut out of my body by an aukward surgeon, who gave me ten times more pain than was necessary. He was particularly hurried, at this time, because the army had just received orders to march in a few hours, and all was confusion in the camp. My wound was excessively painful, and the fear of being left behind with those who were deemed incurable added to my torments. Perhaps, if I had kept myself quiet, I might have escaped some of the evils I afterwards endured; but, as I have repeatedly told you, gentlemen, it was my ill fortune never to be able to judge what was best to be done, till the time for prudence was past.

'During that day, when my fever was at the height, and when my orders were to keep my bed, contrary to my natural habits of indolence, I rose a hundred times and went out of my tent, in the very heat of the day, to satisfy my curiosity as to the number of the tents which had not been struck, and of the soldiers who had not yet marched. The orders to march were tardily obeyed; and many hours elapsed, before our encampment was raised. Had I submitted to my surgeon's orders, I might have been in a state to accompany the most dilatory of the stragglers; I could have borne, perhaps, the slow motion of a litter, on which some of the sick were transported; but, in the evening, when the surgeon came to dress my wounds, he found me in such a situation that it was scarcely possible to remove me.

'He desired a party of soldiers, who were left to bring up the rear, to call for me the next morning. They did so; but they wanted to put me upon the mule which I recollected, by a white streak on its back, to be the cursed animal that had kicked me, whilst I was looking for the ring. I could not be prevailed upon to go upon this unlucky animal. I tried to persuade the soldiers to carry me, and they took me a little way; but, soon growing weary of their burthen, they laid me down on the sand, pretending that they were going to fill a skin with water at a spring they had discovered, and bade me lie still and wait for their return.

'I waited and waited, longing for the water to moisten my parched lips; but no water came—no soldiers returned; and there I lay, for several hours, expecting every moment to breathe my last. I made no effort to move, for I was now convinced my hour was come; and that it was the will of Mahomet that I should perish, in this miserable manner, and lie unburied like a dog: a death, thought I, worthy of Murad, the Unlucky.

'My forebodings were not this time just; a detachment of English soldiers* passed near the place where I lay; my groans were heard by them, and they humanely came to my assistance. They carried me with them, dressed my wound, and treated me with the utmost tenderness. Christians though they were, I must acknowledge that I had reason to love them better than any of the followers of Mahomet, my good brother only excepted.

'Under their care I recovered; but scarcely had I regained my strength before I fell into new disasters. It was hot weather, and my thirst was excessive. I went out, with a party, in hopes of finding a spring of water. The English soldiers began to dig for a well, in a place pointed out to them by one of their men of science. I was not inclined to such hard labour, but preferred sauntering on in search of a spring. I saw at a distance something that looked like a pool of water; and I pointed it out to my companions. Their man of science warned me, by his interpreter, not to trust to this deceitful appearance; for that such were common in this country, and that, when I came close to the spot, I should find no water there. He added that it was at a greater distance than I imagined; and that I should in all probability be lost in the desert, if I attempted to follow this phantom.*

'I was so unfortunate as not to attend to his advice: I set out in pursuit of this accursed delusion, which assuredly was the work of evil spirits, who clouded my reason, and allured me into their dominion. I went on, hour after hour, in expectation continually of reaching the object of my wishes; but it fled faster than I pursued, and I discovered at last that the Englishman, who had doubtless gained his information from the people of the country, was right; and that the shining appearance, which I had taken for water, was a mere deception.

'I was now exhausted with fatigue: I looked back in vain

after the companions I had left; I could see neither men, animals, nor any trace of vegetation in the sandy desert. I had no resource but, weary as I was, to measure back my footsteps, which were imprinted in the sand.

'I slowly and sorrowfully traced them as my guides in this unknown land. Instead of yielding to my indolent inclinations, I ought however to have made the best of my way home, before the evening breeze sprung up. I felt the breeze rising, and, unconscious of my danger, I rejoiced, and opened my bosom to meet it; but what was my dismay when I saw that the wind swept before it all trace of my footsteps in the sand. I knew not which way to proceed; I was struck with despair, tore my garments, threw off my turban, and cried aloud; but neither human voice nor echo answered me. The silence was dreadful. I had tasted no food for many hours, and I now became sick and faint. I recollected that I had put a supply of opium in the folds of my turban; but, alas! when I took my turban up, I found that the opium had fallen out. I searched for it in vain on the sand, where I had thrown the turban.

'I stretched myself out upon the ground, and yielded without further struggle to my evil destiny. What I suffered, from thirst, hunger, and heat, cannot be described! At last, I fell into a sort of trance, during which images of various kinds seemed to flit before my eyes. How long I remained in this state I know not; but I remember that I was brought to my senses by a loud shout, which came from persons belonging to a caravan returning from Mecca.* This was a shout of joy for their safe arrival at a certain spring, well known to them, in this part of the desert.

'The spring was not a hundred yards from the spot where I lay; yet, such had been the fate of Murad, the Unlucky, that he missed the reality, whilst he had been hours in pursuit of the phantom. Feeble and spiritless as I was, I sent forth as loud a cry as I could, in hopes of obtaining assistance; and I endeavoured to crawl to the place from whence the voices appeared to come. The caravan rested for a considerable time, whilst the slaves filled the skins with water, and whilst the camels took in their supply. I worked myself on towards them; yet, notwithstanding my efforts, I was persuaded that, according to my usual ill fortune, I should never be able to make them hear my voice. I saw them mount their camels! I took off my turban, unrolled it, and waved it in the air. My signal was seen! The caravan came towards me!

'I had scarcely strength to speak; a slave gave me some water, and, after I had drunk, I explained to them who I was, and how I came into this situation.

'Whilst I was speaking, one of the travellers observed the purse which hung to my girdle: it was the same the merchant, for whom I recovered the ring, had given to me; I had carefully preserved it, because the initials of my benefactor's name, and a passage from the Koran, were worked upon it.* When he gave it to me, he said that, perhaps, we should meet again, in some other part of the world, and he should recognise me by this token. The person who now took notice of the purse was his brother; and, when I related to him how I had obtained it, he had the goodness to take me under his protection. He was a merchant, who was now going with the caravan to Grand Cairo:* he offered to take me with him, and I willingly accepted the proposal, promising to serve him as faithfully as any of his slaves. The caravan proceeded, and I was carried with it.

CHAPTER III

Self-love is deaf to the Lessons of Experience.

'THE merchant, who was become my master, treated me with great kindness; but, on hearing me relate the whole series of my unfortunate adventures, he exacted a promise from me, that I would do nothing without first consulting him. "Since you are so unlucky, Murad," said he, "that you always chuse for the worst, when you chuse for yourself, you should trust entirely to the judgment of a wiser or a more fortunate friend."

'I fared well in the service of this merchant, who was a man of a mild disposition, and who was so rich that he could afford to be generous to all his dependents. It was my business to see his camels loaded and unloaded, at proper places, to count his bales of merchandize, and to take care that they were not mixed with those of his companions. This I carefully did, till the day we arrived at Alexandria; when, unluckily, I neglected to count the bales, taking it for granted that they were all right, as I had found them so the preceding day. However, when we were to go on board the vessel that was to take us to Cairo, I perceived that three bales of cotton were missing.

'I ran to inform my master, who, though a good deal provoked at my negligence, did not reproach me as I deserved. The public crier was immediately sent round the city, to offer a reward for the recovery of the merchandize; and it was restored by one of the merchant's slaves, with whom we had travelled. The vessel was now under sail, my master and I and the bales of cotton were obliged to follow in a boat; and, when we were taken on board, the captain declared he was so loaded that he could not tell where to

stow the bales of cotton. After much difficulty, he consented to let them remain upon deck; and I promised my
master to watch them night and day.

'We had a prosperous voyage, and were actually in sight
of shore, which the captain said, we could not fail to reach
early the next morning. I stayed, as usual, this night upon
deck; and solaced myself by smoaking my pipe. Ever since
I had indulged in this practice, at the camp at El Arish, I
could not exist without opium and tobacco. I suppose that
my reason was this night a little clouded with the dose I
took; but, towards midnight, I was sobered by terror. I
started up from the deck, on which I had stretched myself:
my turban was in flames, the bale of cotton on which I had
rested was all on fire. I awakened two sailors, who were fast
asleep on deck. The consternation became general, and the
confusion encreased the danger. The captain and my master
were the most active, and suffered the most in extinguishing
the flames: my master was terribly scorched.

'For my part, I was not suffered to do any thing; the
captain ordered that I should be bound to the mast; and,
when at last the flames were extinguished, the passengers
with one accord besought him to keep me bound hand and
foot, lest I should be the cause of some new disaster. All
that had happened was, indeed, occasioned by my ill-luck.
I had laid my pipe down, when I was falling asleep, upon
the bale of cotton that was beside me. The fire from the
pipe fell out, and set the cotton in flames. Such was the
mixture of rage and terror, with which I had inspired the
whole crew, that I am sure they would have set me ashore
on a desert island, rather than have had me on board for a
week longer. Even my humane master I could perceive was
secretly impatient to get rid of Murad, the Unlucky, and
his evil fortune.

'You may believe that I was heartily glad when we
landed, and when I was unbound. My master put a purse
containing fifty sequins into my hand, and bade me fare-

well.—"Use this money prudently, Murad, if you can," said he, "and perhaps your fortune may change." Of this I had little hopes; but determined to lay out my money as prudently as possible.

'As I was walking through the streets of Grand Cairo, considering how I should lay out my fifty sequins to the greatest advantage, I was stopped by one who called me by my name, and asked me if I could pretend to have forgotten his face. I looked steadily at him, and recollected, to my sorrow, that he was the Jew, Rachub, from whom I had borrowed certain monies at the camp at El-Arish. What brought him to Grand Cairo, except it was my evil destiny, I cannot tell. He would not quit me; he would take no excuses; he said he knew that I had deserted twice, once from the Turkish and once from the English army; that I was not intitled to any pay; and that he could not imagine it possible my brother Saladin would own me, or pay my debts.

'I replied, for I was vexed by the insolence of this Jewish dog, that I was not, as he imagined, a beggar; that I had the means of paying him my just debt, but that I hoped he would not extort from me all that exorbitant interest which none but a Jew could exact. He smiled, and answered that, if a Turk loved opium better than money, this was no fault of his; that he had supplied me with what I loved best in the world; and that I ought not to complain, when he expected I should return the favour.

'I will not weary you, gentlemen, with all the arguments that passed between me and Rachub. At last, we compromised matters; he would take nothing less than the whole debt; but he let me have at a very cheap rate a chest of second hand clothes, by which he assured me I might make my fortune. He brought them to Grand Cairo, he said, for the purpose of selling them to slave merchants; who, at this time of the year, were in want of them to supply their slaves: but he was in haste to get home to his wife and family, at Constantinople, and therefore he was willing to make over to a friend the profits of this speculation. I should have distrusted Rachub's professions of friendship, and especially of disinterestedness; but he took me with him to the khan, where his goods were, and unlocked the chest of clothes to shew them to me. They were of the richest and finest materials, and had been but little worn. I could not doubt the evidence of my senses: the bargain was concluded, and the Jew sent porters to my inn with the chest.

'The next day, I repaired to the public market-place; and, when my business was known, I had choice of customers before night: my chest was empty,—and my purse was full. The profit I made, upon the sale of these clothes, was so considerable that I could not help feeling astonishment at Rachub's having brought himself so readily to relinquish them.

'A few days after I had disposed of the contents of my chest, a Damascene merchant, who had bought two suits of apparel from me, told me, with a very melancholy face, that both the female slaves, who had put on these clothes, were sick. I could not conceive that the clothes were the cause of their sickness; but, soon afterwards, as I was crossing the market, I was attacked by at least a dozen merchants, who made similar complaints. They insisted upon knowing how I came by the garments, and demanded whether I had worn any of them myself. This day I had for the first time indulged myself with wearing a pair of yellow slippers, the only finery I had reserved for myself out of all the tempting goods. Convinced by my wearing these slippers that I could have had no insidious designs, since I shared the danger whatever it might be, the merchants were a little pacified; but what was my terror and remorse, the next day, when one of them came to inform me that plague boils had broken out under the arms of all the slaves, who had worn this pestilential apparel. On looking carefully into the chest, we found the word Smyrna written, and half effaced, upon the lid. Now the plague had for some time raged at Smyrna; and, as the merchants suspected, these clothes had certainly belonged to persons who had died of that distemper.* This was the reason why the Jew was willing to sell them to me so cheap; and it was for this reason that he would not stay at Grand Cairo himself, to reap *the profits of his speculation*. Indeed, if I had paid attention to it at the proper time, a slight circumstance might have revealed the truth to me. Whilst I was bargaining with the Jew, before he opened the chest, he swallowed a large dram of brandy, and stuffed his nostrils with spunge dipped in vinegar: this he told me he did to prevent his perceiving the smell of musk, which always threw him into convulsions.

'The horror I felt, when I discovered that I had spread the infection of the plague, and that I had probably caught it myself, overpowered my senses: A cold dew spread over all my limbs, and I fell upon the lid of the fatal chest in a swoon. It is said that fear disposes people to take the infection: however this may be, I sickened that evening, and soon was in a raging fever. It was worse for me whenever the delirium left me, and I could reflect upon the miseries my ill fortune had occasioned. In my first lucid interval I looked round and saw that I had been removed from the khan to a wretched hut. An old woman, who was smoaking her pipe in the farthest corner of my room, informed me that I had been sent out of the town of Grand Cairo by order of the Cadi,* to whom the merchants had made their complaint. The fatal chest was burnt, and the house in which I had lodged razed to the ground. "And, if it had not been for me," continued the old woman, "you would have been dead, probably, at this instant; but I have made a vow, to our great prophet, that I would never neglect an opportunity of doing a good action: therefore, when you were deserted by all the world, I took care of you. Here too is your purse, which I saved from the rabble;

and what is more difficult, from the officers of justice: I will account to you for every para* that I have expended; and will moreover tell you the reason of my making such an extraordinary vow."

'As I perceived that this benevolent old woman took great pleasure in talking, I made an inclination of my head to thank her for her promised history, and she proceeded; but I must confess I did not listen with all the attention her narrative doubtless deserved. Even curiosity, the strongest passion of us Turks, was dead within me. I have no recollection of the old woman's story. It is as much as I can do to finish my own.

'The weather became excessively hot: it was affirmed, by some of the physicians, that this heat would prove fatal to their patients;[1] but, contrary to the prognostics of the physicians, it stopped the progress of the plague. I recovered, and found my purse much lightened by my illness. I divided the remainder of my money with my humane nurse, and sent her out into the city to enquire how matters were going on.

'She brought me word that the fury of the plague had much abated; but that she had met several funerals, and that she had heard many of the merchants cursing the folly of Murad, the Unlucky, who, as they said, had brought all this calamity upon the inhabitants of Cairo. Even fools, they say, learn by experience. I took care to burn the bed on which I had laid, and the clothes I had worn: I concealed my real name, which I knew would inspire detestation, and gained admittance, with a crowd of other poor wretches, into a Lazaretto,* where I performed quarantine, and offered up prayers daily for the sick.

'When I thought it was impossible I could spread the infection, I took my passage home. I was eager to get away from Grand Cairo, where I knew I was an object of

---

[1] Antes's Observations of the Manners and Customs of the Egyptians.*

execration. I had a strange fancy haunting my mind: I imagined that all my misfortunes, since I left Constantinople, had arisen from my neglect of the talisman, upon the beautiful China vase. I dreamed three times, when I was recovering from the plague, that a genius appeared to me, and said, in a reproachful tone, "Murad, where is the vase that was entrusted to thy care?"

'This dream operated strongly upon my imagination. As soon as we arrived at Constantinople, which we did, to my great surprise, without meeting with any untoward accidents, I went in search of my brother Saladin, to enquire for my vase. He no longer lived in the house in which I left him, and I began to be apprehensive that he was dead; but a porter, hearing my enquiries, exclaimed, "Who is there, in Constantinople, that is ignorant of the dwelling of Saladin, the Lucky! Come with me, and I will shew it to you."

'The mansion to which he conducted me looked so magnificent that I was almost afraid to enter, lest there should be some mistake. But, whilst I was hesitating, the doors opened, and I heard my brother Saladin's voice. He saw me almost at the same instant I fixed my eyes upon him, and immediately sprang forward to embrace me. He was the same good brother as ever, and I rejoiced in his prosperity with all my heart. "Brother Saladin," said I, "can you now doubt that some men are born to be fortunate, and others to be unfortunate? How often you used to dispute this point with me!"

'"Let us not dispute it now in the public street," said he smiling; "but come in and refresh yourself, and we will consider the question afterwards at leisure."

'"No, my dear brother," said I, drawing back, "you are too good: Murad, the Unlucky, shall not enter your house, lest he should draw down misfortunes upon you and yours. I come only to ask for my vase."

'"It is safe," cried he, "come in and you shall see it: but

I will not give it up till I have you in my house. I have none of these superstitious fears: pardon me the expression, but I have none of these superstitious fears."

'I yielded, entered his house, and was astonished at all I saw! my brother did not triumph in his prosperity; but, on the contrary, seemed intent only upon making me forget my misfortunes: he listened to the account of them with kindness, and obliged me by the recital of his history; which was, I must acknowledge, far less wonderful than my own. He seemed, by his own account, to have grown rich in the common course of things; or rather, by his own prudence. I allowed for his prejudices, and, unwilling to dispute farther with him, said, "You must remain of your opinion, brother; and I of mine: you are Saladin, the Lucky, and I Murad, the Unlucky; and so we shall remain to the end of our lives."

'I had not been in his house four days when an accident happened, which shewed how much I was in the right. The favourite of the Sultan, to whom he had formerly sold his china vase, though her charms were now somewhat faded by time, still retained her power, and her taste for magnificence. She commissioned my brother to bespeak for her, at Venice, the most splendid looking-glass that money could purchase. The mirror, after many delays and disappointments, at length arrived at my brother's house. He unpacked it, and sent to let the lady know it was in perfect safety. It was late in the evening, and she ordered it should remain where it was that night; and that it should be brought to the seraglio the next morning. It stood in a sort of anti-chamber to the room in which I slept; and with it was left some packages, containing glass chandeliers for an unfinished saloon, in my brother's house. Saladin charged all his domestics to be vigilant this night; because he had money to a great amount by him, and there had been frequent robberies in our neighbourhood. Hearing these orders, I resolved to be in readiness at a moment's warning.

I laid my scymitar beside me upon a cushion; and left my door half open, that I might hear the slightest noise in the anti-chamber, or the great stair-case. About midnight, I was suddenly wakened by a noise in the anti-chamber. I started up, seized my scymitar, and the instant I got to the door, saw, by the light of the lamp which was burning in the room, a man standing opposite to me, with a drawn sword in his hand. I rushed forward, demanding what he wanted, and received no answer; but, seeing him aim at me with his scymitar, I gave him, as I thought, a deadly blow. At this instant, I heard a great crash; and the fragments of the looking glass, which I had shivered, fell at my feet. At the same moment, something black brushed by my shoulder: I pursued it, stumbled over the packages of glass, and rolled over them down the stairs.

'My brother came out of his room, to enquire the cause of all this disturbance; and, when he saw the fine mirror broken, and me lying amongst the glass chandeliers at the bottom of the stairs, he could not forbear exclaiming, "Well, brother! you are indeed, Murad, the Unlucky."

'When the first emotion was over, he could not, however, forbear laughing at my situation. With a degree of goodness, which made me a thousand times more sorry for the accident, he came down stairs to help me up, gave me his hand, and said, "Forgive me, if I was angry with you at first. I am sure you did not mean to do me any injury; but tell me how all this has happened?"

'Whilst Saladin was speaking, I heard the same kind of noise which had alarmed me in the anti-chamber; but, on looking back, I saw only a black pigeon, which flew swiftly by me, unconscious of the mischief he had occasioned. This pigeon I had unluckily brought into the house the preceding day; and had been feeding and trying to tame it, for my young nephews. I little thought it would be the cause of such disasters. My brother, though he endeavoured to conceal his anxiety from me, was much disturbed at the idea of meeting the favourite's displeasure, who would certainly be grievously disappointed by the loss of her splendid looking-glass. I saw that I should inevitably be his ruin, if I continued in his house; and no persuasions could prevail upon me to prolong my stay. My generous brother, seeing me determined to go, said to me, "A factor,* whom I have employed for some years to sell merchandise for me, died a few days ago. Will you take his place? I am rich enough to bear any little mistakes you may fall into, from ignorance of business; and you will have a partner, who is able and willing to assist you."

'I was touched to the heart by this kindness; especially at such a time as this. He sent one of his slaves with me to the shop in which you now see me, gentlemen. The slave, by my brother's directions, brought with us my china vase, and delivered it safely to me, with this message: "The scarlet dye, that was found in this vase, and in its fellow, was the first cause of Saladin's making the fortune he now enjoys: he therefore does no more than justice, in sharing that fortune with his brother Murad?"

'I was now placed in as advantageous a situation as possible; but my mind was ill at ease, when I reflected that the broken mirror might be my brother's ruin. The lady by whom it had been bespoken was, I well knew, of a violent temper; and this disappointment was sufficient to provoke her to vengeance. My brother sent me word this morning, however, that, though her displeasure was excessive, it was in my power to prevent any ill consequences that might ensue. "In my power," I exclaimed, "Then, indeed I am happy! Tell my brother there is nothing I will not do, to shew him my gratitude, and to save him from the consequences of my folly."

'The slave, who was sent by my brother, seemed unwilling to name what was required of me, saying that his master was afraid I should not like to grant the request. I urged him to speak freely, and he then told me the favourite declared nothing would make her amends, for the loss of the mirror, but the fellow vase to that which he had brought from Saladin. It was impossible for me to hesitate; gratitude for my brother's generous kindness overcame my superstitious obstinacy; and I sent him word I would carry the vase to him myself.

I took it down this evening, from the shelf on which it stood: it was covered with dust, and I washed it; but unluckily, in endeavouring to clean the inside from the remains of the scarlet powder, I poured hot water into it, and immediately I heard a simmering noise, and my vase, in a few instants, burst asunder with a loud explosion. These fragments, alas! are all that remain. The measure of my misfortunes is now completed! Can you wonder, gentlemen, that I bewail my evil destiny? Am I not justly called Murad, the Unlucky? Here end all my hopes in this world! Better would it have been if I had died long ago! Better that I had never been born! Nothing I ever have done, or attempted, has prospered. Murad, the Unlucky, is my name, and ill-fate has marked me for her own.

CHAPTER IV

Prudence neither overlooks nor neglects Trifles.

THE lamentations of Murad were interrupted by the entrance of Saladin: Having waited in vain for some hours, he now came to see if any disaster had happened to his brother Murad. He was surprised at the sight of the two pretended merchants; and could not refrain from exclamations, on beholding the broken vase. However, with his usual equanimity and good nature, he began to console Murad; and, taking up the fragments, examined them carefully, one by one, joined them together again, found that none of the edges of the china were damaged, and declared, he could have it mended so as to look as well as ever.

Murad recovered his spirits upon this. 'Brother,' said he, 'I comfort myself for being Murad, the Unlucky, when I reflect that you are Saladin, the Lucky. See, gentlemen,' continued he, turning to the pretended merchants, 'scarcely has this most fortunate of men been five minutes in company before he gives a happy turn to affairs. His presence inspires joy: I observe your countenances, which had been saddened by my dismal history, have brightened up, since he has made his appearance. Brother, I wish you would make these gentlemen some amends, for the time they have wasted in listening to my catalogue of misfortunes, by relating your history, which, I am sure, they will find rather more exhilarating.'

Saladin consented, on condition that the strangers would accompany him home, and partake of a sociable banquet. They at first repeated the former excuse of their being obliged to return to their inn: but at length the Sultan's curiosity prevailed, and he and his vizier went home with Saladin, the Lucky; who, after supper, related his history in the following manner:

'My being called Saladin, the Lucky, first inspired me with confidence in myself: though I own that I cannot remember any extraordinary instances of good luck in my childhood. An old nurse of my mother's, indeed, repeated to me twenty times a day that nothing I undertook could fail to succeed; because I was Saladin, the Lucky. I became presumptuous, and rash: and my nurse's prognostics might have effectually prevented their accomplishment, had I not, when I was about fifteen, been roused to reflection during a long confinement, which was the consequence of my youthful conceit and imprudence.

'At this time there was at the Porte* a Frenchman, an ingenious engineer, who was employed and favoured by the Sultan, to the great astonishment of many of my prejudiced countrymen. On the Grand Seignor's birth-day, he exhibited some extraordinarily fine fire-works; and I, with numbers of the inhabitants of Constantinople, crowded to see them.* I happened to stand near the place where the Frenchman was stationed; the crowd pressed upon him, and I amongst the rest: he begged we would, for our own sakes, keep at a greater distance; and warned us that we might be much hurt, by the combustibles which he was using. I, relying upon my good fortune, disregarded all these cautions; and the consequence was that, as I touched some of the materials prepared for the fire-works, they exploded, dashed me upon the ground with great violence, and I was terribly burnt.

'This accident, gentlemen, I consider as one of the most fortunate circumstances of my life; for it checked and corrected the presumption of my temper. During the time I was confined to my bed, the French gentleman came frequently to see me. He was a very sensible man; and the conversations he had with me enlarged my mind, and cured me of many foolish prejudices: especially of that, which I had been taught to entertain, concerning the predominance of what is called luck, or fortune, in human affairs. "Though you are called Saladin, the Lucky," said he, "you find that your neglect of prudence has nearly brought you to the grave, even in the bloom of youth. Take my advice, and henceforward trust more to prudence than to fortune. Let the multitude, if they will, call you Saladin, the Lucky: but call yourself, and make yourself, Saladin, the Prudent."

'These words left an indelible impression on my mind, and gave a new turn to my thoughts and character. My brother, Murad, has doubtless told you that our difference of opinion, on the subject of predestination, produced between us frequent arguments; but we could never convince one another, and we each have acted through life, in consequence of our different beliefs. To this I attribute my success, and his misfortunes.

'The first rise of my fortune, as you have probably heard from Murad, was owing to the scarlet dye, which I brought to perfection with infinite difficulty. The powder, it is true, was accidentally found by me in our china vases; but there it might have remained, to this instant useless, if I had not taken the pains to make it useful. I grant that we can only partially foresee and command events: yet on the use we make of our own powers, I think, depends our destiny. But, gentlemen, you would rather hear my adventures, perhaps than my reflections; and I am truly concerned, for your sakes, that I have no wonderful events to relate. I am sorry I cannot tell you of my having been lost in a sandy desert. I have never had the plague, or even been shipwrecked: I have been all my life an inhabitant of Constantinople, and have passed my time in a very quiet and uniform manner.

'The money I received from the Sultan's favourite for my china-vase, as my brother may have told you, enabled me to trade on a more extensive scale. I went on steadily, with my business; and made it my whole study to please my employers, by all fair and honorable means. This industry and civility succeeded beyond my expectations: in a few years, I was rich for a man in my way of business.

'I will not proceed to trouble you with the journal of a petty merchant's life; I pass on to the incident which made a considerable change in my affairs.

'A terrible fire broke out in the suburb of Pera; near the walls of the Grand Seignor's seraglio.[1] As you are strangers, gentlemen, you may not have heard of this event; though it produced so great a sensation in Constantinople. The vizier's superb palace was utterly consumed; and also the mosque of St Sophia.* Various were the opinions, formed by my neighbours, respecting the cause of the conflagration. Some supposed it to be a punishment for the Sultan's having neglected, one Friday, to appear at the mosque of St Sophia: others considered it as a warning sent by Mahomet, to dissuade the Porte from persisting in a war in which we were just engaged.* The generality, however, of the coffee-house politicians, contented themselves with observing that it was the will of Mahomet that the palace should be consumed. Satisfied by this supposition, they took no precaution to prevent similar accidents in their own houses. Never were fires so common, in the city, as at this period: scarcely a night passed, without our being wakened by the cry of fire.

'These frequent fires were rendered still more dreadful by villains, who were continually on the watch, to encrease the confusion by which they profited, and to pillage the houses of the sufferers. It was discovered that these incendiaries frequently skulked, towards evening, in the neighbourhood of the Bezestein,* where the richest merchants store their goods: some of these wretches were detected in

---

[1] *v.* Baron de Tott's Memoirs.*

throwing *coundaks*[1] or matches, into the windows; and, if these combustibles remained a sufficient time, they could not fail to set the house on fire.

'Notwithstanding all these circumstances, many even of those who had property to preserve continued to repeat, "It is the will of Mahomet;" and consequently to neglect all means of preservation. I, on the contrary, recollecting the lesson I had learned from the sensible foreigner, neither suffered my spirits to sink with superstitious fears of ill luck, nor did I trust presumptuously to my good fortune. I took every possible means to secure myself. I never went to bed without having seen that all the lights and fires in the house were extinguished; and that I had a supply of water in the cistern. I had likewise learned from my Frenchman that wet mortar was the most effectual thing for stopping the progress of flames: I therefore had a quantity of mortar made up, in one of my out-houses, which I could use at a moment's warning. These precautions were all useful to me: my own house, indeed, was never actually on fire; but the houses of my next door neighbours were no less than five times in flames, in the course of one winter. By my exertions, or rather by my precautions, they suffered but little damage; and all my neighbours looked upon me as their deliverer and friend: they loaded me with presents, and offered more indeed than I would accept. All repeated

[1] 'A *coundak* is a sort of combustible, that consists only of a piece of tinder wrapped in brimstone matches, in the midst of a small bundle of pine shavings. This is the method usually employed by incendiaries. They lay this match by stealth behind a door, which they find open, or on a window; and, after setting it on fire, they make their escape. This is sufficient often to produce the most terrible ravages, in a town where the houses, built with wood and painted with aspic oil, afford the easiest opportunity to the miscreant who is disposed to reduce them to ashes. This method, employed by the incendiaries, and which often escapes the vigilance of the masters of the houses, added to the common causes of fires, gave for some time very frequent causes of alarm.'—*Translation of Memoirs of Baron de Tott*, v. I.*

that I was Saladin, the Lucky. This compliment I disclaimed; feeling more ambitious of being called Saladin, the Prudent. It is thus that what we call modesty is often only a more refined species of pride. But to proceed with my story.

'One night, I had been later than usual at supper, at a friend's house: none but the *Passevans*,[1] or watch, were in the streets, and even they, I believe, were asleep.

'As I passed one of the conduits, which convey water to the city, I heard a trickling noise; and, upon examination, I found that the cock of the water-spout was half turned, so that the water was running out. I turned it back to its proper place, thought it had been left unturned by accident, and walked on; but I had not proceeded far before I came to another spout, and another, which were in the same condition. I was convinced that this could not be the effect merely of accident, and suspected that some ill-intentioned persons designed to let out and waste the water of the city, that there might be none to extinguish any fire that should break out in the course of the night.

'I stood still for a few moments, to consider how it would be most prudent to act. It would be impossible for me to run to all parts of the city, that I might stop the pipes that were running to waste. I first thought of wakening the watch, and the firemen, who were most of them slumbering

---

[1] 'It is the duty of the guardians of the different quarters of the city, who are called *Passevans*, to watch for fires: during the night, they run through their district, armed with large sticks, tipped with iron, which they strike against the pavement, and awaken the people with the cry of *Yungenvor*: or, there is a fire! and point out the quarter where it has appeared. A very high tower, in the palace of the Janissary Aga, as well as another at Galata, overlook all Constantinople; and there is a guard in each of these towers constantly looking out for the same object. It is there that a sort of larum, formed by beating two large drums, quickens the alarm, and conveys it rapidly down the canal, from whence a vast concourse of people, who are interested, run to their shops, as they often find them burnt or pillaged.'—*De Tott's Memoirs*, v. I.*

at their stations; but I reflected that they were perhaps not to be trusted, and that they were in a confederacy with the incendiaries: otherwise, they would certainly, before this hour, have observed and stopped the running of the sewers in their neighbourhood. I determined to waken a rich merchant, called Damat Zade,* who lived near me, and who had a number of slaves, whom he could send to different parts of the city, to prevent mischief, and give notice to the inhabitants of their danger.

'He was a very sensible active man, and one that could easily be wakened: he was not, like some Turks, an hour in recovering their lethargic senses. He was quick in decision and action; and his slaves resembled their master. He dispatched a messenger immediately to the grand vizier, that the Sultan's safety might be secured; and sent others to the magistrates, in each quarter of Constantinople. The large drums in the Janissary-Aga's tower* beat to rouse the inhabitants; and scarcely had this been heard to beat half an hour before the fire broke out in the lower apartments of Damat Zade's house, owing to a *coundak*, which had been left behind one of the doors.

'The wretches, who had prepared the mischief, came to enjoy it, and to pillage; but they were disappointed. Astonished to find themselves taken into custody, they could not comprehend how their designs had been frustrated. By timely exertions, the fire in my friend's house was extinguished; and, though fires broke out, during the night, in many parts of the city, but little damage was sustained, because there was time for precautions; and, by the stopping of the spouts, sufficient water was preserved. People were wakened, and warned of the danger; and they consequently escaped unhurt.

'The next day, as soon as I made my appearance at the Bezestein, the merchants crowded 'round, calling me their benefactor, and the preserver of their lives and fortunes. Damat Zade, the merchant, whom I had wakened the preceding night, presented to me a heavy purse of gold; and put upon my finger a diamond ring of considerable value: each of the merchants followed his example, in making me rich presents: the magistrates also sent me tokens of their approbation; and the grand vizier sent me a diamond of the first water, with a line written by his own hand: "To the man who has saved Constantinople." Excuse me, gentlemen, for the vanity I seem to shew in mentioning these circumstances. You desired to hear my history, and I cannot therefore omit the principal circumstance of my life. In the course of four and twenty hours, I found myself raised, by the munificent gratitude of the inhabitants of this city, to a state of affluence far beyond what I had ever dreamed of attaining.

'I now took a house suited to my circumstances, and bought a few slaves. As I was carrying my slaves home, I was met by a Jew, who stopped me, saying, in his language, "my Lord, I see, has been purchasing slaves: I could clothe them cheaply." There was something mysterious in the manner of this Jew, and I did not like his countenance; but I considered that I ought not to be governed by caprice in my dealings, and that, if this man could really clothe my slaves more cheaply than another, I ought not to neglect his offer merely because I took a dislike to the cut of his beard, the turn of his eye, or the tone of his voice. I therefore bade the Jew follow me home, saying that I would consider of his proposal.

'When we came to talk over the matter, I was surprised to find him so reasonable in his demands. On one point, indeed, he appeared unwilling to comply. I required, not only to see the clothes I was offered, but, also, to know how they came into his possession. On this subject he equivocated; I therefore suspected there must be something wrong. I reflected what it could be, and judged that the goods had been stolen, or that they had been the apparel of persons who had died of some contagious distemper. The

Jew shewed me a chest, from which he said I might chuse whatever suited me best. I observed that, as he unlocked the chest, he stuffed his nose with some aromatic herbs. He told me that he did so to prevent his smelling the musk, with which the chest was perfumed; musk, he said, had an extraordinary effect upon his nerves. I begged to have some of the herbs which he used himself; declaring that musk was likewise offensive to me.

'The Jew, either struck by his own conscience, or observing my suspicions, turned as pale as death. He pretended he had not the right key, and could not unlock the chest; said he must go in search of it, and that he would call on me again.

'After he had left me, I examined some writing upon the lid of the chest that had been nearly effaced. I made out the word Smyrna, and this was sufficient to confirm all my suspicions. The Jew returned no more: he sent some porters to carry away the chest, and I heard nothing of him for some time; till one day, when I was at the house of Damat Zade, I saw a glimpse of the Jew passing hastily through one of the courts, as if he wished to avoid me. "My friend," said I to Damat Zade, "do not attribute my question to impertinent curiosity, or to a desire to intermeddle with your affairs, if I venture to ask the nature of your business with the Jew, who has just now crossed your court?"

'"He has engaged to supply me with clothing for my slaves," replied my friend, "cheaper than I can purchase it elsewhere. I have a design to surprise my daughter, Fatima,* on her birth-day, with an entertainment in the pavillion in the garden; and all her female slaves shall appear in new dresses on the occasion."

'I interrupted my friend, to tell him what I suspected relative to this Jew and his chest of clothes. It is certain that the infection of the plague can be communicated by clothes, not only after months but after years have elapsed. The merchant resolved to have nothing more to do with this wretch, who could thus hazard the lives of thousands of his fellow-creatures for a few pieces of gold: we sent notice of the circumstance to the cadi, but the cadi was slow in his operations; and, before he could take the Jew into custody, the cunning fellow had effected his escape. When his house was searched, he and his chest had disappeared: we discovered that he sailed for Egypt, and rejoiced that we had driven him from Constantinople.

'My friend, Damat Zade, expressed the warmest gratitude to me. "You formerly saved my fortune: you have now saved my life; and a life yet dearer than my own, that of my daughter, Fatima."

'At the sound of that name I could not, I believe, avoid shewing some emotion. I had accidentally seen this lady, as she was going to the mosque; and I had been captivated by her beauty, and by the sweetness of her countenance: but, as I knew she was destined to be the wife of another, I suppressed my feelings, and determined to banish the recollection of the fair Fatima for ever from my imagination. Her father, however, at this instant, threw in my way a temptation, which it required all my fortitude to resist. "Saladin," continued he, "it is but just that you, who have saved our lives, should share our festivity. Come here on the birth-day of my Fatima: I will place you in a balcony, which overlooks the garden, and you shall see the whole spectacle. We shall have *a feast of tulips*; in imitation of that which, as you know, is held in the Grand Seignior's gardens.[1] I assure you, the sight will be worth seeing; and

---

[1] The feast of tulips, or Tehiragan, is so called because, at this feast, parterres of tulips are illuminated. 'This is the flower,' says the Baron de Tott, 'of which the Turks are the fondest. The gardens of the Harem serves as the theatre of these nocturnal feasts. Vases of every kind, filled with natural or artificial flowers, are gathered there: and are lighted by an infinite number of lanterns, coloured lamps, and wax lights, placed in glass tubes, and reflected by looking-glasses disposed for that purpose. Temporary shops, filled with different sorts of merchandise, are occupied by women of the Harem, who represent, in suitable dresses, the merchants

besides, you will have a chance of beholding my Fatima, for a moment, without her veil."

'"That," interrupted I, "is the thing I most wish to avoid. I dare not indulge myself in a pleasure which might cost me the happiness of my life. I will conceal nothing from you, who treat me with so much confidence. I have already beheld the charming countenance of your Fatima; but I know that she is destined to be the wife of a happier man."

'Damat Zade seemed much pleased by the frankness with which I explained myself; but he would not give up the idea of my sitting with him, in the balcony, on the day of the feast of tulips; and I, on my part, could not consent to expose myself to another view of the charming Fatima. My friend used every argument, or rather every sort of persuasion, he could imagine to prevail upon me: he then tried to laugh me out of my resolution; and, when all failed, he said, in a voice of anger, "Go then, Saladin, I am sure you are deceiving me; you have a passion for some other woman, and you could conceal it from me, and persuade me you refuse the favour I offer you from prudence; when, in fact, it is from indifference and contempt. Why could you not speak the truth of your heart to me with that frankness with which one friend should treat another?"

'Astonished at this unexpected charge, and at the anger which flashed from the eyes of Damat Zade, who, till this moment, had always appeared to me a man of a mild and reasonable temper; I was for an instant tempted to fly in a passion and leave him: but friends, once lost, are not easily regained. This consideration had power sufficient to make me command my temper. "My friend," replied I, "we will

who might be supposed to sell them *** ****. Dancing and music prolong these entertainments, until the night is far advanced, and diffuse a sort of momentary gaiety within these walls, generally devoted to sorrow and dullness.' *Vide Memoirs of Baron de Tott*, v. I.*

talk over this affair to-morrow: you are now angry, and cannot do me justice, but to-morrow you will be cool: you will then be convinced that I have not deceived you; and that I have no design but to secure my own happiness, by the most prudent means in my power, by avoiding the sight of the dangerous Fatima. I have no passion for any other woman."

'"Then," said my friend, embracing me, and quitting the tone of anger, which he had assumed only to try my resolution to the utmost, "then, Saladin, Fatima is yours."

'I scarcely dared to believe my senses! I could not express my joy! "Yes, my friend," continued the merchant, "I have tried your prudence to the utmost; it has been victorious, and I resign my Fatima to you, certain that you will make her happy. It is true, I had a greater alliance in view for her: the Pacha of Maksoud* has demanded her from me; but I have found, upon private enquiry, he is addicted to the intemperate use of opium; and my daughter shall never be the wife of one who is a violent madman, one-half the day, and a melancholy idiot during the remainder. I have nothing to apprehend from the Pacha's resentment; because I have powerful friends with the grand vizier, here, who will oblige him to understand reason, and to submit quietly to a disappointment he so justly merits. And now, Saladin, have you any objection to seeing the feast of tulips?"

'I replied only by falling at the merchant's feet, and embracing his knees. The feast of tulips came, and on that day I was married to the charming Fatima! The charming Fatima I continue still to think her, though she has now been my wife some years. She is the joy and pride of my heart; and, from our mutual affection, I have experienced more felicity than from all the other circumstances of my life, which are called so fortunate. Her father gave me the house in which I now live, and joined his possessions to ours; so that I have more wealth even than I desire. My riches, however, give me continually the means of relieving the wants of others; and therefore I cannot affect to despise them. I must persuade my brother Murad to share them with me, and to forget his misfortunes: I shall then think myself completely happy. As to the Sultana's looking-glass, and your broken vase, my dear brother,' continued Saladin, 'we must think of some means——'

'Think no more of the Sultana's looking-glass, or of the broken vase,' exclaimed the Sultan, throwing aside his merchant's habit, and shewing beneath it his own imperial vest. 'Saladin, I rejoice to have heard, from your own lips, the history of your life. I acknowledge, vizier, I have been in the wrong, in our argument,' continued the Sultan, turning to his vizier. 'I acknowledge that the histories of Saladin, the Lucky, and Murad, the Unlucky, favour your opinion, that prudence has more influence than chance, in human affairs. The success and happiness of Saladin seems to me to have arisen from his prudence: by that prudence, Constantinople has been saved from flames, and from the plague. Had Murad possessed his brother's discretion, he would not have been on the point of losing his head, for selling rolls which he did not bake: he would not have been kicked by a mule, or bastinadoed for finding a ring: he would not have been robbed by one party of soldiers, or shot by another: he would not have been lost in a desert, or cheated by a Jew: he would not have set a ship on fire; nor would he have caught the plague, and spread it through Grand Cairo: he would not have run my Sultana's looking-glass through the body, instead of a robber: he would not have believed that the fate of his life depended on certain verses, on a china vase; nor would he, at last, have broken this precious talisman, by washing it in hot water. Henceforward, let Murad, the Unlucky, be named Murad, the Imprudent: let Saladin preserve the surname he merits, and be henceforth called Saladin, the Prudent.'

So spake the Sultan, who, unlike the generality of monarchs, could bear to find himself in the wrong; and could discover his vizier to be in the right, without cutting off his head. History further informs us that the Sultan offered to make Saladin a Pacha, and to commit to him the government of a province: but Saladin, the Prudent, declined this honour; saying he had no ambition, was perfectly happy in his present situation, and that, when this was the case, it would be folly to change, because no one can be more than happy. What further adventures befel Murad, the Imprudent, are not recorded: it is known only that he became a daily visitor to the *Teriaky*; and that he died a martyr to the immoderate use of opium.[1]

---

[1] Those among the Turks, who give themselves up to an immoderate use of opium, are easily to be distinguished by a sort of ricketty complaint, which this poison produces, in course of time. Destined to live agreeably only when in a sort of drunkenness, these men present a curious spectacle, when they are assembled in a part of Constantinople called Teriaky, or Tcharkissy; the market of opium-eaters. It is there that, towards the evening, one sees the lovers of opium arrive by the different streets which terminate at the Solymania: (the greatest mosque in Constantinople) their pale and melancholy countenances would inspire only compassion, did not their stretched necks, their heads twisted to the right or left, their back-bones crooked, one shoulder up to their ears, and a number of other whimsical attitudes, which are the consequences of the disorder, present the most ludicrous and the most laughable picture.*

Jan. 1802

EXPLANATORY NOTES

I HAVE attempted wherever possible to supply information about places, language, historical events, and literary references not necessarily available to the modern reader. I have relied when necessary on a number of general sources for information regarding Islamic beliefs, customs, and practices, including: John L. Esposito, *Islam: The Straight Path* (Oxford, 1991); H. A. R. Gibb, J. H. Kramers, *et al.* (eds.), *The Shorter Dictionary of Islam* (Ithaca, NY, 1953); Albert Hourani, *A History of the Arab Peoples* (Cambridge, Mass., 1991); Joseph Schacht and C. E. Bosworth (eds.), *The Legacy of Islam*, 2nd edn. (Oxford, 1979). The following sources are referred to in the Notes by short titles:

Abbott, *Hawkesworth*	John Lawrence Abbott, *John Hawkesworth: Eighteenth-Century Man of Letters* (Madison, Wis., 1982).
Antes, *Observations*	John Antes, *Observations on the Manners and Customs of the Egyptians* (London, 1800).
Arabian Nights	*Arabian Nights' Entertainments* (London, 1728–30). The *Arabian Nights* originally began appearing in English in 1706.
Baron de Tott, *Memoirs*	François, Baron de Tott, *Memoirs of Baron de Tott* (London, 1785).
Boswell, *Life*	James Boswell, *Life of Johnson*, ed. George Birbeck Hill, 6 vols. (Oxford, 1934).
Davies, *Egyptian History*	J. Davies, *The Egyptian History . . . According to the Opinions and Traditions of the Arabs* (London, 1672).

Johnson, *Dictionary*   Samuel Johnson, *A Dictionary of the English Language*, 2 vols. (London, 1755).

Johnson, *Rasselas*   Samuel Johnson, *Rasselas and Other Tales*, ed. Gwin Kolb (New Haven, Conn., 1990).

OED   *A New English Dictionary on Historical Principles*, 2nd edn. (Oxford, 1989).

Sale, *Koran* and *Prelim. Disc.*   George Sale, *The Koran, Commonly called The Alcoran of MOHAMMED . . . To which is Prefixed a Preliminary Discourse* (London, 1734).

Almoran and Hamet

3 TO THE KING: George III (1738–1820) had succeeded to the throne in the autumn of 1760, less than a year before the publication of Hawkesworth's novel, which appeared the following June. The Dedication reflects something of the short-lived goodwill which followed the accession of the new king. '[N]o monarch', Boswell would write of George III in his *Life of Johnson*, 'ever ascended with more sincere congratulations from his people. Two generations of foreign princes had prepared their minds to rejoice in having again a King who gloried in being "born a Briton"' (Boswell, *Life*, i. 353). Hawkesworth's subsequent reference in the Dedication to the 'free, . . . joyful, and now united people' of Britain similarly recalls Johnson's own praise for 'a King who knows not the name of party, and who wishes to be the common father of all his people' (Boswell, *Life*, ii. 112). The emphasis on national unity may likewise refer to the prominent inclusion of Bute—Hawkesworth's literary patron, the king's 'dearest friend', and, significantly, a Scot—in the new ministry. Hawkesworth had in fact secured permission to dedicate *Almoran and Hamet* to the new king through the influence of Bute, who managed to allay the author's self-confessed fear

of including in the story 'any Sentiment, allusion, or opinion, that would make such an address improper'. On the circumstances of composition, see Abbott, *Hawkesworth*, 115–16.

3 *I think myself happy . . . to bring an humble offering in my hand*: a great deal of emphasis was placed by English writers of oriental fiction in the eighteenth century on the generous procedures of what Samuel Johnson, in his *Rasselas*, calls 'the laws of eastern hospitality' (Johnson, *Rasselas*, 78). Hawkesworth here probably has in mind the narratives of those oriental tales which suggested that petitioners to the sultan would normally be expected to approach the court only if they had some sort of gift to offer. The mother of the hero in the popular 'Story of Aladdin; or, The Wonderful Lamp', included in the *Arabian Nights*, for example, at one point tells her son that 'nobody ever goes to ask a Favour of the Sultan, without a Present; for by a Present they have this Advantage, that if for some particular Reasons, the Favour is deny'd, they are sure to be heard' (*Arabian Nights*, ix. 127).

4 *WHO is he . . . in the dust*: the tone of the novel's opening deliberately recalls the injunction which begins Johnson's *Rasselas*: 'Ye who listen with credulity to the whispers of fancy, and pursue with eagerness the phantoms of hope; who expect that age will perform the promises of youth, and that the deficiencies of the present day will be supplied by the morrow; attend to the history of Rasselas prince of Abissinia' (Johnson, *Rasselas*, 7).

Solyman: unlike William Beckford who, later in the century, would loosely base his popular *Vathek* on the account of the historical Caliph Vathek recorded in d'Herbelot's 1697 *Bibliothèque orientale*, Hawkesworth follows the more casual tradition of earlier orientalists such as Joseph Addison, Samuel Johnson, and Oliver Goldsmith in simply creating a fictional monarch for his vaguely described 'throne of Persia'. The earlier oriental characters in his *Adventurer* had been given similarly fanciful (if at times historically redolent) names such as 'Almet', 'Amurath', and 'Nouraddin'. In naming the father of Almoran and Hamet 'Solyman', Hawkesworth probably has in mind the famous Ottoman leader

Sultain Suleiman I, 'the Magnificent' (1494–1566). This is the 'Sultan Solyman' referred to by the Prince of Morocco in Shakespeare's *The Merchant of Venice*, II. i. 26 ('By this scimitar | That slew the sophy and a Persian prince | That won three fields of Sultan Solyman'). The Old Testament King Solomon (see note to p. 7) was likewise often referred to in eighteenth-century oriental fiction as 'Sultan Solyman'. Hawkesworth had already made use of some of the other names used in *Almoran and Hamet* (e.g. 'Omar', 'Osmyn', 'Caled') in his *Adventurer*.

4 *one hundred and second year of the Hegyra*: Hawkesworth sets his tale slightly earlier than most of those in the *Arabian Nights*, many of which are said to take place in the reign of the historical Abbasid Caliph Harun-al-Rashid ('Haroun Alraschid') who ruled in Baghdad from AD 786 to 809, and whose reign is said to have constituted an early golden age of Islamic civilization. Readers of the *Arabian Nights* would recall the 'Hegyra' (*hijra*) as 'the Common Epocha [*sic*] of the Mahommetans' (*Arabian Nights*, iv. 249). The term—literally meaning 'emigration'—refers to the flight of Muhammad and a group of followers north from Mecca to Medina from July to September 622, marking the beginning of the Islamic era and the starting-point of the Muslim calendar. The action of *Almoran and Hamet* would thus, were Hawkesworth pretending to any historical accuracy, begin in the year AD 724.

the seraglio: often, in the oriental fiction of the eighteenth century, referring specifically to the apartments of a palace or residence reserved for wives and concubines, i.e. the harem. Samuel Johnson, for example, defines a seraglio as 'a house of women kept for debauchery' (Johnson, *Dictionary*). Both Hawkesworth and Frances Sheridan at times in their stories, however, use the term (as Hawkesworth had on several occasions in his *Adventurer*) in its more general sense of 'palace' or 'court'.

5 *the Angel of Death*: angels, in the Koranic tradition as in the Bible, are said to act both as agents of divine revelation and as intercessors and messengers of God. The Islamic Angel of Death in particular (variously identified by the English

writers of the eighteenth century as 'Azrail' or 'Azvail') and his assistants are several times mentioned in the Koran as the messengers who 'precede and usher *the righteous to paradise*' (Sale, *Koran* and *Prelim. Disc.*, 479).

5 *the permanent and unchangeable felicity of Paradise*: the Muslim Paradise or Garden (*al-janna*) detailed in the Koran offers both spiritual and material comforts. Those who enjoy what Hawkesworth characterizes here as the 'permanent and unchangeable felicity' of this Paradise are said to recline on couches of silk and gold in gardens watered by rivers and fountains, feast on fruits, fowl, and wine (from which they can never get drunk), and enjoy the companionship of eternally youthful attendants and the houris (see note to p. 25).

voluptuous: 'given to excess of pleasure' (Johnson, *Dictionary*).

the Prophet: i.e. Muhammad (AD 570–632), whose divine revelations recorded in the Koran over a period of twenty years constitute the sacred scripture of Islam.

7 *the power of the Seal of Solomon*: the 'Seal of Solomon', long familiar to readers of works such as the *Arabian Nights*, was a talismanic ring in the possession of the biblical King Solomon said to have magical properties, and by means of which he controlled the spirits. In describing Omar as one to whom was known 'the power of the Seal of Solomon', Hawkesworth may well be recalling a passage from Steele's *Guardian*, 167 (22 Sept. 1713), an oriental tale in which the physician Helim is said to have known 'the words that were engraved on the seal of Solomon the son of David'. Steele appears in turn to be echoing a passage in 'The Story of Beder Prince of Persia, and Giahaure Princess of Samandal' in the *Arabian Nights*, in which a magic transformation is effected by pronouncing 'certain mysterious Words over [Beder], which were engraven on the Seal of the Great Solomon, the Son of David' (*Arabian Nights*, vii. 120). Several other stories in the *Nights* also refer to the 'Seal of Solomon'.

10 *sofa*: oriental 'sofas' or 'sophas' (the word is of Arabic origin) were not the free-standing couches of Western design, but rather raised portions of the floor upon which were spread carpets and cushions. The platforms, which could be used for

reclining, eating, and sleeping, were thought by many Europeans to be a distinctive and distinguishing feature of Eastern interior design. The *Arabian Nights*, for example, finds it necessary to gloss the word for its readers as 'A Turkish Bench, on which Mats and Cushions are put' (*Arabian Nights*, vi. 158).

13 *a system of laws*: Omar's proposal for a 'system' of written laws here and the subsequent debate in Chapter III regarding the proper form of government most clearly reflect Hawkesworth's stated determination that his story be of practical value to George III (see note to p. 3).

20 *"Let not the eye of expectation . . . thy prerogative to impart"*: not identified.

23 *the scymitar and the bow-string*: i.e. instruments of execution. A 'scymitar' or scimitar is 'a short, curved single-edged sword' (*OED*).

"the feet of the prostitute go down to death, and . . . her steps take hold on hell": a slight misquotation of Proverbs 5: 3–5: 'For the lips of a strange woman drop as an honeycomb, and her mouth is smoother than oil; But her end is bitter as wormwood, sharp as a two-edged sword. Her feet go down to death; her steps take hold on hell.'

24 *the perfumes of Arabia*: Hawkesworth's phraseology may well be recalling the lines of Lady Macbeth in Shakespeare's *Macbeth*, v. i. 57 ('All the perfumes of Arabia will not sweeten this little hand'), although the East, and Arabia in particular—also known as *Arabia Odorifera*—had long been famous as a source of rich fragrances and exotic spices.

the forbidden pleasure of wine: Islamic tradition, as dictated by the Koran, enjoins Muslims to refrain from the consumption of alcohol. Several stories in the *Arabian Nights* make the Islamic practice (or pretence) of refraining from the drinking of wine an important feature of their narratives, as does Frances Sheridan's *Nourjahad*.

25 *Circassia*: a region of the Caucasus, between the Black Sea and the Caspian Sea. The natives of Circassia were prized for their great beauty and many—particularly the women—were sold into slavery in the harems of the Turks and the Persians.

25 *the daughters of Paradise*: the companionship of the 'houris' (*hur*)—'agreeable and beauteous damsels . . . [h]aving fine black eyes, kept in pavilions from public view'—is several times mentioned in the Koran as one of the rewards of the Garden of Paradise (Sale, *Koran* and *Prelim. Disc.*, 433; see also note to p. 5).

27 *her veil had dropped off by the way*: the common Muslim practice of the veiling of women is made a central feature of several of the narratives in the *Arabian Nights*. In his *Adventurer*, 20 (13 Jan. 1752), Hawkesworth had included a passage in which the veil of his heroine, Ammana, similar to that of Almeida's here, slips off in a crisis to reveal her beauty to an enamoured young hero.

33 *till the year should be completed*: the Muslim faith in fact prescribes no necessary period for mourning, and Hawkesworth is unusual among English orientalists in extending such a period to the space of an entire year. One story in the *Arabian Nights* ('The Story of Noureddin Ali and Bedreddin Hassan') notes that 'according to custom' it was usual for a man to remain in mourning for one month (*Arabian Nights*, iii. 101) and another notes that 'it belongs only to Women, to persist in perpetual mourning', and that at the end of one month a man should 'lay aside his mourning Habits' (*Arabian Nights*, vii. 127). The hero of 'The History of Zeyn Alasnam and the King of the Genii' in the same collection mourns for the death of his father, the king of Balsora, for only seven days.

34 *the public baths*: the spectacular public baths of Eastern cities were frequently noted by European visitors, and figure prominently in many of the stories in the *Arabian Nights* and its imitations.

35 *a summer pavilion that was built on a lake behind the palace*: a similar 'summer pavilion' is described in 'The Story of Noureddin and the Fair Persian' in the *Arabian Nights* (*Arabian Nights*, vii. 47).

37 *coffee and sherbet*: both coffee and sherbet were considered by English orientalists to be suitably exotic eastern beverages. Coffee had first been imported into England in 1652, and by

Hawkesworth's day 'coffee-houses' were the centres of various coteries. Sherbet—'the Juice of lemons or oranges mixed with water and sugar' (Johnson, *Dictionary*)—though perhaps less congenial to the English climate, continued throughout the eighteenth century to be thought of as a cooling and characteristically Eastern drink.

42 *poignard*: 'a dagger; a short stabbing weapon' (Johnson, *Dictionary*).

43 *a Genius*: jinn or 'genii', as they are known in the West, would be familiar to readers of collections such as the *Arabian Nights* and the *Persian Tales*, both of which make much of their supposed magical powers and enchantments. According to Islamic tradition jinn are actually supernatural beings, like angels and demons or 'shaytans'. They are said to have been created from 'smokeless fire', as angels were created from light, and human beings were in turn created from clay or dust and the spirit of God. Eighteenth-century oriental tales usually emphasize the playful, magical qualities of jinn, and often (as Hawkesworth does here, and as Sheridan will in *Nourjahad*) describe them in terms which tend to connect them in the minds of their readers with the protecting or tutelary angels of Christian tradition. See Sale, *Koran* and *Prelim. Disc.*, 109.

47 *'Fear not; for thou canst neither perish nor be wretched'*: perhaps recalling Isaiah 41: 10: 'Fear thou not; for I am with thee: be not dismayed; for I am thy God: I will strengthen thee; yea, I will help thee, I will uphold thee with the right hand of righteousness.'

the mufti and the imans: muftis (from the Arabic *mufti*—'one who decides') are judges of Muslim religious law; imams (from the Arabic *imam*, 'to lead') are religious leaders or 'exemplars'.

48 *the mutual promise which was to unite them*: Hawkesworth appears to be aware that Islamic marriages are not sacramental, but contractual. The marriage ceremony itself would therefore not emphasize an exchange of vows, as in the Christian tradition familiar to most English readers of the eighteenth century, but would focus rather on the contract or

'mutual promise' now binding the two individuals (and their families) together.

Volume II

61 *surrounded by mutes and eunuchs*: oriental fictions of the eighteenth and early nineteenth centuries tend often to include at least passing reference to the slaves and eunuchs employed to protect the harem of the sultan from intrusion or violation, and to the mutes, who were frequently portrayed as the silent agents of royal displeasure. See also Samuel Henley's comments on Beckford's *Vathek* (World's Classics edn.), 29 and n.

68 *an emerald of great lustre . . . a different letter*: the multi-faceted talisman given by the genius to Almoran here recalls not only the Seal of Solomon referred to earlier in the story (see note to p. 7) but also, in its power somehow to transform the physical being of its possessor, the ring of Gyges of classical legend. 'The History of King Ruzvanschad and of the Princess Cheheristany' in the *Persian Tales* includes a pair of rings which enable their possessors to assume the shape and features of anyone they desire to resemble. Hawkesworth himself had earlier made use of a magic ring in his *Adventurer*, 20–1 (13–20 June 1753).

70 *hood-winked*: not, as in contemporary parlance, fooled or deceived, but literally blinded by a hood or other covering.

72 *the mountain Kabessed*: Hawkesworth may well have an actual mountain and spring in mind, though in *Adventurer*, 32 (24 Feb. 1753), he had written similarly of 'the mountain Aubukabis, which rises on the east of Mecca, and overlooks the city'.

78 *the bow-string and the mute*: i.e. the executioner; see note to p. 61.

82 *I shall retire, and, like the shaft of Arabia, leave no mark behind me*: perhaps a reference to 'The Story of Prince Ahmed and the Fairy Pari Banou' in the *Arabian Nights*. In the tale, the three princes of India—Houssain, Ali, and Ahmed—compete for the affection of their beautiful cousin, the Princess

Nouronnihar. After an initial contest fails to resolve the dispute, the sultan decides to award the princess instead to the son who can shoot an arrow the furthest. Prince Ahmed in fact appears to have won the contest, shooting his shaft far beyond the others, but his arrow, when searched for, cannot be found, and the princess is awarded instead to Prince Ali.

98 *irremeable*: 'admitting of no return' (*OED*).

109 *Orosmades*: i.e. Ahura Mazda or Ormuzd; in Persian mythology, the wise and beneficent god of creation.

111 *as the sands of Alai from the trees of Oman*: obviously meant to signify a very great distance. Oman is the comparatively fertile coastal region on the eastern butt of the Arabian peninsula, famous for its dates and fruit trees.

112 *At the words of the Genius . . . a monument of his punishment and his guilt*: although recalling for many readers the fate of several characters in Ovid's *Metamorphoses* (most notably that of Niobe, whose grief for the death of her children transforms her into a column of stone), Almoran's own transformation into a 'monument' of stone is perhaps also meant to recall the punitory (and temporary) fate of the princes turned into black rock in 'The Story of the Two Sisters who Envied their Younger Sister' in the *Arabian Nights*. The lower body of the King of the Black Isles in 'The Story of the Prince of the Black Isles' in the same collection is transformed into black marble. In 'The Story of Zobeide', also in the *Arabian Nights*, the entire population of a city is found petrified.

the Angel of instruction: Cf. Hawkesworth's description of Hassan in *Adventurer*, 32 (24 Feb. 1753), 'upon whose mind the angel of instruction had impressed the council of [the hermit] Omar'.

The History of Nourjahad

117 *Schemzeddin*: the names of Sheridan's characters, while—like those of Hawkesworth—reminiscent of those given to figures in the *Arabian Nights* and the *Persian Tales* (e.g. 'Noureddin',

Schemselnihar'), are probably not meant to recall specific narrative or historical prototypes.

118 *Mussulman*: i.e. a Muslim.

119 *seraglio*: see note to p. 4.

   a bank of violets: Sheridan's language recalls Shakespeare's *Twelfth Night*, I. i. 1–7. See Introduction, p. xxxiii.

120 *our holy prophet*: Muhammad; see note to p. 5.

121 *guardian genius*: see note to p. 43.

125 *the ruins of a small temple . . . the worship of the Gentiles*: Christianity had flourished in the pre-Islamic East, particularly along caravan routes. See John L. Esposito, *Islam: the Straight Path* (Oxford, 1991), 6.

   taffety: i.e. taffeta; a thin, glossy silk fabric. The word 'taffeta' is itself of Persian origin.

127 *In the former. . . King Solomon himself shall be outdone*: the Old Testament King Solomon is said in the Bible to have had 700 wives and 300 concubines (see 1 Kings 11: 3).

129 *a thousand crowns yearly*: a crown was a silver coin of Great Britain worth five shillings. English orientalists in the eighteenth century also referred casually and with varying accuracy to oriental coins of different denominations as 'dinars', 'dirhams', 'aqtchas', 'manghirs', 'aspers', 'sherrifs', and 'sequins' (see notes to pp. 176 and 225). Sheridan later in her story refers to the currency necessary for Nourjahad to purchase a villa merely as 'pieces of gold' (p. 144).

   some leagues from Ormuz: Sheridan sets her story in 'Ormuz' or Hormuz, a port near the Strait of Hormuz, on the Persian Gulf, which flourished as a trading town in the Middle Ages and early Renaissance. The fame of Hormuz as a rich trading centre in the 'gorgeous East' for spices and precious stones is reflected by Milton in *Paradise Lost*, II. 4 ('the wealth of *Ormus* and of *Inde*'); it is the setting for several stories in, among other collections, the *Persian Tales* and the *Mogul Tales*.

136 *intoxicated . . . drunk*: see note to p. 24.

142 *blow*: blossom, flower.

145 *Nourjahad . . . broke them open*: the gesture would be a familiar one to readers of eighteenth-century oriental tales. See, for example, 'The History of Ganem, Son of Abou Ayoub' in the *Arabian Nights*, in which the character Mohammed receives a letter from the Caliph Haroun Alraschid: 'knowing the Hand, [he] stood up to Shew his Respect, kiss'd the Letter, and laid it on his Head, to denote that he was ready submissively to obey the Orders contained in it' (*Arabian Nights*, viii. 43).

148 *those mansions of joy prepared for the reception of the faithful*: see note to p. 5.

Epicurean phrenzy: Epicurus (341–270 BC) was a Greek philosopher whose ethical system espoused the attainment of the good through the avoidance of pain and a life of quiet virtue and pleasure. His name later became identified (as it is here) with a hedonistic indulgence in 'licentious pleasure' and 'sensual gratifications'.

149 *the Houriis; those beautiful virgins who are given as a reward to all true believers*: see note to p. 25.

Cadiga, the favourite wife of the great Prophet: Cadiga, or Khadija, was the first and most beloved of the wives of the prophet Muhammad (see note to p. 5), to whom she was married for fifteen years. During that time she bore seven children and, according to Muslim tradition, encouraged Muhammad to accept his call as a prophet. She died in AD 619.

152 *the furies*: referring apparently to the three Furies (*Erinyes*) of classical mythology: Alecto, Megaera, and Tisiphone.

153 *the Temple of Mecca*: the Kaaba (literally meaning 'cube') or House of Allah, located in the centre of the Haram mosque in Mecca. Muslims are asked to make the pilgrimage to Mecca—the centre of the Islamic world—at least once in their lifetime. See also note to p. 199.

165 *a page to one of the emirs of Shemzeddin's court*: an emir (from the Arabic *amir* or 'commander') is an Arabian prince or

chieftan; the term is also 'a title of honour borne by the descendants of Mohammed' (*OED*).

172 *a solemn mourning . . . during the space of twenty days*: see note to p. 33.

173 *in thy slave's habit*: Sheridan's description of Cozro's dress (see also p. 193) recalls several of the narratives in the *Arabian Nights*. The character of Bahader in 'The Story of Prince Amgrad, and the Lady of the City of the Magicians', for example, dresses 'in a Slaves' Habit' in order to further the romantic intrigues of Prince Amgrad. See *Arabian Nights*, vi. 161.

174 *one of the cady's officers*: a 'cady' or cadi (from the Arabic *qadi* or 'judge') is identified by Johnson as 'a magistrate among the Turks, whose office seems to answer that of a justice of the peace' (Johnson, *Dictionary*).

176 *ten sequins*: the *Arabian Nights* notes that 'the Turkish sequin is about 9 s. sterling' (*Arabian Nights*, iii. 14). Sequins were in fact Venetian gold coins, although the *OED* notes that the term was 'also used as a name for a former Turkish coin, the sultanin'. See note to p. 225.

184 *his prime vizier*: a 'visier' (from the Arabic *wazir* or 'porter', and by extension one who carries the burden of government administration) is a minister or councillor of state (cf. p. 202).

185 *saloon*: i.e. salon; apartment, room.

The History of Charoba, Queen of Ægypt

197 *CHAROBA . . . other nations*: the Pharaoh of the Abraham story in the Book of Genesis (Gen. 12: 10–20; see note below) is unnamed and remains unidentified. Reeve's source for the narrative, however, Davies's *Egyptian History* (see Introduction, p. xxxv), notes that Totis was 'the first called *Pharao* in *Egypt*, because he was cruel and bloudy, and put many people to death' (Davies, *Egyptian History*, 117).

In the reign of Totis . . . delivered his servants: the story of Abraham's journey from Canaan into Egypt is related in Genesis 12: 10–20. The Abraham story is recounted in Davies's *Egyptian History* (pp. 109–12), immediately prior to the story of Charoba.

197 *After this . . . Ishmael*: in the Genesis account, Hagar is referred to only as Sarah's handmaid, 'an Egyptian'. Reeve's story draws on a tradition which identifies Hagar explicitly with the 'maidservants' given by Pharaoh (and here Charoba) to Abraham prior to the couple's expulsion from Egypt (Gen. 12: 16).

a Coptess by nation: i.e. a native Egyptian (from the ancient name of Egypt). The term 'Copt' generally refers to native Egyptian Christians.

198 *Agar*: the name Hagar actually comes from the Hebrew signifying 'flight' or 'emigration'. The use of the name Hagar to denote 'wage' or 'recompense' is a later derivation.

199 *Sarah likewise bare a son*: the Bible records that Sarah, at the age of 90, conceived and gave birth to Isaac (see Gen. 17: 16–22). The quarrel between Sarah's son Isaac and Hagar's son Ishmael is presented in the Bible as an etiological myth explaining the enmity between the Israelites (the descendants of Isaac), and the Ishmaelites (the Arab descendants of Ishmael).

Ægyptian linen: Egypt had, since earliest antiquity, been recognized as a centre for the production of fine linens.

the square temple at Mecca: i.e. the Kaaba (see note to p. 153). The Kaaba had existed as a sacred shrine before the birth of Muhammad, who is said to have 'cleansed' it of idols. Islamic tradition in fact credits Abraham himself with having built the Kaaba, with the help of his son Ishmael.

Gedde: i.e. Jedda or Jidah, an ancient port city on the Red Sea, eventually an important port of entry for pilgrims *en route* to Mecca, just over sixty miles to the east.

200 *She also suspected . . . by what persons*: Reeve's source states much more explicitly that Charoba is guilty of patricide: '[Charoba] always endeavoured to prevent the shedding of blood, but could not prevail: Wherefore she was at last afraid they would take away the crown from him [i.e. Totis], seeing him extremely hated by all people, which made her resolve to dispatch him by poison, after he had reigned 70 years.' Davies, *Egyptian History*, 117.

201 *Gebirus the Metaphequian*: based probably on Jubair al Muta-
fiki ('Jubair of the cities of the plain'), a leader of the Hyksos,
the ancient Asiatic invaders of Egypt. Vattier's incorrect
transliteration of Murtada's Arabic (retained by Davies and
Reeve) recalls the 'Geber' (the name means 'mighty man') of
1 Kings 4: 19. On the identification of Davies's 'Gebirus'
with Jubair see Stephen Wheeler's explanatory notes to
Walter Savage Landor's *Gebir* in Landor's *Poetical Works*
(Oxford, 1937), i. 474.

203 *in the same place where Alexandria now standeth*: the port city
of Alexandria, founded by and named for Alexander the
Great in 332 BC, and once famous for a library unequalled in
the classical world, still stands on a narrow strip of land near
the Canopic mouth of the Nile river.

which city was founded by Sedad the son of Gad: the city of
Irem or Arem, the city of the ancient Adites, near Aden.

206 *brazen*: i.e. made of brass.

208 *her own city of Masar*: possibly El Masara, near the ancient
city of Memphis.

209 *a regal garment . . . for that purpose*: the poisoned garment
which Charoba's nurse places on Gebirus recalls both the
shirt of Nessus (the deadly tunic given by the centaur Nessus
to Deianira, the wife of Hercules), and the poisoned robe and
diadem given by Medea to Creon, the king of Corinth.

211 *embalmed with camphire and spices*: the Egyptians were cred-
ited from classical antiquity with having originated the art of
preserving corpses from decay.

Murad the Unlucky

215 *IT is well known that the Grand Seignior . . . as the Caliph,
Haroun Alraschid, used formerly to do in Bagdad*: the opening
of Edgeworth's tale deliberately recalls the beginnings of
several stories in collections such as the *Arabian Nights* and
the *Persian Tales*, in which the Caliph Haroun Alraschid (see
note to p. 4) disguises himself to wander among the streets of
Baghdad and observe his people incognito. It is worth noting,

however, that the historical Turkish Sultan Osmin III (1754–6), who reigned in Constantinople during the period described by Baron de Tott's *Memoirs* (a work which Edgeworth later acknowledges to be one of her principal sources for *Murad*), in fact enjoyed a reputation for wandering about the streets of Constantinople disguised. Baron de Tott himself describes encountering the sultan in the streets on one such occasion 'disguised like a Professor of the law' (Baron de Tott, *Memoirs*, i. 23). References to Baron de Tott's *Memoirs* in the Explanatory Notes are to the first English edition of 1785; Edgeworth rendered her own translations of the original French.

215 *the Arabian story of Cogia-Hassan, Alhabal, . . . human affairs*: 'The Story of Cogia Hassan Alhabbal' is related in the *Arabian Nights*. In the tale each of two friends—Saad, who is wealthy, and Saadi, who is a man of more moderate means—in turn bestows a gift upon the honest rope-maker Hassan. Saadi, who believes that 'most People's Poverty is owing to their wanting at first a sufficient Sum of Money to employ their Industry with', twice gives Hassan purses filled with 200 pieces of gold, and twice Hassan—through the mishaps of ill fortune—loses the money. Saad, who had earlier admitted that while riches were perhaps 'necessary in Life', nevertheless contends that 'the Happiness of a Man's Life consisted in Virtue, and no further Attachment to worldly Goods, than what were necessary in Life, and to do Good withal', and offers Hassan a piece of lead. Through a series of remarkable adventures Hassan manages to transform the seemingly worthless lead into a great fortune. The moral drawn from Hassan's adventures is that 'Money is not always the Means of becoming rich.' See *Arabian Nights*, x. 138–xi. 27.

216 *Murad, the Unlucky . . . Saladin, the Lucky*: Edgeworth is most likely drawing the name 'Murad' from Baron de Tott's *Memoirs*, in which the Baron writes at length of his friendship with Murad Mollach (Baron de Tott, *Memoirs*, i. 14); Murad was also the name of several Ottoman sultans. 'Saladin' would of course be famous as the name of the great Muslim sultan and military strategist (1137–93) who repeatedly frustrated

the designs of Christian crusaders in the late twelfth century AD. See Introduction, p. xliv.

217 *their khan*: the *Arabian Nights* had identified a khan for its readers as 'A Publick House, in the Towns of the Levant, where Strangers lodge' (*Arabian Nights*, v. 4). The sultan and his vizier, as 'pretended merchants', would naturally be expected to be spending the night at such an inn or caravanserai.

the Grand Seignior's turban . . . struck off: Baron de Tott, commenting on the ceremonies surrounding the installation and coronation of Ottoman princes, takes special note of the extraordinary respect paid to the turbans of the Grand Seignior (Baron de Tott, *Memoirs*, i. 120).

Aleppo: located on the caravan route which crossed Syria to Baghdad, Aleppo was one of the busiest commercial and manufacturing centres in the Near East.

219 *the Grand Seignior's seraglio*: on the significance of the term 'seraglio' in general see note to p. 4. The famous seraglio of the Ottoman sultan at Constantinople, begun by Muhammad II (1429–81), is located near the Bosporus.

221 '*Whom the Gods wish to destroy, they first deprive of understanding*': a popular maxim, from a Greek fragment variously attributed to Aeschylus, Sophocles, and (more commonly) Euripides. In his *Life of Johnson*, Boswell notes the Latin phrase ('Quos Deus vult perdere, prius dementat') to be 'one of the sayings which every body repeats but nobody knows where to find' (Boswell, *Life*, iv. 181).

For some time before . . . the bakers: Edgeworth bases Murad's misfortunes here on a passage included in Baron de Tott's *Memoirs* (i. 204–5) in which Turkish methods of ascertaining the proper weight of the bread to be sold at market are described.

223 *the Grand Seignior's army . . . resolved to accompany them*: Turkey had controlled Egypt since the conquest of the Mamelukes by the Emperor Selim in 1517.

El Arish: the ancient city of Rhinoculura, in Sinai, near the shore of the eastern Mediterranean. El Arish might well be remembered by Edgeworth as the site at which the French eventually signed a treaty, in 1800, agreeing to evacuate Egypt.

224 *bastinadoed*: i.e. beaten with a stick, cudgelled. Edgeworth almost certainly has in mind a memorable passage from Antes's *Observations*, in which he describes the procedures of such torture. Antes was himself captured and 'bastinadoed' in November 1779, when hunting outside Cairo. 'Every stroke', he later wrote of the torture, 'felt like the application of a red hot poker' (Antes, *Observations*, 115–32).

224–5 *two hundred sequins*: see notes to pp. 129 and 176. Baron de Tott notes that 'the Sequin is a piece of Gold Coin, but there are Sequins of different Values. That most in use is worth about seven livres (five shillings and ten pence) of our Money.' See Baron de Tott, *Memoirs*, iii. 110.

225 *drink sherbet with them*: see note to p. 37.

226 *Antes's Observations . . . Egyptians*: No such anecdote is recalled in that work.

227 *There were certain Jews . . . exorbitant interest*: although neither of Edgeworth's sources mentions such 'followers', Edgeworth would unfortunately not have had to look very far for stereotypical depictions of Jews as treacherous villains. Edgar Rosenberg notes that the dishonest Rachub is merely a variation on the traditional stock figure of the Jewish villain. Two more of the *Popular Tales* contain similar characters, and the uncompromising, Shylock-like Mr Mordacai of Edgeworth's later novel *The Absentee* is clearly operating in the same tradition. See Edgar Rosenberg, *From Shylock to Svengali: Jewish Stereotypes in English Fiction* (Stanford, Calif., 1960), 56–7.

229 *a detachment of English soldiers*: although the conflation of diverse historical source material here makes any specific reference unlikely, Edgeworth, who was writing *Murad* in 1802, may well have had in mind very recent British successes in the area when placing a 'detachment of English soldiers' on Egyptian sands. Following Nelson's spectacular victory at

the Battle of the Nile in August 1798, British land forces had barred any further advance by Napoleon on Constantinople, and by 1801 had effectively evacuated Egypt of French forces.

phantom: i.e. a mirage.

230 *a caravan returning from Mecca*: Edgeworth probably has in mind a company of merchants travelling together for the sake of collective security, although such a group might also include Muslims completing their annual *hajj* or pilgrimage to the Kaaba (see note to p. 153). Baron de Tott describes an encounter with just such a 'Caravan of Mecca' in his *Memoirs* (iv. 117).

231 *a passage from the Koran . . . worked upon it*: 'Qur'anic passages have been used as decorative motifs not only on religiously significant items but also on fabrics, garments, vessels and service trays, boxes and furniture, walls and building, even the lowly cooking pot, in every century of Islamic history and in every corner of the Muslim world.' Isma'il R. al Fārūqī and Lois Lamya' al Fārūqī, *The Cultural Atlas of Islam* (London, 1986), 175.

Grand Cairo: Cairo, then as now the largest city in Africa, is frequently referred to in the *Arabian Nights* and in English oriental tales and travellers' accounts of the eighteenth and nineteenth centuries as 'Grand Cairo'—one of the greatest centres of the Islamic world.

236 *Now the plague . . . died of that distemper*: Antes includes in his *Observations* (40–1) a lengthy discussion of outbreaks of the plague in Egypt in 1771 and 1781, twice noting Smyrna to be one of the locales from which the disease was 'most commonly brought' to Egypt. He likewise mentions that both brandy and vinegar were commonly used as preventatives against the disease. Edgeworth has drawn upon his account of the 1781 outbreak for several of the specific details of her narrative. Edgar Rosenberg notes that the 'old clothes' Jew figures as a recurrent type in nineteenth-century English fiction. See Edgar Rosenberg, *From Shylock to Svengali: Jewish Stereotypes in English Fiction* (Stanford, Calif., 1960), 55.

236 *Cadi*: see note to p. 174

237 *para*: 'a Turkish coin of very little value' (*OED*).

> *Antes's Observations . . . Egyptians*: 'The natural cause of the plague ceasing . . . in Egypt, is the great heat.' Antes, *Observations*, 44.

> *Lazaretto*: 'a house for the reception of the diseased poor . . . a hospital, pest house' (*OED*).

241 *A factor*: a merchant who earns a commission by selling another's goods.

244 *the Porte*: variously the 'sublime' or 'Ottoman' Porte; the Ottoman court at Constantinople.

244 *On the Grand Seignor's birth-day . . . crowded to see them*: Edgeworth here actually introduces a character very closely resembling Baron de Tott himself ('a Frenchman, an ingenious engineer') into the narrative. Visiting the 'Cham of the Tartars' (see note to p. 254) Baron de Tott notes: 'I had observed he was very fond of Fire-works . . . therefore . . . I asked the Cham's permission to give him this kind of entertainment on his Birth-day; and, he having been only used to see smoaky Wheatsheafs, good for nothing Crackers, and small ill managed Skyrockets, my success was very great' (Baron de Tott, *Memoirs*, ii. 85).

246 *Baron de Tott's Memoirs*: Baron de Tott early in his *Memoirs* includes an extensive account of a fire which is said to have destroyed two-thirds of the Ottoman capital in 1756, as an example of 'those dreadful fires, which too frequently lay waste Constantinople'. In her narrative, Edgeworth asserts the fire to have broken out 'in the suburbs of Pera', while Baron de Tott in fact notes that the residence of the French Ambassador '*situated* in the suburbs of Pera', commanded a view of the city from which the conflagration could be observed.

> *the mosque of St Sophia*: Santa Sophia or Hagia Sophia, the great Byzantine mosque (originally a church) at Constantinople.

246 *others considered . . . a war in which we were just engaged*: the Ottomans were not, in fact, engaged in any foreign wars at the time of the destruction of the seraglio in 1756.

the Bezestein: or 'Bezesteen', from the Persian meaning 'clothes market'; 'an exchange, bazaar, or market place in the East' (*OED*). The designation would be familiar to readers of the *Arabian Nights*, in which such a market is described as 'a publick Place where silk Stuffs, and other precious Things, are exposed to Sale' (*Arabian Nights*, iv. 177).

247 *Translations . . . v. I*: quoted from De Tott's *Memoirs*, i. 133.

248 *De Tott's Memoirs, v. I*: quoted from De Tott's *Memoirs*, i. 21. This note is omitted from the 1832 Longford edition.

249 *Damat Zade*: Damat Zada, a friend of the family of Murad Mollach (see note to p. 216), is mentioned in Baron de Tott's *Memoirs* (i. 14).

The large drums in the Janissary-Aga's tower: see Edgeworth's note to 'the Passevans', p. 248.

251 *Fatima*: the name recalls that of Muhammad's daughter Fatimah, the only surviving child of Muhammad and Khadija (see note to p. 149); she gives her name to the Fatimid dynasty. In *The Absentee*, Edgeworth will refer to a number of fashionable English ladies reposing on 'seraglio' ottomans as 'beautiful Fatimas admiring, or being admired'. See *The Absentee* (World's Classics edn.), Oxford, 1988, 37 and n.

253 *Memoirs . . . v. I*: quoted from De Tott's *Memoirs*, i. 78. The note is omitted from the 1832 Longford edition.

254 *Pacha of Maksoud*: In his *Memoirs* (ii. 95) Baron de Tott recounts at length his meeting with Maksoud-Gueray, 'then on the Throne of the Tartars'. This is the same 'Cham of the Tartars' for whose birthday the Baron had arranged a fireworks display (see note to p. 244).

256 *Those among the Turks . . . the most laughable picture*: Edgeworth again quotes from Baron de Tott's *Memoirs*, i. 141–2, although the source here remains unacknowledged. The omission is corrected in the 1832 Longford edition.

THE WORLD'S CLASSICS

A Select List

SERGEI AKSAKOV: A Russian Gentleman
Translated by J. D. Duff
Edited by Edward Crankshaw

A Russian Schoolboy
Translated by J. D. Duff
Introduction by John Bayley

HANS ANDERSEN: Fairy Tales
Translated by L. W. Kingsland
Introduction by Naomi Lewis
Illustrated by Vilhelm Pedersen and Lorenz Frølich

ARTHUR J. ARBERRY (Transl.): The Koran

LUDOVICO ARIOSTO: Orlando Furioso
Translated by Guido Waldman

ARISTOTLE: The Nicomachean Ethics
Translated by David Ross

JANE AUSTEN: Emma
Edited by James Kinsley and David Lodge

Mansfield Park
Edited by James Kinsley and John Lucas

Northanger Abbey, Lady Susan, The Watsons,
and Sanditon
Edited by John Davie

ROBERT BAGE: Hermsprong
Edited by Peter Faulkner

WILLIAM BECKFORD: Vathek
Edited by Roger Lonsdale

R. D. BLACKMORE: Lorna Doone
Edited by Sally Shuttleworth

The Pickwick Papers
Edited by James Kinsley

FËDOR DOSTOEVSKY: Crime and Punishment
Translated by Jessie Coulson
Introduction by John Jones

Memoirs from the House of the Dead
Translated by Jessie Coulson
Introduction by Ronald Hingley

ARTHUR CONAN DOYLE:
Sherlock Holmes: Selected Stories
Introduction by S. C. Roberts

ALEXANDRE DUMAS *fils*:
La Dame aux Camélias
Translated by David Coward

MARIA EDGEWORTH: Castle Rackrent
Edited by George Watson

GEORGE ELIOT: Daniel Deronda
Edited by Graham Handley

Felix Holt, The Radical
Edited by Fred C. Thompson

Middlemarch
Edited by David Carroll

JOHN MEADE FALKNER: The Nebuly Coat
Edited by Christopher Hawtree

SUSAN FERRIER: Marriage
Edited by Herbert Foltinek

HENRY FIELDING: Joseph Andrews *and* Shamela
Edited by Douglas Brooks-Davies

SARAH FIELDING: The Adventures of David Simple
Edited by Malcolm Kelsall

The Eclogues and The Georgics
Translated by C. Day Lewis
Edited by R. O. A. M. Lyne

HORACE WALPOLE : The Castle of Otranto
Edited by W. S. Lewis

IZAAK WALTON and CHARLES COTTON:
The Compleat Angler
Edited by John Buxton
Introduction by John Buchan

MRS HUMPHREY WARD: Robert Elsmere
Edited by Rosemary Ashton

OSCAR WILDE: Complete Shorter Fiction
Edited by Isobel Murray

The Picture of Dorian Gray
Edited by Isobel Murray

MARY WOLLSTONECRAFT:
Mary *and* The Wrongs of Woman
Edited by Gary Kelly

ÉMILE ZOLA:
The Attack on the Mill and other stories
Translated by Douglas Parmeé

A complete list of Oxford Paperbacks, including The World's Classics, OPUS, Past Masters, Oxford Authors, Oxford Shakespeare, and Oxford Paperback Reference, is available in the UK from the Arts and Reference Publicity Department (RS), Oxford University Press, Walton Street, Oxford OX2 6DP.

In the USA, complete lists are available from the Paperbacks Marketing Manager, Oxford University Press, 200 Madison Avenue, New York, NY 10016.

Oxford Paperbacks are available from all good bookshops. In case of difficulty, customers in the UK can order direct from Oxford University Press Bookshop, Freepost, 116 High Street, Oxford, OX1 4BR, enclosing full payment. Please add 10 per cent of published price for postage and packing.